NAKED BEFORE GOD

NAKED

BEFORE

GOD

The Return of a Broken Disciple

Bill Williams

with Martha Williams

MOREHOUSE PUBLISHING
A DIVISION OF THE MOREHOUSE GROUP
HARRISBURG, PENNSYLVANIA

Morehouse Publishing
P.O. Box 1321
Harrisburg, Pennsylvania 17105

Morehouse Publishing is a division of the Morehouse Group.

Scriptural passages are generally based on the New English Bible, but have been paraphrased for a new generation of readers. Since a portion of this book deals with the Christian experience of the Bible, words and phrases especially unique to the NEB have in some instances been brought in line with other major translations. Some updates reflect the benefits of later academic work unavailable to the NEB committee.

Cover art: Bonnat, Leon. Job. Museé Bonnat, Bayonne, France. Giraudon/ Art Resource, NY.

Cover design: Trude Brummer

Illustration p. 62 by Martha S. Williams; all other illustrations by Bill Williams.

Library of Congress Cataloging-in-Publication Data
Williams, Bill, 1960-
    Naked before God : the return of a broken disciple / Bill Williams ; with Martha Williams.
      p. cm.
    Includes bibliographical references.
    ISBN 0-8192-1739-5 (hardcover)
    1. Suffering—Religious aspects—Christianity. 2. Cystic fibrosis—Patients—Religious life. 3. Williams, Bill, 1960– .
    I. Williams, Martha, 1960– . II. Title.
    BT732.7.W535 1998
    242'.4—dc21   98-11330
                                                      CIP

Printed in the United States of America

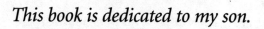

This book is dedicated to my son.

CONTENTS

(Chapter names are derived from the Hebrew and Greek alphabets, except where they are not. Do not be alarmed: it is merely an outbreak of lawlessness.)

A Word about Inclusive Language

The issue of male/female God-talk has evolved to the point of agony. No matter what a writer does, someone will get angry or hurt.

Picture, if you will, two prospective readers…

Claudia had a dysfunctional, abusive father, and whenever God is referred to as "Father," she finds the word so filled with bad meanings that she can no longer relate to God in a positive way. When too many male images clutter up church-talk, she has to rush out. She resents having to do that… she *needs* God.

Doris experienced a loving father, loves the liturgy of the church and is pained by all the furor over the issue. She takes the Hebrew prophets seriously, and whenever she hears phrases like "Mother God" she feels like she has stepped into a pagan cult that will threaten her salvation. She rushes out of the church. She resents having to do that… she *needs* God.

Both of these people are real, many times over. I love them both. I've sat with them for many hours in lounges, living rooms and cafeterias. They have real claims on my life; they have held me up when many other supports dropped away. I not only want to share my story with them, I *must* speak to them.

I have this crazy notion that if I master the rules to this obscure game, both of them might be able to read this book. But I've been playing this game for a while now, and I've figured out something that makes me want to scream.

The game, for a writer, has only one rule to it:

You lose.

What to do?

Some folks try to avoid the issue by avoiding all pronouns. In small doses this can work, but I've seen some atrocious trombone solos, too:

> *God will do this by God's self, because God must be sure God's creatures do not compromise God's freedom to act in God's own best interests…*

After reading an entire paper like that, the reader does, at least, discover why pronouns were invented! It is barely decipherable in an academic paper, and in a book written in colloquial style it stands out like a cyborg among farmers. Furthermore, in our increasingly polarized atmosphere, it is becoming a red flag in itself: a gang handshake indicating whether or not the author is going to stand with "us," or "them." Those who would walk among both Jews and Samaritans are likely to get shot on certain streets.

There are other possibilities: "it," which depersonalizes what Jesus was trying to personalize; "s/he, he/she," and all the other eye-breaking textual speed bumps; alternating genders; the creation of new words such as "isth"; only speaking to God in the second person; or complete, helpless silence.

I've considered them all.

Sometimes silence sounds the most attractive.

Even if you pull the teeth on pronouns, you still have to deal with "Father" language, or "Son of Man" language, both of which are ever-present in Jesus' dialogues. (Note, too, that "Son of HuMANity" simply buries the distinction in syllables—please, laugh with me, I think I'm about to cry—and if in desperation I go to "Son of Earthlings," will you follow that with "take me to your leader" in your best robotic voice?)

The ironic thing about all of this is that very few people are convinced that God has a sexual organ at all. Let's all pause for a minute and contemplate that.

To those of you who hate Political Correctness: I know you wish I'd just be a man and stop whining. But this book contains a cry about things I've found hurtful. Shall I squash others, just because their hurt differs from mine? That would be the height of arrogance.

To Claudia and Doris: I don't want to hurt either of you. I will do my best. I will try to write things so that they are readable and responsible.

But you know what?

I will fail. I am human, and I can't win a game with only one rule such as this.

Forgive me for being human; understand that it makes me hurt, too; and approach this text with compassion. Only your grace can keep this writer from falling silent.

Your weary friend,

—Bill

Unquotes and Misquotes

This book already has too many quotes in it. It's hard to believe that there are some sources who escaped direct quoting, but that is the case. This piece is so shot-through with their work that there was no center from which to hang a credit.

The vision of God's omnipotence and process theology segments are heavily indebted to Anna Case-Winters and her book *God's Power: Traditional Understandings and Contemporary Challenges* (Louisville: Westminster/John Knox Press, 1990). Anna, I sold my house to read your book. It was a good deal.

The "projection theology" (my term) running through this book was inspired by Robin Scroggs' *Paul for a New Day* (Minneapolis: Fortress Press, 1977).

The words of "Rabbi Halverstadt" in Chapter Pi significantly reflect a lecture by Professor Hugh F. Halverstadt in the course "Managing Church Conflict" at McCormick Theological Seminary, Chicago; but his words were more tightly focused. His intent was to discuss the so-called alligators (problem parishioners) that can prolong conflict in an organization. I have, for the purposes of narrative, broadened the scope of his words to match what he inspired in me, and then inserted them in "Rabbi Halverstadt's" mouth. It would be unfair to suggest that Professor Halverstadt was speaking as broadly—but the rest of his description is accurate and deserves credit.

The little smattering of semiotics comes from Jean-Jacques Nattiez, *Music and Discourse: Toward a Semiology of Music*, translated by Carolyn Abbate (Princeton, N.J.: University Press, 1990).

Professor Ralph Klein of the Lutheran School of Theology was the first person to name the negative effects of ellipsis in the Psalms for me; I am indebted to him for his general approach to the Hebrew Scriptures, including his wonderfully accurate characterization of Job, which struck me like a name long forgotten but long known.

Finally, confidence and freedom to finish this piece, as well as a deepened understanding of the Gospels, came from David Rhoads, *The Challenge of Diversity: The Witness of Paul and the Gospels* (Minneapolis: Fortress Press, 1996). Dave, your book was like the final boost over a forbidding wall.

Acknowledgments

Since I've been unconsciously writing this book most of my life, this section is unavoidably abridged. But special thanks…

To Mike DeWilde: for wondering why Christians lose their sense of humor when they "do" spirituality, and for countless well-timed notes that built me up when the destroyer was tearing me down.

To Marianne Zitzewitz: for her patient correspondence, and for remembering to send a paper more than a year after the promise was uttered (a very "Marianne" thing to do!).

To Professor Phil Hefner, who assigned Marianne a devilish task: explaining what Jesus does for us without resorting to church language.

To Professor Vitor Westhelle: for blowing fresh winds of myth and change through my mind.

To my classmates at the Lutheran School of Theology at Chicago: you will never know how you filled my soul.

To Joan Swander, for listening, contributing, pushing, sharpening and supporting: you were the whetstone of this book. Many times I would describe the subject of a chapter to you, then realize I'd found a better illustration than what I'd written.

To Jim McQuinn, for his help with web-work, copyrights, and occasionally loaning his tongue to God.

To Neil Orts, for suppressing burnout long enough to rehash my endless subject.

To Rev. Bob Walters, for thinking my story might make an interesting book. I think this is as close as I'll get to autobiography, so I hope it will suffice.

To my parents, for such extraordinary support and help, for believing in the author and helping with practical details. Thank you.

To the many folks who accepted reaction copies: thank you for your interest and feedback. It was good to hear that it worked on more than a personal level.

To the People at Morehouse Publishing: your kind, respectful behavior, generosity and enthusiastic treatment of this book turned this into an experience that never ceased to amaze me. I thank God for placing each one of you in my path.

To my Editor, Debra Farrington: when I was in the computer game industry, we called it the talent to "Blue Sky"; a free approach to roadblocks that can create something new and fun. You have it, and I'm thankful for that… along with your delightful and frequent laugh, your patient teaching and a phenomenon that I can only call "resonance."

To Managing Editor Valerie Gittings: By the time authors such as I recognize the miracle worker hiding behind your humble mask, their books are almost typeset, and it's too late to expose your true identity. Yet without your persistent genius, our books would never make it out the door. Thank you, and thanks for the easy-going manner with which you perform the impossible. I've truly enjoyed working with you.

To Professor Kadi Billman: Kadi, you taught me that a child of the light is unafraid of shining into dark places. The teaching has been around for awhile, of course, but you taught me with deeds rather than words, and I could no longer deny it. Thus you created the author that could create this book.

Thank you, too, for your ministry during that period.

To Angie Shannon: you were always there, sitting on my shoulder, challenging every word. If I closed my eyes, I could smell the refectory food.

To Professor David Rhoads: for listening to the Holy Spirit and sending your new manuscript when I most needed to hear your wise words again (I was assailed by demons of doubt and quitting regularly, but your book had the answers to shut them up); for your ministry; and for your oral performances of Mark, which gave me visions of Christ's joy in healing that will never fade.

Most importantly, though, thank you for picking up the torch when this runner stumbled. When I finally finished this book, I had no energy left for anything but merely breathing, and the mere thought of contacting publishers was as laughable as a moon-shot. But you took up its cause—as if you needed more to do!—and quickly found a home for this tale. Without you, this book would have remained a forgotten file on an anonymous hard drive.

To Martha Williams: it wasn't until the final stages of the editing process, when you were taking dictation, word-processing the changes, and performing so many of the author's duties I could no longer perform myself, that I realized that this book was as much yours as it was mine. Certainly I wrote the story, but we learned how to survive C.F. together, how to enjoy life in its presence and how to hope in its shadow. How fitting that at the end we write it together!

Just as important, you are a smart lady who is unimpressed by seminarian lingo. If I can't discuss something without resorting to SemiSpeak, then I know I'm behind the looking glass again, playing head games. Thank you for defending the reader from my addictions.

Finally, to all the people who contributed money so that we could deal with the cost of buying oxygen while I edited this book: you not only helped me breathe, you continued to prove the theme of the book in tangible terms. Lovely children of light: thank you.

*The details and ramifications of life with cystic fibrosis and diabetes
are as accurate as the author can describe them.*

THE FIRST TESTAMENT

'Aleph

In the beginning was the word: perfect, pure and holy—and then we started messing with it. It's a wonder God hasn't struck us down yet.

My name is Nathaniel. I am writing this book. It is a piece of fiction. That is to say, it is an irresponsible pack of lies. Don't believe a word of it!

I wish it could be different; I wish I could tell you the truth. I struggle, in fact, after that chimera—look at these smudges, already accumulating on the page—but I know I'm chasing the wind. It's a hopeless task, trying to capture the word. *Vanity*, as Solomon would say.

> I, the Speaker, ruled as king over Israel in Jerusalem; and in wisdom I applied my mind to study all that is done under heaven. What a sorry business it is, this burden God has laid on humanity! I have seen everything done under the sun, and all of it is emptiness: a striving after the wind. What is crooked cannot be straightened; what is lacking cannot be counted. *(Ecclesiastes 1:12–15)*

Listen: I'm about to be removed from the gene pool. This is no laughing matter. I have a demon called cystic fibrosis, a minor twisting in the blueprints of life, and it cannot be straightened. For that I am being punished mercilessly, strangled in my own bed.

I gasp as I write this: got another clot down there, somewhere in my ragged lungs. They multiply like gerbils, fill up my chest. I sleep upside down like a bat to shake them out, but it's not working. I am running out of time, hope and breath. The scar tissue is accumulating.

I am suffocating, striving after the wind.

So here I am: pushing words around on the page, hoping to find a little hope. Vanity, again.

When your oxygen runs low, you run out of hope. Did you know that?

Funny. Here you thought it was your own virtue, your will, your faith, your mind, and it turns out it was the function of chemicals running—or not running—in your brain. You can't even take credit for it.

How disappointing. Where's the vanity in that?

Breathe on me, breath of God; fill me with hope anew. Wipe out these little gerbils in my chest.

Agony.

My back hurts.

When I run out of air, all my muscles seize up—if it goes on long enough, my entire body turns into one big cramp—but it's always the shoulder muscles that go first, just under the blades. They're like a little alarm bell, clanging behind my head, letting me know that my hopeless condition is chemical and not a reflection of reality. This is only my personal experience, here, and it's possibly a little bluer than yours. My wife tells me I change color—she holds my dusky fingers next to hers and says see, see—but I never can tell. My eyes just see *me*, who is always *me*-colored, and they cannot see this alleged blue; they don't know what's going on.

But clang! The shoulder muscles know.

Blueness alert

Blueness alert

Blueness alert

This is possibly not the color of the actual universe.

O.K., try again.

Take a deep breath and start over. Find some hope.

In the beginning was the word…

No. No. I'm sorry. It's no use. Books, I'm afraid, are hopeless vanities. I'm a fool to even get started. Forgive me for my foolishness.

Look at the Gospel of John. *In the beginning was the word*—what a wonderful beginning, surely worth cribbing!

But what is a word, really? To the Greek, *word* meant the Reason, impassionate and immovable, that governed the cosmos. Yet to the Jew, John's word was a reference to Jonah's God, passionate, love-stricken and able to "repent of his anger."

You see how hopeless it all is? John writes a single word with his own private meaning, and already the Greeks and the Jews are reading it differently. Three versions of the truth now, and we haven't even gotten to the Bosnians yet. They have a word for *word*, but no word for *peace*. How shall John write a Gospel for the Bosnians?

Hopeless!

A word is nothing more than a symbol you've encountered over and over again. It is a fragment of your experience, a bit of your past that you connect to other bits.

You point at a thing of life and ask Mommy for it; "Glass," she says, and hands you a plastic cup instead. You drink her milk and her word. In your young world, "glass" now means something that will quench your thirst, give you sustenance. It could be plastic, ceramic, or wood. It is probably safe to throw, if your Mom has any sense.

When a real glass falls, it startles you by shattering. The word of life hadn't meant *fragile* to you yet.

My cup is shattering. Every word looks different to me now. I wish I could describe it to you. All the pieces are flying in the air, and they all look so strange. When you die, every word changes meaning suddenly, radically, like a glass shard twisting in the light.

How can I show this to you? How can I tell the truth?

I can only describe the pieces as they shatter. I can only hope my life is close enough to yours that *some* of the pieces will look roughly similar. Then the meaning you construct around this shard, this *word*, might be roughly parallel to mine— but God help us if our universes are different.

And yes, I have gerbils in my chest.

God help us!

You have more in common with me, by the way, than you do with John.

Beth

I have been singularly blessed.

I have seen a miracle!

This is how it happened: I was sitting under a pecan tree, feeling turgid and angry. The day was a hot oven, the air still and vacuous. I was panting twice as fast as I might have panted in winter, because hot air does, indeed, expand; and when it does this, there's not as much oxygen in a gulp of air. Simple physics. It made me turgid.

I also needed to go to work, and I was too stupid to get any work done. I was a computer programmer at the time, a darn good one, but not when my brain had only bad fumes to burn. I was having another one of *those* days, when I just couldn't juggle all the variables I needed to keep in my head. That made me angry.

Anger, incidentally, is the proper setting for a miracle. All the Gospels generally miss this point, that the realm of God is born with its teeth clenched and lots of howling.

Without anger, change doesn't happen. If you're happy with your life, you go with what's working. If you're depressed, you sit and suffer with what is not working. Anger is the only thing that breaks people out of their chains. It's just the way it is.

In the Gospels the disciples just drop all their things and go off on a pleasant lark with the Lord, like spiritual dilettantes with a funny whim in their heads. What a laugh! You must have thought we were all proper fools, space cadets with stars in our eyes. Don't believe it for a minute. There were plenty of reasons why we were willing to chuck it all. We were occupied people. You've seen the news clips. We were throwing our lives like stones.

Who were the targets? Romans, mostly. We all had our individual couplets— Romans and family; Romans and poverty; Romans and disease; Romans and vocation—but we had this commonality, this universal scapegoat.

Looking back, I see now that we were too heavily focused on the Romans as the source of all pain. It's easy enough to do when you're possessed by that demon called Legion; you forget the other sicknesses in your soul. But it was a convenience to make them the problem… the other things, we might have to take responsibility for changing. The Romans gave us a warm, cozy glow of powerlessness.

Identified problems are rarely the worst ones we have. They're just the ones we like to show to our friends.

Triage is a word you need to know, if you don't already. It might help you make sense out of your universe. It's a medical term, having to do with identifying critical wounds in a hurry. It was invented by army surgical hospitals, but it's big in any Emergency Room, and it might even be one of God's words.

All healers have to do triage. They can't fix everything at once, so they need to pick the most life-threatening things first. That's not always easy, because the obvious wounds may not be the worst wounds. My wife, who used to be a nurse, once attended a seminar on triage. During the class they projected a slide of a woman with a knife stuck in her eye, buried to the hilt—a real, full color slide. Everyone in the room wanted to end the nightmare... pull it out, pull it out, please God, that sight is hurting *me*... but the eye injury was stable. The knife was actually plugging up the wound!

Meanwhile, the woman's other injury was silently bleeding buckets into her chest cavity. She had precious few moments to live, and the difference was whether or not her healers worked according to disgust or wisdom.

That's triage.

A good healer knows this. She can be unnervingly calm in the storm of an emergency room, cool, efficient. She barks orders, thinking fast, moving while she grabs the most needful thing. Martha, Martha, it's not the dishes, come attend to what's happening here... Yes, Doctor, I'm coming...

Maybe that person in E.R. is a caring person inside. Maybe later on she will go off to the atrium and collapse. But while the emergency is on, she can seem a little rough, brisk, to those who don't know the severity of the wound. She might snap when people drag their feet. It's not a measure of what's inside, but what's happening outside: the situation is critical and the patient is dying. She'll hold your hand later on... and she might just leave that knife in your eye for a while.

Yes, you hear me; I've just given you my first sketch of the doctor that came to our ward.

Let's make this clear to all the materialists out there: when all was said and done, the Romans were still in Jerusalem and the poor were still poor. If that's what it was all about, this is the story of one convoluted failure.

And to all the spiritualists: we finished up this story with our bodies, rust, time and decay. If matter is a burden, we were still burdened by it.

When Lazarus was raised from the dead, he still had a pimple on his forehead, a bum knee that went out occasionally and no money to speak of. The Romans were still going to destroy his temple in a few years.

Triage.

Paint the scene red, then. Dull, hazy red. Color it with pain, distraction, denial and misdiagnosis. Make it look like the real world.

Two figures come up the road.

One of them is Philip, a guitarist with the rock band I used to belong to. He likes to play very loud: 900 watts in a closed space, his chords crashing against the walls like a jet taking off. My left ear is still a little deaf because it faced his amp.

We had a great time back then, drowning our powerlessness with sound. Rock is God's gift to the downtrodden, a source of energy for those who need to fight to live.

What a glorious release! James wailed on the drums, John pounded the bass, and I screamed myself bloody raw on an undersized vocal amp from Radio Shack.

> Rise up and
> Fight the Beast that tells us
> Peace is just an order for the day
> Abomination is
> The sheet of inaction
> Don't lie in bed
> And let others risk the way
> It's not your glory
> But dishonor
> To drink the cup that
> Drives our lives astray...[1]

I miss those days. We were angry as hell, but we sure had a lot of fun being angry. It's an amazing feeling, to strike a chord that makes the whole house shake. We called ourselves the "Sons of Thunder." We were very popular in bars.

I listen to wimp music most of the time now.

When my condition gets worse, I still put *The Abyss of Freedom* on the stereo and scream myself bloody raw—just until things settle down—but after a few months of living with my body I figure out the new parameters and quit grieving. Then I rediscover peace, blessedness and light jazz.

The other figure in this scene is Andrew. Poor, tentative Andrew! He was the most nervous kid I'd ever met, just waiting to be bullied. He'd hooked himself up with the Baptist to try to get some help. The Baptizer was strong and confident, sure of his faith, mesmerizing in a crowd—everything Andrew was not.

Andy went into the river hoping to soak up what John was washing off, but it didn't work. He got clean, not confident.

> They are snatching up
> Your children
> To fill their ears

With poison
Steam is not the
Only thing
To warp the
Shriveled mind
Do not bathe
With the enemy
Or frequent public places
They are not our kind.

Andrew crouches down in front of me with a worried-puppy face.

"How are you doing?" he asks.

Ick. I loll up at him with my half-glazed stupid look, trying to piece together an answer that will make him take his weepy eyes elsewhere.

"Don't ask him that," Philip says, putting his hand on Andrew's shoulder.

Andrew jumps at the touch.

"Why not?"

"You're just asking him to say he's fine, and he hates to lie."

Philip has been around me too long. He knows how ugly I can be.

Once, early in the spring, we were in the marketplace, buying yams. An old busybody accosted us after hearing me hack up my gerbils. She ragged on me about the way I was dressed—shorts, bare feet, uncovered head—and told me that if I just wrapped myself up sensibly I wouldn't have such a nasty cold. I let her blab until she was out of wisdom, then looked her square in the eyes and let her have it.

"No," I said, "actually, this isn't a cold, it's a terminal disease that causes a progressive deterioration of the lungs no matter how I dress… and thank you very much for reminding me of that fact, I'd almost forgotten it for a second."

She slunk away low enough to kiss a snake.

True story.

I used to love telling it, but now I confess I'm a little ashamed of it, too. It's the tale of a boy who wants to shoot whoever's responsible, but points the muzzle at a harmless old nag instead. I did a lot of that, back then. I had no tongue, I had a weapon.

Now at least I know who I'm angry at.

"You O.K.?" Andrew asks, wrinkling his nose.

"No," I say. "I'm dying."

Poor Andrew doesn't know what to do with the sudden stab. Innocent Andy! He looks about to cry. I stare at him with dead eyes, unwilling to give him any relief.

What a creep I am. I hate telling this story. Remember, it's fiction. Don't think bad of me, O.K.? I'm much better now.

"Do you think, maybe," he tries, looking for a positive note, "it's allergies? My nose has been a little stuffy lately, too—"

"—no—"

"—the ragweed—"

"—no—"

"—the dogwoods—"

"—no," I say, cutting him off, "it's my genes, Andrew. They're broke, they're killing me. This is not a stuffy nose, alright? This is like having a bag drawn over your head. Every day it gets a little tighter, and the hands pulling it down won't stop."

"—maybe the weather?" Andrew persists.

I press my hands to my temples. Dear God, you can't help but love someone so simple, can you?

Far better than tangled me…

Zzzt.

Zzzzzt.

System failure.

It comes on fast sometimes, without warning. It has a way of happening when I'm involved in a conversation. Stress, probably: my urge to choke Andrew, my mind's command to override it, my increased heart rate and talking more than breathing. My metabolism has leaped to a different state, and now all my chemicals are in the wrong position.

Suddenly my head is swimming. Black spots flood around me, like deadly clouds. My eyes do this upward roll thing when my science lab starts to shut down; people tell me it looks very frightening.

Not half as frightening as it looks from the inside. Imagine purple-black holes appearing in the very fabric of the world. The Void, the Un-maker. My demon is back, ripping up my universe. In a few minutes, I won't be able to see anything at all.

Sugar? Maybe. I have more than one broken part. I have to run too many meters to find out the source of any one crisis…

It might be the lungs, get the pulse-ox… what's the insulin like, prick the finger, get some candy… the pulse-ox is lying again, do you want to go with a pulmonary function, or an arterial sample? You push this spike down between the bones of the wrist—push it slowly until it hits the artery, while I will arch my back into the bed and try to come out the floor below—it feels like crucifixion, but you get a very important number…

too many meters

I have to run too many meters

before I can

lie

down

Once again the day came when the members of the court of heaven took their places in the presence of God, and Satan was with them. God asked him where he had been. "Ranging over the earth," Satan said, "from end to end." Then God asked Satan, "Have you noticed my servant Job? You will find no one else like him on earth: blameless and upright, fearing God and setting his face against evil. You incited me to ruin him without good reason, but his integrity is still unshaken."

Satan answered, "Skin for skin! There is nothing that fellow will grudge to save himself. But stretch out your hand and touch his bone and his flesh, and see if he will not curse you to your face."

Then God said, "All right, then. All that he has is now in your hands; but you must spare his life." *(Job 2:1–6)*

A bar bet!

If you're going to gamble with life, you have to know something about statistics. Let me give you the lowdown on the odds for cystic fibrosis, straight from the bookies.

People have to really work *hard* to get cystic fibrosis. First, they have to pick parents who are carriers. That's not easy. It comes only from North European stock. Furthermore, you can't go looking for them. Carriers show no outward signs of the disease. They have one bad copy of the gene, and one good copy. One's enough to live well. You could have such a land mine in your DNA right now, and never know it—unless you fell in love with another carrier. Scary, huh?

But all is not lost. If you find two unsuspecting carriers, you're still not done. Even if they bang their four genes together, the odds are still only one in four that the land mine will go off.

This is how it works:

Mom	Dad	Baby	
Good *Bad*	**Good** *Bad*	**Good Good**	= Free & Healthy
Good **Bad**	**Good** *Bad*	**Bad Good**	= Carrier & Healthy
Good *Bad*	*Good* **Bad**	**Good Bad**	= Carrier & Healthy
Good **Bad**	*Good* **Bad**	**Bad Bad**	= Boom!

Out of three children in our family, all three were born Bad, Bad.
Three out of three.
It's kind of like winning the Lotto, except your children die.

My brother and sister have already, to use that loveliest of biblical phrases, been gathered to their ancestors. They call across the great divide with Abraham, saying that the water is cool and the breeze is sweet, there is relief at the end of the long walk up Golgotha. They tell me to hold on, show courage, keep walking.

I am amazed they made it. Little kids, just barely teenagers, and they walked this road that is killing me. You brave children, you put this man to shame. How did you do it?

See how I weep and snap!

"What's he doing? Is he alright?"
"Yes."
"He's just laying there."
"I know. He's coming back."
"How often does this happen?"
"A lot."
"What a shame… well, they say God won't give you anything you can't handle."
"Yeah, well, don't say that around him."
A calm hand touches me.
"Here, Nat, I think you need some more."

Three out of three.
It is the central mystery of our family, the crippling load that distorts all our frames. Why the rigged game? Why did the odds pack their bags and leave town?

We have always lived with the unspoken, terrible fear that God had singled us out: *did it on purpose.* My parents never voiced it, but this fear hung in the air, a question over the dining room table, the hospital bed, the two graves. I grew up with it, breathed it in. It formed my very bones. If you look at an X-ray, you will find my spine bent very subtly into the shape of a question mark.

"I don't know how you stand it."
"It's O.K."
"Can't you do something more?"
"No. It's just the way it is. He's a complicated case."
"I have a cousin…"
"Andy, there aren't three doctors in this part of the country that even understand all the interactions. He's not your cousin, alright?"
"Oh."
"See, his eyes are starting to focus. He's coming around."
"My cousin gets violent."
"He usually doesn't. He just gets, um, honest."
"If he's going to be O.K., I'll just go, then."
"He's not your—yeah. Go… go. Just go."

When I'm coming back up there is an awful stretch of time waiting for things to improve, a time in which I'm strongly tempted to overdo the cure. It takes tremendous willpower to stop and wait. Imagine a drowning man deciding that one life preserver is enough, when a second one lies nearby.

I usually don't have that kind of control. When my head starts going under water, I get a little panicky. I don't want something that's *probably* enough; I want a sure thing. I've had enough of gambling. I don't roll the dice, don't buy Lotto tickets.

Don't make bar bets, either.

"Do you need more?" Philip asks.

I give him my terrific pumpkin impression. I'm still cloud-watching inside my head. Dark blue oxen walk by his face, chased by black porcupines. Lava lamp blobs swell and split; a black firework blooms in the center. With all that going on, it's hardly surprising that Philip can compete. It's worse than TV.

I can hear him, but the strange thing is that I can hardly make any decisions yet. When I try to reply, I lock up. I don't know why, but decision making is always the first to go.

I've stood in front of the candy rack in drugstores, telling myself *just pick one, any one, you're going to die stupid, it doesn't matter,* and been paralyzed by the choice. Friends will find me staring at a hundred different candy bars, all of which might save me, but I'll be rooted in place, unable to decide.

I used to pride myself on my intellect.

Vanity, vanity!

"If after all this you do not listen to me, I will then punish you seven times for each of your sins. I will break down your stubborn pride. I will make the sky above you like iron and the earth beneath you like bronze." *(Leviticus 26:18–19)*

The sacrifice acceptable to God is a broken spirit; a broken and contrite heart, O God, you will not despise. *(Psalm 51:17)*

Don't let God find out what your pride is, or you'll be taken down fast. Pick something unimportant to crow about. Take up stamp collecting, and paint a big, juicy prideful bull's eye on it. Remember Babel, and build a decoy tower for pride-seeking cruise missiles from heaven.

I'm not kidding. You've been forewarned.

"For God does speak once or twice—though humans may not notice. In a dream, in a vision of the night, when deep slumber falls upon them in their beds, then God may open the channel and terrify them with warnings to turn them from trouble and keep them from pride, to save their soul from the pit.

"Or one may be chastened on a bed of pain, with relentless aches in the bones so severe that food loses its appeal, and the choicest meal seems loathsome." *(Job 33:14–20)*

"Here," Philip sighs. "Have some more."

We all deal with pain and loss. I'm not applying for a special grant, here. This is all of us, writ large. Our legs slow down, our eyes grow dim, our parents die.

Sooner or later, we all ask, "Why are you doing this to me?"

It wasn't the issue itself, but the way it formed me. Children are not supposed to breathe that question when their heads are getting wired. It's an adult issue. When you expose kids to it, the pattern that is laid down is so foundational that it can never be undone without bulk-erasing their brains.

I'm just now beginning to understand the meaning of growing up in a house where all the kids were dying. It's an obscene psychological experiment on real people.

This fear of mine, it was laid down before I was six years old. It goes beyond learning, becomes architectural. Certain neurons zigged when they should have zagged. I can talk to them, dump new data into them, give them therapy, read them the Bible… and they stay zigged. There is always a child inside me that points at the book of Job and says the only word it knows: "us."

—And *please, please,* don't tell me about the happy ending, because the kid never read that far. When the adult reads it the child remains convinced, down to his very secret core, that chapter forty-two was tacked on by a Pollyanna who couldn't bear the awful truth: the Universe hates us, tortures us, and God gives permission for it to happen. God won't lift a finger to stop it… might even order it to make a point.

Where is that bulk brain eraser, anyway?

As I begin to come back up, my body suddenly gushes sweat. It's like a garden hose that has suddenly sprouted holes, very unnatural. I'm drenched in less than a minute.

I can hear someone moaning repeatedly, softly. Gradually I realize it's me, and I stop it. My body resubmits to my control in stages, and the civil war pauses for another day.

Up… up… I can see again.

Philip stands above me with a Minute Maid orange juice in his hands, half-consumed. A miracle! Philip hath wrought a miracle!

It was an insulin reaction, not oxygen deprivation—though, of course, the stress of poor oxygenation does funny things to the insulin. That's why I'm a "brittle" diabetic. I have a hard time finding just the right dose, because my metabolism is constantly shifting gears, depending on how well I breathe. But though the results are muddled, the science experiment has ended, according to the parameters laid down in a tavern long before. I am still alive.

"Feeling better now?" Philip asks.

I nod. Philip puts the cap on the bottle and it vanishes in a puff of smoke.

He makes no big deal about it. No weepy eyes, no exaggerated concern, just business as usual. Yet he doesn't try to cover it up, deny it, or put a happy spin on it. He is a true Southern gentleman, able to care in the minimal way that leaves you some dignity. I love Philip.

Andrew is gone: scared back into his own private cave, with one more monster added to his list of monsters. I will have to apologize later, see if I can coax him out again.

I feel awful.

Part of that is the aftereffects of the sugar dip—*trampled* is about the best word to put to it—but a lot of it is guilt, too. I run the classic cycle of abusive personalities: hurt, regret, apologize, vow, hurt again. The thing that causes me to lash out remains unaffected by guilt and promises.

"Met a man yesterday," Philip sniffs, in that laconic way of his, already tossing my breakdown aside. He stretches and sits down next to me, under the pecan tree. "John says he's the next David."

"We've heard that before."

"I know," he says mildly, tilting his head. He falls silent and watches traffic move along the old road: a careful, considering eye on the world.

Philip reminds me of an old lizard, too wise and slow to get ruffled, but not so slow as to go hungry. He has good instincts. When he says something, he says it from his gut.

I, on the other hand, always play the part of Mr. Rationality himself. Winning an argument is more important than anything to me, even being right; I have to prove that there's *something* that's not inferior. My demon makes me a logic abuser, the way some people sniff coke. How ugly! It's amazing how diseases can reach down into your soul and cripple everything.

My debating victories, I am sad to say, only last about four months. Then, long after I've worn Philip down to a confession of irrationality, I will have to admit that his gut was right and my head was wrong. This is always the way it is; I don't think my head has ever really been smarter than his gut.

Philip accepts this sequence of events gracefully, bless his heart. He never rubs it in, never leaves me to swing at nothing, never abandons me for more decent friends. I don't deserve it, I can't figure it. I wonder what's wrong with him, sometimes.

"His name is jesus,"[2] Philip says. "The son of Joseph, from Nazareth."

I snort. "Can anything good come out of Nazareth?" I ask.

"You should meet him," he shrugs, "before you judge."

"Philip, you know the prophets say the new David will be born in Bethlehem…"

Philip is mild, but resolute. "Yes, I know, we've been over all that. You're the scroll-reader, Nat, and I won't argue with you. But I think you should come and see."

He won't play our little game. He levels his lizard eye at me, and I know his gut is clicking. I think about wearing him down further, but decide I've been enough of a jerk for one day.

"O.K.," I sigh. "Let's go see the savior."

...the rejoinder identifies Nathaniel as a serious student of the scriptures, a trait confirmed by the evangelist's description of him as having been seated under a fig tree prior to Philip's invitation. In Rabbinic tradition, fig trees were frequently cited as appropriate locales for teachers to discuss the meaning of the scriptures with their students.[3]

Yes, and jesus cursed the fig tree because it would bear no fruit for him. Don't believe John for a second. It was really a pecan tree.

We walk down to the Sea of Galilee at my poky pace, a thirty-six-year-old man doing ninety. Philip walks slowly without appearing to; he ambles along beside me, admires the wildflowers. When we reach the waterside he steps into the wash and wets his feet. He smiles and gives me a nudge with his elbow.

"Nat, look."

A school of mullet is passing by, roiling the waters into green-gold bumps. They are weird little beasts, communal in the extreme. They pack themselves tightly on top of each other, as if there was no other room in the ocean: a busload of fish without the bus, traveling nowhere. What do they get out of it? I don't understand. We watch them weave away, gasping and shoving each other, odd little eyes bugging out, ludicrous.

"Perhaps they feed better that way," says a voice behind me.

I twirl around, startled. It was like he'd dropped out of the sky next to us, rather than walked.

Spooky.

"Maybe bigger fish dine better that way," I say, recovering my wits.

The man's eyes crinkle. "The world is not out to eat you, Nathaniel."

He is emaciated, hollowed out. He looks like he's been starving for forty days—not my idea of a new David. But his eyes are undimmed, and he holds himself as if he's full. He has a very small smile, easy to miss. It's not the smile of a people-pleaser, but a bemused turn at the corners. The countenance of an observer, an analyzer. He makes me feel naked.

"Good guess," I say, holding out my hand. "Yes, I'm Nat."

He doesn't take it—touch is never casual for him—but makes a small bow instead. His dishrag body is surprisingly gracious; he moves smoothly, unselfconsciously, making a formal maneuver seem like the most natural thing in the world. He even gets out of it cleanly, which is the tricky part. It diminishes him not a bit, but I can't help but think critically of it. A king that bows?

Strike two, Philip.

"You must be jesus," I say, "son of Joseph."

A fly buzzes around his face. "Yes, the son of a laborer from Nazareth," he says, brushing it away. "Where nothing but weeds and commoners grow." His eye searches out mine, which runs away quickly—too much contact in that gaze—so I find myself staring at his well-worn sandals. The mark of an itinerant worker, I think.

"Strike three," he says.

I look up at him in surprise.

"But it was no guess," he says. "You're an easy man to know, Nathaniel. A classic Israelite. Telling the truth when it hurts—especially when it hurts."

I freeze under his stare. His smile has gone back into the sky, left a line as straight as a challenge drawn in the dirt. I back away from it without thinking.

"You've been talking to Andrew," I say.

"No." He shakes his head slowly. "No, I knew you under the pecan tree, even before Philip."

"That's impossible. I can see for miles from there; you weren't around."

"It's a small impossibility. You will see greater wonders, Nathaniel."

His words are simple, but there is an intensity in them that grabs the tail of my spine and flops it back and forth, the way you shake out a dirty blanket.

you are
exposed
run
now

"What do you mean?" I say, speaking loud enough to drown out a host of demons. It jumps out unnaturally loud from my throat, embarrassing.

quiet

"You are about to be kidnapped by heaven," he says. "It's going to scare the hell out of you. You will see heaven crash down over your head, and angels will lift you out of the pit you cling to. You cannot stay broken forever, Nathaniel."

we know you
are the son

He says all of this with a burning passion, like Moses' bush. I wish I could get it down right on paper: the words need to glow. Ink just doesn't do it. He is completely serious, and the force of his voice alone is nothing compared to the force of those crackling eyes. I feel it strip the skin off my bone, flay all my secrets open.

"Oh, Christ," I say, falling before him. "Oh God." It comes out like somebody else's voice; I barely recognize it. I reach out to touch his ragged sandals with my finger, but he steps back quickly, leaving my hand stretched out in the dust.

"Get up," he commands. "Get up, and follow."

Then he turns around and walks away.

Upon leaving the synagogue they went to the house of Simon and Andrew. James and John went with them.

Simon's mother-in-law was ill in bed with a fever, but as soon as they told Jesus about it, he took her by the hand and helped her to her feet. The fever left her, and she waited upon them.

That evening they brought to him all who were ill or demon-plagued; and the whole town was there, gathered at the door. He healed many who suffered from various diseases, and drove out many demons. He would not let the demons speak, because they knew who he was.

Very early the next morning he got up and went out. He went away to a lonely spot and stayed there in prayer. But Simon and his companions searched him out, found him, and said, "Everyone is searching for you." He said, "Let's continue to the nearby villages, so I can preach there, too. That is why I have come." So all through Galilee he went, preaching in the synagogues and driving out the demons.

Once he was approached by a leper, who knelt before him, begging his help. "If it is your desire, I know you can cleanse me."

Filled with incensed compassion, Jesus stretched out his hand. "It is my desire," he said. "Be clean!" Immediately the leprosy left the man and he was cured.

Jesus sent him away with a strong warning: "Don't talk about this to anyone. But show yourself to the priest and offer the sacrifices that Moses commanded for this cleansing; that will certify your cure."

But the man went out and made the whole story public; he spread it far and wide, until Jesus could no longer appear in any town, but had to stay in the open country. Even then, people kept coming to him from all quarters. (Mark 1:29–45)

Gimel

There's a wedding today. Don't be late!

I set my alarm for two and a half hours before we have to leave—a bare minimum, allowing for therapy and a shower. I'm the slowest starter in the county.

I can't sleep in one stretch anymore; I have to sleep in shifts. The longer I lie down, the more packed my gerbils become, and the longer therapy takes. So I go to bed for three hours; work for two hours; go back to bed, and get up about lunchtime—except on Sundays. The day that God rested is the day I go short. I don't know how that's going to come out. Or maybe I do know, and just don't want to think about it yet.

Brrring.
Mr. Diabetic rises and takes his sugar reading.

157

I figure out my insulin dose, mix regular and ultra-lente insulin together and inject it into my leg. A miracle will happen in about one hour: I will be able to benefit from my food. Just a tiny speck of insulin is all it takes to make the difference. If you saw how small the amounts were, you'd be amazed.

C.F./diabetic patients are hypersensitive to insulin; even normal diabetics are amazed. A half a unit makes a huge difference.

My insulin is a genetically engineered product. It is being grown in vats by a bunch of yeast cells—the bread of life, literally! Thank God for the people who think of this stuff.

But dosage is tricky. My sliding-scale chart is the most complicated one my doctor has ever seen. He chuckles when he sees it, like an engineer contemplating an absurdly complicated machine built out of tinker-toys. The day he typed it into his computer, he was nearly beside himself with glee. He's a wonderful man who delights in problem solving. That's why I'm his patient.

We worked out this miracle of tinker-toy engineering with a third doctor, an endocrinologist. My doctor sent me to her because he wasn't happy with my old insulin regimen, which was designed for a different species of patient.

The doctor that had set up my old schedule was unfamiliar with C.F., and his routine just kept snapping me up and down constantly. That's dangerous: an insulin coma can kill you right away. So to avoid the coma I was letting my blood sugars float way too high, which was killing me slowly instead—but frankly, C.F. is likely to get me before the organ damage is much of an issue. It takes about ten years to show up.

Besides organ damage, though, the high sugars were also speeding up my C.F. problems. Bacterial infections love sweet blood, so the sweeter I got, the more infections I grew in my lungs. Then, to complete the upward spiral, the C.F. infections were releasing chemicals that made my blood even sweeter. It was time to call in a specialist, quick, before I turned into a human Hallmark card.

Let me tell you about grace:

Up until I met Dr. Wilson, I hated my diabetes care. It didn't work, and in the diabetes community when something doesn't work you blame the patient. But Dr. Wilson didn't blame me. I came whining to her that nothing was working and no one understood—it was different, it wasn't my fault, *weep, sob, pity, pity*—and you know what she did?

She listened.

She not only listened, she calmed me down and *agreed* with me.

Here I was, unloading my frustration and anger—expecting to be blamed once more and already starting to get frenzied about it—and what did she say?

"You're right," she said. "That regimen won't work for you. Your case is different. But we'll work out something."

Then she began to teach me. It turned out it was even more complicated than I had thought. I came prepared to argue with her, and pretty soon she was convincing *me* that I hadn't grasped how difficult it really was.

What if that happened to everyone in heaven, too? Wouldn't it be outrageous?

Or even worse: suppose you had actually *made* the standard regimen, and then discovered you didn't have to? Wouldn't that tick you off?

You could have had cake!

This is how the human body is supposed to work: you eat, and that raises your blood sugar (glucose). Your body's insulin kicks in, converting your glucose to energy and body fat. You complain to all your friends about going up to a size-40 waist. You fork over a fortune for an annual pass to Vic Tanny's, and after sweating on the machines for two weeks, give up, stay home and watch Oprah. This is how the Universe was designed. It is God's intention for us all.

My Universe looks a little different. First off, I must take enzyme pills to digest my food. Without outside enzymes I could eat all day and starve to death.

"Oh, I wish I had that problem," dieters have sometimes said to me.

No.

You don't.

My enzymes are another modern miracle, like insulin. They're not made from genetically tweaked yeast, though. They are considerably more low-tech. To be specific, they are made from grinding up pig guts.

Eeeew!

I know, I know: I hear the animal rights folks stomping off. But listen, the pigs are on their way to becoming pork chops no matter what I do. They're not going to need their enzymes anymore, and if those enzymes can help C.F. patients digest their pork chops, well, there's kind of cosmic economy going on there, don't you think?

Anyway, the pills don't work perfectly, so they complicate my insulin regimen. I get the same punch out of 300 calories of wheat as I get out of 150 calories of oats.

There's no textbook for this, I just have to figure out how it interacts with my system.

The first lesson Dr. Wilson taught me was this: pay attention to what I'm actually absorbing with the pills, and throw those helpful little diabetic food exchange charts out the window. Life data takes precedence over paper data. If reality does not match theory, it's not reality's fault.

Take *that*, dietitians and theologians of the world!

More importantly, Dr. Wilson taught me about timing. If you don't get the insulin at the right time, there's no magic dose that will work. Insulin rises slowly after you take the shot. You want it to arrive when your sugar is rising, not before. It's like throwing a long pass to a wide receiver; if the football isn't at the goal at the same time as the receiver, he's not going to catch it, no matter how wide he is.

My timing is very complicated. The enzymes are coated to sneak through my stomach undissolved, and unload their magic somewhere in the small intestine. Tough foods get digested there. But some easy foods break down in my wimpy stomach without help; some even break down with the saliva in my mouth.

Each meal has a mix of different foods digesting at different times—a bunch of footballs in the air.

I have to take a look at what the mix of food is, and figure out when to give myself the insulin shot. There's no perfect time, just a rough average. If I take my insulin too soon, I can plow my blood sugars into the ground, and if I take it too late, I can go into orbit.

So I've learned to study how each of them digests. It's vitally important that I understand how long each of them will take before they unload their sugars. When I look at a plate of food now, I see time and sugar, rather than taste.

How strange!
- Beef and pork are slow. Turkey is slower, chicken faster. Turkey peters out before the other meats.
- Potatoes are medium speed-wise, but they pack quite a punch once they get there.
- Grains are generally very fast, but their final value varies wildly.
- Corn is fast, peas are slow.
- Grapes can raise my blood sugar if I look at them hard.
- Strawberries are safe and delicious in almost any amount. Pineapple and kiwi are fast risers with little endurance.
- Hot dogs, Chinese food, and styrofoam are in the same basic food group. I may as well eat the packaging and donate the food to a shelter.

Sound dizzying?

After a while, you get the hang of it.

My new insulin coach drew a lot of X's and O's on the board, and together we created a better game plan. She put me on two different types of insulin, worked out a schedule that brought me closer in line, and taught me how to call audibles for myself, rather than relying on canned plays.

That was the most important step. Until then, I was trying to do this with rigid, inflexible systems engraved on stone tablets.

I add or subtract units from the rough schedule, depending on how well I'm breathing, then add or subtract units depending on what's on the menu. I adjust my timing so the insulin rises in my blood at the same time as my sugar. If I've gauged everything well, it works like a charm—and it always works better than the old program. I still throw incompletes once or twice a week, but I used to fumble *every day*. Given the complicated parameters that are going on, that's a near miraculous improvement.

Dr. Wilson was marvelously supportive. When I'd bring in my spreadsheets tracking the ups and downs of the week, I'd come in like a whipped puppy, expecting to be beaten, and she'd study the numbers intently for several minutes, then point out the moments where it *had* worked. Then she'd suggest some modifications for the times it hadn't worked. We'd discuss how I'd handled it, and she'd teach me how to think on my feet about a process that was as messy and complicated as life. I never got blamed once, and sometimes that, in itself, was enough to make me want to cry. It was such a change from my previous diabetic experiences!

I had gotten to where I didn't even feel like trying anymore: I'd settled for the rather bleak hope that C.F. would kill me before diabetes made me go blind or chopped off my feet. In the face of constant failure, crushing condemnation and no other alternatives, I just gave up and tried not to think about it.

Now I actually have a sense of some control. The odds may still be stacked against me but at least I feel like getting out on the field again. That's the kind of thing grace can do.

Dr. Wilson, you are the gift of God to me!

Dr. Wilson is not a lone angel, however, but a member of an advancing vanguard. She is part of a care team that got tired of accepting failure and began to search for new diabetic guidelines that would achieve realistic success in reducing amputations and deaths. This is an example of the new kind of thinking that evolved from that search. As you read it, I would like you to imagine yourself hearing it in a surprising place: a church. Imagine sitting in a church that had moved from the image of jesus as defense attorney and knew him as he was first known: a healer. Replace the word *diabetes*, if you wish, with any word referring to the wounds the church considers within its jurisdiction.

> Sometimes people are just overwhelmed, and shut down. I've coined a new disease I call "Diabetes Overwhelmus." Everybody, from time to time, feels overwhelmed by the demands of their diabetes... Guilt is one of the most pervasive feelings and potentially one of the most destructive. When people feel guilty they tend to beat themselves up. That drains their motivation for making changes. But you can't be perfect. If you think about all the things you need to do to manage diabetes day to day, you couldn't be perfect for a single day, let alone a lifetime.[4]

Imagine what would happen if *that* bit of Life-data became common knowledge. The Dietitians would have a fit!

Mr. Cystic Fibrosis takes over while Mr. Diabetic recedes.

I receive the new dressing kit from the overnight-delivery service. We talked to the people in Bethesda—over a thousand miles away—and told them the last dressing kits stunk. This morning new dressing kits arrive at my door. Amazing!

Fed Ex, you're a miracle. You make the C.F. Foundation pharmacy possible—and the C.F.F. pharmacy's discounts makes our staggering medical budget possible.

Thank you, Fed Ex and C.F.F. You are both gifts of God to me.

The dressing kits are for the Groshon catheter I have imbedded in my chest. We have to change the dressings each week to keep the hole in my skin from becoming infected.

My Groshon catheter is a marvel of medical engineering. It delivers intravenous antibiotics to a spot one inch from my heart, where the blood flow is strong enough to keep the highly caustic drugs from eating up my veins. Until I had the Groshon put in, I had to run my antibiotics into my arms, which mangled my veins fiercely;

sometimes I'd only get two bags through my site before it was wasted. If you look at my body, you can still see the knots and gnarls from that time. Painful, awful.

It was also a painful experience for my wife, who had to start each new site. Starting a new I.V. is an awful lot like pushing a nail into someone's arm; that's tough to do, when the arm belongs to your husband. You kind of hope the site will last longer than two bags. The Groshon made Martha's life a lot easier, and that made my life easier. Martha is one of the great gifts of God to me; I don't like to see her hurt.

Dr. Groshon, your work has been a gift of God to both of us.

One minor oddity: wrapping my chest in Saran Wrap to take a shower.

Just having the familiar green and white box in there looks like a topic for Sally Jesse Raphael—guests come out of our bathroom with funny smiles on their faces.

But without the Groshon, I never would have completed my course of Vancomycin, and without Vanco (rhymes with Drain-O) running through my heart I never would have kicked the staph infection that was beginning to look permanent. The fevers that staph produced were ferocious; I'm glad Dr. Pettigrove decided to pound it with everything he had—even if it took a hole in my chest to do it.

Two months afterwards, I was pronounced free and clear. My staph complained to the Labor Relations Board about unfair working conditions and quit. They haven't answered the phones since then—and good riddance to them. I was doing all the work, anyway.

Thank you, Dr. Pettigrove. I may whine from time to time, but you truly are the gift of God to me.

O.K., time to puff.

My breathing treatment is basically a powered water-hookah. I look like a high-tech hashish smoker while communing with it. The active ingredient, Alupent, is best described as a bottled car accident. It does exactly the same thing to your body that happens when you have a near-miss on the freeway. *Thump-thump-thump*: adrenaline, shakes, nerves. If I have too much, I feel like I'm going to have a heart attack—which, the literature assures me, is a distinct possibility. (Great sense of humor, those folks who write med sheets.)

Why inhale a car accident? Well, it wakes up the sleepy critters in my lungs. They like to sleep like kittens in a pet-shop window, and I have to unpack them from their nighttime bliss. The more gerbils I shake out, the longer and happier I live.

So an artificial car accident shakes them out, and then I can breathe. It's rough on the system, but it's cheaper than banging up Fords, and a whole lot more attractive than suffocation. I do this by choice, and keep the alternative in mind.

Today I estimate the dosage well—it depends on how many fur balls are down there—so my hands don't shake too much when I'm done.

Who figures this kind of stuff out, anyway? Who bottles fender benders and gives them to children? Whoever you are, thank you. It's insane, but it works.

Take one ounce of lactulose, rinse out the little measuring cup, grab something to drink with it. This is to handle Mega-Colon, which is not the archnemesis of James Bond but a description of what lies underneath my stomach. Where the rest of you folks have little garden hoses, I've got the Holland Tunnel. The engineering changes are necessary to accommodate the traffic, which is also a little more impressive. It has many fascinating ramifications that I'm sure you'd rather not hear about.

Sometimes even this architectural marvel comes to a state of gridlock, and that makes me writhe, pant and scream for an hour or so. It is the most potent pain I experience, a kind of fugue on the little one-note melody called "cramp." Think of food poisoning and raise it to a four-voice Bach masterwork, and you'll get the idea. When it happens, my wife does what she can, curls up on the couch to not read a book, and the cats pace anxiously, wondering where the catfight is. When it's done I'm bathed in a cold sweat, deathly white, and have the general posture, ambition and countenance of a ratty old dishrag.

Listen: at the first hint of trouble, I take lactulose *religiously.*

Whoever invented it, give me a call, and I'll put you in my will.

Better take my oral antibiotics now. They work better between meals, if I can stomach it. The current one I'm taking is powerful enough to drop bacteria, badgers and small cows at thirty paces. Great stuff, although they never teach these things how to differentiate between the bad fauna and the good fauna—it sterilizes bowels, which makes you very, um, quick on the feet—so yogurt is part of the treatment. (I like boysenberry, if you're stopping at the supermarket.)

I've been taking this one for a while now, so the effectiveness is starting to fade. Too bad.

All my antibiotics will eventually give in to resistance. Darwin would have been fascinated to meet one of us. Eventually the bugs figure out how to eat my drugs, and they can actually *pass the information on* to other types of bacteria, through free-floating packets of genetic material! (Even my stomach fauna figure out resistance, toward the end of an antibiotic's life! Isn't that amazing?)

Some people debate evolution, some people demonize it... but C.F. patients live it every day.

I'm sorry to be losing the Floxin; I was very grateful for it. It is one impressive pill. I know this because it has impressive side effects. In addition to sterilizing my intestines, it gives me twisted, fever-like dreams, and the feeling it gives my body is... well... try to imagine sand running out a small hole in your veins. All of your arms and legs have a constant, granulated draining feeling, and your energy flows out with it. Sand in the blood, pouring, pouring.

That's almost exactly how it feels, once you work up to the maximum dose. I think of it as Mr. Sandman's candy, since it also makes me sleepy about four hours after I take it.

These kinds of side effects are important for oral antibiotics; that's how you know you're getting your money's worth. If it ain't screwing up other significant parts of your system, it's not going to be able to play in the big leagues. When you have advanced-stage C.F. you want your antibiotics to be toxic to everything two inches shorter than you are—and just a little rude to you, too. Then they just *might* be able to talk back to the full-metal-jacket gerbils down there.

I owe my life to the constant march of these gerbil poisons. Whoever makes these things, thank you—and keep them coming. Quickly. The cabinet's looking a little bare these days.

Time to commune with Flo. She's a big green torpedo in our bedroom: bottled oxygen.

How do they get it into a can? I don't know. But they pump her up to 2,000 pounds per square inch, and I empty her out at 2 to 3 liters per minute, depending on gerbil density. When she starts to work, my legs tingle, my back stops aching, and I stretch as luxuriously as a cat in the sun. Martha laughs at me. She thinks I enjoy it too much.

I *really, really* appreciate Flo.

It's hard to believe I resisted getting her, but I did. I had a fear, common among lung patients, that I would become "addicted to oxygen." My doctor shook his head at my displaced Puritanism and informed me of a startling fact: *Everyone on the planet is addicted to oxygen.*

My problem is that I'm not getting as much of a fix as y'all, and the withdrawal symptoms are hell. So I laughed and edged into the world of bottled air.

Flo was ugly as sin when she arrived, but Martha and I dress her up. It keeps her from turning our bedroom into a hospital room. Today she's wearing jeans and a straw hat, feeling casual. She's worn my old clericals before—praise God from whom all blessings Flo—and she looks great in a satin bathrobe. No hips, though, so some fashion statements are just plain out.

I set her to 2.5 liters, slip on the mask, and continue to work.

Flo has a very long tube. I can almost cover the entire house. If I want to go out, I have two portable units (named Oscar and Oort, if you're keeping a scorecard) which I can sling over my shoulder. Mobility, of a sort. Clunky, but not as clunky as a casket. I also have a cool new regulator for the portables. It's computerized, which is always a sure way into my gadget-loving heart, and it stretches a two-hour tank out to ten hours, which is even better.

It does this with a neat but simple trick: it waits until I start to breathe, then puffs a brief snort of oxygen into my nose. That way I'm not wasting gas during my exhale cycle. The only problem is the sound, which is a little more bionic than I'd wish. Sometimes I feel like Robo-Nathaniel.

Whoever works on this stuff, thank you. You are the gift of God to me.

But think about the sound. A slower ramp-down on the valve…?

Time for percussion therapy: P.T., in the medical biz. Everyone else calls it a beating. I lie upside down on my bat couch and vibrate my chest with a portable hand unit. This isn't quite as good as getting whomped on with real hands—a human can really get your chest moving—but it's something I can do by myself. Later on in the day, I'll have Martha give me a whomp. (Here's a standard joke from C.F. culture, a place where the darkest things are made light: "It's a little perk I get from marrying him—how many women have their husbands ask them for a beating?")

The nine-degree slope of the bat couch is just right: the gerbils lose their footing and tumble toward my throat.

Mom and Dad built the couch. Thanks, Mom and Dad. It's much better than the closet door I was using before you visited.

You, too, are the gift of God to me.

There are other drugs, procedures and tricks:
- I take timed-release theophylline to liquefy my phlegm;
- I drink an expensive herbal tea named Essiac to jump-start my cough;
- When the pink froth of pulmonary edema shows up, it can be reduced by nips of cream sherry (hey, it's in the nursing manual—says right here…);
- Salt loss is a constant problem, so I salt everything, including my ham and Jell-O;
- When I cough too hard I can break open "a bleeder," so I pour a topical decongestant down my throat to keep my lungs from filling with blood. (The doctors thought that was ingenious; but the idea was Martha's.)
- I've discovered that drinking Diet Dr. Pepper during my breathing treatment reduces the bleeders. (Why? Beats me. Life data.)

Then there are more heroic measures for when my system starts to go down; but this is my daily routine.

Artificial insulin, artificial traffic accidents, artificial air, artificial veins, artificial immune system, artificial enzymes… These are the things that make a man out of a child who would have died. When people get all nostalgic and misty about the good old days, I don't sing along. I have no fantasies about visiting a simpler age. I am a product of late-twentieth-century Western medicine. The cozy past would have rubbed me out before my first birthday.

Even in 1960, when I was born, my warranty ran out at 13, and it's been extra mileage ever since. It's this modern set of tinker-toys and procedures that's done it.

I am a science experiment, run daily.

The routine is done. I'm finally ready to roll.
We've still got some day left. Looks like we'll be able to make it!

Martha's learned to cool her jets and wait until I give the thumbs-up. She used to get a little crazy about being late, but cutting my routine short is a VERY BAD IDEA, and you can't tell how long it's all going to take. My drainage, in particular, is completely in the hands of the gerbils. But today they're feeling gracious, and they march out with only moderate effort. Only forty-five minutes, and I can breathe well enough to walk around. I pack up my portable life-support equipment, and we head to Cana.

We get there a little late, so we have to sit in the back row, but we *do* see the vows; and the reception is a big success—except for one little hitch, which jesus quickly solves at the request of his mother. He turns some water into wine so the party can go on. Big deal.

"I am not myself the source of the words I speak to you; they come from the Father dwelling in me, doing his work. Believe me when I say that I am in the Father and the Father is in me; or else accept the evidence of the deeds themselves. In truth I tell you, those who have faith in me will do what I am doing; and will accomplish even greater things, because I am going on to the Father." *(John 14:10b–12)*

Next time someone starts telling you that science and faith are incompatible, remind them that Western science appeared after Christ, not before; that some scholars think Christianity was *necessary* for the development of Western science,[5] and that heavyweights like Johannes Kepler and Francis Bacon saw the exploration of God's mind and method as a kind of praise, not a negation of it.

Christians in the seventeenth century were driven by a vision that still exists today; if we understand the Creator's ways well enough, we might build a better tomorrow. Their explorations and experiments were acts of hope and praise.

JOHANNES KEPLER
FRANCIS BACON
LOUIS PASTEUR
RUDOLF VON EMMERICH
SIR ALEXANDER FLEMING
RENÉ DUBOS…

Thank you for continuing the Healer's work.
You have all been gifts of God to me.

Daleth

When he saw the crowds he went up the hill and sat down. When his disciples had gathered around, he began to teach them, saying "Blessed are they…" *(Matthew 5:1–3)*

They come before the sun, two times two times three: ragged arks of people across the sleeping hills, escaping a flood of misery that's been pouring down on this land since before Elijah was weaned. They are dark shapes bent over with their burdens, clots in the grey twilight, hoping to be first and despairing to see the crowds already forming. Mourning brings them together as the Son rises and dispenses his first communion, a sharing of the bread of life. Broken bread: he puts them back together with a blessing and they return with joy.

Have you seen the change? Once will last you forever, and here there are thousands.

They do not call him *Rabbi* at first, but *Iatros:* healer, physician. Starving children learn no lessons. He gives them bread and the wine will come. Watch.

Tardy Sol rises above the horizon and blinks his eye. Something new under his belly! The surprised clouds begin to glow warm and red, then pink against a turquoise dome. The entire world blushes at its tawdry faith. Why did we ever think life was bad?

God is good, God is good, God is good. He whispers it to them, and they whisper it to each other as they find their place; some in awe, some in tears—some in astonishment.

And then, before any of us would believe possible, it is over. The eating of the five thousand ills. He takes it all into himself and becomes tired, but finishes the plate.

As the satisfied students sit, the Teacher stands. The bread is done; time for wine.

"I have good news to tell you," he announces.

"God is good!

"All you who are poor and heavy-laden: congratulations! Your comfort will outlast the stars.

"All you who toil in the night, you truck drivers, shop rats, nurses, watchmen, cashiers: congratulations! The world is yours. You will eat and play with your children again.

"All you who long for the days of Jubilee: congratulations! Your debts will be forgiven seven-fold, and your credit cards will melt in the noonday sun."

On and on he goes, like a master of ceremonies at a convention, handing out celestial door prizes. It is crazy behavior, but the crowds believe it. As he names them, they make strange noises, find each other, laugh and dance the rumba… all the behavior you see at the Lotto, the bingo parlor, the slot machines. No one questions his ability to hand out the goods. Hasn't he just jangled the keys to heaven? Whoever can command bones to mend; demons to flee; deaf ears to hear and blind eyes to see; isn't he the Son of God? Isn't he David, Elijah, Moses, all wrapped up in one? Yet he only claims one title for himself, an obscure phrase from a book for crackpots: the Son of Man.

Most don't recognize it, I think. Apocalyptic is pretty far-out stuff, radical. I wonder, more than a little anxiously, just how into this stuff jesus is. Who are we getting attached to? Is this one of those end-of-the-world scams?

I ask him about his chosen name in the evening, and his eyes crinkle.

"New paper to wrap new fish," he says. "I think it's high praise to be descended from Eve."

"But we are all—"

"—you are *all* children of God," he responds. "That's nothing special. Do you have any other source? Are you children of Beelzebub? No, you're made by God, like salt of the earth is made by God.

"Can salt be anything but salty? Don't try; even if you managed it, what would be the point? You'd no longer be good for anything, except to be thrown out and trampled.

"Don't claim to be anything less than what God claims for you.

"You are the light of the world. Does anyone light a lamp and put it in a trash can? Of course not! You put it on a stand, so it can give light to everyone in the house. Don't claim darkness and trash; let your light shine. Then everyone can praise the One who lit it."

He walks over toward a single mother named Sara, still trying to bundle together all of her baby things: crib and toys; car seat; blankets and bib; pacifier and formula. The *strick-strick* of Velcro punctuates the evening air.

She looks up at him, embarrassed to still be fumbling with everything.

He smiles down at her.

"Listen!" he roars, turning to the lingerers on the hills. "This is the way you praise God: to be most fully what you were made to be, salt and light, human in every way.

"Does a pot fight with the potter? Does it resist its shape? Then the potter must put it back on the wheel. But the clay that gives itself over to the potter's hand comes off the wheel and sits on the table—and everyone who sees it praises its maker."

He lifts up Sara's baby, tosses it in the air.

"This is the praise of God!"

It squeals as it comes down: *do it again, do it again!*

He touches it lightly on the nose; it goggles up at him in astonishment.

"And this is the praise of God!" he adds, waving his hand at the baby's mother.

Sara looks sheepish and quickly reclaims the baby. She scuttles off down the hill, wondering how to escape the sudden attention.

But the baby just laughs and laughs.

He

I was an unusual C.F. child. I didn't show many symptoms—didn't even develop a cough until adolescence. By that time my brother and sister were long dead, and it was like a rediscovery for me. I didn't remember much of what I'd seen back then.

My mom tells me I took it in stride when I was little. I imagine I did. I do remember loving them intensely.

But I remember sitting in the waiting room to Dr. Chang's office, watching another boy cough into a Kleenex. I hadn't seen the C.F. cough in years. I was disgusted and offended by it; I felt like gagging. My reaction, in fact, was entirely, sadly based on what his illness was doing to me, as if he was doing it on purpose. Does that sound self-centered and ugly? It's pretty normal, I think.

Now that I'm on the other end of the Kleenex, I see it all the time. I'd guess 5 percent feel it in full flower, and 85 percent feel it in some dim way, but shove it out of their mind because it's not nice.

When I started to cough myself, it always felt like punishment for that day in the waiting room. I was now standing in my own condemnation; I knew what I looked like through the eyes of another. Most C.F. kids don't have the chance to view their illness from such a distance.

I wish I'd never been given that chance.

> "Pass no judgement, and you will not be judged. For as you judge others, so you will be judged, and whatever measure you deal out to others will be dealt back to you." *(Matthew 7:1–2)*

This was my first glimpse at the cause-and-effect nature of judging. It's like the law of gravity: it requires no action on God's part at all.

When you create a scale and hold somebody to it, there will always be a secret place that knows you can be held to it, too. You may shove that inescapable knowledge down beneath your day-to-day consciousness, but the nighttime self knows better. It will let you know that you're a pretty small catch, too.

People go two ways with that knowledge. They can be consumed by it, or they can cover it up with massive layers of denial and dishonesty; self-righteousness; religious hyperactivity; finger-pointing.

The thing we call "pride"—that central sin of classic theology—is usually the fruit of fear and self-loathing. I don't think I've ever run into pure, sinful pride, to tell the truth. Whenever I encounter a classic case of it and listen well, I begin to hear a structure as shaky as mine, being propped up with bad wood. I'm not startled by that discovery anymore. I've come to think of it as an entirely natural part of life... as natural as an apple falling out of a tree.

"You may eat from every tree in the garden, but not from the tree of the knowl-edge of good and evil; for on the day you eat from that tree, you will surely die."
(*Genesis 2:16–17*)

When I began to cough, I couldn't bear to see myself in the eyes of others. I knew I was a disgusting creature, making other people gag with my bodily fluids. So I tried to cover it up, not cough in public. That's slow suicide to someone with C.F.; the whole goal of treatment is to get the stuff up and out, so it doesn't turn solid and close off the lungs. Every time I repress the urge to cough, I'm shaving a few min-utes off of my life. Quite a price to pay to avoid looking sick!

But the fruit of judgment, as Genesis warns, is death. It is like heat rising; like oxygen and rust; like the erosion by the wind. The day you bite into the tempting fruit is the day you begin to eat yourself alive.

Maybe, like Adam and Eve, you discover nothing happening right away. Maybe it's just tasty and satisfying to decide who gets what they deserve and who doesn't... but with that first bite you have entered a different world, where thorns, thistles and the pain of childbirth will become *punishments* for your own secret shortcomings, rather than the random shots of life. It is your secret judgment that makes it so.

If people are evil, they must be punished, right? Maybe that's why the storm hit your house.

"Who told you that you are naked? Who made you feel exposed and humili-ated?"
I did, Lord. I thought it was safe to know who was good and who was evil. Now it's cold out here, and I wish I hadn't gotten started.

Through our own judgments we cast ourselves into a world of moral cause and effect, and the best God can do is knit together garments to help protect us in our harder, crueler world—which is the small bit of grace that happens at the end of our sad story: a picture of a mourning God with a sewing needle and thread, vowing that we won't remain maimed for all of eternity.

The final sight from the garden is God as grieving gran'ma, shaking her head and wondering what on earth will happen to her children.

I still see that boy in the waiting room every time I cough—and it still feels like poetic justice.

My own attempts at covering myself were as futile as fig leaves. I had to hide from everyone when my sickness erupted. The more often it happened, the more I began to dread groups of people. The worst was having to use a public restroom—I couldn't control who might come in and hear me. I would kneel in the little stall, puking and spitting into the dirty toilet, dreading those fateful words from outside the door:

"Are you alright?"

"Should I call someone?"

"Are you sick?"

This is what I would hear:

Stop, stop.

You're hurting me with your uncleanliness. You're making me want to puke, too.

Can I do something to make you stop?

"No," I would gasp, trying to swallow it. "It's… O.K. This is—ah—normal for me…"

They would finish their own business and hurry out of the room, and then I'd finish my own in wretched misery. Sometimes they would call the mall security guard. Once I had an emergency medical team break in on me.

I can't tell you what that feels like, to have your own sickness be the source of a false alarm. Everyone is making a big fuss and watching, and you bear the responsibility for wasting the time of professionals who might truly be needed elsewhere—and then there are the quick micro-glances of skepticism, the up-and-down evaluation: *Is he really drunk or high? Is he being punished for yesterday's pleasures?*

> They are fierce waves of the sea,
> Foaming shameful deeds;
> They are stars that have
> Wandered from their course,
> And the place forever reserved for them is blackest darkness.
>
> (Jude 13)

Then, of course, there were the Christian reactions, no less complicated. Prayer is an obvious response to illness; and if the illness is a broken leg or fever, it should not feel condemning. But if the sickness is a part of your very formation, it can also feel like a rejection of *who you are,* who you have to be. To hurry up and pray for a Down's syndrome child may be an expression of your own revulsion; it may be an indication of your anxiety, not his need.

And those of us who were broken right from the start, we don't know how to say any of this without being told that we're *wrong, wrong, wrong, we just want your healing, you should knock and it will be opened…* You won't hear us; and you certainly won't want to admit that some of what we see is true. But we see these little ticks, these tiny confirmations in the eyes and hurried prayers. We know. If the prayer fails to fix us to your requirements, we'll do our best to cover our symptoms anyway, so we won't revolt you. If healing doesn't come, we will struggle mightily to look better.

To be *who we have to be* means to continue to oppress you with our presence; to be the constant source of failed prayers and disappointment; to always be "lifted up" (oh, deadly accurate phrase!) as the broken one.

The cross is a shameful piece of wood, no matter who you nail to it. Imagine yourself hanging naked in front of the congregation, bleeding at the side, with all the world chanting "Come down, come down..."

... and you can't come down.

If we disappear from your sight, it may be because our courage failed. We decided not to burden you, and ourselves, with our presence.

But I've been with people who are not made anxious by my brokenness, and I've seen the difference. It is, in fact, the best definition of ministry I have ever heard; I nearly weeped when I heard it, it so defined what I needed. Engrave this upon your forehead, if you would wish to do good:

Ministry is a non-anxious presence.

You can tell such grace by its care, by its attentive ear, by its pace. When it reaches out to heal you, it is to give relief to you, not itself—and when it prays with you, it lets you declare your own burdens, rather than declaring what it finds burdensome about you. You may be surprised by what we ask for. My friend Joan, a wise minister and gift of God, tells me that she usually is.

As my disease got worse I began to abuse cough drops. You could say I became psychologically addicted to them. I used them in astonishing quantities for many years, unaware of the damage growing inside me. After thousands of such fig leaves, I went to a dentist who was horrified by what he found inside my mouth. He'd never seen anything like the erosion those cough drops had produced. I'd removed the outer layers of my tooth enamel down to the gum line. He did what he could to correct it—which wasn't much—and switched me to sugarless cough drops.

So I began poisoning myself in a sugarless way, to spare my teeth.

I think that's kind of pathetically funny.

My lungs were in their twenties back then, and starting to scar up. Spots were beginning to show in the X-rays. But I still had enough capacity to breathe without trouble; I didn't pant or wheeze yet; I could go up a flight of stairs in one smooth motion. I could still afford to suppress my phlegm so others wouldn't be offended.

It became an automatic, lifetime habit: covering up my nature, like a kitty in the litter box.

An encouraging word from our church fathers:

It is also taught among us that since the fall of Adam all men who are born according to the course of nature are conceived and born in sin. That is, all men are full of evil lust and inclinations from their mother's wombs and are unable by nature to have true fear of God and true faith in God. Moreover, this inborn sickness and hereditary sin is truly sin and condemns to the eternal wrath of God all those who are not born again through Baptism and the Holy Spirit.[6]

The scariest thing about all of this? Everything I've just told you is literally true for me, but it doesn't take much of a metaphoric shift to be about most of us. How sad.

If the mind that is set on the flesh is hostile to God, then the flesh sins even when it performs outward civil works. If it cannot submit to God's law, it is certainly sinning even when it produces deeds that are excellent and praiseworthy in human eyes... This contempt for God corrupts works that seem virtuous, for God judges the heart.[7]

If you grew up in America, you are—like it or not—a child of the Reformation. The folks who laid down the bedrock of your town, state and union also laid down its Protestant culture. Their views on what it meant to be human, their expectations from the human animal, were still mostly preoccupied with the the great debates of the Church Fathers.

Much of what was laid down back then still operates today. This is your heritage.

The quote above, which declares obvious good works to be sinful, lies behind your Aunt Edna's inability to take a compliment on the blueberry muffins she baked for the soup kitchen. She doesn't know the passage, but her culture does.

Charlie Tafta's refusal to show his wonderful carved duck decoys? Same thing.

It all lies in what we expect from the human mammal. If we're ignorant of the design specs, we try to cover up behavior that makes perfect sense. We smile heroically through a funeral. We apologize for emotions that merely come from paying attention to our situation. We tell people we feel no grief, even though our wife died only a year ago.

What are your design specs for humans? It's worth thinking about.

God help you if you set them tighter than the One who actually designed you.

According to the reformers who wrote the Augsburg Confession, "original sin also involves such faults as ignorance of God, contempt of God, lack of the fear of God and of trust in him, inability to love him," as well as such normal human emotions as anger at his "judgments," indignation when we are not immediately delivered from trouble, and even the crime of "fretting" over the notion that bad people seem luckier than good.[8]

Which leads me to one last note about shame. I've heard a lot of talk lately from the "What's Wrong with Our Country" crowd, who seem to fret a good deal about the "bad people" in our midst. They say we need to return to good old-fashioned Christian shame to control our social problems.

Welfare mothers having babies, drug addiction, crime… all that stuff can be fixed with a healthy dose of shame. I'm still trying to figure out what a healthy dose of shame is, myself.

I'm still wishing I could get some of that lung area back.

Vav

Once some of the disciples were arguing about the law. Some of jesus' preaching was becoming disturbing, because he seemed to concentrate so much on the goodness of Creation. He seemed to think that sins were easily forgivable; that people could truly become better; that God found humans fairly likable—lovable, even. This Good News seemed very false at heart. Wasn't the law there for a purpose, to tame our evil natures?

"God called it good," he said, his voice cracking like a whip. "Don't make that into a lie."

But this didn't satisfy them. Was he trying to abolish the requirements of the law?

"I have nothing against the law," he said. "I've come to fulfill it. But it's not a tool to become God. Your lawfulness will have to exceed that of the highest Pharisees and Sadducees, if you want to become perfect.

"You must never be angry, you must never look at each other lustfully, you must never divorce or make an oath."

"We can do that," they said, though some looked uneasy.

"And you must not resist evil. If someone strikes you on the cheek, you must offer him the other. If someone sues you, you must give him all he wants, and more. If you're forced to march a mile, you must volunteer to go a second. If someone wants your money, you must always give it to them."

"We can do that," said a few of the blustery ones, but most—especially the city-dwellers—fell silent.

"That hardly seems fair," someone muttered.

"Your Father in Heaven causes the Son to rise on the evil and the good, and sends rain to the crops of the righteous and the unrighteous alike," jesus said. "If you would be perfect, you must be perfect as God is perfect.

"—oh yes: when you are acting justly, you must also be secret about it, so your behavior is untainted. Don't have impure motives for being good; don't hope that someone notices. In your heart of hearts, don't even have the smallest hope that it will be seen.

"In fact," he added, warming up to the topic, "don't even notice it yourself! Split yourself in two, so that when your right hand gives, your left hand won't feel any secret pride over your charity."

"That's not possible," someone protested.

"No? God does it every day. Gifts flow out of heaven uncontrollably, naturally, helplessly. God is the endless servant, forever handing life to the lowliest creatures without thanks or pride. If you must be perfect, you must be like God."

"That's fine for him to say," I heard a volunteer coordinator from the shelter whisper, "but nothing would get done."

Someone else snickered.

"Do not judge others, either," jesus continued, "but accept them uncritically. Be concerned about nothing but your own imperfections. Flawed vision sees only flaws! If you would make yourself judges like God, you must scrub yourself clean. Survey yourself constantly, pluck out every defect—and experience no tainting pride at your progress.

"When you have finally become as pure as God, your eye will become pure, and you will then see your neighbor clearly.

"You will see them as God sees them!

"Then, and only then, may you offer to remove the tiny speck in your neighbor's eye—those few specks that still remain in your new, Godly sight."

"Humph," grunted a Sadducee.

I could feel the crowd growing angry and impatient. This was not the kind of teaching they wanted to hear.

"God does not worry, either," he added. "Neither must you! Live your life carelessly. Don't worry about where your next meal is coming from, or how you will clothe yourself. Live like a bird, like a flower. Don't give an anxious thought about tomorrow, but simply trust yourselves to God's care. Not a single sparrow falls to the ground without God's awareness—isn't that enough to know?"

"Yes," I commented dryly, "but the sparrow still falls, doesn't it?"

"But God is aware of its passing," jesus chided. "Isn't that enough for you? Are you still so selfish that you care about your own life?" He shook his head slowly. "You have far to go, before you can achieve spiritual perfection. How will you ever climb the rungs to heaven?"

"I will try," said a meek voice.

"Don't be a fool!" his companion snapped.

The muttering grew louder and angrier.

"Children," he said, lifting his head to call to the crowd. "Why are you angry? This is perfection; this is Godliness!"

"No one can match your tests," growled a man at my side. "This is unfair."

"This is what it takes to earn the Seat of Heaven," jesus said. "Anything less will not seize the throne."

Then he turned from his listeners and walked brusquely through the crowd.

They boiled about him like a gathering storm, but no one dared strike him. He was the lightning, and he flashed quickly to ground, leaving the ear stunned and the eye blinded.

Zayin

Jesus loves me
This I know
For the Bible
Tells me so.

The Redeemer loves me, but what about the Creator? Does the same hold true there?

"When you've seen me, you've seen the Father," jesus told Philip. But when I sit in church, I see two very different images—how can they be the same?

In Church I receive this picture of jesus pleading before a wrathful cloud, shielding me from its anger. He has carefully interposed himself between us; he is talking furiously, arguing my case, defending me from certain death. If he should step even a millimeter to the side, the murderous thundercloud will strike.

When I was sinking down,
Sinking down,
Sinking down...
When I was sinking down
Beneath God's righteous frown
Christ laid aside his crown
For my soul, for my soul,
Christ laid aside his crown
For my soul.[9]

In the rigid stubbornness of your heart you are making for yourself a store of wrath for the day of wrath, when God's just judgement will be unveiled, and he will pay everyone for what they have done. Those who pursue glory, honor, and immortality by persistently doing good will find eternal life; but for those who are selfish, follow evil, and refuse obedience to the truth, there will be wrath and fury.

(Romans 2:5–8)

I don't know what's going on. Maybe it's easier for jesus to love me. At least jesus doesn't have to admit that when he made me, he made a mistake.

I was raised with the assumption that the Bible was a book that made sense, that the church made sense, that the hymns and the liturgy and the prayers all made sense. Somewhere, people knew how it all worked.

Trust us: it all hangs together.

If I saw apparent contradictions, I needed to approach the professionals, who would make the problem vanish with a dab of glue and bits of interpretative string. If I was getting burned by the words, it was obviously the fault of my untrained little punkin' head. I was never given permission to argue with it. Nobody ever modeled that for me, even though they did it privately in the lunchroom, with the other God-plumbers.

Yet it's terribly obvious the Church Founders didn't listen to each other very well.

The authors of Hebrews and Romans thought John was kidding when he reported that jesus was of the same mind as the Creator—unless they were groping toward an early definition of schizophrenia.

And the authors of the Athanasian creed—who listened to some parts of John too well and other parts not well enough—didn't pay any attention to Paul's description of jesus' relationship with dear old Dad:

> Then the end comes, when Christ delivers up the kingdom to God the Father, after abolishing every kind of dominion, authority, and power. For he is destined to reign until God has put all enemies under his feet; and the last enemy to be abolished is death. Scripture says, "He has put all things in subjection under his feet..." and when all things are thus subject to him, then the Son himself will also be made subordinate to God, who made all things subject to him, so that God will be all in all. (Corinthians 15:24–28)

Paul has a grand, sweeping vision of a collapsing hierarchy: Creator, Messiah, Creation... even Death is a soldier with his place. That makes Paul a heretic, by definition of the church. The technical term for it is *subordinationism,* a belief that Father, Son and Holy Spirit are somehow ranked in order, and it's been outlawed since the fourth century. (Many translations try to cover that up a little by using the word "subject," rather than "subordinate"; but *subordinate* is also a legitimate translation of the Greek word.)

According to the Athanasian creed, St. Paul has earned himself a ticket straight to hell.

> And in this Trinity, no one is before or after, greater or less than the other; but all three persons are in themselves, coeternal and coequal... one cannot be saved without believing this firmly and faithfully.

What a wonderfully graceful statement that creed is! It goes right past "works righteousness" straight into something that can only be called "doctrinal righteousness." Forget God, Christ, and Holy Spirit. Now you can only be saved by an accurate technical understanding of the Trinity!

That condemns, by my rough estimate, 99.97 percent of the people in the pews to the Lecture Hall in Hell, where they will see St. Paul issue his woeful retractions in a suit made of live frogs, and beg for forgiveness from God, and God's only superior, a Church that dictates who must—and must not—be loved.

Most of the pastors that taught the attendees will be taking notes, too. I have never heard an explanation of the Trinity that did not fall into one heresy or another, usually (like the famous water-ice-steam illustration) the heresy of "modalism."

"Creator-Redeemer-Sustainer" language is also a ticket to the land where the worm does not die—and don't even *think* that the Holy Spirit might resemble its depiction in the Hebrew Scriptures, unless you enjoy very warm climates, bland foods, and Reader's Digest Condensed Books.

The plain fact is that the definitions of the Church Founders, written to combat wild and wooly Christianity, often involve such tightly negotiated wording that the only way to avoid "heresy" is to use exactly the words they specified, and no others. It quite literally defies explanation.

> There is one "substance" of God (or "essence" or "nature"), in three "persons." But these terms had been through none of the Eastern conceptual wars; and when it came to the creative thrusts of such Easterners as Gregory of Nyssa, Western readers invariably missed the point. Augustine himself confessed incomprehension of the key Greek distinction: "I do not know what difference they intend between *ousia* and *hypostasis*."[10]

The notion that belief in this tract is God's litmus test for condemnation is so appalling that it descends to the ridiculous.

I'm so glad my church still stands by this bit of nonsense—even gladder that everyone who becomes ordained must *affirm* it in their vows. That way every one of them can start practicing schizophrenia from Day One.

Yes, grieving mother, our church says your baptized six-year-old has just gone to hell for an inadequate understanding of the difference between ousia *and* hypostasis. *But don't be terrified: our church doesn't really believe what it professes. I find that some comfort, don't you?*

Now let me tell you about the hope we have in Jesus Christ...

The Church is incredibly unconcerned about this—no protest marches, no ringing resolutions—and when you point out that even St. Paul is, by testimony of the Church, toasting in hell, you get a yawn, or a sleepy disclaimer. It all seems so terribly tiring, so... academic.

That one should be damned for bad, or even merely out-of-date, theology has seemed a bit hard... [a bit hard?!? Have you ever lost a child, Mr. Jenson??] It is one thing for future preachers to understand that salvation hangs on their preaching and that they are to preach thus and so. It is quite another thing for a congregation publicly to proclaim curses on the theologically maladroit or anachronistic. At any rate, the retreat of the Athanasian Creed back into the classroom may be regarded as a return to the proper locus of its authority. There, however, it surely deserves the highest respect.[11]

How calm, how erudite. One can almost picture our scholar with unmussed hair, begging for a sense of proportion. This is, after all, only a creed: no one's dying. Theology hardly matters in the real world, does it?

You might think that, against the scale of life and death, I would feel the same way about such academic distinctions. You would think that, because you're not standing where I'm standing right now.

I'm trying to find something that hangs together, something that doesn't make me cringe or turn off my brain, and I just don't have much time anymore. I've lost patience with sleepy attitudes. I want to think sense, and I want to think sense now.

I *know* I don't stand a chance of fully grasping God, but I want to grab something that doesn't fall apart as soon as I touch it. Life preservers made of toothpicks just won't survive these choppy seas.

If I can't understand something, I would rather label it "I don't know." Then, with nothing else taking up the space, maybe I can go back and struggle with it, work with it. But I no longer feel the luxury of shrugging at obvious non-sense—and I'm starting to shake with fury at those who do.

The pastoral response to this is always the same: an appeal to simple trust in the Lord and reliance on peaceful rituals. Don't get all tied up in knots over theology, Nathaniel, just believe in God.

Which god? The god you're telling me about, the one we sing about, the one you affirmed in your vows, the one we read about in today's lessons, or the one jesus says he reflects? They're all *different*.

I can't strike your pose; I can't pretend to be cool. Theology has been both poison and balm to me all my life, and in the current situation I can't tolerate much more poison. I've got too much toxin in my system that I can't do anything about. I don't have room enough for the optional poisons anymore.

Breaking up
Solid chunks
With my ribs
Propelled by Martha's fist
My back

Propped against the edge
Of death my recliner
The air finally hits
And suddenly the sheets are cool
Against my legs
My hand vibrates thank you
And the pillow is soft
Again
Give us this day
our daily breath
Doitagaindoitagaindoitagain

Somewhere along the line, in spite of my upbringing, I became frightfully pragmatic: I began to demand that my faith help me survive this road I'm walking.

Picture someone walking through a room. He picks up an object of the faith: He asks, "Will this help?" If the answer is *yes*, he keeps it.

If the answer is *no*, he asks, "Can I look at it a different way to make it help?" If the answer is *yes*, he turns it on its head, and keeps it.

If the answer is still *no*, he asks, "Does this hurt?"

If the answer is *yes*, he throws it out the window. He may not even open the window first.

This is not sophisticated or calm. It is not the kind of thing to garner accolades, not scholastic. It is reckless, impatient, perhaps desperate. It's what I have to do to survive.

Peace be with you? I just need some reason to breathe tomorrow.

Let us even rejoice in our present sufferings, because we know that suffering produces perserverance; and perserverance produces character; and character, hope.
(Romans 5:3–4)

Suffering produces *hope?*

Let me tell you about the kind of hope suffering produces. I am bowed and beaten, flinching at the prospect of being noticed by God, yet terrified at being forgotten. That's what lies at the bottom of my foundation; that's the wonderful character suffering has brought to me.

Rejoice! Rejoice!

Listen:

It's not enough to say "God loves you." If it turns out that I'm being loved by an angry demon, I would surely find no hope in it; so "love" by itself is no balm. The methodology of love is what makes it destructive or creative.

What is the methodology of God's love toward Creation?

So come to him, our living Stone—the stone rejected by humanity, but chosen by God as most precious. Come, and let yourselves be built, as living stones, into a spiritual temple... My dear friends, do not be bewildered by the fiery ordeal that is upon you, as though it were something extraordinary. It gives you a share in Christ's sufferings, and that is cause for joy; and when his glory is revealed, your joy will be triumphant. *(1 Peter 2:4–5b, 4:12–13)*

When he broke the fifth seal, I saw underneath the altar the souls of those who had been slaughtered for the word of God, and the testimony they had borne. They gave a great cry: "How long, sovereign Lord, holy and true, must it be before you vindicate us and avenge our blood on the inhabitants of the earth?"

Each of them was given a white robe. They were told to rest a little while longer, until the tally of all those servants in Christ who were to be killed as they had been was complete. *(Revelation 6:9–11)*

What if you snuck down to the cellar of heaven
  And dug up the floor? What if you took a pickaxe
    To the wall
      Attacked crumbling bricks and old cement
        Scraped away all the dirt
          And found living sacrifices
            Sealed into the foundation
              With their eyes still bulging
            From the scream they gave
          When the last block was
        Pushed over their face

What if God built The Kingdom on Pain?

What if you saw your own broken bones down there
  Gathering righteous dust?

When you climbed back up the long golden stair
  Could you shout Alleluia
    Could you dance out your praise and sip cool margaritas...

    Could you look God in the eye?

Heth

For God did not send the Son into the world to judge the world, but to save it.

(John 3:17)

"The problem," jesus said to us once, "is that the Creator pronounced Creation 'good,' not 'god'; and you people have been angry and confused ever since."

We were eating a small supper at Martha and Mary's. He was still eating light—when you fast as long as he did, you have to ramp back up slowly—and teaching between every mouthful.

"Look at your plate," Martha scolded, in her best Jewish Mother voice. "Eat! Eat!"

jesus laughed, but didn't take another bite. "My food," he said, "is doing what my father wills."

She brushed his piety off with a dismissive wave. "What your father wills," she said, "is that you don't fall down dead in the middle of a crowd, just because your jaw was too busy with words. Look at my soup; you've barely touched it!"

"Yes, ma'am," he said. The Son of God obediently put a spoon into his bowl, while James smirked.

I studied him anxiously, with more than a little shame tugging on my spine. Ever since he'd preached the Sermon on the Mount, I'd felt even more damned than usual. I wasn't sure I should even be there.

The wretched thing about it was that the heaviest accusations he'd leveled at me—those blissful lilies of the field and unanxious sparrows—seemed so *nice*. But their model was completely unreachable. They were like Precious Moments figurines with the plague inside.

Don't tell me not to worry, O.K.? Speak hopeful words to me; remind me of all the times God pulled my fat out of the fire; but don't tell me not to worry. It's not a choice I have to make. It is a reaction to the fact that I've got a disease that is not only going to kill me, but *torture me for a while,* like a cat with a bug. I've got a sadist of a demon in my genes, and I don't need a civil war inside my head just to add to the fun.

Setting my faith against my emotions just won't help. I've been there, done that. It only works to a certain threshold of pain, and then something *snaps*.

"I'm sorry, jesus," I said. "But you keep confusing the hell out of me."

"Whatever casts out your demons," he responded, mumbling around the spoon.

Martha came by and broke some crackers into his bowl, ignoring his waving hand: more calories.

"Yeah, well, I feel like I've got more of them, not less."

"What's your problem, Nathaniel? Speak, and ye shall be heard."

"On the one hand you say you're preaching the Good News, but on the other hand, the standard you set is something I can't reach. I'm no lily of the valley. I'm a human with a bucketload of troubles."

"That's the Good News."

"Great," I sighed. "Thanks a lot. You can go back into the desert now."

He snorted. "You don't think that's Good News? Where's your faith, boy?"

He bit off a bit of bread, complimented Martha on the honey butter. She received it with a dim eye, knowing he was trying to get back on her good side.

Failing there, he turned to Mary with a look that would have made a stone cry— the Baptizer didn't call him the lamb of God for nothing—and said, "Mary, dear, will you sing part of the Magnificat for me? I love your voice."

She looked around nervously. "With everybody watching?"

"They're your friends; it's an easy crowd. Start with the fourth line."

Anybody else would have gotten a no. But Mary stood at the window and sang.

> He has shown strength with his arm;
> He has scattered those who are
> Proud in their inmost thoughts.
> He has brought down the powerful
> From their thrones and
> Lifted up the lowly.
> He has filled the hungry
> With good things
> And sent the rich away empty...
> *(Luke 1:51–53)*

"Thank you," he said. "That was exactly what I wanted. Beautiful... I wish you'd sing more often."

She slipped away without replying. He watched her go with kind, sad eyes. He's always hoping to build her confidence, but having only spotty success.

"That song," he said, turning back to me, "was written in honor of my birth. My mother sang it to Elizabeth. You might call it a mission statement: afflict the comfortable, comfort the afflicted.

"If you're getting confused, you're probably listening to everything and thinking it all has to work for you. That's deadly, when you're listening in on other people's conversations."

"It seems like a poor version of truth, if it doesn't apply everywhere," I complained.

"Don't be so Greek. What would you think of a doctor that gave the same diagnosis, no matter who walked into the clinic? Would you take muscle relaxers for influenza?"

My eyebrows rose. "No."

"Then why do you think you can take all of my words, spoken to different patients, and swallow them without examination?"

"Oh," I said, confused.

I puzzled that out; it was a little different than I'd been taught.

A *lot* different, actually.

We'd always been given scripture as a package deal, take it or leave it. It was one grand set of prescriptions for all of humankind, God's master plan. Truth was universal, and contextless to boot.

The child that learned all this never left me; I just added an adult on top, and the underlying kid still has powerful, gut-level assumptions about the Bible that don't budge easily. Even though the adult might want to head in jesus' direction, to the child it seems as frightening as—well, hell.

> I shall not be, I shall not be moved,
> I shall not be, I shall not be moved,
> Just like a tree
> That's planted by the water,
> Lord, I shall not be moved.

Sorry, jesus, you just can't compete with Mrs. Henderson, Mrs. Albright and my fourth-grade class.

He could see I wasn't buying it.

"Nathaniel, listen to me," he said. "I'm serious. My words are spoken to different patients with different ailments. Some are lowly, some are high, some are hateful, some are run down. They're all different sermons. But if you can't sense the joints between different sermons, you're going to get lifted up, taken down, and just generally yanked into confusion. It's not my intent to do that.

"Now, if you're a scribe who missed this point, you might try to explain why I'm so perverse and contradictory. You might even build an entire system on the tension between 'law' and 'gospel': the law makes you feel guilty so the gospel can make you feel forgiven, blah, blah, blah… a ton of ink and a forest of trees ruined on a basic misunderstanding: there are different diagnoses for different sicknesses."

"Peace is my parting gift to you, my own peace, such as the world cannot give. Set your troubled hearts at rest, and calm your fears." *(John 14:27)*

"You must not think that I have come to bring peace to the earth; I have not come to bring peace, but a sword." *(Matthew 10:34)*

"If any wish to be a follower of mine, they must leave themselves behind; they must take up their cross and come with me." *(Matthew 16:24)*

"Come to me, all whose work is hard, whose load is heavy; and I will give you relief. Bend your necks to my yoke, and learn from me, for I am gentle and humble-hearted; and your souls will find relief. For my yoke is good to bear, and my load is light."
(Matthew 11:28–30)

"You're saying you're not trying to make me feel damned and saved at the same time?"

"No. Forget the joy of making people feel awfully good and pretty awful. It's a fiction. There's no virtue in it."

"But I was raised—"

"—I know. Once people think they've figured out the program, they start doing it on purpose. You can hone it like a knife: God loves you; God is disgusted by you; you're damnable; you're justified… A lifetime of that is toxic to your soul. You won't know who you are."

Peter spoke up, looking put out.

"Wait a minute. Surely the purpose of the law is to condemn, while the Gospel forgives."

"The purpose of the law," jesus said, "is to give you a picture of what healing looks like."

"Right," Peter nodded. "That's what I said. It's to let you know you're *sick.*"

"There must be some static on the lines," jesus sighed. "Maybe we should hang up and get another connection."

Peter looked to James.

"What?" he appealed. "What'd I say?"

James shrugged.

The Teacher grabbed a napkin and doodled on it.

"Think of the law as a road map," jesus tried, patiently.

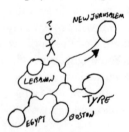

"For people who don't know where healing is, it points the way. It shows you where you're going. And for people that think they're already there, it's also pretty instructive—when they look at the map, they find out that they're still in Boston."

He drew another stick figure near the bottom.

"But that's Good News, too! Now they won't stop in Boston and call it the end of the road. They'll keep walking toward healing—and they won't reject a lift if it comes by."

A poorly drawn horse appeared, labeled *HELP*. He shoved the napkin over toward Peter, who just scowled at it. Lazarus picked it up instead and studied it with dry amusement.

"That's all the law is. Its value is as neutral as a road map until you unfold it."

"But," Peter objected, "you can't say that the law doesn't condemn. We all experience the law's condemnation."

"That," jesus replied, "is an accurate observation. Law focuses the condemnation you hold in your heart. But there's a difference between observing the side effects of something, and saying you've uncovered its *purpose*. Vitamin C might cure scurvy, but God doesn't give people scurvy so they'll want orange juice!

"The same holds for forgiveness and condemnation. If you don't watch out, you'll start thinking it's part of some perverse plan to make people feel grateful."

Peter began to get a little hot under the collar.

"But that's exactly what it does," he complained. "It *does* make you feel grateful. That's what it's all about. You can't appreciate forgiveness until you know what you've been forgiven *for*. You'll wreck everything, make it cheap! It's like being pardoned of a speeding ticket. If you don't know what the ticket's about, you won't value the judge's mercy!"

jesus' eyes widened. "What an intriguing idea," he said.

He turned to me.

"What do you think, Nathaniel? Does that seem helpful?"

I looked at him uncertainly, not wanting to speak.

"You told me, yesterday, how wonderful it was to have the oxygen come back into your legs."

"Yeah," I nodded, trying to sound detached. "It's good."

"You said it was better than sex."

I smiled weakly. "Well—"

"—if given the opportunity, would you forego the chance to be so appreciative?"

I rolled my eyes. "You know the answer."

"Yes, but Peter apparently hasn't figured it out. Would you please tell him?"

"I think you're doing fine by yourself."

jesus gave me a long, piercing look.

"I think he wants to hear it from you, Nathaniel," he said.

Right.

Thanks, jesus.

I looked across the table at Peter and tried to stay calm.

I could feel my stomach boil.

"Peter," I said, closing my eyes, "that's just about the stupidest idea the Church ever had. It's pretty obvious it comes from the people who do the guilting."

"But it applies to us all…" he protested. "We all labor under it."

"Yeah, well, it doesn't apply *quite* so much to the god-like figure in the middle of the room, doling out condemnation and forgiveness like Santa Claus."

"That's hardly fair," Peter said, his voice raising. "It's a serious weight we carry."

"Uh-huh. Take it from me, the presents are a little heavier when you're only on the receiving end; especially if you've already got a whole pack of condemnation already in your head."

"I understand—"

"—the hell you do," I broke in. "You don't understand at all. You don't listen, you don't give—no, that's the problem, you do give a damn, and some of us don't need any help on the condemnation part… and we really don't appreciate the two-penny forgiveness you pass on all that much, either, when it has an expiration date that only lasts until the next time we gather—"

—*armpits dripping in sweat… Peter taken aback… sudden vehemence, like stepping on a land mine*—

"—because the condemnation doesn't have any expiration date. All the junk we've already got has a shelf life for eternity, and the little wafers of manna you hand out just turn *wormy* the next day—"

Blueness alert
Blueness alert
Blueness alert

Starting to shake. Stop. You made the point. Sheath the tongue, already.
I chopped it off, decided to leave the rest unsaid. It was going to get vicious.
Now everyone, I thought, *will hate me.*

They'll know I'm just a mean, un-Christian person that wants to spit on all the good they're trying to do. Peter doesn't deserve being flayed like that—he's certainly a hell of a lot more Christian than I am. jesus chose the Rock, not the Well of Filth.

Christians are *nice.* They are not supposed to tell the truth, when the truth is unpretty. Christianity means confessing to general failure and denying specific ugliness. Everyone knows that.

If you don't figure it out at first, you will when you read the Psalms by yourself, away from the temple. That's where you'll discover the real rules of the family. There's all this nasty, filthy stuff that gets clipped out from the scripture inserts, and the things clipped out are the very questions, screams and curses in your heart.

Now, when I read the lessons in worship, I feel like they have big black magic marker lines running through them: *the censor has been here, the censor has been here… don't take this to God, take it to hell…*

Big mistake, to encourage scripture-reading away from the fig tree! Shame on Gutenberg for deadening the censor's shears.

The 137th Psalm, believe it or not, isn't even in the Lutheran hymnal at all. The space-time continuum shifted while the Green Book[12] was being prepared, and part of the church warped into n–1 hyperspace. If you learn to count from the pews you'll think 138 follows 136. It may not be Euclidian math, but it apparently gets you to heaven faster.

> By the rivers of Babylon: there we sat down and wept... there those who carried us off demanded music and singing, and our captors called on us to be merry...
>
> *(vv. 1,3a)*

Psalm 137 is a starkly honest, heart-breaking lament written by a poet who was asked to write pretty songs in exile. How terribly appropriate that the fabric of church-space might hiccough over it! *The city streets of Babylon will not pound with rap, even if we have to bend the fabric of the universe. Write us pretty songs, please.*

> How could we sing the Lord's song in a foreign land? *(v. 4)*

Exile. Honesty means exile. Having human emotions is exile. Don't show your flesh, don't reveal your sickness.

> If I forget you, O Jerusalem, let my right hand wither away! Let my tongue cling to the roof of my mouth... *(vv. 5–6a)*

I'd show you the rest, but it wouldn't be *nice.*

Peter bent his lip upward seriously. He always got a little red in the face when he felt like his doctrine was being attacked. He straightened his back and put on his didactic robe, as if preparing to explain celestial mathematics to a child.

"I'm afraid you can't just let some special context—"

"Special context?" jesus said. "You mean one that's different from yours?"

Peter shifted uncomfortably. "You have to understand, I regret the excesses that happen from time to time—a lack of caution can sometimes make things worse—but you can't go messing with God's revealed truth just because somebody's feelings get hurt. Gravity doesn't stop just because someone skins their knee."

"*Skins their knee?*" jesus exploded in amazement. "Weren't you listening? Are you that dense?"

"Ah—"

"What if we called you up some morning and told you that your kids had been slaughtered, so that you could appreciate your family more? Would that seem sensible to you?"

Peter tilted his head to the side. "No, but that's a poor analogy, isn't it? You'd be lying, in that case. But this is about condemnation and atonement..."

"—no," jesus said, "it's a perfect analogy. Your scheme is just as much of a prank, just as false. You are giving a confused answer to a bad question, based on a terrible assumption. Your atonement and forgiveness schemes are *hurtful lies built on a hateful lie.*"

Thunk. Peter's tongue hit the roof of his mouth.

Martha picked up a few dishes and scuttled into the kitchen.

"Listen to me," jesus said, taking a deep breath. "Do you have ears? Then use them for a change."

He took a drink of water from his cup, swilled it around in his mouth, and swallowed it. He looked at Peter with a weary ache, then closed his eyes and said a silent prayer. Then he began to tell us a story about the relationship of God.

The Parable of the Prodigal M.B.A.'s

"There were once two teenagers. They were the son and daughter of a wealthy industrialist, living in a tiny city at the edge of the empire. They were impatient to receive their inheritance, as most children are, but these two were especially vehement about it because their father was uncommonly healthy and strong. 'If we wait until he dies,' they thought, 'we may never get anything, the crusty old buzzard!' They managed to feel wronged by their father's health—you know how self-centered adolescents can be.

"So they went to their father and said, 'Give us our share of your holdings now, for we are ready to run it. We know it is only jealousy that keeps you from giving it to us.'

"The father was grieved by their accusation, but he knew the moods of teenagers. So he broke off several subsidiaries, and liquidated some of his assets to give them additional operating capital. He told them that he loved them, and appointed good assistants to help them manage their affairs.

"The first thing they did was fire the assistants, because they were Dad's old cronies, hopelessly out of date. Then they hired many of their friends, fresh out of business school, and other mid-level executives. They spread-sheeted all of the operations and discovered tremendous savings to be had, simply by shifting to some cheaper suppliers and laying off some of the excess labor force. When they needed extra production capacity, they would hire temps, because they wouldn't have to pay for retirement benefits or medical insurance.

"The adjustments had an immediate effect, and their third-quarter profits soared. By the end of the year, they had transformed a sleepy conglomerate into a lean and mean enterprise. They gave all of the top executives large Christmas bonuses, and built opulent new houses.

"The second-year profits sagged because exports fell off. They had quality assurance problems, and some of the temps just didn't have the same commitment as vested employees.

"They drastically cut back on their labor force and paid the remaining workers for double and triple overtime. They found newer suppliers who said they could improve quality with lower costs—the new suppliers used third world labor and paid them next to nothing—and then an accountant noticed that their pension was hideously overfunded, and so they raided it. It was like finding a gold mine!

"That restored profitability, so by the end of the year they could justify their large bonuses to themselves again. It was quite a relief—they had all taken on heavy mortgages.

"But in three more years the company was in ruins. Exports dried up completely, and there were few local sales. They had forgotten they were the major employer in the region. Their ex-labor force had also been their been customers, and now nobody could afford their products.

"The son and daughter had to file Chapter 13. The court put them on a strict allowance, and they found themselves in dead-end data-entry jobs for a struggling local bank. They couldn't sell their huge houses to anyone, but they did get a resale shop to take most of the furniture on consignment.

"They never talked to their father during this time, because they knew he would just blame them and treat them like stupid children. They never asked for help, even when their bankruptcy lawyers suggested it.

"'He was always stern and demanding,' they explained. 'He would enjoy rubbing our noses in it. Look at the way he handled the break-up in the first place—he gave us the sleepiest, weakest parts of his empire. He wanted us to fail right from the start, just so we could come begging to him. No way!' They learned to like macaroni and cheese, and they exchanged their Perrier for tap water.

"But one day the boy was sitting in the back room, and he said to himself, 'What am I doing? If I were a cashier for my father's gas station I'd be making as much, and I wouldn't have carpal tunnel syndrome from slaving over the keyboard all day! What price am I paying for pride?'

"So he went to the personnel department of one of his dad's businesses to fill out an application. He was surprised to find his sister there, too, doing the same thing.

"Well, the paperwork went up through channels. It took a long time before they heard anything. When they called after two weeks, they received no explanation for the delay.

"'It's as we thought,' they said. 'Dad's flunkies found out, and he's trying to figure out the best way to humiliate us.'

"So they went together to the personnel office to withdraw their applications.

"They found their father there at the desk, staring at the forms and weeping. The clerk was trying to comfort him when they were led into the cubicle. He looked very old and grey.

"'How could it come to this?' he asked. 'Why didn't you approach me directly for help?'

"His daughter started to cry. 'Because we could never do anything right for you!' she burst out.

"'Because we knew you'd just punish us,' the son said, stiffly.

"At that the father put his hands on the applications and tore them both in two.

"'You will never be cashiers for me!' he said.

"'I knew it. Come on, let's go, Sis,' said the boy, tugging on the daughter's sleeve.

"'You will share equally in what I have, even if I have only three pennies,' the father vowed.

"As the teenagers looked on in amazement, he told the clerk to call his most trusted vice president and ask him if he might have room for two new positions: training positions.

"'That's right,' sneered the boy. 'Make us grovel. I knew you couldn't pass up a chance to hear us admit we screwed up.'

"His sister looked at him, dumbfounded. 'We *did* screw up,' she said. 'Can't you even give him that?'

"'It's what he was trying to engineer all along,' the boy said. 'And I won't give it to him, even if I have to die first.'

"The father looked a little older yet, but he did not give up. 'I've never wanted anything but the best for you,' the father sighed. 'And the only thing I wish is that you be willing to learn. If you won't learn, you'll end up in the same straits again, no matter how much I liquidate—and it wouldn't be fair to the people who work under you.

"'Part of learning is seeing opportunities for improvement. If you can't go that far, I can't save you from yourself. But to prove to you that I never tried to humiliate you or break you, this is the only thing I ask: Go to my vice president and work with him. Show him that you're willing to learn. That will be enough. You never have to face me with your failures, if you think it will diminish you unfairly.'

"And so the two did.

"The vice president was a good teacher, and he eventually gained their trust. He wasn't burdened by being the father in their eyes, though in truth they had a lot in common.

"As the teenagers became adults, this final gesture on their behalf began to make sense to them. It was undeniable. They had to admit that their father had always loved them. One afternoon when they were all together on the porch, the son confessed that he'd been a terrible jerk, and wondered aloud how his father had ever tolerated him.

"'There were times,' his father admitted, 'when I just felt like braining you. But you're my kids. And I knew it wasn't really your fault. It was just part of growing up. Hormones.'

"Then they went to a good restaurant and celebrated like a family again. The kids found great pleasure in paying the bill—from their own modest, but honestly earned salary—and that filled the father with pride."

jesus finished his tale, and the room fell silent. Mary took in a deep breath.

This, I thought, for one fleeting second, *is true.*
It hung in my throat, like cool water.

"That's um, a good way of looking at it, of course," Peter began.

jesus eyed him dryly. "But...?"

"I do have some concerns."

"Such as?"

"Well, I have some problems with some of the ramifications of your story," Peter said, "theologically speaking."

He looked apologetically toward me, holding his hand up in the air.

"Not to say it's not worth hearing, Nathaniel, don't get me wrong. I can tell that speaks to you, and I'm glad for that." He turned back to jesus. "But there are limits to how far we can bend for personal issues. The fact is that your two teenagers did screw up—as your female protagonist noted."

"Yes?" jesus sighed.

"That raises a few questions, then, about the nature of repentance, forgiveness, that sort of thing. I can assume you didn't mean to say that the industrialist *approved* the way they ran their business into the ground?"

"I thought that was clear," jesus nodded.

"So if the industrialist has an interest in good management, obviously there has to be some true atonement for all their failures. I think you hinted at that toward the end, although it was soft-pedaled a bit."

"The point," jesus said patiently, "was that—"

"—yes, I know, I got it," Peter interrupted. "But let's speak plainly. We have an interest in righteousness, don't we? God can't tolerate unrighteousness. Although he might have a great deal of love for us, he has to place some demands in that direction. Now, maybe you don't like the word *condemnation,* per se. But no matter how you cut the cloth, I think it's going to suit."

He smiled at that, pleased by his manipulation of metaphor.

jesus was less amused.

"If you want to clothe yourself in righteousness," he said, "you might want to find out what it looks like first."

"Right. That's what the point of law is all about. We take a look at all the many ways we fall short, so we can see what righteous behavior is."

"Righteousness isn't *behavior* at all," jesus said. "That's your first misunderstanding. It has little to do with law, and everything to do with relationship and vision. Righteousness is seeing one's self in right relation to God, neighbor, and the rest of Creation, neither too high nor too low. The law is occasionally useful for people who see themselves as above humanity. It's not for shaming. It's just honesty, that's all. They're *not God.* They need to see that."

"Aha!" Peter said, as if he'd caught jesus in a trap. "That's what I'm talking about."

"It is not condemnation," jesus said archly, "to find out that you're not God. Unless you have some ambitions in that line, Peter?"

**An inspiring word from Manoel de Nobrega,
first leader of the Jesuit missionaries to Brazil, 1549:**

If the Indians had a spiritual life and would acknowledge their Creator and their vassalage to Your Majesty and their obligation to obey Christians... men would have legitimate slaves captured in just wars, and would have also the service and vassalage of the Indians in the missions.[13]

Peter fell silent. jesus picked up the cup to his side and examined it, smiling faintly. It was a cartoon mug showing a goofy cat next to a cardboard box, inscribed with the caption "Pizza on Earth." Martha's mug.

"Some people want to be lifted up," he said. "They feel a need to become godly, because they find no value in humans. They need their white robes shortened a bit. But it's not to make them feel *bad*, it's to force them to take another look at what God has made.

"Creation is not *God*, but it is *good*, as God pronounced. I want them to rediscover the value of that extra vowel, which they want to forget.

"On the surface the God-game sounds very holy, but it has at its heart jealousy, idolatry and a rejection of creation. It is an attempt to usurp the throne, not serve it. God-game players need to abandon their fruitless search for godliness, so they can recover a sense of *goodness*. Step one of that process is letting them know that deification is not something they've achieved, or even an option. But this is a reality check, not an attempt to crush their spirits.

"Now, other people play dirt instead. They don't see the value in being human, either. They're already in the pit. They need a hand up, not down.

"But that's righteousness, too: being given pride when you have none.

"Neither too high nor too low, Peter: that's what righteousness is."

Peter hemmed and hawed anxiously. "All this goodness talk makes me a little nervous," he complained. "It sounds like that worn-out old Pelagian heresy we had to thump in Carthage... man can save himself through his own efforts, that sort of thing. If we hadn't stamped that out in the bud—"

"—Pelagius," jesus shrugged, "was just another Godliness player. He was searching for the path to perfection, too. That wasn't a change in the game; that was a spat over the rulebook. I wouldn't be so proud of the thumping you administered, Peter."

"But surely you can't be saying there is no evil—"

"—far from it," jesus nodded. "There is more than I care to see. But most of it is rooted in *playing God*; rejecting the value of Creation; having a feast on the knowledge of who is Good and who is Evil. These things are rooted in evil, and they bear evil fruit."

He turned back to me. "Forget the games. I'm not playing some prank to make you feel awful and unlovable so you'll be glad that God doesn't fry your hide. Lifting up the lowly and bringing down the high is simple honesty.

This is the Good News:

You are human,
and human is good enough.

"Not 'squeaked by on a technicality'; not 'filthy and forgiven,' not 'simultaneously condemned and justified'...

"Human.

"Enough!"

James, who until now had been letting Peter do all the arguing, harrumphed unhappily. "Well, you still have to deal with questions of ethics, living things out. It's a very graceful thing you're saying, and I'm not speaking against the concept of grace—but you still have to address the bottom line: what in God's name are we supposed to *do*?"

"What you *do*, even in God's name," jesus said, "doesn't change your heart. Righteousness can't be *done*. It's knowledge. It tells you who you are, not what you should do.

"Work to find out who you are and who you belong to. If you're rooted in that soil, you'll be like a fine apple tree, producing good fruit as you're able. But if you try to produce fruits without being rooted in good soil, you'll produce crab-apples, thorns."

He set down his spoon and waved his hand toward the window, indicating the city outside. "If you go to a shelter for the poor and volunteer your services, you will find some people serving love, and some serving hate, though they are serving the same law. You will find people that begrudge everything they hand out. They make the clients feel small and abject, unfairly blessed by their ministry. In private, they complain about the luxury of the ointments, the generosity of the Sunday food and the newness of the donated shoes.

"I've stood with those people; I always do. These people are *doing* their Christian duty, and it comes out as hostility. Why? Because they obsessively chew on the knowledge of Good and Evil. It is their vision of humanity that makes them grudgingly serve out bitter gifts.

"But I've stood with other people, people who believe that Creation is *good*, that people are *good*, that God is *good*. And I have seen them pour themselves out, James, like a drink offering. I have wept to see the way they give. Women with two pennies give what they have; men with thirty free minutes give thirty-five. The law, you see, has nothing to do with it. It is powerless to compel love or stop hate.

"Faith and works are *both* dead without clear vision. Clear vision produces good faith, life-giving work and sturdy love—as naturally as the sun gives off light, life and warmth. It is what is fused in the core that shines."

Oops.

"Nice try, jesus," I said, "but that last bit of yours just blew up in my face. When you have a core like mine, you don't want to hear that kind of stuff. I can't change what's in my core—tried already—and now you say that faith and works can't help. Thank you very much, I'll just go slit my wrists, now."

He smiled faintly.

"But did you really believe otherwise?" he asked. "Have you found faith or action working changes in your core?"

"Sometimes... ah... well, no. I mean, I try. I really do. But it seems ..."

And then I stopped dead. I couldn't do it. I found a truth I couldn't speak for any price.

God and I, down to our very cores, are enemies. I can't tell this, I have to hide it. Exile. Hell. Don't let anyone know.

Have a cough drop.

"Nathaniel? What are you thinking right now?"

"Nothing," I said. "Just... thinking."

"I had a sense you—"

"—I'm just reviewing what you said," I said quickly. "Piecing it together."

"Mmm..." He contemplated my expression for a while, then heaved his shoulders. "Alright, I won't press. But Nathaniel, you don't have to change your core to be rescued. Relax. There is nothing so filthy in there that God will hate you for it."

"I don't know..."

"Does a doctor come to patients who are healthy? Of course not. You don't earn the visit by being healthy, you earn it by being sick. It's the same way with being saved: the price of salvation is *needing it,* not having it."

James and Peter straightened as if they'd been poked with a sharp stick. They both looked ready to protest, but jesus stared them down. He didn't want them messing with me right then, just for their doctrinal purity.

I tried to make that work for me. Pushed it around inside my head...

...it ran into mud and wet grass, got all tangled and filthy again. "I wish I could believe that," I said, "but I don't."

He looked unsurprised. "If you could," he replied, "you wouldn't need help. Your unbelief doesn't shove you off the train—it's your ticket. That's what I've been trying to tell you."

"That's it? I'm acceptable because I *don't* believe? That's outrageous."

"It's one of your wounds. Doctors only visit wounded people, unless they're quacks. God is no quack."

"But—"

"—Listen," he interrupted, "you gave me your qualifications yourself. *I'm a human with a bucketload of troubles*, you said. That's enough. You're there! Nothing left to do." He waved his hand in the air. "*Finis.* End of story, roll the credits."

"But it's just too easy to have you wave your hand like that and say I'm acceptable."

"Easy? It doesn't appear to be very easy at all. The Pharisees won't accept it, my own disciples won't accept it… if it's that easy, how come everybody's finding it so hard?"

"Because I didn't do anything! Nothing changed!"

"Good. I'm glad you noticed."

"But then I'm still sick."

"Good news! That means I won't pass you by."

I put my head down on the table, banged it lightly. It felt good, so I did it again. It was something solid. "If you say I've been healed, something ought to be different," I said, speaking slowly and carefully, the way one speaks to foreigners and the hard-of-hearing.

"I said you were acceptable for treatment," jesus corrected. "That's your concern, isn't it? You don't have to be any different to be admitted! Now, when you are healed, you truly *will* be different. But you're not done yet; you've just started treatment."

"When will I be done?"

"Are you still breathing?"

"Yes."

He shook his head. "Not done."

"But if I'm not done until I'm dead, it will be too late. I won't get to heaven."

"Nathaniel, wake up! *Heaven is not your reward, it's your healing.*"

Thunk.

Wham.

Tongue up on the roof like a kitty, afraid to come down.

I saw the holy city, New Jerusalem, coming down out of heaven from God, made ready and beautiful like a bride awaiting her husband. I heard a loud voice proclaim from the throne: "Now at last God has his dwelling with humanity! He will dwell among them and they shall be his people, and God himself will live with them and be their God.

"He will wipe every tear from their eyes, and there shall be no more death or grief or pain; for the old order has passed away!"

Then he who sat on the throne said, "Behold! I am making all things new!" (And he said to me, "Write this down; for these words are trustworthy and true.")

(Revelation 21:2–5)

"Wait a minute," I sputtered. "We're supposed to be cleansed first. John wrote that, too."

"The 'trustworthy and true' words are the ones spoken from the throne," jesus smiled. "As to the rest of his interpretations, give the author some slack; he's waiting for healing, too."

"You mean I can't just—"

"—you don't interpret your own dreams perfectly, either. What makes you think John's any less human?"

"Oh, great!" I complained. "Now I have to pick and choose what to believe—"

"—it's awful to have to think, isn't it?" he asked, unsympathetically. "Nathaniel, use your brain. If people could perfect themselves on earth, why on earth would they *need* the New Jerusalem? They'd have produced it themselves. Even John quietly admits as much:

> Then he showed me the sparkling river of the water of life, clear as crystal. It flowed from the throne of God and Lamb, down the middle of the great street of the city. On either side stood a tree of life, yielding twelve crops of fruit, one for each month of the year; and the leaves of the trees are for the healing of the nations. *(Revelation 22:1–2)*

"Now I ask you: what are the leaves for, if the nations that can reach them are already healed?"

"Um... I never noticed that before."

"Of course not: you've been locked into seeing the New Jerusalem as your reward. When you're in a box like that, you don't even see the stuff that lies outside of the box."

"Now hold on!" Peter objected. "You've gone too far. The tree in Revelation is for physical healing. That's different than sin."

"Really?" jesus asked. "Why are you making the distinction now, Peter? It seemed to have escaped you before. Boils, leprosy, mildew, menstruation, homosexuality, childbirth—even being born a *girl* rather than a boy—weren't these things an offense against God up until five seconds ago?"[14]

Peter looked uncomfortable. "There are some differing opinions, of course. We're still trying to sort this out."

"An alcoholic's genes drive him to degradation," jesus challenged. "What do you call it?"

"Well," Peter said, "There does seem to be new data in some areas—"

"—A boy is abused by his father and he grows up to abuse his children. What do you call it?"

"Um—"

"—A grieving widow becomes bitter and spiteful after her husband's heart attack. What do you call it?"

Peter looked helplessly at John.

"A Tourette's syndrome patient blurts out blasphemies," jesus continued. "What do you call it? A rich woman is taught to confuse money and love by her community. What do you call it?

"A man persecutes others because he himself was shamed mercilessly. What do you call it?

"A baby is born with drug addiction inherited through the umbilical cord. What do you call it?

"A teenager gets high because he finds no hope in the ghetto. What do you call it?

"Peter," he pleaded, "use your ears and eyes: people don't wake up in the morning, look in the mirror, and say 'I guess I'll be evil today!' Everyone limps to the tree from a background of accumulated hurts, ignorances, spiritual and physical wounds. And every time science uncovers a new factor you have to struggle over redrawing the lines. Which conditions will God blame you for? Which not? Is there someone you can pin the blame on instead?

"You turn creation into some sort of slalom course around the singled-out defects, or an endurance test of the spiritually strong—"

"—try demolition derby," Mary interjected.

jesus laughed.

"Or demolition derby," he agreed. "And you spend all of your time trying to figure out *who* and *how* rather than *where* and *when*. That big fight you had with each other back in—oh, when was it…?"

"The sixteenth century?" Lazarus asked.

"Yeah, that'll do… works righteousness, faith righteousness, on and on… frankly, we got so sick of it, heaven just stopped listening. But it all sounded so deathly important to you because you're convinced you have to get 'fixed' to earn your 'reward.' Who's responsible for making you godly so that you can reach heaven? How's it happening?

"But you folks got so tied up in the *who* that neither of you noticed that whoever was supposed to be doing it, *it wasn't happening.*"

He rifled through his robe and found a tattered scrap of parchment. "Here," he said, throwing it across the table. "Read this. It was the first inkling you had."

My Greek stinks. But I stumbled through it.

I don't understand my own actions. For I don't do the things I want to do, but the very things I hate.

Now, if I don't want to do these things, my mind agrees that the law is good by its desires.

But in fact it is no longer my mind in control, but the sin that dwells within me. For I know that nothing good dwells within my flesh.

I can will what is right, but I cannot do it… For I delight in the law of God in my inmost self, but I see in my flesh another law at war with my mind, making me captive to sin.

Wretched man that I am! Who will rescue me from this body of death?

(Romans 7:15–18, 22–24)

"Sound familiar?"

I set the scrap down on the table.

"I could have written it myself," I admitted.

"That's what I thought. He is, at least, honest."

"He sounds tortured."

"Yes. He had his thorns, too."

He picked the scrap back up, folded it and returned it to his inner robe. "Once you've bought into the reward myth, you'll have to claim you're already healed so you can get into heaven—but you'll constantly encounter evidence that you're still sick. Imagine a patient outside the hospital lobby, limping around and coughing wildly, trying to suppress his symptoms so that the guards will let him in the door.

"How absurd he looks from the lobby: all he has to do to gain admittance is to walk up and say 'help!'

"But he's convinced that healing is the entrance requirement: if hospitals are all about health, shouldn't they be only for healthy people?"

"The pressure of trying to reconcile your claim to be healthy with the contrary evidence drives you into mad, whipsaw theories, like your 'simultaneously justified, simultaneously a sinner' double-talk. 'I'm both healthy and sick,' you'll say to the mystified guards. 'Please let me in.'

"'Very well,' the guards will sigh, 'we'll let only half of you into the hospital—which half shall we admit? The healthy part or the sick part?'

"You don't even know that it is the *sick* part that God wants to bring through the door!"

"Wait a minute," Peter objected, truly outraged. "You mean only *sinners* can get to heaven? I'm sorry, but I have a problem with that!"

jesus looked at him out of the corner of his eye. "No," he said succinctly. "You don't."

Lazarus became intensely interested in a hole in his sandal. Mary covered her mouth and looked out the window. I thought I saw her shoulders shake, but I might have been mistaken. She's not usually that petty.

"In the end," jesus continued, "your reward schemes will always come out the same. It will be reduced to mere bookkeeping, as if God actually isn't interested in *real* healing, but merely the *appearance* of it—God becomes a doctor who no longer cares about his patients as long as he can fudge the medical records.

"I say to you now, listen carefully: God does not want to pretend that you're healed! God wants you healed!"

There shall no longer be any curse. The throne of God and Lamb will be there, and his servants will serve him. They will see his face, and bear his name upon their foreheads.

There shall be no more night. Neither will they need a sun or the light of a lamp; for the Lord God shall illumine them, and thus they shall reign for evermore.

Then the angel said to me, "These words are trustworthy and true."

(*Revelation 22:3–6a*)

Righteousness

When God's presence
Is as real
As the sun on your cheek
When you can
Close your eyes and
Turn toward God
As sure as you know
The wind
Then you will have
The knowledge of God
The right-seeing vision:
God is good
Creation is good
And you
Are part of Creation
Rooted you will be like
A flower basking
In God
Drinking it in
Through every leaf and pore
Warm as the lily
In an August field
Splendor
Shines through you
Tender petal, you seem to glow
From the other side of
What you know
I see the face of God.

"I don't know," I said. "I'd like to believe what you're saying, but it's pretty hard. How can I be sure?"

"You can't. It's one of your wounds. You won't know health until you're healed. God brings the imperfect and the failing, the doubter and the hopeless into the infirmary. It will happen. Trust me."

"Prove it. Show me."

He shook his head. "It won't work; if your heart is broken, your mind will just argue endlessly. I've been through this before."

"Please. Try me."

He took a deep breath and steeled himself for a foray into proofs, like an experienced spelunker going into a hopeless tunnel for the benefit of a novice.

"O.K.," he sighed. "Here's your evidence. Look at a stunted tree growing out of the rock. It is a hundred years old, but barely a foot high.

Scene from Walnut Canyon, Arizona, by Martha S. Williams

"Would God hate the tree for being planted with no soil, or for its crippled form? No! It did not plant itself. God loves the tree, even as it carves out its life. Every gnarled limb is testimony to its loveliness of spirit, struggling against a harsh world. It's frailties are, in God's loving eyes, nothing but a history of its struggles.

"Or think of God as a young mother, carrying her unborn child in late summer. It has been a long, wearying pregnancy, and there have been many times when both she and the child wished it was over... but what could the fetus do to atone for its unfinished state? And does the mother really expect such nonsense? 'No,' she sighs. 'Simply grow and be born, and that will be enough. I long to see you face to face.'

"You, Nathaniel: you have two cats. They are the gift of God to you, a message. Think about your own feelings toward them. They can be astonishingly smart and astonishingly dumb. They are venal, jealous and sweet. They think they own the house, but they did nothing to make it. In fact, they think they're doing you a favor to invite you to live with them. They don't understand you. They never will. Lisa wonders why you sing, and really wishes you wouldn't. Greyfuss is annoyed by your preoccupation with machines. Toilets puzzle them both: why do you soil a perfectly good watering hole? You are mysterious, ineffable to them. You are knowable in part, but ultimately unknowable.

"They are terribly jealous of each other. When you pet Lisa, she runs away if Greyfuss shows up. This grieves you every morning: you have two hands; you can love them both. Why can't they get along? You keep hoping it will get better. It doesn't.

"Whenever Lisa thinks you're not around, she gets up on the dining room table. Greyfuss will do it right in your face, just to see if he can get away with it. Nothing that they do earns the food or medical care you give them. It is what they are, not what they do. You love them for the cats that they are—even when they drive you crazy. You don't expect human qualities from them, just a little cat-loving from time to time.

"And even then, they mostly let you down. When they come around, it's usually because they want something. Mostly, you're just a meal ticket. Yet in spite of that, you find it hard to imagine getting rid of them. They puke on the carpet; you clean it up with a sigh. They climb where they shouldn't; you yell at them and then forget about it. Even when they become incredibly sick, you will spare no expense to heal them. If evaluated on a purely economic basis, devoid of love, you get absolutely nothing out of this relationship. Anybody would think you were crazy to put up with it.

"But they'd be wrong. You get more out of it than what you put in. You are, in fact, *gifted* by them. There are times when they have been the sole comfort of an aching day. They have sat by you, stood watch over you, ministered to you. When you've crouched alone and moaned, they've heard your cries. They have tried, with every bit of their limited abilities, to answer them. By the power of their attention you have known they were bringing the love of God."

Ira

Ira
Was an angel
In a cat's body
Who would sit
Beside me when I
Felt low.

An angel
Is a sign of
The presence of God:
We can all be angels
You know.

Tiny paw of God!
Passing on the hugs
That couldn't come
Directly so
Heaven sent
Ira instead
Be at rest
Good and faithful servant:
Rest your fuzzy little head.

"Now, humans, too, can do the same thing. When you visit the sick, lonely and imprisoned, when you feed the hungry and clothe the naked, you are doing this. The moans of God come out of the throats of people, and you can answer them, too, to the best of your limited abilities. But does this purchase love? Think: You loved Greyfuss, Lisa and Ira right from the very first day you brought them into your house. They couldn't earn what you had already given them for free. But that doesn't mean that their love is worthless, even though it buys nothing. Their love is still worth the world to you. You treasure it, you would hate to profane it. You would be insulted if people said it was either cold cash for their care, or valueless. Both would be a terrible distortion of what exists between you. Love is not that way!

"Now, tell me this: if you, with all of your broken and conflicted bits, can feel this way about such creatures that you *found,* why do you think the unbroken God—who knits you together, understands you and intimately labors to heal your very wounds—cannot even love you as well as you love cats?

"Is God so much less than you? Are you that arrogant, to claim greater love than God?"

While he was talking, Lisa sensed that she was being talked about. She tapped jesus on the hip and sneezed, the way she does when she wants attention. He reached down and rubbed the tender part of her chin. Greyfuss sat in a chair by the window and looked bored. Ira sat in Abraham's lap and nibbled on a lily.

Lazarus stood up from the table and stretched. He was a good friend of jesus, unintimidated by his presence. In Lazarus' eyes, jesus was halfway between 'rabbi' and 'prophet-in-his-hometown.'

Lazarus asked, "But what scriptural evidence can you give us? Evidence from the world is very fine, but I bet I can come up with as many counterexamples."

jesus laughed. "Yes, I bet you could… Lazarus, one day you're going to hear a word from me that you won't want to argue with! But alright. Listen to scripture":

"You all know Abraham was loved by God. Yet he was a weak man with tawdry faith, a man who sinned and failed. He was very old, and he had no children. But God promised he would have so many descendants that he would become a great nation. God told him to look up at the starry night and imagine they were his children! And for just a brief moment in time, Abraham felt loved by God. He became right-seeing.

"Now, neither Abraham nor Sarah were perfect, in faith, courage, character or action. When they passed through fearful country, he tried to pass off his wife as his sister, so he wouldn't be killed by other men. And when God's promises did not show up immediately, they did abysmal evil to a slave woman named Hagar: Abraham had a child by her and then pushed her out into the wilderness.

"But God never reversed the word that was spoken. God gave these humans the same grace given to a struggling tree. The fear of evil in alien lands; the fear of old age; the crippling shame of being a barren woman; these were the hard rocks crippling Abraham and Sarah's seed. Fear and shame were at the root of their evil and foolish acts. They hadn't created those rocks—and God knew that! They had been blown into them, and they were trying to survive as best they could. So God loved Abraham and Sarah, and did not hate them for their crooked limbs or bent hearts.

"Neither did God hate Hagar or her son Ishmael; an angel saved them in the desert, and they, too, were built into a great nation, even though Ishmael grew up bitter and vengeful—understandably so, when you think about what happened to his mother.

"But God does not fix brokenness with hate; never has. God loved all of these people and did not abandon them. It was never necessary that they already be healed to be loved.

"Healing is not a *price* for love, it is the *consequence* of love. You can't earn it, you can't pay for it, you can't undo it. God is already hopelessly, irretrievably in love with you, like a mother pining for her willful children":

When Israel was a boy, I loved him; and I called my son out of Egypt. Yet the more I called, the further they went from me, sacrificing to the Baalim and burning offerings before carved images.

It was I who taught Ephraim to walk, I who had taken them in my arms; but they did not know that it was I who harnessed them and led them in bonds of love—that I had lifted them like those who lift infants to their cheeks. I bent down to them and fed them. *(Hosea 11:1–4)*

Did you feel it then
Or was it me
The sense it was all
A bright fantasy
Meant to trap us
Into some dark
Vision of hell
Where the mice all bit Gospel cheese
And felt the law
Snap down on their necks?
God as trickster
The world will beat a path
To your door because
You know how to catch us all
In clever games
The path is narrow
The path is narrow
I know it
You're trying to trick me
I always get suspicious
Even when I build the trap myself.
What a wretched mouse I am
Nibbling at your Gospel cheese

"Nathaniel?"

I shifted around, hid my face. "That's good," I said to the window. "A very good case."

> *What if*
> *What if the light*
> *That blinded Paul was a demon*
> *And it was all a hoax*
> *Or what if it was all a hoax*
> *But it really was God*
> *What if*
> *What if*

jesus studied the back of my head in long silence. He nodded and decided to leave me alone for a while.

"I'm not denying our final healing will happen in heaven," Philip said, frowning slightly. "But it seems to me that we need something to... well, make us acceptable to God's presence. I mean, don't we need a mechanism to let us stand before God in the first place? Then we might be *finished off* in heaven...."

He trailed off, realizing that it sounded as incoherent as anything Peter had so far said. jesus' eyes glinted in amusement. "You're admitting that God knows you have broken and unfinished parts?" he asked.

"Yes, of course," Philip nodded.

"And that God will one day make you whole?"

"I hope so."

"Do you think humans are more loving or sensible than God?"

"No."

"Philip, have you ever met a *human* doctor that couldn't stand being around sick people?"

"Um..."

"Or a pharmacist that only lets healthy people approach the counter?"

Philip began to look sheepish.

jesus leaned forward and held up his hand. "Think about this, now: when I cure lepers, what do I do?"

Philip smiled. "Touch them."

jesus leaned back in his chair again. "When you have seen me work," he concluded, "you have seen how God works."

"In truth, the Son can do nothing by himself; he does only what he sees the Father doing. What the Father does, the Son does." *(John 5:19)*

"The reason you pursue healing," jesus said, "is because healing is *good*. You don't need any better reason. My call to pursue healing *now* is like a call from a clinic nurse. She tells you what to do to stop up the bleeding and ease your pain before you can get downtown. She concentrates on the worst wounds, and tells you to hurry on in. She doesn't ask for radical surgery, just some commonsense measures you can take with what the homeowner put in the bathroom cabinet.

"And don't despair! The one who works downtown is greater than any of your wounds. The healing I bring you is just a tiny foretaste of New Jerusalem, brought to you so you can see how God is working in the world. My healing is a message of hope to lure you back to the true God. I bait my hook with miracles and pull you out of the deep waters.

"Listen to what the message says: There is nothing that can't be healed. There is no cost. Even belief can come after the fact":

> Once again he visited Cana-in-Galilee, where he had turned the water into wine. An officer in the royal service was there, whose son was lying sick back in Capernaum. When he heard that Jesus had come from Judea into Galilee, he came to him, and begged him to go down and cure his son, who was nearly dead.
> "Will none of you ever believe without seeing signs and portents?" Jesus asked.
> The officer pleaded with him, "Sir, come down before my boy dies."
> Then Jesus said, "Return home; your son will live."
> The man took Jesus' word and started for home. When he was on his way his servants met him carrying the news: "Your boy is going to live." So he asked them what time it was when his son began to recover, and they said, "Yesterday at one in the afternoon the fever left him." The father realized that was the exact time when Jesus had said to him, "Your son will live." He and all his household became believers.
> *(John 4:46–53)*

"You don't even have to know what to ask for or how to answer—because it might be your wound that befuddles your spirit, and God knows that":

> In the colonnades at Bethesda a great crowd of sick, blind, lame, and paralyzed people used to lie. Among them was a man who had been crippled for thirty-eight years. When Jesus saw him lying there he knew he had been that way for a long time, so he asked, "Do you want to recover?"
> "Sir," the wounded man said, "I have no one to put me in the pool when the water is stirred by the healing power, so someone else reaches the pool before me."
> Jesus said to him, "Rise to your feet! Take up your bed and walk." The man recovered instantly, picked up his mat, and began to walk. *(John 5:3–9)*

"God can understand the 'yes' in your confused groans and complaints. Your spirit's aches are all the 'yes' God needs."[15]

Judas had been listening in silence for a long time, his face darkening with every word. At last he could hold it in no longer; he leaned forward, jabbing his bread toward jesus like an angry finger. "Teacher, this all sounds very nice. But it almost sounds like you're endorsing sin, saying that it's of no consequence."

"Sickness is its own consequence," jesus shrugged. "But you've heard me say it, Judas: 'Go and sin no more.' That should not be news to you."

"So there is a limit," Judas pounced. "A requirement. When people take advantage of your initial forgiveness—"

"—that would be a very broken thing to do," jesus said. "Something that would need healing, I would think. Don't make more of that command than what's there, Judas. If a doctor cures someone from food poisoning, he tells his patient to stop eating rare meat. If an acupuncturist frees a client from smoking cigarettes, she tells him to stay out of smoky bars. It's for his own benefit. That doesn't mean she won't see him again if he relapses."

"But what about punishment?" Judas complained. "There has to be justice, a reckoning somewhere. I think your doctrine sounds too well calculated to please itching ears."

"Does it?" jesus asked. He studied Judas with a neutral expression, then leaned back in his chair and looked up at the ceiling.

"Justice for sickness," he mused. "A reckoning..." His eyes wandered over the long beam running the length of the house, which was only roughly finished. His hands twitched a little, as if he'd like to get at the beam with a sanding block. "Have you preached much, Judas?"

A micro-frown, slight annoyance. "No."

"Mmm. Well, I'll tell you a strange thing, something I really don't understand. The ears that itch most, they itch for the things you speak of. The most pleasing sermon is the one that lays down the law; the highest compliment paid a preacher is that he gave them hell. Sermons that give people *heaven*—well, they're O.K. for Mother's Day, but you won't get invited back. Brimstone's much more popular. Damnation is hypnotic. Pounding the pulpit is exciting. And this motion you made..."

He imitated the action of Judas' hand, moving it toward each one of us in slow succession. "This is what people want. It confirms everything they have in their hearts."

His finger came to a halt in front of Judas. It wagged toward his eyes. Judas tried not to scowl.

"This is how you scratch an itching ear," jesus said, with curious detachment, as if describing something he'd seen but could never understand. "For some it works if it scratches at them."

Wag, wag, wag.

"For some, it's more pleasing if it scratches at others." He wagged it at me. Judas relaxed visibly.

"But that's the motion," he said. "That's what does it." He put the Accuser's finger down on his chest, and hummed a little to himself. He seemed bothered by something, but unwilling to pursue it further.

"So much sanding to do," he sighed, looking back up at the rough wood, the splinters, the gouges. "Lazarus, you must let me do this for you."

"Oh, I couldn't," Lazarus said, startled.

"It would be a pleasure," jesus said. "I like to do finish work—I used to do it for my dad. He'd do the cutting, mostly... but planing and sanding, that was what I did for Dad." His eyes faded into the distance.

It suddenly struck me that I'd never heard the story of Joseph's passing. What happened that day? Did jesus stand by and watch him go? I wondered why no one ever told that tale.

"You ever wish you'd stayed in carpentry?" Peter asked.

"All the time," he said, sounding wistful. "It's good to work with your hands. Your stresses come out of you. It's my favorite part of this job, though I don't get enough of it... it seems like more and more of my time is getting tied up with church lawyers."

"Maybe you need to just blow them off."

He shook his head. "Can't. I'm afraid the litigation is going to get fierce before I'm done. What I really need is an army of builders, nurses, potters and gardeners. People who like to work with their hands. Artists, technicians. People with dirty fingernails. Then I might get somewhere."

So Jesus went around to all the towns and villages, teaching in the synagogues, announcing the good news and curing every kind of disease. The sight of the people moved him to pity: they were like sheep without a shepherd, harassed and helpless. He said to his disciples, "The crop is large, but the workers are few; beg the landowner to send more laborers to harvest his crop." *(Matthew 9:35–38)*

I heaved myself out of my funk and decided to return to the conversation. "Martha gardens," I put in.

He smiled to hear it and nodded. "Good. Soil between the fingers. Very relaxing. God's first experience with humanity... what a wonderful beginning!"

"Mary works with clay," added Lazarus.

"I didn't know that," jesus said, considering her shrewdly.

"Oh, it's nothing..." she shrugged.

"You should show me some of your work sometime."

She nodded, unenthused.

"Sure," she lied.

"I knew a woman that was a wonderful potter," jesus said. "You remind me a little of her. Now, she really knew something about creation; it was deep in her soul."

"Tamar?" asked Mary. "Down on Austin Street?"

"Mmm-hmm. Gentle woman."

"I remember her. She used to let you play with her clay, didn't she?"

"A little bit."

"I saw you make doves once. They almost looked like they could fly."

He chuckled. "Just goofing off."

"You made them look alive."

"I made them too smooth," he said, shaking his head. "Too perfect. Tamar made them look *real*. I've learned to appreciate real since then."

He reached out and gave her a pat on the hand. "But thank you," he added.

She dimpled, but wouldn't accept his word. "You were better than Tamar, no matter how humble you try to sound. Tamar said so herself, if I remember right."

"It's not humility. Tamar was very good."

"Yes, but you were perfect."

He shrugged. "Sometimes good is better than perfect."

"How could that be? You're talking in riddles again."

jesus sat up straight in his chair again, found some more energy for his voice. He'd been teaching all day, and it was getting hoarse. I suppose I shouldn't wonder that he got cryptic at times. "Sorry. I don't mean to," he apologized. He took a sip from Martha's mug and cleared his throat.

"Good," he taught, "is better because it raises you and all of your kin at once. *Perfect* rescues you alone; but *good* rescues humanity."

We all looked blank.

"Or to put it another way: *perfect* rejects humanity, while *good* embraces it."

Still no light bulbs.

Mary frowned and shook her head. "Sorry, I just can't buy that."

"No?" He looked hopefully at Lazarus. "How about you, then?"

Lazarus shook his head.

"Peter? James? Nathaniel?"

A chorus of no's. His shoulders slumped as if defeated. How long had he been talking, anyway?

"Hmm." He rubbed his face, looked out the window and yawned. "O.K.," he sighed. "One more try, and then we'll call it quits. Some of us have to get up early tomorrow. Listen up: we'll call it *Better Than Perfect*."

"Three women were walking through a city park. One was very burdened and beaten-down. Though the day was beautiful and the flowers were blooming, she didn't enjoy her lunch hour a bit. She saw only her own cares.

"Another had been made, by dint of incredible conjurations, perfect and blameless in the eyes of the Law. None of her coworkers had any complaints about her, and she had none about herself. She was unburdened by any of the doubts and internal conflicts that plague most human souls. She knew that if she had any residual sins, they had been cleansed by both water and blood.

"As she passed through the park, she discovered she could not sit down to enjoy the day because there were so many homeless people sleeping on the benches. So many people! Winos and drug addicts and crazy people; people who looked diseased; people who looked so poor that they might be tempted to rob her. So many poor, broken people. Why couldn't they be saved from the wretchedness of human misery, too? It made her good heart sad to think they might go to hell. She said a prayer, made a mental note to redirect part of her tithe to the local shelter… and ate her lunch in safety, back at her desk.

"Now there was another woman who had never been perfected. She struggled every day with knowledge of the things she might do better. Her spirit groaned, sometimes. But she had one thing the other two lacked, a secret in her heart: she knew it was truly a wonderful thing to be human, even if imperfect.

"When she walked through the park that day, she was troubled to see so many good folks suffering. No one, no matter what their problems, should have to sleep without a roof over their head!

"Now, she often volunteered at the local shelter; she did what she could. But even that experience could make her ache. She learned how difficult it was to make a meaningful difference in these people's lives. They had so many more handicaps to overcome! Even something as simple as getting their laundry done was a fantasy—and without that, who would hire them? What employer trusts the unwashed?

"Some of them were plagued with mental problems that made it impossible to work with others, or even trust others to help them. They had been released by 'reforms' that only ended their care and put them on the street. They were not equipped to compete in the world, no matter how she tried to help. Sometimes it was so overwhelming, she was tempted to quit. But she stuck with it, because people *did not deserve* such misery.

"On this particular day, she ate lunch next to a man who'd lost his job four years before retirement. He had no insurance and no family to help—and, she suspected, the strong odor of whiskey on his breath had some bearing on his situation, too.

"Had he been in to Samaritan House, she asked?

"—Oh, no, he scoffed. They wouldn't do anything for him there.

"She urged him to go in that day and talk to someone; ask for Katy, she said.

"The man smiled ruefully. He'd been 'helped' by Katy before. No thanks, he smiled—but he was glad to learn that such a nice lady as herself volunteered there. After a few minutes of discussion he tentatively agreed to come in Friday at eleven, as long as she'd be there. Maybe, he allowed, she could find him some assistance.

"She went back to work five minutes late, feeling depressed and hopeful at the same time. She said a prayer to God... and God said a prayer to her.

"On Friday, both of them saw that the other had heard, and answered."

He turned to Mary and held her in his gaze. She looked embarrassed, as if she'd had a secret exposed. "I ask you now, Mary: you tell me. Which of the three women most pleased God that day? Was it the lowly woman, the perfect woman, or the uncleansed woman with a secret in her heart? One stayed low: she was crippled by imperfection. One was lifted up: she found value only in perfection. And the third is lifting others up—because she believed in a different word altogether."

Mary sat for a long time and said nothing, her face still and absorbed. When she finally stirred herself to speak, she didn't answer his question, but asked another.

"Are you always watching?" she asked.

"Always," he said.

Then he got up, stretched and walked into the bedroom to take a nap.

Teth

It took me forever to go to sleep that night. Too much racket in my head: my mind was pop-pop-popping off shots at my faith, my emotions were hurling Molotov cocktails at my mind, and my faith was rolling through the streets with big, angry tanks. I tossed restlessly and shouted *stop, stop*, but you know how well that works when the shooting starts.

I picked up a Bible and leafed through it, finding all the parts jesus had left out. He was playing fast and loose with scripture, I knew.

I have not come to bring peace, but a sword.

My spirit wrapped itself in barbed wire and grey-green fatigues.

How, it asked, could you trust him?

The disciples went up to him and asked, "Why do you speak to them in parables?" He replied, "It has been granted to you to know the secrets of the kingdom of Heaven; but to those others it has not been granted. For those who have will be given more, till they have more than enough to spare; but those who have not will forfeit even what they have.

That is why I speak to them in parables; for they will look without seeing, and listen without hearing or understanding... Otherwise, their eyes might see, their ears hear, and their mind understand. Then they might turn again, and I would heal them." *(Matthew 13:10–13, 15b)*

I speak unclearly so that I won't have to save them. What a horrifying vision; it is terror in the night, the Gestapo in the scriptures.

Yet how could I put up any meaningful resistance? It was the *Bible*. Matthew had all the correct papers to break down the door and arrest me. He had the authority, and even worse, he had the damning information. He knew, too, what my heart knew: God was—to borrow a word from wretched Gollum—tricksy.

Matthew's god was the same one I'd met in Genesis: a farmer who plants a tree right in the middle of the garden just to catch the bad kids. The fruit that snared the first couple was not to be eaten or harvested—it was only shiny bait in a death trap. It was hardly a surprise when Old MacDonald sauntered by that evening with some well-prepared questions, was it? It was a setup, an F.B.I. sting. Let's face it, if that hadn't worked, Adam and Eve would have woken up with a suitcase full of marked bills and a bag of crack in bed with them.

Whoever has will be given more, and whoever does not have will have everything taken away from them… such a distinctly American brand of justice, it makes me want to scream. Yet none of this bothered Matthew, because he believed he was a member of the protected citizenry.

"In the same way, a good tree always yields good fruit, and a poor tree bad fruit. A good tree cannot bear bad fruit, or a poor tree good fruit. And when a tree does not yield good fruit it is cut down and burnt." *(Matthew 7:17–19)*

I cannot bear good fruit—no matter how I might wish—because I was made bad. *Yes, hello,* I thought, *welcome to the pig roast. I'll be your fuel for the evening.*

Well, move on. Maybe there's a better passage for the kindling…
Flip, flip.

"Again: the kingdom of Heaven is like a net lowered into the sea, where fish of every kind were caught in it. When it was full, it was dragged ashore. Then the men sat down and collected the good fish into pails, but threw the worthless fish away. That is how it will be at the end time. The angels will go forth, and they will divide the wicked from the good, and throw them into the blazing furnace, the place of wailing and grinding teeth." *(Matthew 13:47–50)*

Flip, sizzle, flip…

"Then he said to his servants, 'The wedding feast is ready; but the invited guests did not deserve the honor. Go out to the main streets, and invite everyone you find to the wedding.' The servants went out into the streets, and collected all they could find, good and bad alike. So the hall was packed with guests.

"When the king came in to see the party, he noticed one man who was not dressed for a wedding. 'Friend,' said the king, 'how did you get in here without wedding clothes?', The man was speechless. The king told his attendants, 'Bind him hand and foot; turn him out into the dark, into the place of wailing and grinding of teeth.'

"For though many are invited, few are chosen." *(Matthew 22:8–14)*

God gathers in street people—without any clue as to what's expected of them—then punishes the one that didn't own a tux. Is it any wonder the poor man was speechless?
Flip, flip…

For when humans have once been enlightened—when they have had a taste of the heavenly gift and a share in the Holy Spirit, when they have experienced the goodness of God's word and the spiritual energies of the age to come—and after all of this they still fall away, it is impossible to bring them back again to repentance; for with their own hands they are crucifying the Son of God and mocking his death.

So if we wilfully persist in sin after receiving the knowledge of the truth, no sacrifice for sins is left: only a terrifying expectation of judgement and a fierce fire which will consume God's enemies. *(Hebrews 6:4–6, 10:26–27)*

Even if you do get saved, it's only good for a single use. Don't sin after baptism, or you'll burn, little baby, burn.

Flip, flip, rattle, boom…

"A good person produces good from the good stored up inside himself; and an evil person produces evil from a store of internal evil. But I tell you this: there is not a thoughtless word that escapes the lips that will not have to be accounted for on the day of judgement." *(Matthew 12:35–36)*

Gag your mouth, if you have evil things stored inside you. Keep them from the light of the day. Whatever you do, don't let them out.

But now another figure raps on the motel room door…

If we claim to be sinless, we are strangers to the truth, deceiving ourselves. But if we confess our sins, God is just, and may be trusted to forgive our sins and cleanse us from every kind of wrong… *(1 John 1:8–9)*

The sting is set up now, the camera rolling.

A gentle-looking man walks into the motel room: the picture is grainy, but it looks like the Good Shepherd. He's speaking to the occupants of the room—what's he saying? Turn up the volume. Missed some of it…

I think he said we have to confess.

Confess! Failure to confess is *prima facie* evidence of evil intent.

But the tape is running, too, and anything you say can and will be used against you…

"For out of your own mouth you will be acquitted; and out of your own mouth you will be condemned." *(Matthew 12:37)*

Bang. Bang. Clank.

The tanks ran over a very small, frightened child that night. I looked out the window and saw his crumpled body, but I didn't dare go pick it up.

The divisions just kept rolling through, backlit by flickering flames and thick, oily smoke. I was paralyzed. I just sat there and watched it all happen.

Everything jesus said, as soon as it hit my heart, it got twisted around.

What would he have said if I had brought out my charges? How would he have replied to them?

I don't know. He didn't get a chance.

He was always so well-spoken, so alert. Part of my soul said that I could trust this man. He wasn't like Dad, no, he wouldn't make me grovel just to feel big. This man was safe; Teacher, Rabbi, Good Shepherd.

And yet people kept coming dressed in his clothes, leering wolfishly at my rotten roots, growling out of one side of the mouth and purring out of the other. They urged speech and practiced silence, covered up ugliness and said truth would make me free... I didn't know who I was speaking to half the time.

Did I dare say anything? Was it really safe? Or was the tape rolling?

Paralysis.

I didn't dare bring up the real things, the hateful things, the blasphemous things. Damning doubt and questions had to hide; my charges remained in the dark, untouched by the light. I couldn't speak any true words. They were kept safely out of sight, fifty feet down in the Well of Filth that was my soul.

I tossed and tossed, but found no oblivion until, in desperation, I started counting sheep.

Funny how that works.

134

135

136

138...

Yodh

From the Elder, to the Lady chosen by God, and her children, whom I love in the truth… Grace, mercy, and peace shall be with us, from God the Father and from Jesus Christ, the Son of the Father, in truth and love. *(2 John 1, 3)*

Morning in the old house. The grackles whizzed and whistled outside the window, traffic purred down the road.

Elizabeth sighed and opened up the black book. The morning sun shone through the curtains, blazed white and warm onto the paper. She sat and looked at the page for a long, still time. The house was quiet and nearly empty; most of the guests had gone out to get ready for the day's labors.

jesus and another disciple, a teenager named Aquila, watched the sun illuminate her bony face, frizz up her hair.

Light. You can't read without it.

At last Elizabeth finished. She wordlessly handed the book back to jesus. Her face did not look pleased.

"Too hard?" he asked.

"Well, yes," she said, with faint accusation. "Have you ever lost a child?"

"Six million in the Holocaust alone," he nodded.

She winced.

"Being Jewish leaves you no room for illusions," he added.

A bitter curl of the lips. "I suppose that's true," she muttered. She stood up and methodically cleared the table of its breakfast remains, shaking her head sadly. Her young friend reached out for the book, and read the open page.

Psalm 137
(A Contemporary Version)

There by the waters of Babylon
We sat down and wept
Exhausted and hungry
For hope
We hung our joy on a tree

With a noose around its neck
Made of patch cords
And guitar strings,
The tools of our trade
We couldn't bear
To plug them in
And sing pretty
No, the words stuck
In our throats
Our tormentors, our captors
Asked us for laughs
And we wanted to howl
Like dying dogs
How could we sing
The Lord's joy
In this foreign land?
If I forget you that much,
O Jerusalem
Let my right hand whither
Before it touches the first
False Note
Let my tongue stick in my mouth
If I do not set you above
My highest, meager hope
In this broken land
And you, Lord
Don't you dare forget
The ones who
Tore your city down
—You hear me?
They brought it down
To its footings
Reduced your temple
To rubble
And
Laughed.

O Babylon
You Destroyer
I wish I could do it myself
I wish I could pay you back

I wish
I could take your
Babies
And dash
Their heads
Against those stones.

Aquila slid the book back across the table. It reminded her of what she'd seen at home, a long time ago and far away, but her face was controlled and careful.

"That's not pretty," she said, quietly.

jesus shook his head. "No. What the Babylonians did to them wasn't pretty, either."

"Don't tell me; I don't even want to hear. It makes my skin crawl to think about it." She pulled her shoulders together into a near shiver. "I don't see why we can't just burn those pages."

"You might unintentionally burn out one of the graces in the Bible," jesus said. "Don't set fire to the paper, if the flames still burn in human hearts."

Elizabeth, coming back from the kitchen, flared up at his choice of words. "I find no grace in it," she spat, growing angry. "It's simply evil, and it's obscene to call that graceful."

"The grace isn't in the text," jesus explained, "but in the presence of the text— think of where you find it. The psalms tell you that the ugliest, most vengeful coals you can harbor in your soul will not throw you out of God's presence. Hear the Good News, Elizabeth: bitterness and wrath nearly consumed the psalmists… *and God used them anyway.*"

Elizabeth jerked as if startled.

Herod was in awe of John, knowing him to be a good and holy man, so he kept him in custody. He liked to listen to him, even though it often left him feeling perplexed. *(Mark 6:20)*

Herod had killed her son, as a party favor to a little girl who danced. He'd been afraid of being embarrassed, that was all. Fear of exposure. Her *son.*

"These people wrote scripture sung in churches week after week after week," jesus continued, waving his hand at the small black book. "Their words have given courage to millions of souls passing through the doors of death and destruction. One of their hymns may be on your lips the day you die.

"That's how God punishes 'filthy' people with nasty human emotions, Elizabeth. They help write the Bible."

Elizabeth sat down heavily.

he knows...
dear God
I choke at the part
about forgiving and I always prayed
you wouldn't notice
that I hurried on to
leading into temptation and
how could I ever be
forgiven
I can't possibly
bring myself
for a little girl
that was all
how could you ask me to
I couldn't
Oh dear
Lord
he knows...

Aquila thoughtfully fingered the leather.

he knows...
I shook her
and nearly dear God
how can you...

jesus sat back and enjoyed the clear sunlight pouring through the window. He sipped a cup of tea and smiled at each of them. He wasn't going anywhere.

Many Samaritans of that town came to believe in him because of the woman's testimony: "He told me everything I ever did."
So when these Samaritans had come to him they pressed him to stay with them; and he stayed there two days. Many more became believers because of what they heard from him. They told the woman, "It is no longer because of what you said that we believe, for we have heard him ourselves. We know this: this man truly is the Savior of the world." (John 4:39–42)

Kaph

I am in turmoil. Things are stirring in me that I would rather not disturb.

After another long day of managing jesus' mullet, a gang of us decided to hit the beach for some R & R. I'm not in the *in* crowd, but the Apostles let me tag along occasionally—John says they need someone with a sharp tongue to deflate Peter, in case he starts to puff up like the Pope. Everyone laughs when he says this, but James laughs a little less than the others, even Peter. He struggles with his scabbard, too. Poor guy: he's always so *intense.* James needs an hourly application of the beach for the rest of his life.

Philip, Peter, James, John and I are waiting for the ferry, arguing about figs and prime pickings. As usual, now that they're away from the boss, they're planning who gets what when the revolution's over. John wants to run the State Department, James wants to head Internal Security, Philip is after Missions and Peter wants to enforce Doctrinal and Racial Purity. Everyone's got to have ambition, I guess.

My ambition is to live another day. The schedules of this traveling road show are playing havoc with my insulin routine; I'm beginning to have way too many sugar dips. Some of these are into the low 30s. When they get that low, they're more like Near Death Experiences—which I suppose they are, though I try not to dwell on that—and they leave me shaky for the rest of the day. Just one wipes me out. Two of them, and I feel like the turf at Churchill Downs.

I've had three today.

"It's not so much that they worship the wrong God. It's just *where* they worship. If you don't have some sort of centralized authority, everybody's going to be teaching something different."

"You can't ask them to trek down to Jerusalem every weekend."

Samaritans again. It's a constant sticking point.

Peter and Philip are hotly debating policy guidelines, while John hums "Amazing Grace" with an ironic smile. He takes another swig from his Coke and looks over his sunglasses at Philip, who ignores him.

James thumps his hand impatiently on the dash. "Come on, come on," he mutters.

We're one of the first ones in line, so we have quite a wait. This time of day, there's not a lot of traffic. The sun is hot and the air is stifling in the crowded car. The empire requires you to turn your engine off, so you lose your air conditioning. Around here, that turns your car into an oven in about twenty seconds.

I'm listening and wilting, propping myself up on the door handle, and taking occasional potshots at Peter when I see an opening, because that's my job. I have my oxygen mask on, which muffles my voice a bit, but the others are courteous, and they don't seem to mind my bitter moods too much. Even Peter has been good-humored today.

Usually, after a visit with friends, I will think back over all the things I've said and get embarrassed. So cocksure, arrogant and desperate at the same time! I often tell myself that I really ought to stay away, stop exposing myself.

But I can't stay away forever, no matter how much my inner voice taunts me. I love being around these people too much. They make me feel alive, useful. They are healers, every one of them. I hope that doesn't get lost amidst the gory details.

"You can't depend on High Holy Days alone…"
"Why not?"
When we've been there ten thousand years…
"You know how much they pay attention."
"Maybe a P.A. system…"
…bright shining as the sun…

A young woman, still high from the rally, spots my oxygen mask and leans out of her pickup, interrupting the debate. She motions for me to roll my window down, which I reluctantly do. "Praise God!" she whoops."Do you know jesus?"

"Ah, y-yes," I stammer. I motion to the others in the car. "These are his disciples. They work with him."

"Great!" she leers. She turns her attentions back to me. "jesus is going to heal you, ya know that?"

My tongue bangs against my teeth. Complete system crash. Cursor frozen.

How to be Christian and honest at the same time? No telling. I remember the old lady at the fruit market—old buggy programming, nothing to replace it.

A friendly window appears with a bomb icon on it.

SORRY, AN UNIMPLEMENTED TRAP HAS OCCURRED.
ERROR CODE – 4.
DO YOU WANT TO REBOOT?

Yes, yes. Hit the button.

Nothing happens. Press soft reset. The debugger prompt appears. But I don't know how to debug this system: it's in my head. I don't know the op-codes. Press hard reset, then. The screen clears.

A melodious, pleasant tone hits the air.

"Yes," I say. "I'm sure of it."

Chung! What a nice sound.

The guy in the fluorescent orange jacket is waving impatiently: time to go. The woman's pickup clears its throat, and it scurries off the ferry.

End of encounter.

"Don't let it bother you, Nat," Philip says, quietly.

Hope

The unknown mice of Jerusalem
Shuffle down their holes
Bearing their burdens
On bent grey backs
Which never show
In the colorful
Photographs
Of city life
You gave
Them

But they will claim to know
Those streets for you
Even while they
Pick
Their way through rubble
Where
Hope is another weight
With despair

Where are the shadows
On the clean streets?

Where is the broken brick
Of life?

They can't begin to share
Without some bright squeak of scripture
Stopping up their
Tears
Freezing

Smiles
Upon brave faces

Aren't they so courageous
They're quite an
Inspiration
Don't they feel
Discouraged
I don't know
How they bear it
Just one time
I saw her weary
And I gave her
A wonderful prayer
That
Always
Worked for me
When I was
down

The unknown mice of Jerusalem
Creep through the gleaming streets
Trying to cast no shadow
To spoil your
Shining
Town.

Mem

Wack.
Wack.
Mary sits in her workshop, wedging clay. She presses it against the bench with her palm, a little like kneading dough. Then she raises the formless glob in her hand and throws it against the wood.
Wack.
Air bubbles.
Wack.
Wack.
You've got to get rid of air bubbles, or the piece will blow up when it's fired.
A figure stands in the doorway.
"Mary."
She looks up, startled. She shows a moment's naked hesitation—*don't invade my inner sanctum*—then lets it go and nods her come-in.
jesus steps into the room and searches for a seat, then settles for a crate. He says nothing, but watches. She returns to the clay.
She's bought books, videos. She's the Queen of Self-Help. None of them were worth a nickel.
Wack.
Wack.
There was always something faintly damning in them. They made it sound so easy, when it was really so hard. *Just* think this, *just* do this, *just, just...* It all makes her very weary. She's given up believing in improvement, now. It's apparently something that only happens to the Just.
She sits at the bench, builds up the sculpture. Her nose itches. She scratches it with her arm, because her hands are coated with wet slip. The shape grows. Hours pass.
jesus says nothing, but watches her work with dark, pensive eyes. His head is cocked to the side, his face still.
Her piece is a half-formed woman rising out of a block. It has a hammer and chisel in its hand, yet it is bent over with exhaustion, ready to drop the tools. The figure has etched herself down to the waist and come to a stop. Everything below looks like raw granite.

This Eve's face is stretched and drawn with fatigue, her shoulders sag. Her breasts are mere angular suggestions, her neck is fine and smooth. The arms are thin-boned and graceful at first, then coarse and roughly chiseled near the tools. The effect of the arms is staggeringly ugly; all the weight collects to the clubby wrists. The tools themselves are held in rough, numb folds—claws, really.

How does one create one's own hands? Eve is staring at her left claw, as if dully contemplating the same problem.

The sculptor looks as weary as her subject. Time for a break. She rocks back from the table and finally looks her visitor in the eye. Her face is mute anger only partially exercised, tamped down into cold frustration and nameless irritations. She brushes a loose hair out of her eye with a bothered swipe, and it settles right back into place again. Her mouth squeezes shut, she cracks her back. Annoyance and dissatisfaction seethe in every bone.

jesus nods, understanding.

"Forgive me if I push too hard," he says, quietly.

Her mouth twists into an ironic smile. "You want *me* to forgive *you?*"

"Anything wrong with that?"

"No."

He waits.

"You're forgiven," she says.

jesus rises and kisses her hair—she leans stiffly in to take it, looking down and away—and then he tenderly releases her.

As the door closes, Mary stares at her half-finished piece. Her fingers are drying, flaking at the joints.

Nun

As they were traveling, Jesus came upon a village where a woman named Martha welcomed him into her home. Her sister, Mary, sat at Jesus' feet, listening to all that he said.

Now Martha was distracted by her many tasks, so she came to him and said, "Lord, my sister has abandoned me to do all of this work myself. Tell her to help me."

But the Lord answered, "Martha, Martha, you are fretting and fussing about so many things; but one thing is necessary. The part that Mary has chosen is best; and it shall not be taken away from her." *(Luke 10:38–42)*

The Gospels have been giving Martha a bad rap for centuries; it's time to set the record straight. She does the dishes because she gets impatient when theology junkies go on and on, endlessly debating the fine points of their addiction. They're likely to talk until dawn without actually getting anywhere. She'd rather see clean spoons in the dish drainer.

It's not that she doesn't understand theology; far from it. She simply has a different relationship to it, a different set of demands. Some like theology to be intricate; but Martha thinks theology should be straightforward, untricky. She cares that people not be excluded by obscure points and paradoxes. She cares that God's love not be turned into a game of chess. She cares that God heals the simple, too, and not just logic addicts.

And she *especially* resents being told one thing, then another.

"I was taught," she complained to the Master, "that confession was a precondition for God's forgiveness. It sounds like you're preaching something else."

"Who taught you that?" jesus laughed. "A bunch of Lutherans?"

"You know my roots," she said.

"Teach me about your traditions," he suggested. "What would you say is the core of Lutheranism? What is the gift they give to the world?"

"You're the Rabbi," she said.

"You're the Lutheran," he countered.

She hummed and thought for a moment. "I assume you mean something positive," she said. He smiled without comment.

"You know where—"

"—yes," he said, dryly, "let's try something positive."

"Alright." She thought some more.

"Salvation comes from God," she decided, "and not from anything humans do."

jesus nodded appreciatively. "Good," he said. "That's very good. What a wonderful way to set down the temptation to play God!" He paused as if to savor it, then observed, "But your confession talk picks it back up again. It makes God dependent upon *you*, not the other way around. If you don't do X, God can't do Y."

She demurred. "I suppose... but what about what John writes":

If we claim to be sinless, we are strangers to the truth, and we deceive ourselves. But if we confess our sins, God is just, and may be trusted to forgive our sins and cleanse us from every kind of wrong. If we say we have committed no sin, we call God a liar, and his word has no place in our lives. *(1 John 1:8–10)*

"Another popular part of your heritage," he smiled. "I like it, too—but read it carefully, now. What is the thing that makes the word fail? How do you read it, Rabbi Martha?"

She shrugged. "It says it plainly. The word fails when we don't make a place for it in our lives."

"The word fails in your life. Does John say anything about what happens in *God's* life?"

"No."

"So then, the change is in your life, not God's. God is still free to love you regardless. Confession simply alters your perception of God's love. The benefit is in this world, not heaven."

"Now I *know* you're not Lutheran," she said.

He grinned and pulled a Bible off of Mary's bookshelf. "You have to stop thinking of it as a mechanism," jesus said, flipping through the pages. "Confession is not some cog in a grand machine designed to excuse you from your sins. Confession is simple honesty, and honesty presumes growth, not failure. It seeks to learn, not absolve. Honesty is part of a healthy life. It's not restitution for being sick. How silly! You may as well say that light is the penalty for darkness. Light *ends* darkness.

"John is trying to coax you out of Satan's shadow. He's talking about living in the light as a way of life, full-time. He doesn't want you to flee to it from time to time. He wants you to take up residence. He's not trying to give you an excuse for darkness. In fact, he's pretty convinced that there is no excuse for living in the dark. Why should there be, if God loves you already? Satan tells you to *fear God's wrath* and hide. But John tells you to *trust God's love* and come forward."

Martha frowned. "You see, that's what I'm talking about! Confession is supposed to be about getting God to stop being mad at us. Forget about Lutheran—I'm beginning to wonder if your teaching is even *Christian*."

jesus' eyes grew tattered around the edges. Sometimes, while sitting in the temple, he'd wondered about that himself. Who owns the trademark, he wondered?

Probably the lawyers.

"You can't reach health through fear," he argued. "Confessing to save yourself from wrath has an internal contradiction that robs it of its power."

> God is love. The person who lives in love is dwelling in God, and God is dwelling in that person. In this way love is made complete, so that we can have confidence on the day of judgement, knowing that even in this world we have been like him.
>
> There is no fear in love. Perfect love banishes fear, for fear is about the pains of judgement. *(1 John 4:16b–19)*

"When people think the light is a laser, they stay in the darkness and shove others into its path. They learn nothing from that, and it heals nothing. It's only by stepping into the light *yourself* that you discover that the truth is far gentler. God's love is not, after all, an angry beam. The light of God is *more* like dawn lighting a glen, gradually showing you what lies at hand. Once you know that, you are free to explore what's growing in you, without fear of condemnation.

"John knows that your own heart is far harsher than God's, because it judges in the shadow of ignorance. Only God understands the full extent of your situation, because 'in God there is no darkness at all.' That knowledge makes God *more* compassionate than you can be, even with yourself."

> My children, love must not be a matter of words or talk; it must be genuine, and show itself in action and truth. This way we will know that we belong to the truth, and we can convince ourselves in his sight, even if our consciences condemn us— for God is greater than our consciences, and knows all! *(1 John 3:18–20)*

"This is the meaning of confession: it gives you a God's-eye view, which is clearer and less downcast than your own. It changes how you see yourself.

" 'I am only an unfinished pot,' you whisper, 'and no more.'

"And this is the meaning of forgiveness: you discover acceptance in the Creator's eyes, in spite of this awful truth. The Potter hears you and says, 'You think I'm surprised? Listen, you think I contracted out the job of making you—like I don't know the specs or something? What do I look like? Give me a break. *You're* the one who's surprised!' "

Martha smiled; he'd used a New York Jew accent. As my friend Neil has observed, God should usually be quoted that way. God as a WASP, now—we hear that all the time. Some folks don't even think it's an accent.

"Wait a minute," Martha said. "You've got that upside down. Confession is to *tear down our pride*, not lift up our hearts. We have to hear God's opinion of all the things wrong with us: we go through the list and find out that we're much worse off than we think."

"Martha," the teacher asked, "who is it that's doing the talking when you confess your sins?"

"Well... I am."

"So how are you going to find out something new? The only charges being spoken are coming out of your mouth. If you're telling them to God, don't you already know them?"

She blinked. "Oh."

"The point is not finding accusations, and it's not grinding your nose in what you already know," jesus said. "Preaching, scripture, self-reflection and the world in general will give you plenty of charges to deal with! The point of confession is finding an *answer* to the charges. Because when you come to God with this awful knowledge, do you know what happens?"

"A priest pronounces your forgiveness?" Martha said.

"Something even more amazing and reliable than that," jesus said.

> The sun
> still rises,
> the rain
> still blesses
> the land;
> there is no earthquake or lightning
> or consuming fire; there is no wrath
> or fury; your
> heart is still
> beating; and
> your life is
> pretty much
> the same
> as it was.

"You have stepped into the path of the fearful light, which the Accuser told you was death—and the only consequence is that you can see better. That's it. Imperfect life going forward, still being supported by God in the most basic, fundamental ways. All that anxiety for nothing! Now you have a reply to the Accuser's voice. The Accuser will still berate you and run you down, but now you have something to add on to all of his charges. You have found a place for God's word in your life."

"I am imperfect and unfinished... but God loves me."
"I am tentative and fearful... but God loves me."
"I am aggressive and domineering... but God loves me."

"The Accuser's word has to scoot over and give God's word some space, too," he said, making a little shoving motion over his heart. "And when that happens your secret judgments become instructive, not destructive. You can look at yourself in truth, become confident in God's love and change yourself in freedom rather than crippling fear."

"That's all that happens?" Martha asked, brightening.

"That's all."

She digested it and decided she liked it, Lutheran or not. "That seems very straightforward," she said, with approval.

jesus put his finger to his lips and nodded toward the next room, where the theological junkies were still holding forth. They were going at each other with great enthusiasm and raised voices. The word *soteriological* floated out the door and wafted down the hall, raising a big stink as it passed everyone. jesus wrinkled his nose.

"Don't say that so loud," he whispered. "I could lose half of my grad students."

Samech

It's a beautiful day: clear blue with white puffs, dry, a good wind bringing cool sighs from the northwest. Picture perfect, except we're too busy to enjoy it. Crowd control is becoming a major headache. Philip, Andrew and I are sweating like cold beer bottles in the sun, hustling up and down endless clots of people that refuse, absolutely refuse, to form aisles.

For every person that wants to touch jesus, there are a hundred that just want to watch it happen. The rubberneckers don't understand how desperately important this is to the broken ones—at least, they don't think it's important enough to sacrifice their curiosity. So they press closer to get a good view, and nothing happens because the sick folks can't get up to where the action is… so they wonder what's going on and press in even closer. They are like sheep without a shepherd, mindless. jesus tells us to take pity on them, which we do for the first hour, but after that things get tense.

"You need to clear an aisle," Peter tells his brother, Andrew.

"What a great idea," Philip interjects. "Why didn't we think of that?"

Peter glares at him, sweat dripping off his nose. He decides not to dignify Philip's shot with a reply; he turns and slaps Andy on the back. "Come on, buck up. You can do better." Andrew just nods his head meekly and promises to try harder. *The day Andy stands up to his big brother,* I think, *is the day cows fly.*

"Why on earth is he inside?" I demand irritably. "What's he doing in there?"

"Teaching," Peter shrugs.

"Teaching? Why can't he do that out here?"

Peter just shakes his head wordlessly.

A fight breaks out thirty yards away from us; the bigger disciples run over to put a stop to it. Andrew and I stare at each other for a minute, then roll our eyes and wade back into the herd.

Bah, bah, black sheep, can't some of you go home?

I make my way down the west street, flashing my roadie button. The graphic on our buttons and letterheads is highly effective and recognizable: two simple yellow arcs, forming the outline of a fish. Classy. Levi designed it in a burst of enthusiasm after his conversion. It's clever in its simplicity, very minimalist.

Peter and John thought it was O.K. for a first pass, but I can tell they're going to entertain more designs. The first rule of volunteer labor, I guess, is that you don't speak criticism clearly—like every other potential conflict, you avoid saying what you're thinking and hope that telepathy will cure things.

Good thing I'm not management.

The crowd begins to thin out. I call a few times to see if anyone needs an escort to jesus, but nobody replies. I turn and tarry at the edge, reluctant to plunge back in. It's not so much the physical crush, it's the emotional one that's getting to me. The need to see a miracle is bulging out of their eyes.

Take a break, the wiser part of me says. I nod and step free of the throng. The relief is almost like a cool bath. The noise begins to drop off; then I round a corner, and it shelves dramatically. I wade deeper into peace.

This is the corner of Levi's house. Nice place—he made a lot of money before he got religion. Last night jesus attended a party here, to the outrage of the local clergy. The place was really hopping, full of disreputable types. Advertising execs, producers, starlets, gun nuts, politicians, insurance salesmen… you name it. A real motley crew.

About halfway through the evening—right after the sausage cheese balls, I think—a delegation from the local churches came around to save jesus from his choice of company, figuring he didn't know the seamy background of his fellow revelers. They were full of helpful information, and eager to share it. Charity, of a sort.

jesus listened patiently with a drink in his hand—which didn't reassure his visitors any—and when they were done assassinating everyone's character, he gave them scant gratitude.

"All their sins and blasphemies will be forgiven them," jesus said mildly. "God is attracted to brokenness like a young girl finding an injured bird." He swirled the ice cubes in his glass and downed the rest of his drink. "But when you leave here, watch what you say. The one who calls the Holy Spirit evil will never find forgiveness."

A plump, ruddy-skinned priest blinked in surprise. "We say no such thing," he objected.

jesus looked at him coolly. "Good, if that's true. But watch what you teach," he repeated.

"All our teaching is scriptural—"

"—then watch what you read," jesus continued. "The heart finds the word it seeks. Your heart accuses you of being children of the devil, so that's what you read. Then you teach others the same."

"We are children of Abraham," the priest spluttered, "not of the devil. Where are you hearing these lies?"

"By listening to you," jesus said, surprised. "You know a tree by its fruit, don't you? A fig tree produces figs, a lemon produces lemons, eh?"

"Of course," the man admitted.

"Then if the fruit is poisonous, the tree must be poison. You are either children of the devil, or God is not good."

A horrified scribe, listening in on the exchange, burst out uncontrollably, "No! Never! God is perfect, and all his works are marvelous!"

jesus gave him a faint, ironic smile, and bowed. He gestured toward his fellow partyers. "Then come join us, my friend."

The scribe looked confused. "But they're sinners. Sick."

"Then leave the physician to heal the sick," the master said, his smile evaporating; and then he wandered into the weaving mass of dancers, leaving the churchmen in apoplexy. They muttered to themselves, looking darkly about the room, then strode self-consciously out, as stiff as boards. So much for being neighborly.

Later that night, jesus sat on a couch next to a woman that had grown weepy from too much beer. She told him everything she had ever done to earn money, which was quite an earful.

jesus listened patiently, with no evident shock. When people came by he nodded slightly, sending them a message with his eyes that said *later*. He didn't move until the woman realized that she had been monopolizing him—I guess she'd sobered up a little—and she started to get up in embarrassment; that's when jesus finally laid his hand on her sleeve. "You are acceptable to God," he said.

The woman looked startled, then shook her head violently. "No, no, you haven't heard what I've been saying—"

"—I've heard more than that, Sandra," jesus said. Her eyes widened into two wide dishes of abject terror at her real name, and she made a little choking sound; she'd only given him her stage name. Anonymity was the only way she'd endured her career.

"Listen to me now," he said, laying a finger to her lips. "Are you listening?"

She nodded, mutely.

"Your broken ways are over. Ben was a broken man, and his father before him. Sin gathers like a rolling stone down a hill, and each generation passes on its wounds. But you are a child of God, not Satan. Satan can only destroy. You were *made good*"—she flinched as he said that, dismaying him; but he rushed on before the moment could slip away—"and you were broken," he said urgently, "so you have followed broken ways; but tonight you can begin to mend." He flicked his eyes up toward the ceiling. "The clay is still good," he whispered. "The wheel is spinning, the potter willing."

She nodded her assent, not sure what she was agreeing to; but she submitted to his touch. He smiled, then, and laid both of his hands over her head, like an artisan beginning a new bowl...

...and firmly, invisibly, returned her to the center of the wheel. His eyes shone with genuine pleasure while he touched her—and when he took his hands away she looked as astonished as a new babe.

She never made any indecent money again. What she had she gave away to charity. "I am trying," she told me, "to remember who I am."

A Word of Advice to the Dietitians of the Universe:

Don't tell jesus not to heal. It won't do any good. He's addicted to it. I've seen his eyes—workaholism doesn't even *begin* to describe it. He will stay at the office until the very last light is turned out. Count on it.

> Jesus declared, "I am the bread of life. Whoever comes to me shall never be hungry, and whoever believes in me shall never be thirsty. But as I have said, you have seen me and still do not believe.
>
> "All that the Father gives me will come to me, and I will never turn away anyone who comes to me. I have come down from heaven, not to do my own will, but the will of the one sending me. This is his will: that I should lose not a single one of all that he has given me, but raise them all up on the last day." (John 6:35–39)

Well, how long can one rest before guilt sets in? Not long. I step into the shade of Levi's house, check my sugar, take some pills and decide to get back in gear. I move out into the street, walk toward the bus stop around the corner.

I'm feeling low, I must admit. My run-in with the disciple on the ferry has started a predictable cycle going. This one is going to be ferocious. Senseless anger is flitting back and forth across my soul like heat lightning.

Yes, jesus, I am unhappy with imperfection. There is a part of me that screams *I was made poorly,* and there is no answer I can find for it.

It's an unwinnable longing, I know. No matter how much I may have—and I have a lot—there will always be something wrong, or something limited about me. Who is limitless, besides God?

Every one of us has wounds, demons and limitations, no matter how blessed. We are doomed to jealousy. We might set our sights only on the demon of the day, but I've seen the ratchet effect set in. Remove one obstacle, and the next one is waiting for you. Unhappiness expands to fill the space available to it, like junk in a three-car garage.

Not me, you say? You're quite humble and satisfied with everything you have? No tinkering in mind, no improvements or acquisitions planned? Bless you, child. I hope you can hold on to that feeling until the day you die.

I've had those little peaks, too—but then my condition shifts, and suddenly I start to rage, rage at the limitations placed upon me. It seems like I am enclosed in a steadily shrinking box with no way out. Shoot, right now I'm just glad to have an extension tube on my oxygen tank, so I can reach the kitchen sink! My portables are too expensive to refill for home use, and my H-tank in the bedroom is nearly as tall as I am; so I must weave through the house with a tube trailing behind me, trying to get my chores done—chores that used to be so easy and now are so hard. The tube feels like a leash. It catches on chairs as I move, yanking my head back, ripping at my mask. I hang my head like a dog caught by the collar, and scream helplessly at the chairs.

Sometimes, when my infections start to rage out of control, I still don't get the dishes done and Martha, in enormous frustration, finally has to do it—making me feel like a lousy husband who's too lazy to help. She wants me to give up the chore; I refuse. I don't want to give in.

Limitations, horizons. Walls.

The word *invalid* keeps blowing around my brain, like an out-of-date parking sticker.

Back into the crowd. Up the street, take a deep breath... *Excuse me, excuse me.* Flash the pass, maneuver people aside. The canister on my back thumps into a hurrying businessman, trying to thread his way to the bus. He shoots me an annoyed glance, then hurries on.

No star can be made without horizons. It's a fact of life. No matter how big the body, something constrains it: a leash. It's a by-product of existence. To create things, God had to invent *not-God* stuff, which by definition is finite. If it had been perfect and limitless, it just would have been *more of God.* To make us, even God became self-limiting!

Creative renunciation, Simone Weil called it: God renounced the ability to fill the entire Universe. A stepping back, the making of a protected area where something else might exist, grow into its own being.

Mothers know the same pain. They must let their children differentiate, if their kids are to be something more than simply an extension of Mom. The terrible twos ("No! No!") are the beginning of that long process. It's an awful time, but necessary if the new creation is ever to have its own identity. It just has to be that way.

All of Creation is in its terrible twos. We're very unhappy about the process of being brought forth. Not that we mind being created; we just always wish we were a little bigger, a little longer lasting, a little stronger, a little brighter... the terms of our conception seem terribly unjust when it gets down to the specifics. Maybe it's O.K. *for God* to set limitlessness down, but that was, after all, a choice God could make. We never had that chance.

Our urge for Godliness is an urge to undo the choice that was forced upon us. We yearn to reverse the process of Creation. We're not so sure that humanity is such a great idea; nor are we sure a universe inhabited solely by *us* is a bad idea.

Hey mister, if you don't want that ball, can I have it?

Comparison to others intensifies the rejection of our creation. There is always a heavenly body who has more. God, by being in contact with us, unintentionally sets off the chain of unhappiness. We sense perfection behind the veil; we feel our lack. Imagine how much worse it would be if we experienced it full force!

I had this epiphany when trudging across a hot parking lot outside of Kmart, where all great epiphanies occur. I suddenly saw every shopper with an oxygen mask, dragging their load. I saw them all planning their lives for an unknown number of shortened days; I saw the whole of humanity as if it had cystic fibrosis.

It is your proximity to healthier people that makes your condition seem so unfair, I heard. If all had C.F., none would have it. Now do you understand why I must hide my face?

Yes, Dear God. If I came into the full force of your glory, I would be consumed... but the flames would come from my angry heart, not yours.

Satan, they say, was one of the brightest angels, a powerful being named Lucifer. But he, too, was made out of *not-God* stuff, and eventually his jealousy got the better of him.

How you have fallen from heaven, bright morning star!
  Cut down to the earth, sprawled helpless across the nations!
  You had thought, "I will scale the heavens; I will set my throne high above the stars of God. I will sit on the mountain where gods meet in the far reaches of the north, rise high above the cloud-banks, and make myself like the Most High."
  Yet you shall be brought down to the grave, to the depths of the abyss, and those who see you will stare and ponder your fate. *(Isaiah 14:12–16)*

We might do well to ponder Satan's fate. It is our own. We yearn for limitlessness and call the lack of it evil. We ache and chafe, we feel our boundaries as a powerful curse. *Sin, brokenness, imperfection, ungodliness, sickness, evil:* they are synonyms in our gut. They all scream the central accusation that we weren't made well enough. To exist with *not-God* stuff feels like condemnation, a damnation rather than a creation. But the condemnation comes from our own confused hearts, not God.

Most folks won't own up to their anger at being created. They say God's mad, instead. They say God demands what he never gave, tries to reap what was not sown: perfection, Godliness. God is a spoiled eight-year-old boy, they say, making soldiers out of clay, just so he can punish them for not being gold.

Projection, the psychologists call it. When you look at God, you see your own dissatisfied face.

There's a woman in distress, her eyes as ragged as old corn husks.

"Hello, sister. Do you need help?"

She snaps tight at my word, gives me a frightened glance and edges off into the crowd. I recognize the look. She wants help, but doesn't want anyone to know it. It's a burden to admit to sickness. Exposure of our sin. I try to catch up to her, but she's more mobile than I.

Sister, come back. I won't blame you.

Too late. Argh!

One day I'm going to arrange a special race in which every runner must carry a heavy metal canister upon their back, and then I will be able to demonstrate my true expertise.

Until then, I get frustrated a lot.

Sorry, jesus. You picked a lame horse for this race.

I scan the crowd for sign of her, but fail, sigh, and return to my old course.

The crowd is even more agitated than when I left; something is happening.

I pick up my pace, split the crowd like a bow through troubled water.

Sometimes the Leprosy Effect helps more than a roadie pass. People flee from imperfection, they don't want it to rub off on them.

It's not really the threat of infection, though folks might tell you that. It's another way to externalize the condemnation of our Ungodliness. Society picks out easy targets, symbols of imperfection, and it pushes its rage and self-dissatisfaction onto them.

Sometimes we get so furious we push them off a cliff.

...Then Aaron shall lay both of his hands on a live goat, and he shall confess all of Israel's wickedness. He shall lay them on the head of the goat and send it away. The goat shall carry all their iniquities into the barren waste. *(Leviticus 16:20–22, highly condensed)*

You remember Mr. Wilson
   Four doors down
     Always so cheerful
And the way you fidgeted
   In his strange-smelling house
     When your Mom made you

Visit
With her
In the dark
Life drowning
In strange
Impediments

                  The oxygen man
                  Left a sign today
              Dear he says we have
                    To hang
              It in a prominent
           Place I'll be damned
                    If I do

   You remember
     Mr. Wilson
       Four doors down.

"Why was this man born blind, teacher? Whose sin was it?"
"Why did that tower fall on those people? They must have been evil, eh?"
"How about those folks whose blood was mingled with the sacrifices in the temple?"

The poor, criminal, malformed and alien stand as powerful symbols for us, easy targets for our dissatisfaction; and the scream we aim at them is directly proportional to the burden we feel in our hearts. This shame of being human has to go someplace, and we find outlets. The ones least compassionate with society's scapegoats are also the ones most concerned with Lawfulness and Godliness—check out the roll-call vote in the Senate sometime!

The more wrapped up we are in the evilness of *not-God* stuff, the more we try to crush it. Yet we are made of the same stuff. We ritually destroy ourselves through substitution.

jesus always gave short shrift to such nonsense. He understood the topic wasn't really the stated one. It's not about the victims; it's about you. No matter what you say about victims of AIDS, you are are talking about yourself.

> Jesus answered them, "Are you imagining that those Galileans suffered their fate because they were greater sinners than others in Galilee? I tell you they were not— but unless you repent, you will all come to the same end. Or the eighteen victims who died when the tower fell on them in Siloam—do you fancy that they were more guilty than all the other people living in Jerusalem? They were not, I tell you! But unless you repent, you will all of you come to the same end." *(Luke 13:2–5)*

There is only one logical outcome, jesus knew, from the urge to eradicate the Ungodly. Destruction of all Creation.

Yes, something's happening, all right. There are people on the roof! They have chipped a hole in the ceiling and lowered a paralytic down to jesus. There's going to be hell to pay with Peter later on. It's absurd that this should happen. I push myself up to a window, intent on finding some way to make amends. But the scene inside is mesmerizing; I soon lose all thoughts of myself.

jesus is surrounded by teachers of diet, faith and law, who have been arguing with him all day. They think he represents evil; some are calling him a child of Beelzebub openly. jesus, of course, has been cheerfully returning the compliment. The Good Shepherd is no milquetoast when it comes to judges.

> "And so I tell you this: no sin, no slander, is beyond forgiveness—except blasphemy against the Holy Spirit itself. Even those who speak a word against the Son of Man will be forgiven! But if anyone speaks against the Holy Spirit, he will find no forgiveness in this age or the age to come." *(Matthew 12:31–32)*

He's not going to be invited to many church conferences any time soon, I can see that. He looks at the poor man lying on the mat, looks around the room. Broken clay and straw are strewn everywhere. There is dust on people's heads. He gestures at the rubble, stretches out his hand and smiles that observer's smile of his, the one that laughs inside.

"Such faith," he chuckles, shaking his head in admiration. He turns his head to the lawyers and dietitians surrounding him, as if to share the joke with them, but they return nothing but a scowl.

jesus sighs and turns his attention back to the man. He speaks kindly. "You are acceptable to God."

There is a gasp, a hiss. They can't believe their ears. Blasphemy! Who can forgive sins but God alone?

jesus knows exactly what they are thinking. "Why are you thinking this?" he asks, rounding on them in a flash. "Which is easier? To pronounce God's acceptance to a paralytic, or to say, 'Get up, take your mat and walk?' But to show you that the Son of Man has authority on earth…"

He stands up and points his finger at the lame man. "Get up!" he commands. "Take your mat, and go home. Find more forgiving company!"

It is a healing done in sudden anger; I have not seen one like it before. It comes down like a hard slap on a table. The man jolts upright, as if a bolt of lightning has passed through his body, and nearly leaps to his feet. The room breaks up into a furious babble. I don't know what happens after that. My eyes are filled with tears.

He didn't even *touch* the man; it was his word alone that healed! No hesitation, no recuperation, no long training of the legs: the muscle atrophy is simply gone, gone, like a bad dream. jesus has fast-forwarded the man through two years of therapy—and he did it *just to prove a point*. The man has had his life rejuvenated as an object lesson.

Dear God, make an object lesson out of me!

I confess to an ugliness here. My joy for this man lasts exactly four seconds. And then? Dark, burning jealousy. Uncontrollable rage. Cries of injustice, self-pity, murderous hate.

People step away from me. I am suddenly alone at the window, but I can no longer see through it. There is an impenetrable red wall around me. I imagine jesus can see me, but I don't know that. I certainly can't see him anymore.

I turn around and flee. Not a man touches me.

They all know I am bound for hell.

'Ayin

Blueness alert
Blueness alert
Blueness alert

Too tired today, drowning. My body aches. Sucking on oxygen all day, but it barely helps. Hopeless again. Oxygen is no cure for cystic fibrosis. Antibiotics are no cure. They stretch out your time, but C.F. will get you in the end. In the final stages, in fact, they stretch out your pain. Morphine, I hear, is the drug of choice, when you get there.

Am I there? Don't know. I hate to add anything more to this mind-numbing fog. Already I feel like a potted plant. Yet I need some sort of relief. I can barely write this. My pencil is shaking.

Think of the time you most yearned for something. Now make it a physical thing, this yearning ache. Plant it deep in every muscle, so strong that it makes you feel nauseated.

Sometimes I can't help but moan or whimper. I hate that: chronic lung patients are infamous for being whiny. I don't want to be whiny.

I used to think my personality was mine to determine! Just as I took pride in my mind, I took pride in my demeanor. Vanity, vanity. Everything can be stripped away from you. Don't forget that. If you take pride in who you are, how you act, what you do or what you think, you are skating on thin ice. Don't justify your existence that way. Find something that cannot be taken away from you, or you will crumble, like me.

Right now I have up days and down days. Sooner or later it will be all down days. What then?

Pro-lifers tell me to be strong and carry my cross. So easy to order others to carry their crosses! Who will pick mine up? God, I hurt. Make it stop.

Blueness alert
Blueness alert
Blueness alert

Pe

One day a teacher of the law, an earnest man named Nicodemus, came to jesus asking how he might be saved.

"What is it that makes your joy incomplete?" jesus asked. "How do you read it?"

"We were polluted in the garden," Nicodemus replied. "God made us whole and good, but we chose evil ways and became corrupted."

"And what let this stain into paradise?"

"We were tempted by the snake," Nicodemus hissed.

"Was this snake another god?"

"Of course not!" the scribe said. "There is only one God."

"The snake was made by God," jesus nodded. "So then, your temptation was designed by God…?"

"—The snake was acting on his own Free Will," Nicodemus interrupted, before he could get turned around. He'd been in that maze before. "And in any case, that was only *temptation*. We are the ones who chose to give in, so the failure is ours alone."

"So it is your Free Will that lets the evil into paradise," jesus concluded. "You have the ability to choose, and you choose poorly."

"Except our Will is no longer completely Free," Nicodemus amended. "It is corrupted now, so that we inevitably choose sin."

"And why is that?"

"Because Adam chose poorly."

"And why did Adam sin? Was he a child of the devil?"

"No," Nicodemus answered, "he had Free Will, but he chose poorly. That doomed the rest of us."

"I see," answered jesus. He thought a minute and said, "Nicodemus, do you want to be in heaven?"

"Of course!" Nicodemus replied.

"And will you be happy there?"

"Yes!"

"But if it is as you say, you must have your Free Will taken away. You will become a mindless robot. You won't be yourself at all, but a partial image."

"No," Nicodemus corrected, growing impatient. "I will still have my Will. But I will want the Good instead of the Bad. I will choose correctly."

"Do you want the Good now?"

"Yes."

"But you do not choose it."

"No. I choose what I shouldn't," the man lamented, earnestly. He was a good man at heart.

"Then what will be different in heaven?" jesus asked, with genuine curiosity.

Nicodemus answered as if talking to an obtuse child. "I will be perfect. I will have my Free Will, but I will choose wisely. My Will will no longer be corrupted."

jesus' eyebrows narrowed in concentration. "Let me see if I'm getting this right. You will be restored..."

"Yes."

"...to the state of Adam..."

"Yes."

"...who chose to sin."

Nicodemus started to pull on his beard in exasperation. "Bother!" he exclaimed. "Well, I'll be made better than Adam, then," he decided, looking annoyed. "I will still have Free Will, but I will naturally choose the good."

"Better than Adam..."

"Yes."

"...who was made without blemish in paradise..."

"Stop that!" Nicodemus snapped. "You're getting me confused."

"Sorry," jesus said.

The scribe tapped his finger to his lips.

jesus chewed on a fig.

"If Adam's a problem," Nicodemus said, thinking aloud, "we could get rid of him..."

"Discard the premise and retain the conclusions?" jesus smiled.

Nicodemus huffed. "I'm not talking about discarding him entirely. I'm suggesting rethinking him on mythic lines; a story describing us all."

"If you do that," jesus noted, "you don't get rid of Adam, you make *everybody* Adam. Same problems." The teacher wiped the juice off his lips and began to enumerate with his fingers. "God supposedly made you perfect; yet you are obviously imperfect. You are responsible for screwing up the world, yet everything you have comes from God..."

"—Right, right. I get it," Nicodemus said impatiently. He held up his hand for silence, so he could think of a way out that wouldn't make him leave home.

jesus waited patiently.

The scribe grew despondent.

At length jesus threw the remainder of his fig toward the garbage dump called

Gehenna and put his hands on his hips. "You are a teacher of Israel, and yet you cannot answer?"

"I keep falling into a trap," Nicodemus sighed. "Either there are two gods, or the one we've got didn't make us well enough."

"It's worse than that," jesus warned. "You've lost your hope in heaven by protecting your myth of the past. If 'Freedom' causes sin, God can't make a Paradise that lasts—or at least, one that can endure *free humans* stomping around in it. You can't enter Paradise without taking evil in with you, unless you leave your Free Will at the door like a pair of muddy boots."

An excited gleam came into Nicodemus's eye just at that moment. "I've got it!" he exclaimed. "God will come up with a way to pardon us for our impurities, so that we may enter Paradise."

"You'll continue to do evil in heaven, while God looks the other way?" jesus said. "That sounds more like Earth to me."

Nicodemus moaned. "But if it is as you say," the scribe protested, "it is impossible to enter heaven."

"That seems to come out of your teaching," jesus agreed. "It appears that heaven must be occupied solely by God."

Then he turned to the listening disciples. "Woe to those," he said, "who love their traditions more than hope."

Tsadhe

I applied my mind to all this, and I understood that the righteous and the wise and all their doings are under God's control; but is it love or hatred? No man knows.

(Ecclesiastes 9:1)

The Devil's Playground is a plain of immense boulders strewn without organization, or any discernible attention to aesthetic detail. It earned its name for two reasons. First, it looks like the results of a tantrum on an enormous scale; second, it is a popular hiding place for robbers. It is more dangerous to go there than any other place in the country, if you don't belong. You definitely don't go there if you have something to lose. It's kind of like the commodities exchange in Chicago.

I don't feel like I've got much to lose, though, and I like rocks. I've always been a rock sitter; picked it up from my Mom. Our happiest vacations always involved a pile of rocks and a tide coming in. Give me a sunny day and a block of granite to lay on, and I'm happy. I can't really explain what I get out of it; maybe I'm half-snake.

I am also attracted to the interplay between randomness and chaos. Back when I still designed video games, I tinkered constantly with chaotic functions that seemed natural. Fractal geometry, chaotic math and 1/f noise, that was cool stuff back then, a whole new lens for the world. Science was just getting out of its cocky adolescence, learning that reality was more complicated than our equations. It was fun to be there when science grew up.

Until chaos came along, people were pretty sure that you could predict the future, if you could only measure all the forces involved. Quantum theory started to challenge that, but people compartmentalized that bit of bad news ("I refuse to think God plays dice with the Universe"—Einstein) by relegating it to the realm of the Very Small. When it came to the realm of what you could actually see, Newtonian thinking still ruled. To a pre-chaos, pre-quantum scientist, the world was like a bunch of balls on a billiard table. Measure the vectors, and you're a prophet. Easy.

The ball didn't land in the pocket after all?

Hmm. Must be something wrong with the meter. Let me jiggle this wire here...

Chaos theory finally told people to stop jiggling the wire.

When the prophets of chaos came down from the Holy Mountain, they had a new idea inscribed on their tablets:

The notion is that a very tiny amount of stuff, impossible to measure, can have huge implications over time.

Weather systems are the prime example. You'll never be able to nail down the weather, no matter how many meters and satellites you put up. The roil of a butterfly's wings will be enough to change your thunderstorm prophecies.

Sound fanciful? In truth it's just a bold way of saying that the world is complicated: it was not created just so we could have simple equations to solve. When we started doing our equations on the computer, we could finally see that. Bulk-processed equations on supercomputers still couldn't predict the future, so our faith matured.[16]

Incredible benefits have come out of this new lens. The most important, I think, was humility, and an appreciation for the complexity of God's thought. Suddenly Creation became more impressive. Machine metaphors of the Universe—popular since the heady days of the Industrial Revolution—disappeared. The world looks a little more artistic now, a little less automatic; and when your view of the watch changes, maybe your view of the watchmaker does, too.

But there are many "practical" benefits marching out of the factories, too. You can build better heart defibrillators, for example. New defibrillators can think chaotically to restore the heart to its natural, somewhat chaotic rhythm, and end its phase-locked heart attack. Chaos theory revealed that too much strict regularity (a loss of chaos) in the human heart is brittle, anti-life! The Pharisees were surprised to hear this, but jesus wasn't.

I spent countless hours playing with the toys of chaos, getting a feel for how to shape numbers without completely pressing out their impulses. I loved it. I think I just made up the games so that I could get paid making random worlds.

There are many clever ways of filtering complete randomness and placing some order on it. Pinking, we called it. *White noise* (so named because, like white light, it contains all frequencies in random amounts) sounds like harsh radio static, but *pink noise* sounds like waterfalls, surf, wind and rain. When you sample pink noise, you get pink numbers. Such pinking functions can be used to create digital mountains, continents, oceans and trees. Let there be earth! That was my joy for over a decade.

When I look at graphs of these functions, I feel like I'm looking at the basic methodology of God. It's as different from Newtonian, cause-and-effect engineering as a snowflake is from a billiard ball. Forget the "God is white/black/brown" silliness. God is bright pink.

In the beginning, the earth was without form and void, and God's spirit moved over the frothy white foam... *(Genesis 1:1)*

God has some funky filtering algorithms. Light out of darkness, land out of water...

This is what I see when I read Genesis: God comes across randomness, meaninglessness, and starts to play with it, grow things out of it. It's not linear engineering, but chaotic structuring, pinking, filtering. The character of things is not brute-forced but shaped into something more pleasing than white noise. Light separates out. Water and land clump together in fascinating ways. Once things get a chance to hang together, their nature is revealed: salt, quartz and diamond reveal their different beauties.

The earth coalesces, becomes fertile. Life itself starts to show the potential hidden in acids and chemicals. The goal isn't some ramrod-straight buildings, but Sense applied to what was first entirely Senselessness. A spider web; a thunderhead; inertia; the color wheel; Leonardo da Vinci; Einstein.

What is the difference between Einstein and da Vinci? What are the similarities?

You can see both wild genius and similar structure in Creation, the pattern and the noise; there is endless diversity and yet recognizable similarity at the same time. There is no Platonic Ideal of a "horse" from which the Real is degraded. The ideal *is* the diverse. Variation lies at the very center of it, like a fugue.

As the Hebrews testified, God is "The God of History." The Hebrew God is involved in the flow of things, not like an aloof Greek god at all, but more like a kid playing in rainwater on the road. There's always something that could use a little tinkering. It's irresistible to the Sleepless One: *I bet if I cut a trench here I could get a lake going...*

But God is also not senseless or arbitrary. The mind of God is always radically respectful, honoring the raw materials; teaching them, you might say, toward excellent forms. Order is pulled out of disorganization, always with an eye for inherent beauty.

God's still doing it, and so are we. We have that little piece of the Creator built inside us.

So God created us in his own image; he made us in the image of God; male and female he made us. (*Genesis 1:27*)

Don't you love the look of a good, hand-crafted wood cabinet? Or a beautifully designed bridge? Or a song?

In my second year of seminary, one of my classmates suddenly became a widow. It was an enormous, devastating blow, a senseless death without warning. The void broke in upon us and threw us back into the Devil's Playground. We rushed to her house and tried to help in whatever way we could.

I remember sitting outside, helping Bob and Ann pull weeds. We were mowing her lawn, straightening her garden. It was a heartbreakingly pitiful gesture, but we were compelled to do it. It was, I think, a physical creed; and it was not, in the end, pitifully small, but the most heroic act we were capable of at the time. It was word-less faith thrown in the face of terror. The void—the No-Thing that was impervious to words, comforts, flowers and cards—had just rolled into our world and taken a big chunk out of it. But life could still act out the creed.

Our hands dug into the clay, scissors clipped the grass, and this is what we told the void:

You will not win in the end. You may come and take a husband, a wife, a son and a daughter; you may strike us down with diseases and depression; you may maim us and cause us to hurt each other. But look here: I am taking back this little corner of the Universe. You can't have this bit. It may be small and insignificant, but it's something you can't take. I am going to weed, weed, weed, until this garden is bigger than you are. We are cleaning up, God is going to help us—and someday, evil, you are going to be history.

That is the creed we all instinctively act out when life falls apart. We straighten things up, clean house, rearrange the cupboard. When my condition worsens, Martha gets lots of landscaping done. I do theology. It's pretty much the same thing.

Will the light-gatherers eventually win over the darkness? Will the senseless waters—as the author of Revelation suggests—eventually give up its hold on the human condition? I don't know. There's plenty of evidence to the contrary. Sometimes our weeding does more harm than good. The housing projects in Chicago, so hated by liberals such as I, were the creation of an earlier generation of liberals who thought affordable housing would be an improvement. They didn't set out to sow despair in poor people; but that's what they reaped. The world is a complicated garden.

God help us all!

There are mines for silver and places where gold is refined; where iron is won from the earth and copper smelted from the ore... Humans set their hands to the granite rock and lay bare the roots of the mountains; they cut galleries in the rocks, and gems of every kind meet their eyes; they dam up the sources of the streams and bring the hidden riches of the earth to light.

But where can wisdom be found?

And where is the source of understanding?

No one knows the way to it; it is not found in the land of the living. The depths of ocean say, "It is not in us," and the sea says, "It is not with me." Red gold cannot buy it... no creature on earth can see it, and it is hidden from the birds of the air.

Destruction and death say, "We know of it only by report."

But God understands the way to it, God alone knows its source. (From Job 28)

What are you doing here, Elijah?

A still, small voice breaks in on my thoughts, whispering through the valley; it's like a tentative finger probing through murky water, trying to find me. I look up anxiously toward the clouds, but see nothing.

I have a neat spiral of stones and seashells laid out in front of me, smallest to largest, coming out from the ineffable center.

What are you doing here, Elijah?

Just trying to make some sense, Lord; just doing a little theology.

A quiet chuckle. *Better stick to the stones,* it advises.

I went to Chicago to become a minister. I thought I was going there to help other folks. Maybe I did. People tell me I did, but it's hard to believe, with that whirlpool swirling around me, all that foam and noise. One thing I know: whatever benefit other folks received, I got more out of it than I ever could have put into it. It still stands right next to marrying Martha as the smartest two things I've ever done.

But it did not turn out as planned. Too much time had gone, too many gerbils had collected in my chest, and I had to stop.

If I could only go back to the old days, to the time when the Lord was watching over me, when God's lamp shone above my head, and by its light I walked through the darkness! If I could be as in the days of my prime, when God protected my home... *(Job 29:1–4)*

This still grieves me, though every month I understand it a little better.

One thing I studied in seminary was the problem of evil. It was my attempt at gardening, I guess, but I picked a nasty weed to pull. Might have done better with crabgrass.

I won't rehash all the endless tangles that grow around the subject. Suffice to say that we come down to unpleasant thickets, no matter how clever we are.

Some of us make Satan into a competing God to explain it. That way we won't have to deal with the uncomfortable notion that God made Satan, too, and obviously didn't make him *good enough.* So we say Satan made evil, and stop there.

Some of us cling strictly to the notion of a single God, and there encounter our suspicion that God is malignant, unjustly punitive, or unskilled in the God-trade: kind of a C student, no matter how you look at it.

If God made *everything,* then God is ultimately responsible for our plight. Why do we hurt? Why do we steal, whip our kids and build slums? Blame God, who made us stupid.

Some hope that "free will" saves the issue, but it's a red herring, as jesus pointed out. It doesn't explain the poor equipment which exercises its freedom so brokenly, and—even worse—you can take that tack in only two directions: preserve your explanation of the fall, or preserve your hope of heaven. Which do you prefer, your past, or your future?

I need my future. I need a very real heaven these days, because I'm entering a long, dark, painful tunnel—these current trials, they're nothing compared to what's ahead. If I'm going to survive it, I need a real light shining at the end. And I don't give a fig for anything that makes the light go out, or turns it into a freight train.

Don't tell me that God will make a Nathaniel-machine that looks just like the real thing, O.K.? We can do that already. If I wanted to, I could digitize myself from every angle and plug predictable conversational responses into a computer. I could make holograms and neural nets, use artificial-intelligence functions and motion sensors, robotic effectors and synthesized stereo vocal tracks with Dolby surround. I could leave it all behind for Martha to hug, and she wouldn't, because she would know it wasn't really me.

Don't tell me God's going to do the same thing. Don't say God will populate a sterile city with similar ghosts of my sister, brother, grandmother and poor old Abraham, and say the job's done. Don't even suggest that God is not as smart as Martha.

No, there has to be an answer that respects what has gone on here. Is God such a petty dictator that millions of white-robed automatons bowing and scraping would really be pleasing? If so, why bother with earth? Why pass through all this pain and torture if the final chapter represents a bunch of gadgets God could have picked up in Wal-Mart? And it is a torture at times, too. We need to hold on to that, not forget it. Life *costs*.

What is it buying? When I've been struggling with an infection for months, gradually losing steam, I really wonder what the point is. Is it really worth this pain? I need to know that; it's not a remote issue. It is a matter of life and death.

Most theologians aren't that interested in heaven, you know. Most seem embarrassed by it. In seminary, about the only time you hear heaven discussed is when liberation theologians use the faintly derisive term "pie in the sky."

Yeah, well, I've got news for you, fella. The pie you've got down here is going to get moldy someday.

The more I think about it, the more outrageous I think it is that we didn't discuss the hope of heaven, talk about how to think about it. It's no less accessible than any of the other topics, and of far more import than most of the subjects academics get excited about. This is something people in the real world cling to—and if you think they're stupid, deluded or naive for it, you are being overly obnoxious, arrogant, healthy or young, and you need to grow up. Period. When your life is irretrievably deteriorating into a constant din of pain, heaven is a part of hope.

What shall heaven do with the memory of Earth's pain, then? Can it be salved, or must it be erased? I've been talking to others about heaven lately—picking out the furniture while waiting for moving day, I guess—and I've discovered that memory itself is a problem when we contemplate resurrection. It seems that the conflicting claims, bad blood and grievous losses that go on here are so overwhelming that we can't even imagine having it resolved, so people are forced to believe in heavenly amnesia. Peace, acceptance and understanding seems impossible, so a lot of folks figure that God will zap that part out of our awareness.

"It wouldn't be heaven if I could relive what we did in the war."

"Well, if my son was in hell, I couldn't be happy in heaven—so God will make me forget that I had that son."

"All our earthly sorrows are supposed to pass away."

"What if I remarried after my wife died—how could we all coexist together?"

"How could saints have joy if others were still suffering?"

"Maybe God can forgive me for what I did to my kid, but I can't."

This took me aback at first—I'd never thought that way myself—but after a while I began to spot where it was coming from. I think it says a lot about who we are right here on earth. Denial and suppression are so endemic to Christian culture that we can't envision any other solution to the memory of pain and sorrow. If we tell people to "rejoice when they suffer"; if we blot out the angry bits of scripture; if we worship a God whose main struggle is to forget that we turned out sinful... is it any wonder that heaven begins to sound like one long druggy stupor?

The pearly gates, it turns out, are made of Valium.

You come up to your mother, and find out that she barely remembers you... only a vague sense that you were related somehow... all of the tense bits were wiped out, and there were a lot of them... but she's happy.

The same thing has happened to you. It is the state of everyone around you: numbness, deadened quiet, grey bliss. You wander the foggy streets, looking down at gold, which you remember. Something is odd about that, but you can't quite put your finger on it—tar is no longer a word that means something to you. What was it that we paved earth's streets with?

Must have been gold.

Forget about it. There's a harp concert today at noon. There always is.

No. I already know what that looks like. I don't have to wait for heaven to see it. I've already seen Alzheimer's disease.

Life remembers who it is, where it came from. If our life is supposed to be more abundant, shouldn't memory be more abundant, too? What if our comprehension of the past was greater than it is now—so great that we understood it and found peace with it?

Must the past always wound us?

Yes, and how much luck are you having getting free of your beginnings, Nathaniel?

I know, I know...

But might it not be possible? Is there really no hope of serenity?

Here's another stone to play with; we've touched on it before, but bring it into the pattern now. It's the Dilemma of Existence, Lucifer's problem. We dream of perfection without stop; we feel our lack as something wrong.

In God's presence, this aching sense of inadequacy would reach critical mass. What's God going to do with people like us?

God could remove the limits, deify us to a level that even God does not aspire to; let us be the entire Universe. But if that's going to work for more than one soul, there would have to be a merger, a swallowing. We would be taken up into one big Unity, lose our individuality.

Is that the meaning of St. Paul's "so that God may be all in all"?

Yikes! Now God begins to sound like the Babylonian God that eats you.

That kind of stuff might sound philosophically interesting, as long as you're not contemplating it personally. It might work if you didn't have a good dose of mortality thumping you in the behind.

Along that line, here's a little bit of *real theology* for theology tyros contemplating resurrection. I found it in the Devil's Playground; it comes from Paul Tillich, the master of modern systematics. Those of you who—like Martha—have no patience for this sort of thing can sample it, thank God you never went to seminary and hurry on:

> From the point of view which assumes separate individual destinies, there is no answer at all. The question and answer are possible only if one understands essentialization or elevation of the positive into Eternal Life as a matter of universal participation: in the essence of the least actualized individual, the essences of other individuals and, indirectly, of all beings are present... he who is estranged from his own essential being and experiences the despair of total self-rejection [*au. note: that's me!*] must be told that his essence participates in the essences of all those who have reached a high degree of fulfillment and that through this participation his being is eternally affirmed. This idea of the essentialization of the individual in unity with all beings makes the concept of vicarious fulfillment understandable. It also gives a new content to the concept of Spiritual Community; and finally, it gives a basis for the view that such groups as nations and churches participate in their essential being in the unity of the fulfilled Kingdom of God.[17]

Thank you, Paul. I feel essentially so much better now, knowing that I can look forward to vicarious participation in the great big After-Glob. In fact, I feel so essentially affirmed, I think I'll go drink some essential Drain-O now, and just get it essentially over with.

—I keep on wondering if that worked for him, when he died. Does anyone know?—

Is it possible to deal with our longing for Godhood another way? Rather than catering to it, is it possible for God to heal it? I don't know.

This horizon of mine, it feels like a curse. I tell myself that it's a function of existence; but my heart does not listen. My heart says that God is punishing me.

Reconciliation, I think, must be reconciliation to the fact of my creation; and hence to my Creator. But how am I going to do that? I can't even be comfortable with who I am among *people*.

Strong as I am, I stumble
Under my load of misery
There is disease in all my bones.

I have such enemies
That all men scorn me;
My neighbors find me a burden...
When they see me in the street
They turn quickly away.

I am forgotten
Like a dead man
Out of mind.
(Psalm 31:10–12)

Thunk.

I finally ran out of little black pebbles. I still had some brown and white ones. The shells were there, too. But no more black ones. If I kept going, I'd just add more disharmony to the pattern. Time to stop.

I brought my knees up to my chest and stared down at my stony creed. What did I have?

Three arms circling, but never reaching, the center. An orbit around something that couldn't be touched.

What was in the center? Heaven. I needed it as surely as I couldn't find it.

All of the conflicts I have in this life show up when I think about the afterlife. My talk about heaven isn't about heaven at all, but about my hopes for this world. Yet I need a hope greater than this world...

Spirals.

I brushed the pebbles away, sighed and looked around me. The light had shifted; I hadn't realized how much time had passed.

Yet I saw also that one and the same fate overtakes them both. So I said to myself, "I too shall suffer the fate of the fool. To what purpose have I been wise? What is the profit of it? Even this," I said to myself, "is emptiness. The wise man is remembered no longer than the fool, for, as the passing days multiply, all will be forgotten. Alas, wise man and fool die the same death!" *(Ecclesiastes 2:14–16)*

I was lost in the Devil's Playground, surrounded by a jumble of hot rocks and senseless patterns. My faith was collapsing, my despair increasing. I was like a young sun burning out, falling into itself under the pressure of enormous gravity. A black hole beginning to happen.

I had stopped following the crowds for three days now. I was alone, dead alone.

It was a Sabbath, I remember. A day of rest, although workaholic jesus was pretty much putting an end to that tradition. He had to do what the Father was doing, he kept saying, and he had very little time. So he pulled the weekend shift and sparred with the Pharisees about it. *I've come to fulfill every jot and tittle of the law... as long as it doesn't get in my way.*

Which of you, if a sheep was lost, would not go and fetch it?

I heard light feet on stone. I instantly knew who it was. I felt a pang of guilt, then, to be adding to his burden. Another blot on my soul: there were so many folks that deserved his help. There were people out there he could touch—how dare I pull him from them?

He sat down beside me and said not a word. I looked at him cautiously, expecting an angry face, and found a troubled one instead. He was in the Devil's Playground, too.

He hadn't come to condemn me, but to be with me. Even as I condemned myself, so would he be.

The sun walked over the sky. The shadows stirred uncomfortably around the rocks, trying to hide themselves from the light; but even as they dodged, every nook and cranny was exposed, thrown out in stark relief. A gecko found his lair bathed in radiance, and puffed up an angry red bellow around his neck.

"Do you have something to do?" I finally asked. "I... I won't keep you."

"This is fine," he said. He shifted his weight back onto a flat, broad boulder.

Fire ants picked over the rocks, looking for something to sting.

We fell silent again.

The day edged on. Out of all the things he ever gave me, the simplest was time.

Just as it is written: "Jacob I have loved, but Esau I hated." (Romans 9:13)

I have told you about my special ailments, whined a bit. But now you need to know something. I am not terribly unique. There are plenty of folks whose *principal wound*—the point of triage—is not the church's preoccupations, but an inability to accept the way they were made. This inability feels like an unending condemnation, an especially singular punishment for reasons undisclosed.

For some it is a physical defect;
Or having the wrong kind of "subhuman" skin or shape to the eyes;
Or being "ugly" in a world that worships perfection;
Or giving birth to a child with defects;
Or being barren or sterile in a world that deifies parenthood;
Or growing up in a sect that glorified shame;
Or having the wrong gender or sexuality in a place that calls you inadequate or evil;

Or having parents who crushed body and soul;
Or being pushed to "excel" in a way that said *never good enough;*
Or being dyslexic; or having a short attention span; or possessing mechanical intelligence in a school system that only recognizes agile, literate minds;
Or being freakishly smart;
Or being as Jewish as Christ in an aggressively Christian nation;
Or just being human. In some circles, that's bad enough.

The particulars of my experience are unique; but I am certainly not alone. In fact—and I admit, this might be the buy-a-van-and-see-all-the-vans-on-the-road effect—when I look around, I have this awful feeling that we may be the *majority.* I am like the proverbial canary in the coal mine, a weaker creature who chirps first and flops on its back before the miners do.

When I begin to chirp, the miners must use me correctly.

If they say that the air is bad *for canaries,* my purpose will be lost. But if they say the air is bad and get out of the shaft, then I will have served my purpose, and my death might mean something.

When I went to stay with one of the Twelve—a woman named Joan who made it, bless her, into the hallowed circle—we stayed in her internship apartment on a road called Speedway. It may be the most accurately named street in the world. Every day I breathed in car exhaust from this busy corner, and every day I got a little weaker. By the third day, I didn't have enough life left to talk more than three minutes without panting. We fled back to the clean coast, feeling miserable.

But Joan's a smart woman. When she heard the canary chirp, she realized how bad the air was for us all. She began to notice just how dirty and polluted her beautiful city was. She saw something new that had always been there, something that was eroding many, many folks. She heard the canary, and thought about the *air.*

This is my plea to the Twelve. It is, quite possibly, why I'm spending so much time filling up this paper with smudges and scribbles. I can't get out of this cage, you know. It seems my purpose is to chirp, choke and fall over on my back. When you go into the coal mines, you Twelve, will you remember me? Will you think about the air, and not just canaries? Will you think about gophers, cats, sheep, bats... and miners?

The sun is setting. The heat of the day is gone. Gulls are squealing in the air, sheep bleating away in the valley. In the red light I can just see the peak of Mount Horeb.
jesus takes a deep breath and turns his face from the horizon.

As soon as she heard that Jesus was on his way, Martha went to find him, while Mary stayed at home.

"If you had been here, sir," she said to Jesus, "my brother would not have died. Even now I know that whatever you ask of God, God will grant you." *(John 11:20–22)*

"Nathaniel," jesus asks, "are we kin, you and I?"

He searches for my eyes, which avoid him. I can only watch the clouds.

The Jews said, "How dearly he must have loved him!" But some of them said, "This man opened blind men's eyes! Could he have not done something to keep Lazarus from dying?" (John 11:36–37)

The rocks still retain the heat. I can feel it on my back. Sunset lasts a long, long time when you add in the dying warmth of the rocks. Most people don't—they rarely show up in the postcards and the made-for-TV movies—but they're always there. Even when the cooler breeze starts to blow over you, you can still feel the burning granite against your skin. You go hot and cold at the same time. You have these moments when you grasp something resembling peace, and then it all falls apart again. The burn returns.

Throw away all your graphs, charts and postcards; throw away your textbooks; throw away your lectures on the dying and your TV movies. They mean nothing, nothing at all. Look at a young man sitting against a burning rock while the cool breeze blows.

That's how it is.

"Nathaniel," jesus asks, "who is your maker?"

You know the right answer; say it and be done. You're wasting his time. What's the fine for tying up 911, Nat? He could be with others right now.

"Nathaniel?"

"God," I choke.

"And does God love you or not?"

I open my mouth, but I can't answer. I can't tell him.

He tries again. "Nathaniel, who is your maker?"

"God," I repeat.

"Is God good?"

I try. Oh, how I try. But here I fail jesus' opinion of me again. I can speak no truth. It hurts too much.

"Nathaniel, do you hurt?"

I moan. "Yes."

"Do you want to be healed?"

I nod, tightly. I can't say the "yes" anymore, not to that question. Christ, if you only knew how many times I said "yes"—but they're all gone now, withered up like dead petals of *he loves me, he loves me not.*

"Listen to me," jesus pleads. "If I took away your pain right now, what kind of God would you have?"

I shake my head silently, and the tears fall off my cheek to the dusty rock, little tiny footprints of a son who fears to come home. *I don't know, I don't know, I just want to stop aching for a while… I want you to stop punishing me for something I can't fix…*

"Nathaniel, which is your greater wound: your suffering body, or the fear that God hates you?"

"—Ah, ah… h-hate," I say. "Hate." It comes out like needles in my throat, but it finally comes out. Hate, hate, hate.

"And if I took away your body's pain right now," jesus says, "would that cure your greater wound? Or would you simply feel that God had repented of his anger? Would you live in freedom with a God that loves you—or would you live in fear that God would change his mind again?"

I cannot follow this line of reasoning. It has no hope, I think, no hope. It means I will never be free. jesus waits for me, but I can give him no reply, it just doesn't work, it doesn't work, and I need something more than spirals, God. This *hurts.*

A second line of tracks follows the first in the dusty rocks.

"Nathaniel son of Job son of Esau son of Eve," he vows, "you will be healed, and not one second later than is absolutely necessary. I stake my life on it. But I will not sacrifice your soul, Nat, to bring your body peace. I'm struggling with the Accuser who wants to make you his child. You do not know the war that is raging all about you, every minute of this life. But he will *not win,* Nathaniel. You have been given to me and no one can tear you from my grasp. I will follow you and break open the gates of hell myself, if that's where you must walk."

He does not touch me, but he pats the rock beside me, as near as he might. Then he rises quietly and walks back out of the wilderness. He walks slowly, as if carrying a heavy burden, a healing hand wrapped in chains; yet he passes quickly out of my field of vision, for I stare not at him, but at the parallel tracks of tears walking over the granite. These tiny marks, they bring to my mind a small scrap of scripture; the shortest verse in the Bible, and the truest.

jesus wept. *(John 11:35)*

Qoph

...Nevertheless, despite all the implied elements of faith, neither Qumran, nor John the Baptist, nor yet the ancient zealot movements made any explicit demand of faith. Only in the post-Easter situation of the primitive Christian mission was the programme developed: "Repent and believe the Gospel" *(Mk 1:15)...* Faith in God means for Jesus being open to the possibilities that God presents *(Cf. Mk 11:22: echete pistin theou, have faith in God).* It also involves a reckoning with God which is not simply content with the thing given and the events that have come about.[18]

She has fought for twelve years. Every charlatan in the country has had a piece of her, every bone-rattler, every self-proclaimed savior. And insurance companies! Don't even talk to her about insurance companies. Oath-breakers, spawn of hell, demon's scum! If you roped them all together and threw them into the Mediterranean, it would be a blow for truth, justice and the keeping of covenant.

When she thinks about any of this, her stomach tightens in the most sickening way. She has installed steel bands around the barrel of her anger, and it's the only thing that keeps her from exploding. Sometimes, she breaks open a pinhole and splurts out all over somebody, just spatters them with all the hot grease she's saved. But most of the time, she's mild. Too mild. She lets people back a truck over her, and then thanks them for using new tires.

But give her this: she has not quit.

There are some people who search for healing and don't find it. They are like a single swinging lantern, never resting. Most folks, though, are different. They could have healing, but they never pursue it. They are like the uncountable stars, like Abraham's unwinking children, hanging motionless in a dark sky. The greater tragedy is there. They have been frozen by the void, scared into silence or had their flames extinguished by forces who hate all light.

This woman, she's still swinging. Give her that.

It might be a fool's errand, but she will not settle; no; she will not settle for the way things appear to be written. She goes to the door of every savior in the land and knocks for justice. It won't force any miracles, but at the same time, miracles generally don't happen without it. This is the first meaning of the phrase *hay pistis sou sesoken se;* a formulation translated as "your faith has made you well" by scholars; as magic by would-be conjurors; and as assignment of culpability by those who have lost patience.

She has not lost patience. Neither has she succumbed completely to shame, a small miracle in itself. Her affliction has been described as the woman's curse: a punishment, like childbirth, for the sin of a woman she has never met but nevertheless blew it for them all. At the Dawn of Pain she was the Eve, and one of the things God apparently did after Eve fell to the serpent was vow that she and her descendants would bleed. For twelve years of twelve months—four thousand and four hundred days straight—she has done exactly this without a break, Rabbi, and can you tell her again who sinned? Because she'd like to go and break her scrawny little neck. She is sick of being sick—and it doesn't help to shout "unclean" when she passes by, either.

But she has not lost hope, and she has not yet been so shamed that she thinks she deserves her fate. She still thinks God is worth coming to. That's a miracle of preservation against uncountable odds... and the second meaning of the explosive phrase *hay pistis sou sesoken se:* It is your trust, sister, that kept the door open. Heroic faith and trust that God is not as people say.

And yet, she is eroding. Simple chemistry: try losing that much life, water and iron and stay strong. Simple psychology: try standing up to the unremitting blame of an entire nation—your nation—and stay proud.

Try, try, try... She continues to try, but she is eroding like a strong rock under a constant waterfall. She seeks her healing furtively now, and she's reluctant to speak of it. Too many people have used it as a weapon. She gets her iron back, all right: in daily supplements of knives in the back. How many more months can she go on like this? No one knows.

But this needs to be said: we believe that when someone asks God for healing, the answer is *always yes,* and the only variable is the delivery time. Which of you, if your daughter asked for a fish, would give her a snake instead?

And this, too, needs to be said: it will arrive not one second later than necessary. Triage may seem cruel, but it is not heartless. God suffers while the clock ticks, and watches the second hand move anxiously.

jesus is speaking to a crowd. She has come to hear him. Should she hold the door open? Or is this another trust-breaker? She edges within earshot and then stops, blocked by elbows and sweaty shoulders.

"Oh Jerusalem!" jesus is calling. "Hear me weep for you! God is not like a ravenous wolf, but like a mother hen, longing to round up her chicks. She wonders why her children have scorned her; she is not angry, but frustrated and fearful for you. She wants you to hear her voice, yet you have stopped up your ears!"

The crowd is disturbed by his figure of speech. They rustle and look at each other with worried glances. Is he speaking of the God of Abraham? Are they in the wrong place? Some of them back away.

Their discomfort is her chance: the aisle is suddenly open. She rushes into the gap, starts to climb the long way which had been barred, the forbidding hill *Iatrotha*. She covers half the distance in a cold sweat, fearing that her chance may evaporate. So many times it has been a mirage...

A commotion breaks out; someone is crying.

> Then an officer of the local synagogue, a man by the name of Jairus, came up and threw himself down at Jesus' feet. He pleaded with him. "My little daughter," he said, "is at death's door. I beg you to come and lay your hands on her to save her life." *(Mark 5:22–23)*

Sudden movements, a turning. The Healer is passing by, called to a new crisis. She plunges after him, another Moses demanding a piece of God, if only his retreating back. Wait, Lord, wait... even his robe, she thinks, even his sandals even his footprints even the dust...

She stumbles, falls, reaches out—

> And then the second hand moves...
> Touching the glory of God in heaven...
> Who screams for joy...
> Stunning jesus...
> Who stops dead in his tracks.

The crowd doesn't know what's happening. They can't hear the forces of heaven shout like the voices of many waters, they can't hear the Accuser gnash his teeth, they can't hear much-maligned Eve let loose a whoop that ricochets off the stars. But all of this happens, yes it does, and it happens because a courageous woman did not lose hope or trust, because she decided to *take back* her piece of the garden. The void roars and retreats like a wounded lion, and the angel lifts the sword. Eden—a little corner of it—has just been opened for planting.

"Someone touched me," jesus says.

Thomas laughs.

"Who didn't touch you?" James asks. "You're in a crowd."

"Yes..."

He pays them scant attention while he searches for her. He knows her, she can't hide. Healing is knowing; knowing is healing. Intimacy. She has tried to shrink away with her gift, but God won't let her off that easy.

There is a coin that God asks for healing, you know; but we've got the coin all wrong, backwards. It's a debt with a reason, something that invests in more healings, more hope, more shouts of joy. It's not being pure or perfect, or even outrageously faithful, and it's not sent like a bank check with the order. It is payment *after the fact,* purely voluntary, but nevertheless requested of all that have felt the second hand move.

This is the coin: Testimony.

"I touched you, sir," she begins, and then she drags out the whole story, half-embarrassed and half-amazed.

She has never spoken in public before. She is convinced that she'll speak it poorly; but the spirit of God is still glowing within her. She loosens her faltering tongue and puts out a witness, a witness so strong it will be remembered after the words of kings have been forgotten. God, Eve and Abraham listen to her words, and Jesus smiles for them all.

"Dear lady," the Healer whispers, humbled by her spirit, "your reaching was your healing. Go in peace. "

Then he rushes forward to Jairus' dying daughter... not one moment later than absolutely necessary.

Resh

Then Jesus told them: "The light is among you still, but not for much longer. Make your way while you have the light, so that darkness does not overtake you. He who walks in the dark does not know where he is going. Trust the light while you still have it, so that you may become children of light." *(John 12:35–36a)*

John's hand shakes me awake at about five in the morning. I come up hard, only an hour into my second sleepshift. It's darker than pitch, moonless, just a few stars poking through smudges of cloud. John's got a little oil lamp in his hand, which he's shielding to give my eyes a break. "He's going," he whispers.

I look at him blankly, unable to remember the context.

"Jerusalem. He's going to Jerusalem."

I groan. "They'll kill him."

"I know," John replies. "He doesn't dispute it. He made a joke about it—asked what kind of prophet he'd be, if he didn't die in Jerusalem—said it was big career move…"

I chuckle. "One of those moods, then. You'll never talk him out of it."

"I know. Peter's furious."

"I can imagine."

We fall off to our own complicated thoughts. It's a very dark night, too dark to see.

What is God's Will, anyway? Where is it written? Is it carved in stone, or sketched in pencil?

"Now my soul is quaking, but what am I to say? 'Father, save me from this hour?' No: it was for this hour that I came. Oh Father, glorify your name!"

Then a voice sounded from heaven: "I have glorified it, and I will glorify it again." The nearby crowd said it was thunder, while still others said, "An angel has spoken to him."

Jesus said, "This voice spoke for your sake, not for mine. Now is the hour of judgement for this world; now the Prince of this world shall be driven out. And I shall draw all nations to myself, when I am lifted up from the earth."

This he said to indicate the kind of death he was to die. *(John 12:27–33)*

This season is toughest, I think, for John. Out of all, John is probably the most loved, and most loving. He's not much of a manager type, but he's serious and passionate. Things *matter* to John more than most folks. When he is suffering, he suffers greatly, and when he is happy, he is transcendent, almost manic. I doubt he'll ever get married; a woman would find him too exhausting.

The prospect of lasting bachelorhood hasn't seemed to faze him, however. God is love; he loves God. It's been a simple exchange for him, up until now. Now his bride appears to be running off.

"None of you asks me where I am going. Yet you are plunged into grief because of what I have told you. But I tell you the truth: it is for your own good that I am leaving you. If I do not go, the Advocate will not come, but if I go, I will be able to send him to you." *(John 16:5–7)*

John shakes his head at his own thoughts, then comes back to the present. He slaps me on the thigh.

"Well, anyway... Phil said you needed extra time. This enough?"

I nod.

"Great. I'm going to get some gear together. See you in a bit." He turns around as if to go, then completes the circle and returns to my face. His worried eyes, tanned and crinkled, shine darkly in the light of the little clay lamp, but he gives me the best smile he can find. "Welcome back, by the way," he says.

I grimace. Painful embarrassment, gratitude, love and grief compete for control of my face; I'm like a chameleon on a plaid tablecloth. "Thanks," I mutter.

"You're a good guy, Nat," he says. Then he swirls off.

A bobbing will-o'-the-wisp floats down the hill, and I'm left to my own thoughts. Bless you, John. May your love sustain you through the coming hours.

My chest is packed this morning, and I don't really want to disturb it. I know I'll be better off in the end, but that doesn't make that first minute any easier. Sometimes I'm tempted to just breathe shallow and hope it stays down there. Slow suicide, of course—but it's not easy to do this procedure on purpose. Coughing fits are normally something you try *not* to do.

Get going, Nathaniel. It won't be any fun to do it on the road.

O.K., O.K...

I start my wake-up routine, thinking about jesus, marriage and jealousy.

There is a lot of unauthorized ownership in our hearts when we hear jesus' plans—and a lot of guilt-tripping, too. But jesus has resisted all attempts to be owned by any of us, as much as we would like to do that. We are like the farmer who found a perfect pearl, sold all that he had to buy that one pearl—and then discovered, to his great chagrin, that the pearl belonged to the world. We want him to be *ours,* and we want him to stay right here, in this setting we've made for him. See, isn't it a nice chain?

Once we found a stranger casting out demons using jesus' name. We were all over the guy in a flash, shouting him down as if he'd stolen something. He was a real quack: one of those greasy faith healers who would just as soon sprinkle you with chicken blood as give you a prayer. His use was callous, cynical and entirely self-serving, and it was partly concern for jesus' reputation which motivated us. In other words, he wasn't the kind any of us would have chosen to hang around—and we were pretty sure jesus would have felt the same way.

"Did it work?" jesus smirked, when we eventually detailed the man's outrages.

"Oh sure; after a fashion," Thomas harrumphed. "Somewhere in between fast talk, hysterics and slapping the kid on the head, he managed to yell out *Cheeee-zus*, and in a few minutes the boy came around. Whether it'll stick or not, nobody knows."

"Yes, follow-up is often a problem," jesus nodded. "I know of a man who was cured of one demon, only to have a whole band of them move into his soul. You have to fill the hole, not just empty it."

"That's what we thought," James added. "No way does this guy have the kind of network necessary to make anything last. He's a fly-by-nighter, a barnstormer."

"I thought you said he'd used my name," jesus said, dryly.

"Yes, among half a dozen others."

"He'll come to depend on my name more. And he does have a support network, James. God is his support, just like yours and mine. There is only one source for healing in the world."

Matthew was kind of taken aback by that. "We just thought—"

"—you just thought you could see clearly," jesus nodded. "But flawed vision sees mostly flaws. Look to your own eye, before you start throwing stones. You do not see as God sees, but as the prince of this world sees."

He said it to us all, but I saw Peter flinch as if struck. I didn't know it at the time, but he was still aching from a previous argument that hadn't ended well.

He spoke about his death and resurrection plainly. At this Peter took him by the arm and began to rebuke him. But Jesus wheeled around quickly and, in front of the other disciples, rebuked Peter. "Away with you, Satan!" he said; "you do not have God's interests in mind, but think only of human things." (Mark 8:32–33)

Ownership, again. Sometimes, I fear we would rather bury this pearl than share it.

O.K., starting to get a little air down there. It's easier to cough, the more I've already coughed. When I'm all packed in, my metabolism goes into a low-power conservation mode. It's very difficult to find the energy to even move anything. But every little bit of sputum brings a little more air, and with that a little more energy. My skin loses its blueness, I start to move quicker. My eyes wake up, turn brighter, lose some of their pain-fog.

Martha can always tell how therapy's going without asking. The real clue is my feet; when they start to wiggle like eager cattails she knows I'm making progress. Wiggle, wiggle.

I have to get this done quickly, if I want to keep up with the rest; jesus will likely be getting under way early, before the crowds form. If he wants to get anywhere these days, he has to slip away. Otherwise he'll get bogged down in another mass of crying need. It must drive him crazy. It seems like he can sit in one spot, work until the pyramids fall and never empty out all the misery there is to be found. I recall very few times when he ran out of things to do before he moved on—except, of course, in his hometown, where they all knew he was just Joseph's son. They weren't about to let him be *uppity* there, so he could do very few miracles.

We were embarrassed for him (and for ourselves), but he was unsurprised. Could he have healed them anyway? I asked him about it later.

"No," jesus said. "Not really. You're talking about an impossibility, an oxymoron. Forced love is rape, no matter who is doing it. God has to be very careful."

"What is the use of being God, then? It sounds like a helpless state."

jesus laughed. "You are very, very close to the realm of God!"

That shocked me. "God is *helpless*? You can't be serious."

He sobered a bit. "No, I guess not. Not entirely..." He rubbed his chin and looked up to the heavens. "It all depends on what you mean. God does have power," he said, frowning faintly, "but it's a different kind of power than the kind men lust after." He waved his hands at the clouds, as if pointing to an invisible throne.

"Who wants to be above everything, remote, unaffected, able to push things around and never lift a finger? Who wants to have people marching in uniform with no serious quirks? Who wants to be changeless, unyielding, unrepentant? Who wants lightning bolts, dynamite, fusion bombs?"

"Sounds pretty recognizable," I admitted.

He gestured to the ground. "And who feeds the praying mantis?" he asked. "Who serves the caterpillar, helps the orphan, kneels before the lowly?"

"That doesn't sound very kinglike."

"It's not; it's dirty work most of the time," jesus said. "God's work is being the ground under the ground. That's the job description. God has sent prophets to this land—time and time again—to set the record straight, but nobody has listened for more than a day. People are so attached to the vision of themselves on the throne, they can't see that Godliness is beneath the lowliest servant. They don't want to hear that."

"If they won't listen to the prophets, who will they listen to?"

"No one," he said, with some despair. "If the prophets aren't enough, I'm afraid no one will be enough."

"'They have Moses and the prophets,' Abraham said. 'Your family can listen to them.'

"'No, father Abraham!' the rich man cried. 'If someone from the dead visits them, they will repent.'

"Abraham said to them, 'If they do not listen to Moses and the prophets, they will pay no heed even if someone rises from the dead.'" *(Luke 16:29–31)*

"I never believed Dickens had that right, either," I nodded, recalling his take on *A Christmas Carol*. "Old Marley was wasting his time."

jesus looked at me with an eye that spoke volumes, but said nothing.

"So why rattle the chains?" I asked him. "You don't have to do this, you know."

He shook his head quickly, emphatically. I think even the question hurt him.

Looking back at it now, as I lie here running the vibrator over my chest, I think I understand why our denials hurt him so much. It's a small example—please don't be offended by the comparison. I understand that the scale is vastly different. But this is what I see: when I'm struggling to begin therapy, I don't need anybody telling me to skip it, either. I've already *got* that devil's voice in my soul. The thing I need most is a voice that says I must begin, that healing lies at the end. I know it myself, but I can still use a little support from time to time. I certainly don't need anyone arguing against me, talking against what I must do to fight this demon in my breast.

I didn't realize it at the time, but I was adding my own weight to the pressure. I was part of the void, calling for more darkness. What a jerk. I should have known better. At least he didn't call me Satan.

jesus looked pained, but he bore my question with patience.

"It's time to send the Son," he sighed. "I won't have it said that we didn't try. It is only *pistis*, the unacceptance of what is, that makes possible what could be. The persistent widow, she knocks at the heart of every judge, hoping someone will listen. She knows the judges of this world are hard and unjust, but nevertheless she goes to every one of them and knocks, looking for justice."

"She sounds foolhardy to me."

"Indeed, she is. God is the most foolish widow you will ever meet, Nathaniel." He kept quiet for a long time after that, watching the road pass by under his feet. His shoulders sagged and his brow was sweaty with the exertion of the walk. He was only thirty-three.

The story of the cross is foolishness to those on their way to ruin, but it is the power of God to those being saved. Scripture says, "I will destroy the wisdom of the wise, and bring the clever to nothing." *(1 Corinthians 1:18–19)*

Why???

I went to seminary hoping to discover the answer to that kind of question. It was what drove me into the wilderness. Why must pain be such an indiscriminate part of this world? Why must the innocent suffer meaninglessly? Imagine my shock when they took away the answer I'd already been working on, and handed me back only more questions! The scholars did give me something, though: a name for the question that bends my spine.

Theodicy.

Whenever you ask why evil exists, why sin seems profitable or why bad things happen to good people—*why, oh God, did a train hit this young man's car?*—you have entered the dark realm of theodicy.

> O Lord, I will dispute with you, since you are just; I will plead my case before you. Why do the wicked prosper, and traitors live at ease? *(Jeremiah 12:1)*

Some folks claim that the question is only a brief pang in a sea of certainty. I'm suspicious of that claim; when I did my chaplaincy rotation, I saw plenty of evidence that theodicy was where the action was. I suspect it's the primary reason for human interest in religion. Read the uncensored Psalms, sometime!

Almost half of Christianity is theodicy. We dress it up with other words—soteriology, atonement, blah, blah, blah—but if you close your eyes and listen to it, you'll recognize the duck by the quack it makes. Atheism generally makes the same sound, too; it just faces the other direction, unhappy with what it hears. We're all out here in the swamp, trying to make sense out of conflicting data.

Start with the assumption that God is good and that God is in control: right there you've got some explaining to do, when you stand at the memorial of Pearl Harbor, Nagasaki or Vietnam—and don't even *think* about the Holocaust, where all reasons break down into a singularity.

Look at John, struggling already to make sense out of his grief. He's trying to find a defense for what is happening, something to explain the existence of an evil that is roaring down over all our heads. Is there really any difference? jesus is a train wreck about to happen, and the survivors are going to have to live with it.

> They came together in Galilee, and Jesus said to them, "The Son of Man is to be given up into the power of men, and they will kill him; then on the third day he will be raised again."
> And the disciples were filled with grief. *(Matthew 17:22-23)*

I don't know if theodicy bothers you in your season, but for me, at least, it is a full-time occupation. My Job, you might say; my childhood preordained that theodicy would be my life's quest.

That was another irony, too. The good folks at seminary wasted no time in letting me know that theodicy was a hopeless task, unsolvable. All theodicies are unstable. They may exist briefly under unique circumstances, like antimatter in a particle accelerator, but they all blow up when they encounter the real world. The only way you can keep one alive is by enclosing it in a protective bubble that fends off all threatening material.

Well, I tried them anyway—you know how young snots are; we just have to discover some things for themselves. So I read the heavenly Sears Catalog of answers;

the great ones, the minor ones, the quirky ones. And as soon as I let any of them out of their bubble, they made a tiny popping sound and disappeared. Listen, most of them didn't even make a good bang.

So there I was, surrounded by the greatest thinkers of all time, just beginning to realize that my life's work was a put-up job, a sucker's bet.

Your task, should you choose to accept it, Nathaniel, is to fail.

Oh, thank you, thank you! Who put me up to this task, anyway?

My mind leapt to the answer. God, of course. It's *always* God's fault.

Lord, look and see! Who is it that you have tormented?

Must women eat the fruit of their own wombs, the very children they have brought safely to birth? Shall priest and prophet be slain in the sanctuary of the Lord?

Young men and old men lie in the streets; my young men and maidens have fallen by the sword, and by famine. You slew them in the day of your anger, slaughtered them without pity.

Like men assembling for a festival you gathered my enemies—they were against me on every side, and not a man escaped, not one survived.

Here, on the day of your anger, all whom I raised were destroyed by my enemies.
(Lamentations 2:20–22)

The derivation of the word *theodicy* is probably worthy of mention at this point. It comes from

theo,
which means God, and
dikaioo,
to justify.

That's right. The prime motivating force of religion…

The hopeless task…

The question that bends our spines…

Is the justification of *God.* And here they kept telling you that Christianity was all about *our* justification.

"You are making me very unhappy, jesus," I said.

He nodded, regretfully. "I was about to say the same to you. Shall we talk about something happier?"

"If you can find it."

He lifted his shoulders and took in a deep breath, searched for a moment. "O.K.," he said. "You thought God sounded powerless. But let me tell you about a different kind of power. Unknotting chaos is like untangling a rat's nest of many ropes: patience is the only thing that works. If you get frustrated and start to yank, the knots get tighter, not looser. God knows that, so God pulls with infinite care.

"Imagine being intimately connected with every single thing in the Universe. To know it, feel its needs. To hear the prayer of the sparrow, the ache of a vine, the confusion of a cancer cell. That's one kind of God's power: to be infinitely influenced by the longings of Creation.

"Now imagine being able to whisper to everything in the Universe. To suggest a tree to the sparrow, a direction to the vine, a protein to the cancer. To lure the world out of senselessness with a vision of the future; to shape it, not by force, but with dreams and compassion. Picture what it must be like, to teach birds how to migrate! They use the stars, the sun and the compass in their heads, all provided by God.

"Imagine giving wasps the secret of paper. Think of leading bread mold to become penicillin. Picture painkillers growing out of frogs, and new yeast learning how to make wine. Look at a cotton plant, and see the clothes hiding in its fibers, waiting for only a little human initiative to be revealed—and that initiative is also a link in the chain of growth!

"Imagine looking down the road of time and seeing the best course; steering through all of the conflicting needs. Imagine walking ahead, calling Creation to follow.

"That is another kind of power: to infinitely influence everything in Creation.

"You desire great force because you have never experienced magnitude like that. If you want to stop a river, you build the Hoover Dam. You don't know what it's like to whisper like a wind over the waters, and have it leave a dry path for your children. But that's what it's like to be God. Because you've never felt such power, you can't imagine it could be much good. But if you can speak to everything in Creation, you don't need a loud, commanding voice. You just need a clear vision of what needs to be said.

"God knows what needs to be said. God has an ear for the surf sounds in static; an eye for the colors hiding in light; a dream of abundance flowing out of the wilderness. God's word leads people out of bondage to the void, splits the waters, brings food to the desert.

"There is loss and hardship; the void extracts its price. In a world of conflicting claims and enmeshed brokenness, there is no ideal solution to everything. But time is on God's side. God just keeps dreaming of a place that makes greater sense, and speaking that word that creates it.

"This is part of the Good News I have to bring you: God is no murderer, no molester, no demon with a sickle. God's love is not rape. Think of it as a courtship, a sweet song on a harp. That's the power you fear."

I shook my head doubtfully. "That sounds very nice," I said, "but if we have to wait for all of Creation to sing along with God, your harp strings will break first. The noise will never subside."

"You don't think God's power is enough?" he asked, raising his brow. "You think New Jerusalem will only be built by force?"

"I'm hardly alone," I said.

Bypassers hurled abuse at him. They wagged their heads and cried, "You would pull the temple down, eh, and build it in three days? Come down from the cross and save yourself, if you are indeed the Son of God."

So, too, the chief priests mocked him with the elders and lawyers. "He saved others," they said, "but he cannot save himself. King of Israel, indeed! Let him come down now from the cross, and then we will believe him. Did he trust in God? Then let God rescue him, if he wants him. For he said he was God's Son!"

Even the bandits who were crucified with him taunted him in the same way.

(Matthew 27:39–44)

"No," he sighed, "you're not. But I thought that maybe by now—well, your reaction mostly reflects on your judgment of the song, doesn't it—that it can't win on its own merits? Doesn't it simply say you haven't yet believed in the superiority of love over hate? Isn't it a measure of your own wounds?"

"I'm not saying that God's methods are bad," I said. "I just think—"

"—that hate can only be destroyed by hate?" he asked. "Or that good must mimic evil in certain extenuating circumstances?"

"You can't expect things to work out just because of love and charity. I lived in Chicago, for crying out loud, and I can tell you that—"

"—evil done in God's name is good?"

"Stop putting words in my mouth. I'm just saying…"

"Yes?"

"Ah—"

I'd lost the thread of it by then. By the time he gave me space to say it, I'd lost what I was going to say.

Too bad: I knew it was a killer argument. The really *clever* point being lost, I had to settle for a synopsis. "Well," I said, feeling frustrated, "I just think you're being a little naive, thinking people are going to lie down and let you love them into submission."

"No lions lying down with the lamb?" he asked, wryly.

"Not unless they recline while they eat."

"No desert blooming for you? No society of justice? No shining city?"

"I don't know about the desert, but *people* aren't going to bloom just because you water them and speak pretty words. Not in this world."

"I'm not talking about this one…," he began, then trailed off.

He looked at the other disciples—none of whom had voiced any more faith than I in God's tune—and seemed to lose all his energy. "I don't know," he muttered. "Maybe I *am* wasting my time." But he kept walking down that damned road.

Sin

An inspiring word from Saint Augustine, father of Western theology, 425 A.D.:

Of the two first parents of the human race... Cain was the first-born, and he belonged to the city of men; after him was born Abel, who belonged to the city of God... whence it comes to pass that each man, being derived from a condemned stock, is first of all born of Adam evil and carnal, and becomes good and spiritual only afterwards, when he is grafted into Christ by regeneration; so was it in the human race as a whole...

God, like a potter... of the same lump made one vessel to honor, another to dishonor. But first the vessel to dishonor was made, and after it another to honor.[19]

Firm Foundations

This shard is rough... careful
Popped
Like a firecracker
On the way down
When it knew

Suddenly knew
It was made for breaking

Frags, we call 'em
Here in the bar
Washing down what
Women know and
Men
Only guess

In a flash
And a bang

Have another drink
Your leak is showing
What a pity, too
That bit on the front is nice I like
The way it glitters when the light hits it
Pity it
Couldn't be saved—

                                                    McGhees?
                                            Third on the lane
                                        By the Old Refinery

—You'll like it here but pick a gang fast
        It's for your own
                Protection you know
                        The Host don't pass
                        Twenty Third
                        And you gotta have friends
                                Even if they're broken, they're better

Than nothing.

Shin

Martha and I went to a show last night. It was supposed to be a kid's movie. We haven't felt that assaulted in years. It was about a beautifully pure, smart and wholesome girl trapped in an evil family. Her relatives are ugly, stupid and hostile. They neglect and despise her, and each little detail of the abuse they give is meticulously—one might say lovingly—recorded. After we suffer with her at home for a while, the good girl is sent to a school run by an evil principal. The principal (an ugly, brutish woman) tortures, humiliates and beats up kids.

All is not lost, however: there she also meets her good and pure teacher. The good teacher (a pretty, waifish model) is also cowed by the villainous principal. As the story unfolds, we discover that the good teacher is also the evil principal's niece. The evil principal killed her father, stole her house and money, and abused her in ways both great and petty. Our two paragons of purity are thus united by their opposition to the forces of impurity.

According to the producers, humans are pretty easy to figure out. Everyone was flaming evil or snowy good. Evil people were ugly, stupid and crude. Good people weren't always beautiful—a nod to the enlightened nineties, I guess—but the important ones were, and all of them were tenderly portrayed.

The first half of the movie makes it clear that the evil ones deserve whatever comes to them. In the second half it comes to them. The girl discovers magic powers, then uses them to lead the good folk in an attack on the evil principal. In the climactic scene, all the kids stone the principal. The attack is just as brutal as anything the principal did—but there's a crucial difference: the good people are *righteous* in their brutality. The magic power is used, we are reminded several times, to "teach them a lesson."

I don't know exactly what the lesson was. Don't have less power than your enemies, I guess.

In the end, the evil parents abandon the child and run away to Guam to avoid the law. The girl is adopted and lives happily ever after with her good teacher... who laughed at the principal's stoning.

The candy counter in the lobby sold Juju-bees, M&M's, popcorn and the fruit of the Knowledge of Good and Evil. Everybody had the fruit that night. It wasn't the knowledge of good and evil *acts,* mind you—all the acts were the same. It was the knowledge of good and evil *people*. What makes violence good is who does it. Good guys do good violence.

At the end of the movie, the kids clapped and cheered. Martha and I were sickened and stunned; what we ate was churning in our bellies. We made our way out through excited knots of kids, dazed to hear their opinions float across the lobby.

"That was funny, dude."

"Did you see that glob hit her right in the eye?"

"That was totally awesome."

"Righteous!"

It took a while to make our way out to the parking lot. The lobby floor was littered with discarded apple cores, some already turning brown.

Listen: The prime myth of our nation is so endemic that even "Christian" lobbying groups swallow it without a thought—even while they rail at the comparative gnats of sex and violence. This is the principal message preached in our dark shrines:

- The most satisfying pleasure in life is righteous retribution. If you can get back at someone and be *justified* in doing it, it will really make your day.
- The thing that justifies retribution is doing it to bad people.

We are just itching to commit murder, as long as we can feel good about ourselves while doing it. The trick is finding targets that make the murder seem righteous. We had a war against some dirty foreigners a while back that was very popular. It made us feel "tall in the saddle" again, like all good cowboys riding off to whip the savages. The army's name for the operation was "Just Cause."

Martha laughed bitterly when she heard the name, because she heard the playground echo lying in it.

Why are we doing this?

Just 'cause.

Where is jesus in all of this? Where is the one who forbade the stoning of a woman until a sinless person could be found?

Nowhere. The antithesis of the messiah is what Hollywood gives us; the exact opposite. Literally, and most accurately, the anti-Christ. But don't call Hollywood the "other"—call them the "we." They give us back the same myth we gave them, the very same anti-Christ that flourishes in church. It is what we are founded on, our manifest destiny. It is not exclusively an American delusion.

Even God can do acts that we would call evil if done by Hitler; but they are good acts because of the intrinsic quality of the person doing them. Murder and abuse are legally justified if the victims are evil.

In the scheme of the church, the division is as simple as in the movie: there is God, who is pure and holy, and there is humanity, impure, fallen and unholy. God wants us to know who is who—and if we don't recognize who is kind and merciful, there's going to be plenty of kicking butt and taking names. There will be, literally, hell to pay.

"I love you," says the Lord.
You ask, "How has He shown love to us?"
"Was not Esau Jacob's brother?" the Lord answers. "I love Jacob, but I hate Esau; I have laid waste to his mountains and turned his ancestral home into an inheritance fit only for jackals."
When Edom says, "We are beaten down; let us rebuild our ruined homes," these are the words of the Lord of Hosts: "If they rebuild, I will tear them down again. They shall be called a Wicked Nation, a people cursed by God forever. You yourselves will see it with your own eyes; then you will say 'Our Lord's greatness extends even beyond the borders of Israel!'" *(Malachi 1:2–5)*

We are called, they say, to be like God. We do the best we can, I guess.

I pursue my enemies and destroy them, I do not return until I have finished them. I strike them until they rise no more and fall beneath my feet. You arm me with strength for the battle and subdue foes that rise up against me. You set my foot on their necks, and I make the people that hate me into nothing. They cry out, but there is no one to help them. They cry to the Lord, and receive no answer.
I pound them fine as dust on the ground, like mud in the streets I trample them.
(2 Samuel 22:38–43)

When will this fruit turn sour in our belly? I don't know. I'm not encouraged.[20]

Black and white; good and evil; justified and condemned; we are a digital people, moral computers with impulses that veer on or off. Things are either a one, or a zero. We don't know how to number Creation any other way. The best approximation we can give—and this is the church's math—is to say some things are both one and zero at the same time. This is how you spell human in the binary church:

01001000
01010101
01001101
01000001
01001100

—ASCII digital code for "human"

But let me tell you a secret about binary math:

It can't do thirds.

In binary, we generally extend the decimal fraction out far enough so most people won't complain. But no matter how many ones and zeroes the computer sticks together, it can never capture the simple essence of a third. The same goes for sixths, two-thirds… anything based on the simple concept of division by 3.

Divide 2 by 3 on your calculator sometime. After a long succession of 666s, you'll finally see the poor thing give up and use a 7.

Now print the results. Tear the paper off and fold it like a letter.

Yes, that's right. In the real world, you can do thirds. Reality is not digital.

There are many numbers besides 1 and 0; an infinite number of voltages between On and Off. There is a ratio called Pi which has been calculated to over 100 million decimal places and still not nailed down exactly—although a real-world circle does it every time, effortlessly. There are many colors in the rainbow; 108 elements; 212 degrees between boiling and freezing; over 300 species of hummingbird…

…and somewhere in the midst of all this variety is a curious animal called "homo erectus," whose spine is too often bent with the notion that Creation is made only of Gods and Devils. The best approximation this poor creature can make of a third is God/Devil, and there's always a rounding error somewhere. If we like the person, we round up. If we don't like them, we round down.

Like most novice seminarians, I thought I'd escaped all that when I reached Chicago. I expected a place of contemplative peace: Bible study without conflict. But my professors had other plans: when I got to seminary, I was force-fed feminist theology by my teachers. I really, really resented having to read so much of it. There were times when I literally hurled books across our tiny apartment. Yet once I got far enough away (in both time and distance) from school to digest what I'd been fed, some of the stuff that fed me the most was…

Feminist theology.

I think that's pretty funny, considering all the whining I did.

Looking back, I see it was only natural that their words would speak to me. When I grew up I was—to use the liberal-icky-poo-spit-spit phrase—a marginalized person. I not only had no expectations of being part of the power structure, I had no expectation of living past 13. That puts you out of the running for even *voting* for President, let alone dreaming of becoming one!

When I got to high school, I preferred to hang out with burnouts, because I found them more accepting. They had no ambition; they knew they were on the outside. They had been told, in various ways, that they would never amount to much. We had something in common! Imagine knowing, from age 11 or 12, that your warranty runs out at 13. The phrase *midlife crisis* doesn't even begin to capture it—a 40-year-old still has many resources to combat his sense of mounting futility.

The first true song from the heart I ever wrote was called "Waiting to Die."

They'll find me in the morning
With a razor in my hand
My faded jeans stained with scarlet blood

The aftermath of slashing pain
That cut my cord of life and
Tore all the fibers that it could.

If you've read the papers lately,
Only good kids die
I wonder where the others are
And where their bodies lie
Maybe they've been buried
In some field far away
Forgotten, faded memories
Of tainted yesterdays.

I had a dream last night
Filled me with fright that dream,
In that dream
God spoke to me:

"I hated you
from the day you were conceived
From that point on
I had decided you'd bleed
Now you stand before me
On your judgment day
I need no excuses
I'll just throw you away, away."

I keep this song in my heart as a measure from where I came from. It is my Vietnam War memorial, saying *Remember, remember.*

I sang it incessantly.

I think back to those times, and wonder how my parents could have possibly withstood hearing that sustained scream, over and over again. The music was very loud; the synthesizers sounded like sirens.

Here's another fragment I wrote at about the same time:

From the barren tree
Many wants of me
Feed my lambs and tend my sheep
But you know no tree's going to
Grow from me.

Yep, yep…
Thank God for music; it was the only way I pulled through.

If being passive is part of "women's experience," then the experience of being a patient is womanly. Chronic illness is a very passive world. You have little control over the most intimate parts of your body, especially as a child.

Why do I have to have another enema?

Because...

... so you lie down and take it.

There were many such invasive moments, some truly necessary, some probably not. The science of C.F. was in its infancy—even the basic defect was a mystery—and everyone was groping for ways to cope with its myriad effects. The whole thing had the air of panic about it, and there was little room for giving a sense of consent to the little ones.

I also endured extra testing because I wasn't sick enough, and they wanted to know why. I underwent more procedures than I actually needed, given my state of health.

It wasn't until I graduated to Dr. Markowitz (about 16 years old, and *thank you, God, for creating that man*) that Medicine gave me permission to have a say in what happened to my body. Until then, I was a good little girl that did what she was told. I could automatically enter the posture for many diagnostics before most kids had learned how to play shortstop.

Many of those diagnostics were scary and incomprehensible to a small child: tubes, wires and circling graphs, dark little closets with windows. I remember being surrounded by terrifying tangles of equipment, isolated from my family, hearing beeps and hisses. I remember hating the pulmonary function machine.

Why do I have to sit in the pressure chamber again?

Because...

Strange, strange. It was not your average childhood.

My context was as different from most folks as Greek from Jew, Slave from Free, Woman from Man. That's why the work of marginalized persons was destined to speak to me. When you read the texts from the margins, they look different. You see different things than folks reading it "straight up."

I was reading from a very odd corner of the page, but I still had more in common with the margin-folk than I did with the ones holding the book.

Why, then, was I hurling feminist books across the room?

Many of the folks that wrote those books—and some of the ones who discussed them—had bit into the same fruit that had poisoned them. They were an amazing example of on/off, black/white, oppressed/oppressor thinking. You might want to think that being forced to play zero in the human binary system would make you yearn for a different math, but it apparently makes you yearn to play the role of the One That Counts. It's hard to get out of the digital mindset.

In their minds, I had the shape of a one, so I had to be a one. I couldn't be a third; and in many of our discussions I was relentlessly rounded down by those doing the approximating. I encountered the same oppressive assumptions. I was white, I was of Welsh descent (qualifying for "European"—in ignorance of the uniquely dispiriting history of Wales) and I had a penis. Therefore, I was part of the power structure, *by definition of my own body,* exclusive of my experience.

That really, really hurt. All of the pain I suffered—growing up with the conviction that I would never have a family, job, house or any of the other things normal boys and girls expect—none of that meant a thing to some of these folks.

Let me tell you about pain and shame. It's applying for adoption and being told to get a divorce. Pain and shame is finding out that you're *worse than no husband at all;* that your wife could adopt as a single parent but not when she's married to you. A soon-to-expire C.F. patient is worse than nothing in the eyes of our society; we are a net loss.

Imagine being such a liability to the woman you love! Martha has desired and loved children ever since the day she was created. Being childless is a very real cross that she bears, and she bears it because she is married to me.

Imagine causing that kind of tremendous, life-changing pain to the person you love more than anyone else in the whole world—and that the pain is not because of something you did, but simply *who you are.* You can't atone for how you were created, no matter what the church might say. It doesn't work. You may come to peace with it, you may learn how to work with it and you may even learn how to stop being shamed by it. But if you search for atonement for your creation, you're playing a sucker's game. It's not something you did, and it's not something you can un-do. It is the ultimate in helpless condemnation.

But that doesn't matter, either. The important thing to know is what I have between my legs. If you know that, then you'll know what I've thought, how I've felt and where I've been. You'll be able to tell me who I am and how I think.

I write this with hurt. It still hurts. The very literature that spoke to me, that liberated me, that crystallized what I had felt all my life—that stuff was also being framed to imprison *me.* How awful!

Out of all the stuff I read, the most galling was the contention that a society run by women would be one of justice and goodness, without any oppression. That was incredible to read, from my perspective.

My perspective was that of Clover in George Orwell's *Animal Farm,* who looks through the window and discovers that the heroic leaders of the Revolution—once they put on the oppressive farmer's overalls—look just like the farmer again.

My dear friends:
You have freed me from many basic misconceptions. Let me return the favor.
You are neither God nor Devil. You are human.

Tav

(A conversation continued)

"…Woe to those," jesus said, "who love their traditions more than hope."
Then he turned back to Nicodemus.

"I tell you the truth," jesus taught, "no one enters the realm of God without the second birth."

"What do you mean?" puzzled Nicodemus. "Is it possible to crawl back into the womb?"

"You don't need to crawl anywhere," jesus answered. "You're already in the womb. Look around you!" He gestured at the nearby hills. "A little bigger than the first one, perhaps, but you're a bit bigger, too…"

Nicodemus looked at jesus like he'd lost his mind.

"The first womb," jesus explained patiently, "is for the water birth; and the second is for the spirit birth. In the beginning God drifted over the waters and called you forth. The waves released you reluctantly and with pain; your mother gasped and heaved as the water broke, and then 'flesh gave birth to flesh.' Surely you've seen this happen! But that's only the beginning. You are still looking at what God has conceived, not what will be born."

"But I've already been born," Nicodemus laughed.

"Nicodemus, you are only beginning the birth pangs," jesus said. "The void still has its grip on you. Didn't you say that your will seemed broken and incomplete?"

"Yes," the scribe admitted.

"Then give in to the evidence and admit to the obvious: you're not finished. Is that such a hard observation to make? *Paradise hasn't happened yet.*"

"But Paradise was in the past," Nicodemus objected.

"If Paradise is in the past," jesus sighed, "then God obviously can't make a Paradise that lasts." He nodded toward the city walls, where broken people begged and pleaded for coins. "Look around you. Do you really want to claim that this is the best God can do?"

"But *we're* the ones who—"

"—we've been through this before, Nicodemus. You asked me for hope in heaven, and I'm trying to give it to you. You have to choose to look back or look forward. Is it really so horrible to give up the claim that God made Creation in six days?"

Nicodemus groaned. "You're saying we have more to go through," he complained. "I want to be done."

"Now we come to the real reason!" jesus exclaimed. *"You don't want to die."*

The scribe looked bereft. He clutched at his robe anxiously, as if searching for a better cover. "No! Can't this be enough?" he pleaded. "Can't we call it finished and stay here?"

"I'm sorry," jesus said, sympathetically, "but this is as temporary as your first womb. You must pass through the grave, my friend. This world is not the end of the road."

"That can't be what you mean…"

"To be born again? Yes, I'm afraid so. Then you will be born of both water and spirit. But listen to the Good News: you will come out whole and complete on the other side.

"Think of two siblings in the womb. The twin sees her companion disappear and never return. She thinks he has died forever and been destroyed, because she can no longer feel his presence in the dark. She hangs in the amniotic fluid and suffers doubts that there is any point to the womb at all. But her twin is still there, still very close—and separated only by a few inches of the womb. He waits naked, stunned by the richness of a world never suspected. They will meet again, in a greater light. They'll see each other the way they never saw each other before. They will touch again. That's the way of the second birth, too. The first womb is your promise, your sign."

Nicodemus didn't seem reassured by his promise. His eyes seemed to be swimming in darkness.

"Trust me," jesus said. "I will show you the way."

"I don't… maybe… aren't you talking about baptism, then?" the scribe moaned.

Baptism means participating in the life, death and resurrection of Jesus Christ… By baptism, Christians are immersed in the liberating death of Christ where their sins are buried, where "old Adam" is crucified with Christ… Baptism initiates the reality of the new life given in the midst of the present world.[21]

"There is no ritual substitution that will stop death," jesus said. "I'm sorry, Nicodemus, but you truly will be born again, whether you like it or not. Birth is not something that can be tamed—and when it happens, you won't need a theologian to explain what the difference is. You won't be standing around in the same clothes, in the same place, eating the same cookies. Trust me; it will be as wrenching and as radical as your first birth."

Nicodemus turned pale. "But the water…"

"Is the water of your first birth," jesus said. "And your second birth is quite a different animal. You won't be *invisibly changed*; you will be *made invisible* to those who still wait in this womb. You will be on the other side of the veil.

"Listen closely. Clear your mind of stale words and hear the words fresh—for this is how our conversation ends":

"Flesh can only give birth to flesh; it is spirit that gives birth to spirit. You should not be astonished, then, when I tell you that you must be born again.

"The wind blows where it wills; you hear the sound of it, but you do not know where it is comes from, or where it is going. So it is with everyone who is born of spirit." *(John 3:6–8)*

Nicodemus ran off to the hills sobbing. It just wasn't what he'd been hoping to hear that day.

BREATHLESS

Apocryphal Addition to
Ma Bell and the Dragon

(Septuagint version only)

Sometimes, when I'm finishing up a cold, I get into phases where things start to break up inside. Chunks start to come off my lungs like icebergs calving off the arctic shelf. Some stuff gets lodged halfway in, halfway out. Coughing becomes terrifying: I can't breathe back in for the next cough, and I can't cough without breathing in. Trying to inhale lodges the junk harder across my windpipe. They tell me to do the Heimlich maneuver on myself, but by that time I'm too weak and panicky to think straight. I just freeze, become very animal-like. There's a reason people choke on food and die without help.

The only thing that comes into my mind is to breathe in slow to keep the junk from moving backwards. That's not easy when you're suffocating. It hardly seems like the moment to be calm.

There have been at least three times that I would have strangled, if it hadn't been for Martha whomping me on the back with all her might. It's a frightening experience, a horrible way to go. I don't want to go that way.

Do I have to go that way?

I don't know.

Dear God, finish me off another way, please. If the end is non-negotiable, can we at least discuss methodology?

I'm in one of those frightening phases again. Martha had to cancel a plane trip. She was going to go to a family event, but she didn't dare leave me alone—afraid of what she might find when she got back. I asked her to stay, but I felt miserable pulling her away from the reunion. I don't want her life to stop, just because mine has.

Talk about feeling wretched. Do you realize that even a baby can breathe without depending upon another person?

Even a *baby*.

The Lost Lecture to the Essenes

jesus stood in front of the blackboard and surveyed his class. Everyone was getting uncomfortable with the way things were going; some of the students looked like they were nearly ready to freak out.

"Scripture," he said, "is not God. Don't deify it. You don't need to. God is still alive and present with you. Scripture was written by folks who looked out at a certain world and felt the need to speak. The God who moves humans to speak is omniscient; but the ones who hold the pen aren't. Humans must stand in one place. They can't be viewpointless. Only God can stand everywhere and know all perspectives."

"Nevertheless," a young, distressed Essene protested, "there is One Truth, and scripture reveals it. Truth is not contextual."

"*Life* is contextual," the Teacher responded. "Is there a word that has meaning outside of its language? If I say the word *sowaoo*, and you don't know Ceygolian, will you know that I'm speaking of snow?"

"Of course not," the student said. "But if you translate it into my language, then I will."

"Who shall translate the mind of God?" jesus asked. "If I tell you about snow, you may listen to all I have to say and never understand it, if you've only lived in the tropics. Language is a shared experience, referring to other shared experiences. Can you teach a sparrow about thermodynamics? Does an ant understand internal-combustion engines?"

"I understand your point," another Essene said, "and I won't claim to have the mind of God. Yet I know there is a single Truth, and it will shine consistently through the minds of men, without a varying origin."

"Yet the minds of humanity vary," the Teacher said. "A Malay may see snow and think of salt; a baby might recall talcum powder. A blind man will feel icy wetness; a New Englander may recall a Nativity scene—in which there was, in fact, no snow. If you perceive snow so differently, how shall you share the experience of God? God can only use the words you know, and those change from place to place, and age to age."

"But I want to know what the real truth is," the first student said, growing impatient.

"The real truth," jesus said, "can't be spoken outside of your life. But there is freedom in that, too. It means God can always speak a new word that will make sense to your new life. Hear the Good News: *You can never grow so different that you fall out of conversation with God.*" With that, he called for a break.

The class filed out in retreat, their eyes looking sunken and weary. A Greek exam; five papers; shaky foundations tested; universe redefined; synod essay. Long day. jesus dug an apple out of his sack and thought about the frightened one in the back.

As a collection, the New Testament writings themselves witness to the significantly different visions of life and diverse theological beliefs that were forged out in this period...

The diverse writings of the New Testament are only the tip of an iceberg of diversity among traditions in early Christianity. The writings of the New Testament are merely representative of a much greater diversity in the scattered communities of the early Christian movement. Diversity is fundamental to the biblical witness. The later Christians who decided which writings to include in the Christian canon were well aware of the differences among the books they selected. Instead of choosing only those books that agreed with one theology and church order, they chose the writings closest to Jesus in time and influence, and they allowed the pluralism to stand. By including such variety, they chose wisely—for their own day as well as for ours. Diversity in the New Testament is not, therefore, a cause for concern but a reason for rejoicing...

An overall harmonizing of all the stories about Jesus does not work well, precisely because each Gospel writer has offered a somewhat different portrayal of Jesus. For example, in Mark's Gospel, Jesus keeps his identity a secret. His disciples do not know until halfway through the story that he is the Messiah, and no human calls him Son of God until the centurion does so at the foot of the cross. In John's Gospel, on the other hand, Jesus proclaims his identity as Son of God openly before all from the start, and early in the story his disciples know him as the lamb of God. We cannot simply put these two portraits of Jesus or the disciples together into one story. When we do, we distort both Mark and John, and we come up with a strange story unlike either one of them. The Gospel writers shaped their stories about Jesus in order to bring out the meaning of the events as they understood them. Mark is showing that Christian life is ambiguous and that people have a hard time recognizing Jesus as Son of God and accepting a persecuted Messiah, while John is showing that no matter how open Jesus is, some people will instantly recognize him and others will still not recognize that he is from God...

Luke and Mark, for [another] example, do not show Jesus' death to be an atoning sacrifice before God; in their view, forgiveness is integral to the Christian proclamation apart from any connection to Jesus' death. And many writings in the New Testament do not depict Jesus "paying a price" for sins with his death. For example, in Luke's view, Jesus' death is depicted as the consequence of a life of obedience, and by his death, Jesus showed followers how they too should face persecution and death. In John's view, Jesus' death and resurrection restore an alienated creation back to a relationship with God.[22]

The Apocryphal Poem

Then there was the day
When the stereo found its voice again
And the cats wondered what all the shaking was
And why he was dancing
Lisa stuck her head in the Kleenex box
And played hammerhead shark
Like only she can do
While Greyfuss stretched and watched
Spring cleaning of the soul
And a prayer sung to heaven with a bobbing head
Do you remember Lord
When I could breathe like a teenager
What a time!
Yes I want life again
Let's move the furniture around
And throw out this dusty old carpet in my mind
Can you do it again for me
Please
I'm tired of being low
Let's clean the soul

It's spring somewhere in the world
Why not here
Peter Gabriel tells me so
And all the host of heaven with guitars, flutes,
Synthesizers and drums
Oh sickness, you can just stuff it today
I'm going to sing
Give me one more breath, God
There's another verse
I really love
Coming
Up.

THE SECOND TESTAMENT

Alpha

Zion County Hospital is a big, sprawling complex, built before the insurance companies took over the world. It is also forbiddingly medical and sterile-looking, very old-fashioned. New hospitals are built to look like three-star hotels to attract the shrinking health-care dollar—of course, they also kick you out on the street as soon as your D.R.G.[23] says you should be well, whether you are or not. Win some, lose some.

Personally, I liked the days when you went to see your doctor, rather than purchased attention from a "health-care provider." Healing is a relationship, not a bulk food. But what are you going to do, when The Beast puts his stamp on everything? I sure can't keep my hands clean.

"Look, teacher," I quote, "what massive stones! What magnificent buildings!"

jesus smiles. "I tell you the truth," he quotes back, "there will come a day when not one of these stones will be left on top of each other; every one will be thrown down."

"You warm my heart," I say, "if you're talking about the Corinth Medi-Gold offices over there... but don't touch Dr. Pettigrove's clinic. He's alright."

"Duly noted," jesus nods. "But the destruction comes from human hands, not God's. It will be like a fever running its course, and no one will survive, but that God's hand might reach out and stop it... then all the world will come to grief, and know who it is they've pierced."

His eyes grow glassy, faraway. I thought we were joking, here, but suddenly I feel a chill.

"jesus, warn me before you do that, O.K.?"

"I told you, it won't come from—"

"—I mean before you get apocalyptic. It scares the bejeebers out of people."

He nods, slowly. "It should," he says, frowning slightly. "It scares me, too." He tries to force a smile onto his face, but it comes out wan and thin. "Nathaniel, when you go in there today, I will be with you."

If I haven't been nervous before, *that's* certainly taken care of it.

"Why? What's going to happen?"

"I don't know," he says. "Only the Father knows—"

—I race across the parking lot, eager to escape Mr. Doom before he turns into opaque glass again.

The crowds have been shrinking lately, and it's hard to blame them. jesus' preaching has really taken a pessimistic downturn. I don't know if it's just the lectionary or lack of sleep, but he's gotten so bad that Peter volunteered to fill in for him on Sundays— "to give a him break." jesus ruefully declined.

The automatic door slides away. I enter a tile-and-ammonia world. Indistinct voices over the sound system, the brusque walk of people in white, the measured pace of folks in blue, huddled families lost in street clothes… it's as familiar to me as the supermarket.

I pass the somnolent visitor's desk and the ATM.

First bank of elevators on the right.

The stairway door is constantly flipped open by the People In The Know, because one of the things they Know is that the elevators are too darn slow. I'm a committed stair avoider these days, though—much the same way tomatoes avoid Cuisinarts—so I watch the yellow lights blink through five and four, stop at three.

Dr. Hudson, Dr. Hudson, you're wanted in CCU.

This shouldn't take too long. It's just for gerbil inventory. I shall yield some of my pets to the Lady in Pink, who will count heads. Hopefully, she'll find the usual zoo of critters, nothing extraordinarily nasty.

There are some classes of infection that C.F. patients come to fear and loathe, some that ask the biological question *have you made out your living will,* and some that just mean you're plugging along pretty much the same. Many of them have different colored pelts, and I usually know what the Gentle Lady will find. These days my doctor listens pretty closely to what I tell him—I've been around the block a few times.

Here is a color guide you won't find at the carpet store: yellow is good, white is near miraculous, clear a fantasy, green troublesome, brown worrisome, fluorescent green very bad, and slate grey means my worst enemy is back for another round. I don't know what future, deadlier gerbils look like; only God knows. I don't want to find out. I don't think I will today, either, though jesus' last comment has got me a little jumpy.

Ding, ding.

The elevator slouches into the lobby, and I file in with a crowd of similar supplicants. We smile at each other. Sometimes I make a joke. People aren't as standoffish in medical elevators as they are in bank elevators. Money makes you want to be alone, weakness makes you want friends. Makes you wonder what the greater affliction is.

The Lady in Pink is on the third floor. I get out of the elevator, enter the lab and sign in, even though she's already waved and called me by name. They tell me I don't have to use the sheet, but I don't want to appear like I'm getting special treatment.

The dirty little secret is that regulars do, though. When I call the clinic with no advance notice, saying my condition has shifted, miraculous things happen to the computerized scheduling system. Slots appear out of nowhere, the fabric of space-time bends. I get in regardless. Pharmacies are the same story. Some of the folks at the Wal-Mart pharmacy even recognize my voice over the phone before I give them the refill numbers.

Science experiments are a team effort, all the way from the receptionist to the techs to the nurses, doctors and the cleaning staff. When you make a little progress, everyone cheers. I have a very, very large army of angels pulling for me.

Even though I feel a little ashamed of the personal attention, I appreciate it. I try very hard not to abuse it, but there have been a few times when it really made the difference between a height of five feet up or six foot down.

When I went through Clinical Pastoral Education (C.P.E.), I had a bit of an edge falling into the routine. Not only was I a professional patient, but my family had always been stuffed with nurses. I've had many long years of dinnertime conversation that would make Frankenstein feel right at home—"subdural hematoma" *is* what you say when you pass the biscuits, right? But that edge disappeared fast in the dizzying stress of becoming a rubber chaplain. I kept wondering where the rubber patients were, so I could practice safely.

I couldn't help but remember all the times our family had been zapped by the void, and how one careless word could multiply pain in a few minutes. The weight of responsibility was fearsome. I didn't want to multiply pain, I wanted to subtract it. I lived in fear of my tongue, knowing how it could cut when it started to swing.

There were many days I came home with a deep-seated psychic cramp, a kind of fourth-level version of second-guessing that made my whole world seem like an opportunity to screw up. After a month I couldn't say "boo" without teetering on the edge of paralysis.

And yet, I can honestly say it was the most rewarding thing I've ever done. They tell me the feedback that came from the floor was appreciative—the sword wasn't quite as reckless as I'd feared—and I, too, saw some healing in the process. There I learned lessons that continue to resonate to this day. There I received tools to survive. And there, ironically enough, I ran into just enough personal healing that, six months afterward, I was able to do what I needed to do next. I stopped the ordination track, transferred to a different program and graduated ahead of my chums. C.P.E. healed me out of a job.

The Lord said to Moses, "This is the land which I promised I would give to Abraham, Isaac and Jacob's descendants. I have let you see it with your own eyes. Yet you shall not cross over into it."

There in the land of Moab Moses the servant of the Lord died, as the Lord had said. (*Deuteronomy* 34:4–5)

I still look over the River Jordan and grieve. There are moments when it feels like a crushing failure to stand in Moab. But there are also moments—occurring with increasing rapidity—when it feels like a victory, too. I would have been very unhappy, if I'd tried to cross that river. It would have swept me under.

And the freedom that recognizes such circumstances: that's some real serious healing, there.

Reverend Noel Brown and Mildred Dordal, you are the gift of God to me.

What was it like, to be a rubber chaplain?

It was listening to a gentle, soft-spoken woman tell how she met her husband, while he lay in a bed and died.

It was listening to inner-city parents tell of their life's greatest achievement: keeping their kids out of the gangs.

It was being awed and humbled by the faith of everyday people in outrageous circumstances.

It was listening to folks be brave and strong on the outside while the inner side crumbled.

It was standing up for meek patients being railroaded into choices they didn't have to make.

It was spending five minutes talking about the broken body, and two hours talking about the spouse that died last year: I was amazed to discover how poorly our society provides for psychic hurts—and I began to see how the need for help drives people's health into the ground, just to obtain some socially acceptable caring.

It was hurting with a woman who didn't want to get out of the hospital, because of what was waiting for her at home.

It was days when an odd, risky thought popped into my head... and a patient's eyes widened in relief and recognition because I'd said it.

It was the dying man who wanted to confess something, but couldn't. I pronounced a blessing over his head, trying to work in an absolution for what had not been revealed... and I felt so very, very small and human.

It was saying the Psalms as prayers for the first time in my life.

It was reviewing events and tearing myself up for hours, both at the hospital and at home.

But probably my most powerful impression was of God's disinclination to follow our orders.

There were times when all medical authority had given up, and we simply commended the patient into God's hands, expecting her to die—and she lived. There were other times when I prayed so hard for someone to live, and he simply died. Here, in the midst of all our struggling, I found a God who did not share our burdened overestimation of our knowledge and capabilities.

"You think you have the power of life and death," I heard, "but you swing a very small bat, my friend." It was a constant lesson in ironic humility, applied hourly.

I came to see the time of death as a collaboration between God, patient, family and medicine, with maybe a little void thrown in, too—but by far the heaviest weight was God and patient, again and again. Medicine had an enormous impact on the quality of life, certainly, but there was a mystery surrounding death it could barely touch.

As to the chaplain, if he figured in at all, it was to help the family find their voice. Beyond that, his efforts were nothing, mere striving after the wind. He was there for the living, no matter what he might think he was there for.

Martha was doing a little art therapy at the time. One day I painted two hands in the *orans* position, the position of supplication before an altar. The hands were poised before an immense, swirling, uncontrollable tornado. That's what it felt like to be a rubber chaplain.

The gerbils are produced and handed over, labeled, and banished to a back room. I sign a credit slip and walk to my waiting room seat…

…where one of my pouches no longer sits.

Panicpanicpanicpanicpanicpanic…

Calm down, you don't know it was stolen. Search the other chairs. Did you take it with you into the lab? The tank is still here.

This is not an ordinary purse. It has the stuff of life in it, not money. I frantically comb all the possibilities, hoping it will materialize, but it remains obstinately gone. My glucose meter, $20 worth of test strips, a thermal pack, syringes, candy and two different kinds of insulin: everything replaceable, but how long, O Lord? I'm going to need that insulin in two hours.

Syringes are useful for drugs. Could that be what they were after?

Arghh!

I have my candy, at least. Prudent paranoia causes me to stuff it in everything that will hold it, like a squirrel with precious nuts. It's the stuff that can be the most life-threatening to lose. Ironic: candy wasn't all that important to me, until I became diabetic.

Well, no use looking five times. Four's enough.

There's a pharmacy in the building. I've heard that in emergencies diabetics can just walk in without a prescription, tell them what they need and get it. Time to find out if that's true, I guess. I leave the clinic, feeling fragile and dejected.

"I'll be with you, Nathaniel."

Yeah, well, I wish you'd stayed with my purse instead, and spooked the creep that nipped it.

I pop in the elevator, try to recall what floor the pharmacy was on. The Lobby? No; where the walkway comes in. Level Five. I punch the button a little harder than necessary, but the elevator gives no special response, no synthesized "ouch." Too bad.

I get out, spot the hamster-tube walkway, look around. No pharmacy. Maybe it's this way… Or that way…

A nurse greets me by name. I march over to her in relief.

"I'm so glad to see you."

"So am I. Can you tell me where the pharmacy is?"

"On the lobby level, Reverend."

I keep telling them I'm not a Reverend. I stopped. Went off the map. Failed. But the ones that worked with me just remember me as their rubber chaplain—guess they've never met a real one—and I've just about given up trying to correct them, though it feels like fraud.

"Can you help me out?" she asks.

I look surprised, pause.

"There's a couple I'd like you to see."

You don't understand, I'm in the middle of a personal crisis…

"Sure," my mouth says.

Why, you ask?

Because I'm stupid. Because I can't stop. Because I'm a geek with a theology degree. Because I keep trying to make my life mean something more. Because I'm trying to get on God's good side. Because God doesn't listen any better than floor nurses do. Because I'm going to weed, weed, weed, until my hands are sore. I don't know anymore; take your pick.

I'm ushered through into a familiar looking room. It isn't much bigger than a closet. When you sit in the chairs, your knees meet your companion's knees. Perhaps this is by design; it certainly makes it easy to pray together. I suspect it's just cheapness, however. This is not an income-producing room, it's where you put grieving family members. The chairs are worn, the magazines old. Styrofoam cups of coffee and little white tear-ghosts linger side by side. There are no windows. The place is, I think, a little coffinlike itself. Architectural empathy?

There are no tears here today. The mother is in shock, locked up. The father is in the middle of a holy rage. Their baby has just died, and no one will baptize it. It's against the rules.

Most of the time, ministers break the rules and hope that God understands. But there are others who are paralyzed by that kind of leap: good ministers who just can't turn their back on their theology. None of this is their fault, I think. It's the Church as a whole, for failing to clearly enunciate a rationale, and a rite, for the more timid and lawyerly. If we're going to call those folks, we have to support them. Shame on us for putting them in that position!

I listen, mostly, for about ten minutes. The father pours invectives over the room, and the mother sits in numb isolation. I suspect Mom just wants to go home. But

Dad wants to win, and he needs to pour his anger out on somebody. The Universe and God are both hard targets to hit, so the man needs a stand-in… and the hapless Reverend Miller, caught between theology and pastoral care, is a good candidate.

"I give you a new commandment. Love one another; as I have loved you, so you are to love one another." *(John 13:34)*

I guess catching the heat is one way to do it, though personally I would have taken another path.

"It's not right, it's just not right. He's a—"

"Mike," the mother, Diane, warns.

"Self-righteous little prig?" I suggest.

Diane's eyes widen at that, while the father nods in appreciation. Risky comment, but it works. Mike feels like he's the only one in the universe who's upset—injury upon injury, injustice upon injustice, why, oh world, haven't you stopped and wailed?

"Mike, let's just go home and forget about it."

"I'm not going to just forget about it."

"That's good," I say. "I don't think you should try. Wouldn't work, anyway."

"Damn right. He's a—"

The mother winces. The conflict is making her just sick inside: *turn it off, turn it off.*

I don't know if it's a good idea to break in here, but I'm feeling caught between a rock and a hard place. Mike's relief is tightening the tension on Diane, and he has had plenty of venting already. The plain fact is that the minister didn't kill his son, so all the venting in the world isn't going to satisfy his rage; he's aiming at a minor target.

So I decide to walk into the stream this time. Good decision? Bad? I'll take it apart later and find a million ways to blame myself, but the fact is you just have to pick a lane and drive. Real life happens fast.

"There's a lot of un-rightness going on today," I interject. "I'm glad you're mad."

My comment brings him up short. Mike knows I was brought into the room to calm him down. Hospitals think chaplains are the emotional fire department, and people sense it instinctively. It's the way you're brought into the room: *Fix this person, we need to get on with things.* People resent being treated like a broken widget—and it doesn't work, in any case. They just get more frantic.

"What do you mean?" Mike asks suspiciously.

"Just what I said," I reply. "I'll be honest with you, Mike. I was brought in here to make peace. But I'm not going to play along. The truth is, I'm glad you're angry."

"Why?"

"Because it means you're paying attention. Your son just died."

Thud.

It's not the minister that's your problem.

He doesn't say anything at that. Hearing the word is painful. His face closes up in anguish. So does mine.

I really hate to name things sometimes. I sweat all over; my throat hurts. The only reason why I do it is because a courageous counselor named Kadi Billman— another gift of God—taught me the value of it, and I saw, time and time again, that she was right.

But I hate it. I just hate it.

"I can't take the day away," I say after a moment of silence. "Wish I could; but I can't."

He nods, wearily, and sits down in a chair.

Time to look at the real thing, now.

I was taught to do ministry with an image in my head. If you fill your brain with do's and don'ts, you'll be thinking so much you won't have time to be honest; you'll become a manipulator. But you have to find something to keep you on course, or else you'll flit from one role to another and get lost in your own tangled responses. So we were taught to pick an image that summed up what we wanted to be, and stay true to it. This is one of my images:

Several people are walking across a blasted, hellish plain of missile craters and scorch marks. There are mountains in front, mountains in back. Which of the mountains are lush, which are rocky? I don't know. I can only see the hard-baked mud below me, the cracks in the ground.

There is a wagon to pull across the plain, loaded down with all of the stuff of life. Good, bad, pretty and ugly, it's all there. And it's got to get from one point to another. Why? Again, I don't know. It's just the way it is: you've got to get there.

The stuff on the wagon isn't mine. It's my companions'. I've got my own stuff with me that I have to carry, but it isn't my job to put it on this cart. I have to remember that constantly, or else I'll weigh it down even more.

It's also not my job to pull the load. It took me a long time to realize that, but it's true. When I first got started, I kept trying to take the burden away. It doesn't work. This cart is theirs, and no one else can pull it. If either of us gets confused about that, things get worse rather than better.

What's the point of being there, then? Well, sometimes the wheels get stuck in a rut. It's O.K. to help push when that happens. That's not trying to steal their wagon, it's just being neighborly. And sometimes folks get tired. In that case, it's always good to suggest a break, massage some shoulders, help make camp. They might want you to pull instead…but it will do more good if you help them recuperate from the day's work.

Mostly, though, it's just non-anxious companionship. They know they're not alone in the universe, they've got some help for the ruts—but they also know that their companion sees them as capable and viable, fully able to pull their own cart.

Now they have an image, too: *I am a good, capable person who has hit a rough patch or two. I'm not an invalid.* That gives them hope, even when they've begun to doubt their own strength. How much better than trailing along uselessly, watching a stranger haul their stuff!

If people appreciate your help, they might talk over what's on the wagon. They might think aloud about whether or not something is really worth the weight, toy with the idea of leaving it behind. If you listen well, you might hear their tongue say something their ears didn't hear. If you pass that back to their ears, they might more clearly hear how they feel about things. Our tongues are pretty perceptive, once they relax a little.

They might decide to take that object off the wagon, once they hear how they feel about it. That's usually a good decision that lightens their load—as long as they're the ones doing the sorting. If I tell them what to leave behind, I always get it wrong. I don't know that their cheap bowling ball came from Grandpa.

Well, that's my image. Back when I wasn't so burdened with my own wagon, that's how I tried to do ministry, once my teachers got through with me. I still try to do it that way, when called upon.

And when my wheels get stuck, that's the kind of help I appreciate, too. If you find me out on the dry plain someday, remember that, please. I will truly appreciate it.

We talk about a lot of things. Mundane details, arrangements, history, love of God, hope. The talk eventually swings back to Reverend Miller again, as I knew it would. He's not going to get off the hook that easy.

"When we asked if Joe would go to heaven," Diane says, "Reverend Miller said the Bible doesn't make that clear. He wasn't washed of his sins—"

"—ten minutes old," Mike mutters. "Not even ten minutes—"

"That's a shame," I say. "It sounds like he has a pretty small God, to be handcuffed like that. Just because we didn't dump water on Joe's head, that's going to stop God? I'm sorry, I can't believe that. St. Paul wrote that jesus is lord of both the dead and the living. I'll go with him, I think."

"Wouldn't lift a finger…"

Diane shushes him with a look. "I don't see why we can't have him baptized."

I take a deep breath. "Well, it's tough. Miller isn't really a self-righteous prig, you know. He's just thinking about God a little too much. There's not much theology for baptizing the dead—and, to tell the truth, if he did the ceremony, it might not really seem right to you. You're saying goodbye, too, and baptisms don't address that."

"I just want… I want…" She sighs, giving up. "I don't know. Forget it." She puts her hands up to her eyes, as if shielding herself from a bright sun, but the room is dim; it's her life that's glaring.

"You don't know, and you want to know," I agree. "And there's nothing wrong with that." I pull out my little pocket Bible and squint at the microprint. "But Reverend Miller's wrong about what the Bible says…" Flip, flip. The page comes mercifully quickly to my fingers—but this is no miracle: the binding has learned my habits.

"Reverend Miller was taught that babies start out invisibly stained—they have to be scrubbed before God will remember them—so for him, unbaptized babies are unclean. They fall off the books, and he's not too sure what God is going to do about that. But Peter also had a super-legal outlook about who was clean and who wasn't, and God cleared him up on that point. God used a dream about unclean food as a way of talking about human cleanliness":

Peter went up on the roof to pray, then grew hungry and wanted something to eat. While they were getting it ready, he fell into a trance.

He saw a rift in the sky, and a thing coming down that looked like a great sheet of sail-cloth. It was slung by the four corners, and was being lowered to the ground. In it he saw every kind of creature, whatever walks or crawls or flies. Then there was a voice which said to him, "Get up, Peter. Kill and eat."

But Peter said, "No, no, Lord! I have never eaten anything profane or unclean."

The voice came again a second time: "It is not for you to call profane what God has made clean."

This happened three times; and then the thing was taken up again into the sky. *(Acts 10:9b–16)*

"While Peter was still thinking about the vision," I continue, "he was called to minister to non-Jews—and he had always thought they were unclean! They were like pigs to him: a dirty part of Creation. But he went to them, because of what God had shown him. He went to the house of a man named Cornelius, and he baptized all of the household… Why? Because God had *already called them clean*, and God told Peter to not deny the word that had already been spoken.

"Do you hear that? The cleanliness was already there, before Peter even entered Cornelius' house! When Peter got there, he preached to them. He saw the same signs he'd learned to associate with the Spirit's presence, and he was amazed. They were non-Jews, they hadn't been baptized yet—but here they were, already filled with the Holy Spirit, babbling excitedly after his sermon, praising God and carrying on. The gospel was just as effective in their hearts, too. This is what he said at the time":

Then Peter spoke: "Is anyone prepared to withhold the water of baptism from these people, who have received the Holy Spirit just as we did?" *(Acts 10:46b–47)*

"You see, Peter had been asked to wash these people as a sign of the cleanliness God had already created, long, long ago. The cleanliness came *before* the washing, not after it. It was the world that was calling them dirty—Peter included, until his vision.

"And that's what we still do today. Baptism is a sign of something we can't see. It shows us a cleanliness that the world says isn't there and tries to talk us out of. We lose sight of the cleanliness that God sees; so God has given us a tangible thing to do that we can remember and hold onto. It's full of sights, sounds and the feel of cool water. From thereafter, when the world calls us dirty, we can look back and say 'you're a liar; I have seen my cleanliness. I was baptized.' It's a sign of what has always existed in God's mind; of what God dreamed of at the very conception of the Universe. This is what Peter learned from his vision":

> He said to them, "I need not remind you that a Jew is forbidden by his religion to visit or associate with a man of another race; yet God has shown me clearly that I must not call any man profane or unclean." *(Acts 10:28)*

"That is the command of God: don't call anyone impure or unclean. Miller's lost hold of that command, somewhere down the line, just as Peter lost hold of it. But don't be too worried about Miller and his friends—God has more seniority, I think. It'll all get straightened out in the end."

She smiles bitterly. "I'd like to be there when he finally gets the word."

Her husband nods in angry agreement.

"Well, we're all human… I won't start calling him unclean either," I say. "Just a little… ah… confused. Church law can get you dizzy, sometimes—but I'm not worried about him. I *am* concerned that the Good Reverend has put a stumbling block before you. Maybe we need to do something to visually wash off that stain he's put on your son, so you don't remember him as unclean, too. Let's see Joe the way God sees him, not Reverend Miller."

"But you said baptism wouldn't work for Joe," Diane says.

"Not the baptism you were thinking of," I answer. "But the heart of baptism is simply water and a promise; and the promise holds for everyone. We just need to say it in a way that makes sense. I think I know how we can do that."

Then I explain what I would like to do, and they agree.

The hospital doesn't have a true chapel, but it has a bowl, and water. That's all you need—along with some people. Even Peter admits that baptism is within range of the laity. I try to remember that, whenever I'm stranded on a desert island, a point of theology or a stumbling block.

We have three people, and three times to use the water: a coincidence, which I don't believe in… *what are you saying, God? Speak fast…*

—That's it. We will do it together. So much better, to wash your own baby! Especially here, where thousands of imagined washings will get compressed into one small moment, a mere blip in the day. I briefly describe the additional instructions, which brings a warm color to Diane's face, a nervous one to Mike's.

"Are you ready?" I say. I try to be as hospitable as possible with God's invitations, even when the occasion is sad. It's not disrespectful, but simply reduces anxiety. They both nod, tightly.

We know that power comes from God, but it's hard to stay centered on that fact when the hands doing the ritual are human. It sure looks like we're the ones doing the heavy lifting.

Look at what happened when jesus first sent the disciples out to work in his name: the thing that jazzed them was the power they felt, not the joy of those who were healed; and ever since that demon-chasing day, how we have labored to remember the true source of our power and protection! How many times have I told someone that my new antibiotic was working fantastically for me, and the automatic reply of "We've been praying for you" was too quick for my comfort? How many times has this phrase been said with such an undercurrent of proprietorship that I felt twisted to thank them, rather than God? A hundred times? A thousand?

The greater the act, the greater the struggle to leave the credit in God's hands. I've heard Christians lay claim to performing incredible miracles, with only the weakest formulaic nod to the Creator. And some churches, if you listen closely to their baptismal language, betray a similar tendency. It's not enough that God honor us by letting us help; we want the whole enchilada.

Look at me, here. Why am I so nervous? Do I think the ritual will *fail* if I'm a poor performer? Or am I simply concerned that I minister well?

Questions worth asking myself.

Diane knew Joseph first, so she will wash him first. Then his father met him briefly, so he will wash him second; then I, last of all—as a sign of the Church that got there very, very late in the game.

> He said to me, "Man, can these bones live again?"
> I answered, "Only you know that, Lord God."
> He said to me, "Prophesy over these bones and say to them, O dry bones, hear the word of God. This is the word of the Lord: I will put breath into you, and you shall live." *(Ezekiel 37:3–5)*

We will take our time, as much time as needed. This is a timeless need, isn't it?

We step around the bowl, and together the four of us enter God's dimension, where death is not an ending but a transition, and anxiety is transformed by the expanse of history.

Time is the key to the promise we make. The Hebrews did not testify to a God locked in infinity, but to a God that changed and breathed with the world. It is only God's *promises* that are fixed. Everything else is created, creating, or will be created. This is the eternity of God: a moving, breathing eternity where the oak shall be moved and the mountains really do dance, but the Word shall never, ever be moved.

Time: take your time, Nathaniel.

My heart is pounding. I take a deep breath and hold up an invisible hand to my invisible partner and wrestling companion. *Don't let me screw this up, God. You love these people. They deserve someone better. You better be here.*

I feel the answering squeeze. *I'm here. Relax.*

O.K.

Diane dips her hands into the water. "We wash you in the name of God the Creator, who says you were made a child of God... and we knew you that way, Joseph."

The water trickles over the baby's head.

"We wash you in the name of the Son, who says you *are* a child of God... and we know you that way, Joseph."

Again the water trickles.

"We wash you in the name of the Holy Spirit, who promises you will *always be* a child of God... and we will know you again that way, Joseph."

—Why is it that my voice locks up at these times? Why is it such a struggle to express hope? Help me, jesus, I would not have my broken soul get in the way of your healing—

"This water and word is a sign of a promise that has no beginning or ending, no weakness, no fading. No one can take it away. It is as eternal as your Maker, who has always known you and loved you, and will never stop. The earth might pass away, but God's word will never pass away. And the word is this:

It Is Good."

The water trickles...

...And then the baby cries.

God drives me *crazy.*

Beta

The seventy-two came back jubilant. "In your name, Lord," they said, "even the dev-ils submit to us!"

He replied, "I watched how Satan fell, like lightning, out of the sky. Now you see I have given you power to tread on snakes and scorpions and all the forces of the enemy, and nothing will harm you. Nevertheless, what you should rejoice over is not that the spirits submit to you, but that your names are enrolled in heaven." *(Luke 10:17–20)*

"Every time I come up with a highly thought-out way of saying goodbye, you create a hello," I accuse jesus.

He smiles. "You'd think that might tell you something."

"It tells me what my word is worth in heaven, I guess."

"Mmm. Be thankful. People who know which way to pray have even more trouble waiting for them. At least you know who's doing it, and who isn't."

We are walking down the road again, heading toward Jerusalem. I have my sugar kit back. jesus tells me, with a straight face, that a suspicious-looking character bolt-ed out of the hospital, ransacked it for money and then threw it in the bushes.

"Thanks," I say, dryly.

"You're welcome… Did you really believe what you said back there?"

"Yes."

"But only for Joseph?" he asks, looking a little sad. "Not for you?"

I think about that a bit. "My brain believes it for everyone," I say. "But there's a kid inside me that resists argument. It just clings to fear and feelings. I don't think it even understands the words."

"You had a bad start," he agrees. He nods and says no more, understanding.

Sometimes he'll do that; I'll expect him to say more—argue with me a little—but instead he'll just nod a few times, as if he's just learned something interesting. It's a bit disconcerting, when you're used to talking to normal folks. Most of us just listen long enough to find the next spot of silence to fill.

"Is there any way to rip that part out of me?" I finally ask.

He looks pained, but considers the request seriously.

"I love children, too," he says. "New Jerusalem would be pretty poor without them. I don't want to rip the kid out with careless weeding; I want to see him in heaven, too."

"Am I stuck with this weed forever, then?"

"Patience. Maybe not forever. Maybe just for life…"

I snort.

"…or maybe," he continues, "maybe not even that long. We'll see what happens."

He looks at the horizon, then, and his eyes narrow onto the way ahead. It's a hard-baked road, scored by wind and dry weather. I can see the cracks and ruts. We walk on in silence.

You want a real faith crisis? Witness a miracle. It will rattle you like nothing else. You'll find yourself in the middle of the most cussed questions of the universe: *Why this person, and not that person? Why is there a need for miracles at all?*

We say we want proof of God's existence, but that's really not what's going on. We want proof that God is good. Agnostics may be showing instinctive shrewdness. They know that the first, easier question might be better left unknown.

"God called my bluff," a shaken friend said to me, once. "Can I go back to pleading for a sign, now?"

Later that day, we come to a man who has been blind from birth. Some ask jesus whose sin it was, that he be punished so.

"Neither this man nor his parents sinned," jesus replies. "It is not a punishment but an opportunity, to show what the work of God is—to burn evil and pain out of the world." He spits on the ground, makes some mud with it and puts it on the man's eyes.

"Go," he says. "Wash yourself in the Pool of The Sent."

The man walks away. It will be years before I hear from him again—a marvelous story told with bright, shining eyes.

Miracles.

Miracles and spit. What the hell is *that* supposed to mean? God makes you blind, spits in your eye and it comes out for glory…

Is that the message? I wonder. *Be glad when God spits in your eye?*

Two more miles down the road, I can hold it in no longer.

"Did you mean to say," I ask jesus, "that God gave that man blindness, just so you could take it away?"

jesus groans. "There is no word I can say that can't be twisted by the Accuser," he says. "If your heart hears that, it has become very hard, indeed. You are a hanging judge, Nathaniel."

I am one step away from being called Satan myself, I know—Peter's eyes are silently warning me—but I can't let it go. This is the thing I must know. It is one of my demons. Must a man be born blind so that we can give him sight? Why must babies die in the first place? Just so jesus can show off? And why did my brother and sister have to get cystic fibrosis? They were good kids, jesus.

"That doesn't answer the question," I say. "I want to know why these things happen."

"Everything has to have a reason for you. You can't live, die or get a headache without a reason. Can't it be reason enough to say that God isn't done yet? Can't we say that New Jerusalem is on its way?"

"No, because there is still the question of responsibility. The rabbis say that we can't discard the principle of *ex nihilo*, which says God made everything out of nothing. To my mind, that means God is responsible for everything—including blindness and cystic fibrosis."

"If God is against evil and pain, why would you think God also created it?" jesus asked. "Perversity? Boredom? Trying to make a stone too heavy to lift, just to please the graduate students?"

"But the problem with moving evil—"

"—the void," he corrects absently. He frowns and begins digging through the pockets in his robe.

"*Evil,*" I insist, not allowing him to slip by on semantics. "The problem with moving evil out of God's responsibility is that it makes evil the product of something else, possibly an evil god. We're thrown into a world where evil might win. The Evil One might be stronger."

"Oh, I'm not worried on that score." He pulls out a paperback.

"Your problem, Nathaniel, is that you are asking a question that isn't even solved by God. You're under the impression that the word GOD somehow answers the question of BEFORE. But it doesn't. Even if God *is* responsible for everything you see— what was that phrase, ex..." He snaps his fingers impatiently. "Ex... ex..."

"*Ex nihilo.* It's Latin for 'out of nothing.'"

"Thank you. I'm afraid I never encountered your core principle in scripture," he says with a grin. "But suppose we granted *ex nihilo* was true, just for argument's sake. What stops you from asking the question 'Where did God come from?' Nothing! You can ask that question, too. You still have a concept you cannot stop: the word BEFORE. Who made GOD? Same problem."

"That's what my atheist friends complain about," I admit.

"You need to listen to more skeptics," he says, flipping the paperback into my hand. "You need to get out of church more often."

That afternoon, I read Stephen Hawking's *A Brief History of Time.* His work grows out of the Big Bang Theory, which has become accepted as the standard model for the origin of the Universe. It is worth reading, if you haven't yet. His religious conclusions might be different than the Church's, but his reasoning is fascinating, and his view of time is liberating.

Mr. Hawking helped me realize that part of my problem—and that of theology in general—has grown out of a certain mental image of time. It is the straight line:

Religious folks like to label the start GOD. That's a pretty fearsome word to most of us, so it makes us swallow our other nagging questions. But nonreligious folks aren't afraid of God, so they keep on looking, and this is what they see:

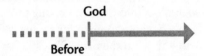

No matter how much you back up that line, you can always find a BEFORE. GOD doesn't fix it, if you leave your brain turned on. There is an edge, and you can visually extend the line past that edge.

"But," you say, "GOD is the one making the line, the hand holding the pencil."

All this drawing and pencil holding, though, is just another sequence of events, removed to a higher level than the previous one. You've created a Meta-Line of time events to encapsulate the other:

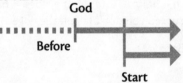

Ex nihilo is also a symptom of timelines. It's a fancy way of saying that we want GOD to be a neat and tidy knot in the rope. We don't want there to be God and *other stuff* at the start, because that leads to two disturbing questions:

• Is the *other stuff* a competing God?
• If not, who made the *other stuff*?

Scary questions. Let us pray.

Now imagine, if you have to, that you're a skeptic. Pretend you don't fear God quite so much. Just call GOD a black box, a container with unknown contents. You might notice that, since you can still ask the question "Who made GOD?" you didn't really change anything by limiting the number of objects at the start. No matter what you do, you have a time line with a set of initial conditions. The initial conditions can be one thing, two things or a thousand things, and it's pretty much the same problem.

You can ask the rude question BEFORE if it's God alone, or God on a barstool or—as Genesis would have it—God and a wild and wooly mess of space-time quantum foam. (That is what it says in the King James Version, isn't it?)

Get it? There are two issues being scrambled together.

One is the problem of the line *(BEFORE)* and the other is the problem of initial conditions *(GOD)*. We've tangled them together because we want one to fix the other, but they're distinct issues that cannot solve each other, in the same way that the question "Who is my mother?" does not solve the question "What is the square root of negative one?" Tying those two together just makes bigger knots.

Physicists and cosmologists ran into the same vexing problem. They labeled the knot in the rope THE BIG BANG (an apt synonym for an angry God!) and discovered that they hadn't changed anything but the name. You still have an accusing BEFORE to wrestle with: "What came before the THE BIG BANG?"

Shoot. Thought getting rid of GOD was going to help, did you? Wrong again.

It's a common problem. Science, at least, has continued to try to think its way out of the tangle. Having failed to fix Time with God synonyms, it's continued to tinker with Time by itself; they're starting to separate the issues.

Listen now to Mr. Hawking talk about the continuum called space-time:

> Space-time would be like the surface of the Earth, only with two more dimensions. The surface of the Earth is finite in extent but it doesn't have a boundary or edge: if you sail off into the sunset, you don't fall off the edge...[24]

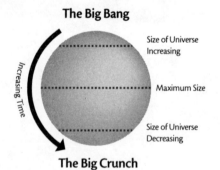

The Big Bang

Increasing Time

Size of Universe Increasing

Maximum Size

Size of Universe Decreasing

The Big Crunch

From *A Brief History of Time* by Stephen Hawking Copyright © 1988 by Stephen W. Hawking. Used by permission of Bantam Books, a Division of Bantam Doubleday Dell Publishing Group, Inc.

That's right. Throw out the image of time as a line, with its troublesome edge. There are other things you can travel on besides a straight line; and there is nothing about time that should suggest a line to you. It's just a convention we've gotten used to, not reality. None of our images are reality, and they all carry their own clarifications and distortions.

Imagine time as a sphere, with the beginning up at the North Pole. Now you've got some place to travel forward (south), but the edge is gone. Now the question BEFORE reveals its nonsensical nature. You might as well ask "What is north of the North Pole?" When you stand at the North Pole, everything is south.

The universe starts at the North Pole as a single point. As one moves south, the circles of latitude at constant distance from the North Pole get bigger, corresponding to the Universe expanding with imaginary time... The Universe would reach a maximum size at the equator and would contract with increasing imaginary time to a single point at the South Pole. Even though the Universe would have zero size at the North and South Poles, these points would not be singularities...[25]

Cool, huh?

I will not pretend that I have picked up what Stephen Hawking laid down on paper. Let's just say that he pushed me out of a mental image that was causing me trouble. After that, I started to dream...

Picture Mr. Hawking's image through the eyes of faith. Don't be rigorous about it; it's just another image, and not reality. But dream with it a bit. Think of it as a History of Creation.

Genesis 1:1 lies up at the North Pole; it represents either the Void, or Senselessness, depending on how you want to read it. Now put the New Jerusalem, the world that makes sense, at the South Pole.

Let the latitude marks represent pain. When the Universe was an expanding cloud of particles rushing out from the Big Bang, pain was at a minimum. Then life appeared; then nervous systems; then—hoo boy!—the human brain. Big mistake, probably, but it's too late to go back now.

The equator, in this image, marks the height of the Birth Pangs, the moment of maximum resistance by the Void. I pray to God that we're not still in the Northern Hemisphere; let's hope we're in the south half. Or maybe the author of Revelation is right. Maybe the history of Creation's pain looks more like a teardrop:

That looks about right to me. But you can pick your own shapes. The faith statement lies at the South Pole: a minimum of pain.

Stand there for a moment and look around. The volume of pain has returned to its beginning point, but with one crucial difference: we're born now. The birth pangs of Creation have yielded something complete and new from the Void.

Us.

I think that's a very liberating way to think of the Alpha and Omega of existence.

Let me tell you what this suggests to me, and see what you think about it. You don't have to buy it, just chew on it.

1. We can see that the BEFORE problem is growing out of our difficulty imagining time. It has nothing to do with God. We're struggling with images of physics, not theology.

2. When we look at the North Pole, we see that the quandary of *ex nihilo*—the statement that God created everything out of nothing and is hence responsible for all of the pain and stupidity of the world—becomes nonsensical. The accusation is a setup with no possible reply, as is the question "Where is more north than the North Pole?"

> *There is no "before" filled with "nothing" from which God created.*

God alone…
God with the Void…
God with a big Space to Fill…
God with the Unlit, Vasty Deep…
God with Chaos…
God with Evil and Entropy...
God and the demons of the Void…

…they are all just starting conditions up at the top of the globe. You can pick any one of them—whatever works best for you. All of these initial conditions carry the same characteristics when it comes to time-related questions. Even the word *nothing* at the start, as cosmologists discovered, has no special advantage over any other set of initial conditions. Since none of them can fix the time line quandary, you are free. Move on to a time-sphere or time-drop, and you can start to think rationally about the second issue: what's in the set of initial conditions.

As Mr. Hawking points out, you may not need to actually postulate a God at all—at least, to explain the origins problem.[26] That's what he buys with his freedom. But that's never been my issue. I've always felt the presence of the living God in the here and now. I don't need to look to the past to find God's fingerprints.

For me, the question was whether or not those fingerprints were left at the scene of a crime.

What will you buy with your freedom?

I'm feeling generous today. Got some new coins jangling in my pocket, my angst is at an ebb… breathing well… and I'm in the mood to buy something. So walk into the candy store, take a look at the shelves. Each theory has amazing *incompleteness-es* built into it. Mystery riddles them all like air in a Three Musketeers bar. None of them captures reality. So read the labels on the wrappers, and find the one that nourishes you best.

Here's a candy bar called "Big Bang." It has nothing in it, yet it spontaneously expands to become a full meal. An effect without cause. Flip the wrapper over, and you'll find it's made by the same company that makes the others. They've just switched logos: this brand is called Nature, rather than God, but the holding company is the same. You'll hear her advertised on PBS from time to time. Conglomerates!

Here's a candy bar named "Genesis." Let's look at the ingredients list: God, a random, wavy sea and a wild wind; an abyss; and an almost suffocating darkness (made up of sugar, cystic fibrosis and BHT added to preserve freshness).

You don't have to view the non-God stuff as physical ingredients if you wish. Just call it the urge to dissipate, to deconstruct. It could look like nothing at all; it could sound like silence or radio static. If you're inclined to physics, call it entropy, another name for a world that keeps wanting to break down. Genes keep breaking down, forgetting how to spell proteins correctly. Societies keep breaking down, forgetting how to protect their weakest members. Churches keep breaking down, forgetting how to help folks survive all the other breakdowns.

This, to me, is the Senseless Sea. It is the experience we have of brokenness and pain.

If you prefer more spiritual terms, a literal use of the word *demonic* is terribly appropriate. Anti-life: the sucking Void that gets into your goodness and tears it apart. Sometimes I've felt *that* in such personal force that it goes beyond metaphor— and the people that regularly feel it that way are quite definite on this point: it doesn't come from God. Ever. To even suggest that God made it is an abomination.

Here's another candy bar named *Ex Nihilo*, or "Out of Nothing" in the Canadian wrapper. It appeals to those with a taste for simpler recipes: it has only one ingredient. No other stuff to worry about! But there are some other important nutrients I won't find here: hope and trust. What an awful price to pay for simplicity.

If I eat this one, when I start to *really, really hurt*, I won't be able to come to God in full confidence and ask for help. Because no matter how you slice it, this candy bar says that God has made my pain. Maybe it's a part of the candy-making process; maybe I'm a quality-control problem; or maybe I'm being "tested, refined, and purified like gold…"

No matter how many synonyms you put on it, God has chosen this path for me. Rather than rescuing me from pain and senselessness, God is plunging me into it for heavenly ineffable purposes. How, then, can I come to God and ask for the end of the fire that's cooking me? It's God's Will; it's…

For My Own Good.
For My Own Good.
For My Own Good.

Just shut up, lowly mortal, and let the Chef cook you until you're done. My ways are not your ways. This hurts me more than it hurts you. Or—to use my favorite euphemism from the dentist's chair—*it's not painful, but you may feel a little pressure.*

Well, I used to eat that candy bar. It works with a modicum of pain. It can even turn some pain around and make it a virtue: *I'm being purified through this, I'm building a better character, etc.* That's where some people are, God bless them. I hope it continues to work.

But somewhere along the line my pain passed over the threshold of tolerability, and suddenly this candy turned sour in my belly. It meant that when I was down on my knees, moaning and wishing that someone would just put a gun to my head and *end this...* I was completely alone. I had no one to turn to.

The only one I had to turn to was the Master Chef who was putting me in the oven.

I can't be alone anymore. I just can't. I need someone with me when I'm down on the floor. The cats help, but I'd like God to be there, too. I need a God who is offended by pain, outraged by it, struggles with it day and night without end.

I will choose an origin that says God weeps at blindness and wants to heal it, aches at the sight of sin and wants to cure it, and howls when children are slain in refugee camps.

I will choose a system that says God is untangling the knots of creation as fast as possible; that the knots are not part of some Master Plan, but what the Master is *Planning Against.*

I'm going to hang out with the Hebrew God of Abraham, Sarah, Isaac, Moses and Christ himself. I will come before a God who calls light out of the suffocating, senseless darkness, not—as the Church sometimes slyly says—a God who made them both.

In the beginning of Creation, when God made heaven and earth, the earth was without form and void, with darkness over the face of the abyss, and a mighty wind that swept over the surface of the waters. God said, "Let there be light," and there was light; and God saw that the light was good, and he separated light from darkness. *(Genesis 1:1–4)*

Listen: my back is aching right now, telling me to lie down. The darkness is inside me, it wants me to stop writing. I have to hurry.

When I encountered an odd little offshoot of theology called "process theology," I sucked it up like a dry sponge hitting water. There I found a vision that started to address my parched existence. It was a vision of God as lure, calling us forward into a world that makes sense: the realm of God, New Jerusalem. This vision says that God has always worked as we see God work today: incrementally. This is God's style.

This is another parable Jesus put before them: "The Realm of Heaven is like a mustard-seed, which a man took and sowed in his field. As a seed, mustard is smaller than any other; but when it has grown it is bigger than any garden-plant; it becomes a tree, big enough for the birds to come and roost in its branches."

(Matthew 13:31–32)

New things don't just pop into existence; they grow out of what has come before. Canyons don't appear at once; a river carves them. Tree leaves come from buds. Forty-year-old tax accountants don't just materialize in an office but start (incredibly) as babies. And babies come from the tiniest of starts, sheltered in a womb that will keep them from destruction.

None of this should be a surprise to us; the only surprise is that we think God got a personality transplant in the distant past. *That's* the weird part.

Process theology says God didn't *make* the world; God is *making* the world. And the implications of that are far-reaching; many familiar doctrines are turned upside down. Some church answers find their fundamental questions unasked.

"Responsibility for sin" takes on a new meaning. It no longer means "who gets the blame" (either us or God). Responsibility does *not* mean that you're to blame for being unfinished. Only a fool would condemn an infant for not knowing how to set the table.

Responsibility takes on the meaning given when a doctor tells a diabetic to be "responsible." That doesn't mean she's to blame for her condition (criminal responsibility); it also doesn't mean that she's *alone* in trying to get better (financial responsibility). But it does mean she's responsible for doing what she can for health, and that she's got the power to help or hinder wellness (responsibility for life).

That's the truth, and we all know it.

Evil truly exists. It is incompleteness and active brokenness springing from incompleteness; the parts that have not yet been put to rights. Evil is still a real choice; our brokenness can cause us to work against God. God doesn't want that. We are called to be light, not agents of the night.

But neither are we to shoulder the blame for the creation of darkness—and neither is God. We are all responsible for *growing beyond it*. We are responsible to heal what we can, and limit the damage of what remains enslaved to the void. This is the proper boundary of human responsibility.

Process theology was, obviously, heavily influenced by Darwin.[27] It describes a creator who is not inimical to the evolutionary process, but author of it. In fact, process is one of the few Christian theologies to absorb Darwin, rather than uncomfortably accommodate him. Most churches have given up their claim to six-day instant creation, yet ironically ground their thinking quite firmly upon its assumptions. Redemption presumes prior completion and a willful fall, in most schemes.

Once you start to really listen to what observation has to say about God's methodology, you find yourself with a different, more patient God. Grace is no longer a fix for the question of *whodunit*. Grace is an entirely logical evaluation of the One Who Is Not Yet Done. A good potter might get frustrated with clay that is too dry and stiff, but doesn't blame the clay for that state; and neither does the potter call the clay wet and continue to work. A good potter gets a sponge and squeezes a little water onto the piece. Patient artistry is the mode of God.

What could be more Christian?

> He also told them this parable: "The Realm of Heaven is like yeast, which a woman worked into a large amount of flour till it was all leavened." *(Matthew 13:33)*

This is a vision that I judge by its fruits. It is congruent with the revelations of God by Christ and natural observation; it resonates with the cross (where the Crowbar God is conspicuously absent); it matches the experience of creation I have felt in my own soul; and it draws me closer to God. It tells me that I am not the damaged creation of a lesser God. It says that our current state will end, that God really does know something about the God-Trade. It says that we're not trapped in a miserable slog back to recover what was lost and cannot last, but heading toward something that has not yet been known.

> As it is written, "Things beyond our sight, sounds beyond our hearing, all that lies beyond our imagination, have been prepared by God for those who love him."
>
> *(1 Corinthians 2:9)*

> No wonder we do not lose heart! Though our outer humanity is in decay, day by day we are inwardly renewed. Our troubles are slight and short-lived in comparison, and their outcome far outweighed in unending glory. Therefore we keep our eyes fixed, not on that which can be seen, but on the things which cannot be seen; for what is seen passes away, and what is unseen is eternal.
>
> For we know that if the earthly frame housing us should be demolished today, we have a building which God has provided—an eternal house, unmade by human hands—in heaven. In this present body we do indeed groan; we yearn to have our heavenly frame put on over this one—in the hope that, being thus clothed, we shall not find ourselves naked...
>
> We therefore never cease to be confident. We know that so long as we are at home in the body we are exiles from the Lord. *(2 Corinthians 4:16–5:3, 5:6)*

I think this vision also gives a little more understanding to the corollary cry: *How long, oh Lord?* You don't put a steeple in the air until the walls are built; one thing has to be built before another. Our consciousness is filled with the perception of that necessary sequence.

We experience being built in rational order. We call that experience "Time." We wait, like the watchman waits for the morning, for the order to be complete. The

Senselessness that God is working against continues to riddle and burden us, but we say with faith that one day the structure will be finished. If some walls cannot go up right now, we can at least hold on to the notion that the builder is working with skill and all possible speed.

"Signs will appear in sun, moon, and stars. Confusion will freeze the earthly nations, who will not know which way to turn from the roar and surge of the sea; men will faint with terror when they see what is overcoming the world; for the celestial powers will be shaken.

"And then they will see the Son of Man coming on a cloud with great power and glory. When all this begins to happen, stand upright and hold your heads high: your liberation is near." *(Luke 21:25–28)*

Process theology—specifically the kind unwrapped by Anna Case-Winters in her remarkable book *God's Power*—was such a blessing to me. I'd been looking for it all my life. It gives me someone to pray to. It lifts up my eyes to look for God again. I can't tell you how important that has been to me over the last two years.

Some might find a feminist theologian and a skeptical physicist an unlikely pair to come down off the Holy Mountain. But I was very glad to see what was engraved on their new tablets; they helped me find a rationale for the hope of the Messiah.

Anna and Stephen, you are both gifts of God to me.

Thinking about Doubt

"And again, the Father does not judge anyone, but has given full jurisdiction to the Son." *(John 5:22)*

"But if anyone hears my words and pays no regard to them, I am not his judge. I have not come to judge the world, but to save the world." *(John 12:47)*

Lutheran theology has a particularly outrageous notion that faith itself is a blessing from God. It came as an extension of the central theme that there is nothing humans can do to earn their salvation. Although it remains in the tradition, this startling assertion seems to excite little interest. In particular, its relationship to evangelization—spreading of the word—is only tepidly mined. Odd, because it can be either a minefield or a goldmine in that regard.

I had never heard this bit of good/bad news until I got to seminary, and was truly offended by it. Hoping to have the matter cleared up for me, I eagerly sopped up the literature that was there, especially the great debate on free will between Luther and Erasmus. I love old Martin, but I thought Erasmus did a little better in the debate. No knockout punches, though, on either side.

The best summary of the outcome is the wonderfully colorful description from the editor of the definitive volume on their clash:

At best, Erasmus prodded Luther into some splendid epigrams and into uttering hermeneutic principles of worth. At the worst, their debate slammed the door on any reconciliation between two great men, and embarrassed their common friends. To use the image of another day, it was a duel in which the two participants got up at crack of dawn, one armed with a rapier, the other with a blunderbuss, where shaking of fists and mutterings usurped the place of battle, and which ended with the two antagonists going their separate ways, undamaged but shaken, and with a frustrating sense of honor ruffled but unsatisfied.[28]

So, once again, no salvation coming from the humans! I was left in the minefield to fend for myself.

The Minefield

Here is the explosive side of Lutheranism: how can you go to people who have no faith, and tell them that God has *done it to them on purpose*—singled them out for lack of faith—yet at the same time will punish them for it?

And what shall be their response? Shall they pray to a God they have no faith in—to plead for faith so they might pray? Do you have the chutzpah to tell them to do that?

For quite some time, I remained outraged by the minefield questions. Organizational loyalty bid me accommodate it, but I just couldn't empathize with another variation on that old theme of God as Crazy Boy, making mud soldiers to smash. By that time, I'd already gotten allergic to such visions.

But then, one day, I realized that as an experiential observation, it matched exactly what my non-church friends were telling me. Seeing the comforts of faith in times of illness and death, they might vaguely wish they had something like that… but it just never worked for them. They listened and tried to understand, but there was no click, no inspiration. It just didn't work for them. I realized, ironically, that every skeptic ought to be an honorary Lutheran. At least it described their experience of the real world.

Yet I could not accept the ramifications streaming out of that notion; so I sat on the fence between the minefield and the goldmine again, torn between theology and experience.

Then I forgot about it, because my own experience started to go to hell in a hand basket. I had plenty of more personal problems with God to work on—and most of them, too, dealt with the vision of God as Crazy Boy.

But when I came back to the question, after many long walks with jesus and friends, I discovered that I'd unintentionally come down off of the fence—and there were no land mines going off! I'd stumbled into consonance between the atheist's experience and the faith statement—my canon—that God is Good.[29] The trick of consonance happens once you change your vision of heaven from a place of reward to a place of healing.

Once you move into that realm, John's notion of a God so real that no lamp or furnace is needed—that God's presence can be physically felt upon your brow—speaks powerfully to the experience of those who wonder why they feel nothing. It says, "One day you will feel my spirit as naturally as a warm August wind." Belief then becomes one of the many healings to take place; and the theodicy issues are at least restored to the normal proportions of other wounds: the cry of "How long, oh Lord?"

Faith is a healing, just as I wait to be healed. Although faith comes from God, God does not inflict doubt and uncertainty upon people, any more than God inflicts us with sickle-cell anemia. I think it is part of the void which will be conquered at the end of Creation, when all things shall be made new.

I realize this inspires cries of blasphemy amongst the faithful. We've gotten so attached to the notion that faith *must* be in "the unseen," that it seems fundamentally wrong. The image of God as trickster, hiding behind the curtain to test our powers of imagination, runs deep in our blood.

We imagine a kind of spiritual Darwinism, wherein God's presence is only hinted at in this world, and those who survive the selection process are then rewarded with a face-to-face encounter with the Grand Riddler himself. Once the weak ones are weeded out, everyone takes off their masks and throws a party.

The fact that we are *untroubled* by such mean-spirited behavior—and *troubled* by the notion that God might not play such games—speaks powerfully about where we stand, doesn't it?

"Faith in the unseen" was never meant as a guiding principle of creation, or a statement of the underlying purpose of this world. It was an expression of hope, that's all. Don't make it into a litmus test, or it will become anti-hope.

"The vineyard owner turned to one of them and said, 'My friend, I am not being unfair to you. You agreed to the usual day's wage, did you not? Take your pay and go home! I've chosen to pay the last man the same as you, but surely I am free to do what I like with my own money. Why be jealous because I am kind?'

"So," Jesus concluded, "will the last be first, and the first last." (Matthew 20:13–16)

jesus, of course, talked about the many benefits of faith. But would you like to hear his final verdict on unfaith?

Christ, they say, forgave the very people who slew him. The murderers were unbelievers—many of them Romans who worshiped foreign gods. All were firmly convinced that his teachings were false, including the leaders of Christ's own church. None of them fulfilled any of the little requirements we attach to God's love. They committed the most heinous crime in their power, and they were unbaptized, uncommuned and *completely unrepentant.* In view of all the prerequisites to salvation added by the Church, many Christians would find them the most likely candidates for hell in human history. Yet their victim pronounced forgiveness upon their heads, based upon one flimsy reason: ignorance.

Jesus said, "Father, forgive them; they do not know what they are doing."
(Luke 23:34)

They just didn't know any better, that's all. They heard the Gospel (even better than we), they rejected it for various personal reasons; and Christ found that as forgivable as any other human condition. But that, evidently, is a cross that's just too hard for believers to bear.

The Goldmine

Rather than the Grand Riddler, we could tell people about the Creator who:
• Loves people enough to save them beyond their ability to save themselves.
• Knows the deep circumstances that create doubt and lack of faith.
• Understands the difference between evil and inquiry.
That's the deity jesus portrayed, to the very end.

But why evangelize, if it doesn't leverage people into New Jerusalem?

Because the reward of faith is on *earth,* not in heaven. Those that receive it will find strength and endurance for their other wounds—as Christ says, faith makes you well. That's reason enough, isn't it?

We do it for the reason we pursue all healing acts; because we're called to be healers. And if the soil is rocky and the seed dies, this is no more of a judgment on a person than cancer or Tourette's syndrome. It is yet another expression of the Not Yet: the waiting for healing that we all endure.

Perhaps part of our responsibility as believers is to spread that healing more effectively: to create an environment that is more hospitable to postmodern disbelief. A starting point would be to honor skepticism as a positive faith statement, as it truly is. It is an expression of faith in Creation being so *well-founded* that it doesn't even need a founder. What a powerful testimonial to the work of God that is!

Can we not honor such faith, even as we respectfully disagree with the conclusion? Can't we see it as a useful critique of our own occasional temptation to view Creation as a hopeless invalid, always needing miraculous props? And can't we give our own testimony with patience and love, understanding that doubt may be, for some folks, a fact of their creation as much as cystic fibrosis is a fact of mine?

The New Testament writings express numerous visions of inclusive unity—all meant to embrace greater diversity than what the writer's previous experiences of unity had embraced. For example, in the Gospels Jesus is recorded as the one who broke down boundaries between those included and those excluded—unclean, Gentiles, sinners, tax collectors. Paul includes Gentiles in his vision of a time when "Every knee shall bow and every tongue confess that Jesus Christ is Lord." The author of Ephesians celebrates God's act in Jesus, which creates out of Jews and Gentiles "one new humanity." Luke cites the prophecy that "All flesh will behold the salvation of God" and describes the Christian mission to "the ends of the earth." The author of Revelation depicts the worship of God by people from "every tribe, tongue, and people" uniting in one glorious hymn to God and to the lamb.

Each of these writers sought to embrace great diversity in a broad vision of unity. Each of these visions of unity is predicated on allegiance to Jesus as the great unifying force that holds diversity together. Such a commitment to inclusivity provides the impetus to keep pushing out the boundaries of unity to include greater and greater diversity.[30]

What if God was still moving over the face of the waters, still uncovering new land? Wouldn't you just *hate* it?

Delta

Come on.
Come on.

Sometimes my body runs out of insulin, and my blood sugar starts to soar, even though I haven't eaten anything. It's a stress response. Dr. Wilson warned me about it. Most diabetics have to worry about it only when they do exercise, but my whole life is exercise, now. Breathing is work, walking is work. When my infections are pounding me, my heart stumbles and whams. And percussion therapy is like running a mile—having someone play drums on your chest is a lot of work, even if you're only playing the part of the drum.

Your body, see, responds to exercise by calling for energy reserves. Fat. The fat is turned into sugar and reenters the bloodstream. That's why you jog to lose weight. But if you have absolutely no insulin at all, the cells can't pull sugar out of your blood. The fat is sacrificed for no purpose; you continue to run out of fuel, and your sugars go higher and higher while your body waits for the payoff to all this fat-burning. It doesn't know what's going on. It keeps eating more and more fat, wondering how come it's starving. Even worse, high blood sugar is more stress on the body. More "exercise" on the system, more fat-burning. Feedback. Your blood sugars walk a spiral staircase into orbit.

It takes me a while to figure out what's happening. It's just a gradual sensation of therapy taking a bad turn, of things not working as well. Then it starts to really hurt. Once I *do* finally guess what's happening, I'm in for a harrowing ride. It takes hours for the insulin shot to kick in. I rocket away from earth fast, waiting for the insulin to pull me down.

How long? Two to four hours before maximum dose, one hour before you start to feel it. It's a curve. I can draw it in my head. I know these curves in my heart, body and soul. I *feel* them. The feeling is much worse than the usual kind of high sugar readings, which mostly make me sleepy. I don't know why; maybe it's the starvation. It's wrenching to have one part of your body starve while the other feels the effects of gluttony. Two sins doth not make a right.

How to avoid the moon-shot? I don't know. I can't take insulin before every therapy session: *most* of the time that would drive my sugar into the ground instead, which is even worse. Low sugars can kill you right away.

Normal diabetics time their exercise with their insulin program, but I can't time my therapy to coincide with my insulin; breathing isn't yet optional for my kind, and sometimes the only thing that lets me breathe is a beating. I'm not going to hold my breath until lunchtime.

I also don't know how well the therapy is going to go. Sometimes I'll dislodge a plug; then oxygen pours into my lungs, and my insulin burns like gas on grill. But if the mucous plug stays in, my insulin smolders like warm charcoal. Argh!

You know what I need? I need a meter telling me how much insulin is left, so I can see what's happening. Somebody invent one, please. You will have my undying gratitude. Install it under my wrist, where a watchband goes. I feel like half a machine anyway. I may as well get some better instrumentation, right? Let's build this cyborg better!

First time the sky-cycle happened, I didn't know what was going on. It was a Sunday and I was supposed to be up on the hill with jesus. That was the day I knew my service days were done. I just couldn't be dependable anymore.

Martha went, because she was the Sunday School department. I thought I'd be O.K. alone. But then the wild ride began. I tried calling four times, but kept getting the answering machine. There I was, shooting away from the ground, and I didn't know what to do. I started to keep this journal for distraction.

Yep, that's how this foolishness started.

Several hours later, I remembered what Dr. Wilson had said about exercise, and made the mental connection. I took my sugar reading, and the meter just said "Hi." It wasn't being friendly; it meant my sugar levels were so far up it couldn't count them anymore. Yikes.

Look, there he goes! The main booster has detached... It should really say goodbye in that instance, I think.

Now I know what's going on, at least. Take the insulin at first indication, and wait for two hours. Hold on. Keep your mind busy. Write. Yeah. That's what I'm doing right now.

I'm not making this up. Wish I was. Wish I wasn't running out of time, too. Wouldn't it be wonderful if this were fiction? Wouldn't it be great if the author got up, wiped the fake blood off his chest and went on to write another forty books?

Don't think so.

All flesh is grass
And burning mist
Fading fast the flower is missed by
None so long as it might have wished

We hold the stem for but a day
And then we pass
To brighter roses and fresher plants
Searching for scents of
Things to come
We pursue the EverNew and EverYoung
Like restless, roaming cats
Nibbling on blades of new-sprung grass
While dreaming
Always
Of the EverLast.

Writing, programming, poetry, music, theology… projects of distraction and release, cries and fiddly stuff. Keep going, find something new to concentrate on. I've always retreated when my body started to betray me. Cramps and enemas were a big part of my preadolescence. It was a miserable time. I'd disassociate myself from my body, go into a mental other-world: body's hurting, ugly things happening, dive, dive, dive. Pull the hatch behind you and wait for it to blow over. Think about fusion… or starting a cool restaurant… Or wouldn't it be great to have a boat that you could just sail away in? It'd be a hundred feet long with everything you wanted, but you could be free…

Is it done yet?

No.

What about a *flying* boat…

Come on, come on. Work!

I hate this.

It's hard to know how much insulin to give yourself, because you're going to be eating your own flesh for at least an hour. While the system is out of balance, your food is your own fat, and you can't stop eating. Self-cannibalism.

Where's the chart for that? What's my body's exchange value, oh Dietitians of the Universe? Am I two breads and a fruit? Well, guess. Add 50 percent to the normal dose. End the crisis. If you take too much, you can always eat candy later.

It feels awful. Not as soul-wrenching as intestinal blockage—that's more like a racing-car blur of constant, maximum pain. This is more like a gnawing… It's hard to describe. This is a moan, the other is a yell. How many words do the Eskimos have for snow? Don't remember. Looked it up in the encyclopedia, but they didn't say. It's probably apocryphal, anyway.

Drying out, now. My body's water is trying to dilute the sugar in my blood before it gets toxic. Dried phlegm don't breathe. More stress: panting, choking.

Cycles within cycles. Orbits. Going into space.

Have some more water.

Martha says not to use diet drinks: keep it clean. I hate clear water, but alright.
O.K.
O.K.
Come on, come on.

It just became a habit, diving inside. It paid off in a good career. I had a hyper-developed imagination. Even in the video game industry, people would look at my ideas and say, "Well, *that's* esoteric." Sometimes they even said it with a smile.

I'll never forget my first Consumer Electronics Show. I spent day after day trying to explain my game to confused distributors in business suits.

First the wizard plants these trees, see, then he takes the trees off to assault the den of spider eggs…

Companies did not come to me to make the two hundredth conversion of the latest hit. They didn't come to me for hits at all. I was the computer equivalent of an art-folk singer: couldn't write a pop hit if my life depended on it. Sometimes I'd try to be more mainstream, but you know, this kid was just always a little too warped.

When I decided to become a pastor, my teaching-parish supervisor told me the same thing. Probably just as well that I bombed out. The Council never would have understood. First time I suggested meeting out on the lawn they'd have had my hide.

—But don't you miss the trees, when you're in church? Don't you think Church is a subset of Creation, instead of the other way around?

Or is it just me?—

Programming is a very internal mind game; it's five-dimensional chess played solitaire. That's why the geeks that play it are so uncomfortable around people. We just spend too much time spelunking in our own caverns.

I spent 12-to 16-hour days for months on end without a break, bolstered by lots of junk food and caffeine. It was the norm, nothing special. I was a state-of-the-art technological hermit.

Eating is something programmers do to make their stomachs shut up. Our body is the enemy, always dragging us back to the physical world. It's no mistake we gave the world "virtual reality"; it's every techno-monk's longing. We *hate* the demands of reality impinging on our digital dreaming. Another point in my favor. I was already very practiced, by the age of twelve, at viewing my body as the enemy. I could play that game very well.

Somewhere in my genes, right next to the misspelled ion channel, it said "Computer Game Designer." It was my destiny.

What a shame! Always staying inside, shutting out the world. I ignored Martha way too much. She saw the back of my head for the first ten years of our marriage. I'd spend my time differently now—but what are you going to do? No one lives their life as if they're mortal. But then, when you're dying, no one looks back and says, "My God, I wish I'd spent more time at the office."

Dear God, it's easing.

I tried a new trick this time. Ate a handful of cereal and a tomato, just to let my body know food was on its way: a false signal to turn off the fat-sacrifice. I got the idea from an article about dieting. They recommended having something acidic at the start of your meal, to fake out your system. Counterintuitive, but I think it may actually work. I did another check: 269. It doesn't hurry the insulin up, but at least I avoided the 400s. Only 45 minutes before the insulin peaks, and I'm already coming back down. Cool.

Thank you, thank you, thank you!

Sometimes thinking is more than distraction. Sometimes it's survival.

My lungs are letting the oxygen back in. Here comes the endorphin rush. It starts with waves of goose bumps running down my arms, then turns into chills running down my back. I shiver as if I've been dropped in a cool bath. Then... ecstasy, the rebound from torment. Glorious, incredible.

When the pain cuts off, you suddenly find out how many natural opiates your brain was pumping out. You didn't know it at the time, because it was barely keeping up—but when the crisis ends you go sailing off on painkiller inertia.

Imagine a rattling, thundering ride, like John Glenn in *The Right Stuff*. Everything's shaking one second, and then the next second there's nothing but a light sound of the wind.

woosh - ahhhhhh. Like that.

Isn't the brain amazing? Cocaine is just an analogue of what your brain *does for itself* under high stress!

There go the calves, then the shins. Knots come out of my back in random bursts. Click: the water comes back to my system like a thrown switch. My nose runs, my stomach comes out of stasis. My fingers slowly unbend, my toes unbend. I crack my knuckles, and every movement of my feet makes snapping sounds. The muscle tension had driven all of my joints all deep into their sockets. Pop, pop. My thighs, ah. I can feel the inner tendon ease.

Cool breeze, the sound of a parachute...

Thirty minutes to go, Houston. We have acquired the landing site on our instruments; awaiting visuals.

God's Page

Haven't I
Ended every drought
With rain?
I don't know what to do
This frustrated bellow in my throat
Unheard
I have met every fear with
Real bread
And wine from the west
Poured over your
Stubborn head and yet
You never stop
To remember.
You are making me old
When I should be young
This world is green
And new
Can't you stop and see?
Have you forgotten
The one I made for you
And you for her
The way you filled each other
Like lock and key
She the presence
For your absence
You the confidence
For her timidity?
The way silence and raucous laughter
Came together
To make quiet jokes
And long Saturdays?

Hamsterquinn stories and
Watercolor hearts
Still pinned to your wall
Where you look at them and grin...
That dream house you
Never thought you'd have
Nuthouse I'd call it not a square angle
In the place but I built it for you
Anyway
Do you remember
The time your furnace blew
And a game dead for three years
Paid for it
With a good dinner to spare?

I tried to get it close
Enough so you
Couldn't ignore the message.

And when you most needed to serve
I used it
And when you most needed to stop
I stopped it.

I built a school of angels for you
In Chicago
And gave you
Cats.

The glowing shield in the sky
That frozen night;
The rain that stopped;
The dreams that came
When you'd lost all posts;
The words dropped
On other helpful tongues;
And twenty-three extra miles
On a very leaky boat.

I've moved Heaven and Earth
For you

And you forget
So fast.

I don't know how
To get through

You're not
The only one
Screaming.

Zeta

Wealth is also a poor predictor of happiness. People have not become happier as their cultures have become more affluent... even very rich people—those surveyed among Forbes Magazine's 100 wealthiest Americans—are only slightly happier than average Americans... Indeed, in most nations the correlation between income and happiness is negligible—only in the poorest countries, such as Bangladesh and India, is income a good measure of emotional well-being.[31]

"I don't know why he bothers with them," Judas grumbles.

"They're people, too," Philip says, reaching for the orange marmalade.

"Who says?"

I smile.

We are sitting at an oh-so-classy table in the breakfast room of the *Pierre' La Something or Other,* an incredibly classy establishment in a mega-classy hotel called *The Centurion.*

The oh-so table is classy because the proportions are absurd: it is about the size of a plant stand, no more. In the oh-so world you must go very big or small to be known as such. This is the small version, very fashionable right now.

Our dishes balance precariously about the edges. Our knees keep knocking together. A thimble of orange juice costs as much as an entire orange tree, and the steaks are postage-stamp horrors, covered with a darling little herb sauce.

Oh-so, very oh-so.

The exquisiteness of it all seems lost on my companions. They munch unhappily on the bread, which is all they can afford or recognize, and look anxiously at the table near the veranda. There, jesus is listening to an eager young prince, who is waving his arms expressively, and jabbing the air to punctuate important points. jesus is sipping water, the prince is having a full meal. We all want to get back outside as quickly as possible. Everybody groaned when we saw the prince's order arrive.

I am no more comfortable than anybody else, but I am, at least, familiar with the sensation. God blessed me with an incredible range of experiences while doing video games. A few of those experiences landed me in places that were so above my station that I couldn't even identify all the bathroom fixtures. ("It's a bidet," my wife laughed over the phone.)

So how much did you make in video games, Nathaniel? Tell the truth, now. It's part of your context, heh-heh.

Did you know, I saw a poll that indicated that we are more willing to discuss our marital problems with strangers than reveal our incomes? If we're so comfortable with the current state of capitalism in the free world, why is everyone acting so ashamed?

And why is there such a resurgence of interest in vampire stories?

I know: same question.

O.K. Truth-telling numbers.

I saw my income swing between $600 to $100,000 a year. I had a few years where I paid more in taxes than the average American grossed. Honestly, I was embarrassed by it. I wasn't even doing anything productive, just killing people's time, rotting their brains.

We had one of those Christian Children's Fund things going, where you sponsor a child for $25 a month. Our child's father was a fisherman in one of the poorest communities in one of the poorest countries in South America. Whenever I wrote to Alex, I never quite figured out how to explain what it was I *did* for a living. The contrast was just far too absurd to make sense. Even my *career* turned into a theodicy issue!

Currently, we're counting our pennies again. I went to seminary, the royalty payments ran out some time ago, and I'm too sick to work. That isn't a great way to improve your bank balance—especially when you have no medical coverage. I spent close to $9,000 last year on body maintenance, and the boiler still needs replacing. Thank God we saved our Monopoly money!

But you want to hear something very weird? The tension level, economically speaking, has stayed about the same. You can either worry about your bills, or you can worry about your money. You can worry about being disabled, or you can worry about the pressures of your job. Anxiety expands, like a noxious gas, to fill the volume available to it.

"For life is more than an abundance of possessions." *(Luke 12:15b)*

We don't really believe that, do we?

The social scientists may as well save their breath. Luke already tried telling us, but it's just one of those things you have to find out for yourself.

Judas is singing the Magnificat, now. He sings it quietly, but the melody carries. jesus looks momentarily at us, his ear catching the familiar strains. The song has a stinging accusation in it coming from Judas' tongue, but jesus' face betrays no reaction: his face is as steady as a patrolman's.

"He has brought down the rulers from their thrones, but has lifted up the lowly," Judas sings. "He has filled the hungry with good things, but has sent the rich away empty."

Peter looks over the rich food sitting in front of the young man, grunts and gnaws on another hunk of bread. He, like several of the others, has horny-monk syndrome when it comes to financial matters. Several times he has reminded jesus that he's left all he had to follow him—he wants that sacrifice *noticed*—so Judas' taunt lands on fertile ground.

"True enough," Peter nods. "I don't see *him* hurting for food." Crumbs spill from his mouth to the pure linen below him.

He casts his eyes down at them, studying them quietly. Jealousy is taking root, blossoming in his eyes, spreading its leaves into his hands. He suppresses a surge of anger, flicks the crumbs away. His swipe is more forceful than necessary; our water glasses clink together.

"Come on, now," Philip says, "you know that's not being fair. He's a child of God, too, isn't he?"

"I'd say if he is, he's already come into his inheritance," Judas replies dryly. "As jesus said, *Woe to you who are rich, for you have already received your comfort. Woe to you who are well fed now, for you will go hungry.* That's the plan for the Kingdom of Heaven. Those that have been waiting get theirs, and the ones who have been keeping it from them go up against the wall."

"That's right," Peter agrees. "Didn't he say not to store up treasures on earth, but to store up treasures in heaven?"

Judas nods wisely. "Whenever I've heard the Master," he adds, "he's been blessing the poor, and heaping curses on the rich. I can't see why he's messing with them now." He pushes his chair back from the table, his eyes glittering with something that looks very wounded and betrayed.

"Was that all just talk, when he was preaching to a bunch of fishermen and burnouts? What's he telling Mr. Big Shot, I wonder?" He waves his head derisively toward jesus' table. "Do they get their own little pep talk?"

This is getting dangerous-sounding to Philip. "Wait a minute. You don't know what they're talking about. Don't go making up your own conversations, Judas, and then start blaming jesus for them."

"I'm not saying anything about that," Judas sniffs. "Just wondering what's going on, that's all."

The waiter comes to our table with the check. Peter looks at it and his eyes bug out. "For bread and water?" he says, shocked. He passes the bill to Philip, amazed.

Philip's eyebrows shoot up. "That's steep," he agrees. He whistles and lays the check back down.

"You've got the money, Judas."

Judas looks at the total, grunts, and picks up as many jelly packets as he can find off the table. "I reckon we paid for these, at least," he says. He stuffs them in his purse and stands up. "They'll come in handy, maybe, when we're out wandering with Rabbi You-Feed-Them."

Peter laughs, then cuts it short when Philip looks displeased.

Judas saunters over to the register to pay the bill. While he waits for the cashier he pulls a few chocolate mints out of a plexiglass holder and stuffs them in his pocket.

Break their teeth in their mouths, God.

Break their jaws, the unbelievers!

May they melt, may they vanish like water. May they wither like grass in a busy road… or like a still-born that never even sees the sun! Root them up like a thornbush before they even know what is happening to them; clear them away like weeds!

The righteous shall rejoice to be avenged, to bathe their feet in the blood of the wicked.

Then everyone will say, "There is, after all, a reward for the righteous; there really is a God that judges on earth!" *(Psalm 58:6–11)*

"Sometimes," Philip says, "I wonder why Judas tags along. Everything seems to be about power and revenge for him. Do you remember when James and John wanted to call for fire from heaven to burn the Samaritans? I thought Judas was going to have a baby when jesus rebuked them."

"James and John didn't look too happy, either," I remind him. "We've all got a little retribution lurking in our souls."

"Yes," Philip says with a worried look, "but Judas has that suit in aces."

Peter waves his hand impatiently.

"I think you're missing Judas' point, Philip. It's a good one. Why is jesus courting the fat cats when he's been cursing them to us? *Ouai* is not a light word, you know."

Philip shrugs. "I've heard it used as an expression of pain, too," he says. "And sorrow. It doesn't always mean *damn*."

"You heard how he said it."

Philip tilts his head to the side, partially conceding the point. "Well, regardless, jesus is a healer. You've seen him work! I don't think he's going to be different, no matter who he's talking to."

"You can hardly call his words to the ruling class healing."

Philip leans across the table. His impatience with Peter finally blooms fullflower—it takes a long time for Philip to get to that point, but it can happen.

"You've got no right to be that dense, Peter. Andrew's told me about your Dad."

Peter's mouth tightens into a hard, thin line. The one thing he does *not* want to talk about is his own background. He gets furious with his younger brother for blabbing about it. If he could, he'd lock up his past into a box and heave it into the sea.

"So?" he says, stiffly.

"What was it that got your Dad to the A.A. meetings?"

"I don't see the point behind rehashing—"

"—Intervention, Peter. Your whole family got together and nailed him. You told him how he was screwing up everybody he loved. You laid all the *ouai* you'd ever experienced right at his feet to stare at. You told him that if he didn't stop hurting himself and everybody else, you would all walk out on him."

"Thank you very much for reminding me," Peter says. "I guess I haven't had my nose rubbed in it for a while."

"Oh, come off it, Peter!" Philip snaps. "I'm not trying to make you feel bad; I'm trying to make you think. Were you glad when your Dad got help?"

"Yes."

"Was it healing for him? For the family?"

"Things got better, but they were never perfect."

"I'm not asking you if things were perfect; I'm asking you if hard words can be healing words."

Peter's eyes turn down. "O.K.," he says. "Yes, they can."

"Some can't handle money any better than an alcoholic handles liquor, right?"

"Right," Peter says, wincing.

"And their binging hurts others," I chime in, intrigued.

"O.K., O.K., I get the point," Peter says irritably. "Can we stop now?"

Judas returns to our table and passes out toothpicks. He's got enough to pick the teeth of an army. He doesn't seem to notice the smoldering tension at the table.

"I'm ready for the next five thousand," he grins, waving them at Peter's face. "—hey, he's done."

He nods toward jesus, who is sadly getting up from his chair. The rich young member of the ruling class has already disappeared, his grand breakfast barely eaten.

"Guess the pledge drive failed," Judas says, with minimal sorrow. "I wonder if we can get a doggie bag to stuff that omelet in." He wanders off to catch a waiter's arm.

Come, all who are thirsty; come here to the water! Come, you poor, hungry people; come have some of my corn. Buy wine and milk without money, without price.

Why spend money on what is not bread? Why work hard for that which does not satisfy?

Listen to me, and you will have good food to eat. Listen, and you will have the bounty of the land. Listen closely. I will make a pact with you: the same faithful love I promised to David. King David was a leader and commander of the people, and I made him my witness to the nations, to all the races of the world. Look: you shall summon nations you never knew, and they shall come running to you because your glory rests in the Lord your God, the Holy One of Israel. (Isaiah 55:1–5)

jesus comes over to stand by Peter. "How hard it is for them," he says, looking old. "He lacked only one thing." Peter looks surprised, but jesus doesn't react. "Sometimes," he adds, "I think it's easier to lead a camel through the eye of a needle than to lead a rich person to God."

Philip never really had more than the rest of us, but he's a lot better at counting his own blessings. His eyes widen at jesus' words. "Then can anyone be saved?" he asks, dismayed.

jesus gives him a rueful look. "By the efforts of man, I suppose not. But by the efforts of God…"

He looks off toward the veranda, where his prior host is conferring with a colleague. "Well, anything is possible," he says, thoughtfully.

"We've given up everything," Peter reminds him. "I gave up my family, my birthright, my trade, everything."

"Yes, I know," jesus smiles. He puts his hands on his shoulder. "I know what you walked away from." He kneads the tension out of Peter's shoulders. His skilled hands find the last leaves of the tree Judas watered and plucks them out with easy care. "You will have family, Peter. More than you can count. I will make you the foundation of a great house; a house that will fill the earth. And later on, I will bring you into a mansion with many rooms, where the light is healing. You will arrive exhausted, and you will find a bed; naked, and be robed. And when you're ready, you will be brought to the banquet hall, where you will feast with all you thought you'd lost—and more than you'd ever dreamed of."

Peter closes his eyes and tilts his head back, giving himself up to jesus' hands. He almost groans.

"Will I stop hurting?" he asks. It comes out like a quiet, anxious prayer, startling me. I guess I've been so busy being hurt by him, I've forgotten his own pains.

"Do you remember cutting new teeth?" jesus asks. "How, as a child, your bleeding gums were the focal point of the world? Or do you remember how you fought with your sister, anxious over a new toy? Your suffering will heal like that. It will be like growing up, that's all.

"When you come home to stand before God, it will be like being born all over again. You will look back with a new perspective, and the past will no longer have a hold on you. I'm going to show you how to come into that spot, out of the womb's darkness. We're going to stand in the full light of God together. I'll be your midwife."

Peter nods, relieved more by his touch than his words. He seems to have become almost drowsy.

"I don't care how it happens anymore," he says wearily. "As long as *you* do it."

> You shall go out with joy
> and be led in peace.
> Your mountains and hills
> shall burst into song before you;
> the wild trees will clap their hands!
> Pine trees will replace your thorns,
> and myrtle will chase away your briars.
> All this will be for the Lord's great name,
> an imperishable sign for all time.
> *(Isaiah 55:12–13)*

Eta

She has learned to be so cool that she barely exists anymore. Her words are tentative probes peppered with *you know, like,* and eye-rolls that indicate she doesn't buy anything, it's all a game. The superficial conversation of a stranger at a party has moved inside, overcome her soul. People quickly hand her off and escape, weary of endless foam without the beer.

He is a failure, a washout. Tried to build a tower, but he didn't count the bricks ahead of time, and that's not how the realm is made. The few walls he got up are crumbling—see, the rain is washing it away already. Fool!

Stay, jesus says, *and talk.*

So he does, out of habit to the Master's voice. He's like an arthritic old dog, still coming to the Victrola. He limps, wheezes and can't play fetch anymore, he's a hopeless old idiot. But he just can't stop.

The Broken Church meets the Empty Conversation.

Ten minutes go by. Nothing but foam. *You're not all that busy,* jesus chuckles. *We taught you better than that.*

O.K....

Fifteen minutes. A year's loss comes tentatively forward. The traumas of life, still not over, and not too many people to share it with. But she shares them now, with this weary ruin slumped over with tubes and life-support machinery. Not the most inviting companion, I would think, but when God sends a buzzard you don't hold out for doves.

How long ago, he asks?

She tells him.

That long? And it's still this fresh and unexpressed?

He suddenly wants to cry.

She should have had this conversation before; she should have a healing community. But they usually insist that she buy before she try—sign on to mysterious words and alien concepts as soon as she enter. She's not that easy.

Here's an alien concept for you: The Church is willing to provide food and shelter without subscription. It feels the call to minister so strongly that it wades into the street with life in its hand, rather than a pamphlet. Its witness is its action, not words. The people that do this are not embarrassed by their faith; but they will let it speak through their lives. They are living letters of Christ, written for you, and you, and you. And it works. They know this.

They know if they forced these lost ones to sign on, they would stay lost. Their wounds would keep them in the wild. So they hold out simple bread, and the birds come. The spirit fetches them, as it promised.

It's not that hard.

It saves lives.

Here's a mysterious word for you: The Church does not meet spiritual and social needs with the same commitment. Where are the churches with ears? Where is the simple service with no creeds and confessions?

Imagine a place where people could experience the healing love of Christ without subscription. Imagine a place that didn't make you get up and say things you didn't believe.

There is a church I know of that does an evening service called Compline, one of the great services of the world. The room is dark and people are safe; they come and hear. The psalms and prayers lift up to heaven, and they breathe them in like incense. There is no argument of force here, but one of peace. It is a balm to modern life. But then they go out again, into a dark world. What if they could stay?

Imagine a shared community of believers and doubters; call it the Church of St. Thomas. "Come," it would say, "press your fingers into this wound. Approach this flesh without fear. I will be quiet and let you touch." The liturgy would be based on the Psalms and humble prayers; music would come from willing volunteers. No one would ever be manipulated or pressured to say a word.

Perhaps there is a homily, but it's different in scope. It's one person talking about getting through life, and what's been helpful. The "I" overcomes the often erroneous assumption of "we." Texts are brought in if they fit, but the point of this is to hear an honest person talk about life, that's all. We don't get too much honesty in this world. That would be a ministry in itself.

This Child of Light is not a searchlight aimed at the pews, but a candle held in trembling hands. A model is shown: how to walk toward light and life in darkness; how to search, how to struggle with God, how to live amongst shadows without being overcome. A premium is placed on not having all the answers, on admitting one's own struggles.

When they look at texts that show rage, hate and broken understandings of the divine, they talk about the ungodly elements in a matter-of-fact, uncondemning way. They are not made anxious by traces of humanity; neither are they completely credulous with all words, wherever they're found.

Perhaps even a doubter speaks without rebuttal. Her words are followed by a Psalm that likewise struggles. Imagine the power of sitting in a Church that had that kind of quiet confidence! What strength do these people have, to be so resilient in the face of honest life?

Afterward, there is an open table of cookies and coffee, and a lounge of conversation with incandescent lights, never mind the cold energy savers. The people chat; they are friends. Some of them have committed themselves to listening ministries and trained for it. The community stays open. They watch and listen for the hurts that wander in. They are not fixers, but supporters.

Am I dreaming? No, I'm feeling convicted. We have shelters for the homeless. Where are the shelters for the friendless? Where are the simple Christian churches for our increasing legions of cut-loose and drifting souls?

I'm not talking about social ministries or crisis counseling; I'm not talking about "doing to" but "being with"; I'm suggesting reforming our very own homes to be open houses. It's the ultimate respect and sign of love, to let the "unwashed" into your own home. It's something you might find the Master doing.

The great outreach efforts of our time, the new Mega-Growth churches, are very loud and brassy. They preach and dance well. But where is the listening place, the place that seeks to know you before it changes you? Where is the place that is unanxious about questions and estrangement—so graceful that it admits to its own?

Tongues are important, and I see plenty of them. But where are the ears of the body? We are a strange beast indeed, with a thousand mouths.

The fact that we have not built churches with ears all over this lonely land tells me something about our own beliefs. It tells me that we, too, think only bread, water and shelter are important. We number as the world numbers, no matter what our rhetoric.

We don't think emotional and spiritual support are on God's map for the world—only for the select few who can stand up, stand up for jesus.

Do you see the need? jesus asks. *Do you see what I see?*

Yes, Lord, I ache. *But what can this ruin do?*

Speak what I see, he says.

The empty conversation ended some time ago; now the real one does, too. Time to go. She leaves a little less foamy; he leaves a little less eroded. I see a cup with some wine in it, a partially rebuilt wall. Nothing extraordinary, just a little less void in the world. Miracles are often small.

Incremental.

"I am the good shepherd; I know my sheep and my sheep know me—just as the Father knows me and I know the Father. I lay down my life for the sheep.

"But there are other sheep of mine, sheep not from this fold, that I must bring in; and they, too, will listen to my voice. Then there will be one flock, and one shepherd."

(John 10:14–16)

Theta

If hard words are healing, we all had a good dose of healing waiting for us that week.

A Pharisee invited Jesus to a meal. He came in and immediately took his place for the meal, surprising the Pharisee, because he had not washed up first. But the Lord said to him, "You Pharisees! You clean the outside of cup and plate, but inside you there is nothing but greed and wickedness. How foolish! Did not the one who made the outside make the inside, too? Give what is inside your cups to the poor, and then everything of yours will be clean.

"You pitiful Pharisees! You pay tithes of mint and rue and every garden-herb, yet you take no care for justice and the love of God. It is these things you need to practice, without neglecting the rest.

"You are to be pitied! You love the most important seats in the synagogues and the most respectful greetings in the marketplace. How sad! You are like unmarked graves, giving no warning to unsuspecting pedestrians, no clue as to the nature of the ground they tread."

In reply one of the lawyers said, "Master, when you talk like this, you insult us, too."

Jesus rejoined: "Yes, you're just as pitiful, aren't you? You load people down with unfair burdens, and lift not a finger to help carry them. You build the tombs of the prophets your fathers murdered, and so show that you approve of what they did. They commit the murders, and you provide the tombs!

"This is why the Wisdom of God said, 'I will send them prophets and messengers; and some of these they will persecute and kill,' as they always have—so that this generation will have to answer for it, every prophet slain since the beginning of their world; from the blood of Abel to the blood of Zechariah, who perished between the altar and the sanctuary. I warn you, this generation will have to answer for it!

"You sad, pitiful experts! You stole the key of knowledge, yet you did not use it yourselves—and those who were on their way in, you stopped."

After he left the house, the lawyers and Pharisees began to assail him fiercely and ply him with endless questions, hoping to trap him with a careless answer.

(Luke 11:37–54)

Then he got after me for tearing into Andrew at McDonald's.

This is how it started:

I'd gone off to take my insulin in the bathroom, and Andy had gone with me, not for the usual reasons but because he was worried about the way I was walking. It was another of my sluggy days, and even my oxygen seemed like syrup—if I was going to name the days of the week, "Turgid" would definitely be one of them—so I oozed into the bathroom like day-old bacon grease. The facilities, as usual, looked like they'd been cleaned by minimum-wage teenagers—public washrooms are a poor mix with sterile medical equipment—so I ripped a bunch of paper towels out of the dispenser and lined the sink, then balanced my pack on the narrow lip and unzipped it. You have to be careful with these little sinks: I've spilled everything before, and there's nothing like picking your medicine off a muddy floor to put you in a special mood.

I got everything ready, all the little bottles, wipes and testing equipment, and waited.

And waited.

When Andrew finally exhausted the obvious reasons for hanging around, he took his time washing his hands, then spent three button presses on the dryer. Then he put his hands in his pockets, leaned against the wall and watched me with his sad-puppy eyes. I *hate* sad-puppy eyes. Especially when they're looking at me; I feel like they're showing me how much distress I'm causing by being alive.

That's when I tore into him. I don't think I actually hit him.

"There's no reason to punish people just because they're worried about you," jesus said, when he broke us up.

"He makes me crazy," I repeated.

"He didn't make you anything, Nathaniel. You make yourself crazy. Stop pretending the world is trying to provoke you; the thorn is in your side, not someone else's hand."

"But he doesn't have to make it worse by being so—"

"—You are so wrapped up in how everybody else thinks about your illness," jesus interrupted, "it's a wonder you've got time to be sick. Why did you go in the bathroom, anyway? You're wearing shorts. You could have given yourself your shot in the leg."

I fumed. "I just don't want people to—"

"—do you have any idea how many people in that restaurant would have cared? Stop thinking the whole world revolves around you, Nathaniel. People are not watching you as intently as you think they are. *You* are the one feeling ashamed, and *you* are the one you're trying to hide from in dirty bathrooms. Grow up!"

Then he rounded on Andrew.

"And what did you think you were doing? You know Nathaniel's a jerk when it comes to his body."

"I just—"

"—you just wanted to let him know you cared. Did it work?"

Andrew looked miserable.

"Of course not. Andy, that boy's got enough stripped gears to fill three crankcases, and *you know it.* If you want to show you care, watch Philip, O.K.? He knows how to behave around broken heads—and what were you doing, letting him run all over you like that?"

"I didn't know what to do."

"Of course you did. You just didn't want to do it. Why not?"

"We're supposed to be gentle shepherds."

"A good shepherd is gentle with sheep," he said, casting an angry eye in my direction, "not wolves."

"But you said we should turn the other—"

"How much cheek-turning did you see me do with our last host?"

"Um…" He thought about it for a moment, then looked helpless. "Now I'm confused."

"Good," jesus said. "Maybe you'll start paying attention to what's going on, and stop trying to follow one recipe."

"But *you* gave me the recipe," Andrew protested, growing frustrated. "You said we should love our enemies…"

"—If you loved Nathaniel," jesus interrupted, "you wouldn't let him be a jerk. When he goes to a new town, people will think poorly of him for being so touchy. They will shut him out and he will become isolated. He won't know why, and he'll become even more explosive. All because you, who claim to love him, sacrificed his need to know for *your* need to be a doormat. I ask you again, did you see me play doormat with the Pharisees and lawyers last night?"

Andrew looked down to the ground. "No."

"That's because I love them, Andrew. Love gives to the greatest need. Sometimes that's a cloak… but people need truth more than cloaks."

Then Matthew and Bartholomew caught it for keeping babies away.

"We just thought you were too busy."

"You 'just thought' your issues were more important. But the realm of God is full of children. No one comes into it any differently… even you two. If you could see straight, you'd recognize that."

He took a baby in his arms and rocked her. "You see this? This is total dependence."

He gestured at them. "And now you're a little more able to stand on your own feet, aren't you?"

They nodded.

He gave the babe a kiss and handed her back to her mother.

"That's the way the realm of God is. You come into it with nothing to stand on, helpless, confused and naked. You can't even see straight. But God takes you in, feeds you and protects you. But it's so that you can grow up—*not* so you can stay babies forever."

He whirled away from them and plunged down the road.

"Grow up!" he commanded.

Then James, Thaddaeus and Simon got in trouble for trying to cast out a demon on their own power. For that they got called "unbelieving and perverse," which pleased them to no end. "God saves; God heals. No one else!" he said. "Do you want to be wizards, or do you want them to be healed? If you want them to be healed, bring them to God. If you want them to stay sick, play Mr. Wizard. The choice is yours."

And down the road again.

Everyone was rebuked that week. He was like a frustrated music teacher upbraiding his students before their last recital. Patience was no longer a preferred strategy; short, sharp shots were becoming the norm. Our thickheadedness was a source of constant pain to him.

We all began to snap at each other in private, and speak less in public. When jesus wasn't away praying, all the disciples grew tense and watchful in his presence. No one wanted to become the special project of the day.

"Can't you see?" he asked plaintively, every night and every morning. He'd shake his head in amazement and stare at us all, while we'd examine our shoes with intense preoccupation. "Can't you hear?"

Well, no.

One evening I approached him with a peace offering in my hand: candy orange slices. The nectar of angels, the stuff of dreams! I hoard them for special moments, like when my sugar is sinking, but not so fast I won't enjoy them. I'd never profane them by gobbling them down like candy corn or Sweet Tarts, never. I brought him *three*.

"I'm sorry if we're driving you crazy," I mumbled.

He looked tired and regretful.

"I have very little time," he explained, setting a scroll down. He shoved a chair over in my direction with the heel of his foot; an invitation of sorts. "Less than you, even."

I didn't know what I could say to that. It was bewildering to me. He looked so *healthy*. What could possibly—

"—I'm alive and I'm speaking up for God," he reminded me. "Around here, that's a terminal illness."

"Oh."

He looked at my gift and summoned a smile. I held them out and he took one.

Even his anger was wearing out, I think. He was beginning to accept that there was a limit to how far he could take us; he'd have to pass on the baton. It took some doing to come to peace with that—he went away to pray a lot—but I think he was starting to hear the goodbye he'd been saying for the last few weeks. It was becoming real, finally. He was really going to have to stop teaching us before we were through.

"What can I do to help?"

"Don't be sorry," he said, wearily. "Stop driving me crazy instead." Then he took a bite of an orange slice and chewed it slowly. His eyebrows lifted in surprise. "You like these?" he asked.

"Yeah."

"They're awful."

Then, at the end of the week, Matthew got called into the woodshed over his scholarship.

Matthew's big interest is in the fulfillment of scripture. He wants to show that jesus has the correct interpretation of the law—*not to overturn it, but to fulfill it*, etc.—and he wants to prove that it all fits together like a well-made cabinet. His gospel rings with confidence that everything happened according to plan.

"This happened to fulfill what was spoken by the prophets," he writes, and then he pulls out a scrap of scripture to prove his point. Great idea, if he'd only given the job to a better student of scripture. If you actually look up his references, though, you find him doing the kind of out-of-context scrap pulling that turns the Bible into a wildly surreal ink blot.

In fact, Matt reminds me of other Christians I have met: wild-eyed enthusiasts who see it all *fitting together*. They grab you by the lapels and start to blurt out scraps of scripture, snippets from the newspapers, something Aunt Kate heard in the grocery store… it all fits so wonderfully, the world is amazing, *can't you see…*? It's endearing, once you get used to it.

—Well, almost. Not when you're standing on the porch in your bathrobe. But I'm trying to be gracious, here.

Remember the slaughter of the innocents?

…an angel appeared to Joseph in a dream, saying, "Rise up, take the child and his mother. Escape with them to Egypt, and stay there until I tell you; for Herod is going to search for the child, to do away with him." So Joseph rose, took both mother and child to Egypt, and stayed there until Herod's death. This was to fulfill what the Lord had declared through his prophet: "I called my son out of Egypt."

When Herod saw how the astrologers had tricked him he flew into a rage, and gave orders for the massacre of all children in Bethlehem and its neighborhood, everyone aged two years or less, corresponding with the time he had obtained from the astrologers. So the words spoken through Jeremiah were fulfilled:

"A voice was heard in Ramah, wailing and loud mourning; it was Rachel weeping for her children and refusing all consolation, because they were no more."

Eventually the time came that Herod died; and while they were still in Egypt an angel appeared to Joseph in a dream and said to him, "Rise up, take the child and his mother, and go with them to the land of Israel, for the men who threatened the child's life are dead." *(Matthew 2:13–20)*

Matthew pulled that passage out of Jeremiah 31:15. Jeremiah, however, was talking about the children of Israel in exile. God is promising them that their tears will end, that they will return to the land God had given them.

This is a fuller piece of what Jeremiah wrote:

These are the words of the Lord:
Hark! Lamentation is heard in Ramah, and bitter weeping: Rachel is weeping for her children. She refuses to be comforted, because they are no more.
Hear the words of the Lord:
Cease your loud weeping, shed no more tears; for there shall be a reward for your toil. They shall return from the land of the enemy. You shall leave descendants after you, and your sons shall return to their own land. *(Jeremiah 31:15–17)*

Mark and Luke, the authors of the other two synoptic gospels (synoptic meaning "having the same vision"), look the other way and whistle uncomfortably when it comes to all of this. Luke, in fact, doesn't yank jesus to Egypt at all, but has jesus head to Jerusalem after his birth in Bethlehem:

Eight days later the time came to circumcise him, and he was given the name Jesus, the name spoken by the angel before he was conceived. Then, after their purification had been completed in accordance with the Law of Moses, they brought him to the Lord...
When Joseph and Mary had done everything prescribed in the law of the Lord, they returned to their own town of Nazareth, in Galilee. The child grew big and strong and full of wisdom; and God's favor was upon him. *(Luke 2:21–22, 39–40)*

jesus forgets to visit Egypt in Luke because Luke was interested in the issues of healing and justice, rather than prophecy fulfillment. Thus when Luke compiled the jesus stories, he felt no reason to fulfill Matthew's little Bible scrap, "Out of Egypt I called my son," a snippet from Hosea 11:1...

... a scrap which refers—you're ahead of me, aren't you?—to Israel's escape from bondage under Pharaoh. In that case, the prophet was speaking of the nation as a personified "him," a common method of speaking for prophets that Matthew, characteristically, misunderstood.

Ah, Matt. What are we going to do with you?

But first note this: no prophecy of scripture is a matter of one's own interpretation. For no prophecy had its origin in the human will, but men spoke from God, as they were carried along by the Holy Spirit. *(Peter 1:20–21)*

All scripture is inspired by God and is useful for teaching truth, refuting error, or for training in righteousness, so that all who belong to God may be efficient and equipped for good work of every kind. *(2 Timothy 3:16–17)*

Well, let God sort it out, then, if the Spirit's going to breathe so sloppily.

Tap-tap-tap-tap-tap.

jesus sits at a table with his head resting disconsolately on one hand, going over Matthew's homework. His pencil restlessly bounces up and down off the eraser tip. Matthew shifts uncomfortably with each page turn. jesus sighs, sniffs and turns another page. The sound of turning leaves is deafening in the stillness.

No one has said anything for a long time.

"Tell the daughter of Zion, 'Here is your king, who comes to you in gentleness, mounted on a donkey, and on a colt, the foal of a donkey.'" *(Matthew 21:5)*

Tap-tap-tap.

jesus brushes his hair back from his forehead. He frowns and flips back two pages, looks at it again; grunts; then flips forward again. He opens his mouth as if to speak—Matthew's shoulders tense up—then jesus changes his mind and closes his mouth. He slowly circles something without comment.

Matthew cringes. They've been going over his work for two hours, and there isn't a page that's survived unscathed. How much honesty can one place on a human back before it gives way?

When they had reached the Mount of Olives at Bethphage, near Jerusalem, Jesus sent two disciples with these instructions: "Go into the village opposite, where you will at once find a donkey tethered with her foal beside her; untie them and bring them to me." *(Matthew 21:1–2)*

"Mmm…," jesus murmurs.

"What?" Matt blurts out, as if he'd been hit with a cattle prod.

"This, um, quote from Zechariah 9:9…"

"Yes?"

"It's about a colt; the foal of a donkey."

"Right," nods Matthew. He licks his lips nervously. "Isn't it marvelous?"

A rub on the chin. "Yes, certainly…" He flips back a page. "Um. Did you—"

"—yes?"

"You know, sometimes people…"

He looks at Matthew helplessly, and sighs. He can't do it. "You like Zechariah, don't you?"

Matthew beams. "He called it all!"

"Yes," jesus nods, unhappily. "Yes, he certainly did."

He flips the papers over and briskly neatens them into one pile. "Very good," he announces, with abrupt cheer.

Matthew is elated. "Really?"

jesus clears his throat and hands the book back to his friend. "Just work out the bits we talked about, and I think that will be enough."

The relief on Matthew's face is palpable. This was his seventh rewrite, and it was beginning to look like seventy times seven was his destiny. "Thanks!" he says, brightening. He takes the book and dashes out of the room, eager to hit daylight.

jesus watches him shut the door with a bemused look.

"That wasn't so bad," floats back his voice through the window.

Peter's reply is unintelligible, but sympathetic. Everyone's been painfully aware of his tribulation.

"Great truth-telling," I say. "Andrew should be here."

jesus casts a jaundiced eye in my direction. "Don't start."

"Mark and Luke will be thrilled, I'm sure. Are they supposed to jigger their own accounts, now?"

"Don't tell them. It's bad enough."

"Wow. Situational ethics, and little white lies, too… what are you going to do about it?"

"It's not situational ethics," he objects. "It's pastoral care."

I nod as if enlightened, and make a big, round "O" with my mouth. jesus sees it and laughs for the first time in a week.

"O.K., so it's situational ethics," he says. "So sue me. Wait until you hear Paul. You'll think I'm a regular drill instructor."

"We do now," I say.

"I know," he says, glumly. "I know."

Well, whether you eat or drink or whatever you do, do all for the honor of God: give no offense to Jews or Greeks, or to the church of God. For my part I try to please all, regarding not my own interests, but the good of the many, so that they may be saved. Follow my example, as I follow Christ's. *(1 Corinthians 10:31–11:1)*

"What are you going to do about it?" I repeat. "It's rather glaring."

He rubs the back of his neck and frowns moodily. "I don't know… I'll think of something."

The Holy Spirit's Page

Even the law of light is gentle
Even the exposure is humane
Not some searchlight on
Quivering cattle
But a candle
To guide you home

You grew up
With dark God-Kings
Rattling in your bones
And ancient prayer was blood
Poured on altars
For the beneficence of seasons
Fertility, good crops, and
Victory against fear;
The only tongue
You could imagine
Was laid upon stones.

But I came to you
Slowly
Took up your conversation
With the only prayers you knew
Brought you mercy
In sweeping stages filled
With haunting lilts of love
That caught your ear by surprise

You turned from
Sacrificing each other
To goats,
Turtledoves.

Not the end,
But a beginning;
A step along the road.

If I'd rushed
You'd have fallen silent
I can't give it all at once
I slow my smoking tongue
To teach you mercy
The very way I say it
Like a mother
Teaching words to her boy
I work with what you know.

I grow angry only when you cling
—Like you do
When you're
Scared—
To age-old conversation
I won't wait forever
When it's time to grow up.

The slaves groaned
And half the human race
Waited endlessly for you
To hear it
Paul spoke it and it scared him
But give him credit
He spoke the words

And we're still
Bringing you along...

Israel
I chose you
To bear the brunt
Of the conversation

But I love you
All enough
To slow
My smoking tongue.

Kappa

I am sunk in misery; therefore I will remember you from the land of the Jordan, from the heights of the Hermons and Mount Mizar.

Deep calls to deep in the roar of your waterfalls. All your waves, all your breakers, pass over me. *(Psalm 42:6–7)*

The bay is full to the brim today, *thwupping* against the high boulders of the pier, erasing beach, drowning grass. Storm-tide, they call it: somewhere in the Gulf a tropical depression is swirling its white arms counterclockwise, shoving the ocean onto the land. I've never seen picnic tables at the water's edge before. It changes the feel of everything, makes it seem oddly British, manicured.

A sand bar is growing fifty yards out from the usual shore. The gulls think it's for them. They stand in ragged clumps, enjoying the novelty. Some peck for food. A few big ones saunter through the crowd, looking for little ones to bully.

All of the gulls in this area have black marks on their heads that look like headphones. When the east wind is wailing the effect is hilarious, for they stand in precisely the same direction, looking for all the world like a battalion of air traffic controllers. You can almost hear the sound of squelched radio static cutting on and off.

The world is full of tiny winks from God, but they're easy to miss when you're stressed out.

We came to this place to be healed. We still find it healing. When the tension builds up in our heads, we come to the sea and wash it out again. If we get too busy to reach the shore, we coil into slow balls of dry skin and autumn leaves. Life is nothing without water.

What is the attraction? I guess it's the vision of eternity it gives me, doled out in endless, rolling waves. It never stops; it's never the same. It's not static timelessness, but eternal change. The water can be emerald green or battle grey, pale or deep blue, green like spruce or the color of old grease. At sunset it runs through an amazing display in a short time: milky white serenity; silvery molten suffering; roseate passion; golden radiance; darkling mystery. In the morning it will rise again to a new life, and no one knows what it will be. It is life, death and life again.

It says something amazing about God that I just can't put down. You'll just have to come out and see.

Call ahead, though. The house is usually a mess.

Rua-ru-ruashh, the bay says to the startled land.
The bugs crawl onto the pier to keep from getting wet.
The stones spit and cry *choap, choap.*

Pity the poor pelican this morning. To eat he must dip his beak into the water, grab a fish, then throw back his head to swallow it. Seagulls know this, so they hover nearby, waiting to steal his breakfast on the backstroke.

Martha and I have seen gulls actually sit on pelicans' heads! That's how pushy bullies can get.

The pelican tries to shorten his swing to hide the fish, but it's really quite an unsatisfying way to eat. He nearly chokes on his food without the full speed of the arc. The poor bird looks miserable, but there's nothing he can do to stop it. He ducks his head in the water, the gull waits until he comes back up. He snaps, the gull springs into the air for a moment. He tries flying to a new spot on the bay, and his tormentor follows him.

He's like the boy with thick glasses in ninth grade, suffering through another day of "keep-away" with his lunch sack. He wishes it would end, but it goes on and on and on.

It's one of the first hard lessons of the young: the hall monitor is never there when you need her.

Where are the blissful birds, Matthew? Where are the contented little Christian sparrows? You're not only a poor student of scripture, but a poor observer of Creation.

We're all out here scrabbling to survive, fending off aggression and mishaps. Of the flock of gulls on the sandbar, I see three one-legged birds and one with a painfully dislocated thigh. The wounded one keeps limping and struggling, wincing and falling. It makes my heart hurt to watch him. I feed him some bread, but it hardly seems enough. I say a prayer for him, wondering if it makes a difference.

Maybe he's doing the same for me. We're both ratty old birds.

There is, however, a subtle grace in this raucous scene for the beleaguered human. He's been working the old "sparrow" condemnation overtime again, feeling bad for feeling bad. He's been fretting about bankrupting Martha with his medical bills, and wondering why he can't let go of his anxiety. Nothing like feeling guilty and unfaithful on top of being scared!

But today he hears another voice. God speaks with a scree and a wild "hah-ah-ah."

These birds, here, they tell me that anxiety and strife are part of living in this world. I'm not sinful for feeling scared, I'm just paying attention to my life. Sometimes life is anxiety-producing. Big deal—this is supposed to be a surprise?

Get real, Matthew, God whispers in my ear.

I always used to think God was supposed to be a safety belt against worry, but the belt always snapped. Now I know that God is the hopeful statement *within* the worry.

In the Psalms, prayer is two-handed: one hand grasps God's activity in the past, one hand holds our fears for the future. The Psalmist lifts both up to God. It may be the finest offering we make—for what is more precious to us than our worry, and what is sweeter to God than our memory? Together they make an effective, real prayer. If I let a few verses in the Bible shame me into holding one hand behind my back, my prayer will be false: I will keep the fear for myself. How much better to share it with God, instead.

Dear God,
I know you've always saved us before. I'm frightened you'll forget this time.
Remember Martha, please. I know you will, even if I believe you won't. You always have. That's why I love you, in spite of my screwed-up head.
Amen.

Well, time to get a move on. I'm supposed to meet Andy for lunch at Wendy's, try to have a good time.

Fretful about it? Sure.

I sling my tank over my shoulder, tell the pelican to try reading Matthew 7, and trudge up the driveway. I meet Andy at the door, looking like a pelican, too. We're each other's seagulls, Andy and I. What a farce!

We stand in line, exchange some small talk about the weather, study the menu board with acute intensity. Should that be a small or medium fries? How about a drink? Hmm. Weighty considerations, when you're uncomfortable.

The food materializes at a snail's pace—folks down here just don't get the concept of *fast food*—and we find a seat. No-smoking section, of course; I don't know what I'll do come Pentecost.

Well.

Here we are.

O.K. Lord, I'll try it.

I pull out my black insulin bag, set it on the table. It's actually an insulated lunch cooler; not too conspicuous. It certainly seems to take up an awful lot of space, though. I have to shove the salt and pepper shakers out of the way. Andrew looks quickly out the window.

I unzip the bag, get out the meter, pop it on. READY, it says. It tells me the date and time, and then orders me to INSERT STRIP. I retrieve an official One-Touch strip—there used to be cheaper generics, but some lawyers put a stop to that right quick—and slide it into its mouth.

WAIT. It thinks for a minute, blinking its little red light.

APPLY SAMPLE.

All of this dialogue, thank God, happens without any helpful little beeps. My last meter was incessant about calling attention to itself. I remember a choir concert in Chicago that was being recorded for all posterity: I got sick and simply had to check my blood, as much as I dreaded it. I snuck away as far as possible, which wasn't far. The piercing little beeps carried through the stone chapel like a car alarm, and I came close to smashing the damning little speaker.

I never bought the tape. I was too frightened I'd discover the evidence of my sickness preserved forever, like electronic squeaks in a beautiful poem.

Whoever you are that gave us the silent option: you have my undying gratitude.

Andrew is looking so studiously out the window that I feel ridiculous. Parking lots are just not that interesting this time of day.

"Andy, you can look. It's O.K.…I'll try not to be a jerk."

He keeps looking out the window. "That's alright," he says. "I don't mind."

I sigh. "Andy, if you don't turn your head and look I'm going to scream."

His eyes edge over, but his head stays turned. "Is that enough?"

"No, I want the whole face, front and center."

He brings his head around. "How's that?"

I grin. "No, your eyes aren't weepy and sad enough."

He smiles sheepishly. "How about this, then?" he says, leaning over the table to stare directly at it.

"That's better," I say.

The tension's gone. He looks relieved enough to cry. Things feel more… normal. How about that. O.K. jesus, you win the first round.

I take the poker and jab it into my finger.

"I don't know how you do that," Andy winces.

"It takes a while to get used to it," I say, squeezing my finger to get a big enough blood sample. "It took me a year to get to the point where I didn't jump." The drip hits the strip, the meter starts counting. "I don't think it's the poke so much, it's the suspense. I used to linger forever on the cusp of clicking the little trigger."

"I saw my cousin use the needle without the gun, once."

I smile. "I'm not that brave yet."

30, 29, 28…

"How long have you been doing this?"

"About five years. I'm still a novice."

27, 26, 25…

He looks at the meter. "What's it doing now?"

I explain what I know about it, which isn't much. Like most modern gadgets, it's just magic to the user. But I know that the strip has some special chemical that turns a different color, depending on how much sugar is present. The flashing light reads the color at the end of the sequence. That's the limit of my technical knowledge when it comes to this demon. But it's kind of a relief, I discover, to talk about it. Confession of my sin: *I am sick… but Andrew is not revolted by me.*

4, 3, 2, 1...

The meter declares its verdict:

137

I show him the reading.

I can eat right away. My sugar's low enough to skip the insulin ramp-up time.

"Now what?" he asks.

I pick up my chart and describe the adjustments I'll make. As I talk I enter the values into the meter, then turn it off.

A new problem comes up: where to put the used test strip? It's gross, bloody. I can't put it back in my bag, or it will smear blood all over. There's no trash in sight—Wendy's is overly aggressive about having you *not* bus your tables like you do in McDonald's—and I can't imagine leaving it with the used coffee creamers. The girl that busses the table would see it. Blood means infection; AIDS; biohazard... I hesitate for a moment, trapped with my own bodily fluids again.

Inspiration comes in a flash: I stick the test strip into the aluminized wrapper that held my alcohol wipe. That's better. Now it just looks like a discarded sugar packet or something.

O.K. Round two, and jesus is still on a roll. Here goes.

This is the moment I really hate. I don't want to spoil anyone's meal. I remember reading a letter in the newspaper—

—well, that was a long time ago, wasn't it? The writer's probably gone on to harangue the editor about bicycle trails—

—but you know, it's amazing how something can stick. I have a Velcro heart—

—shoot, Nathaniel. You can pull things off Velcro, too—

—people hate needles—

—then they don't have to watch—

—O.K., O.K.—

I pull out the needle, take off the bright orange top. It makes a tiny sound that, in the seventh dimension of heaven, sounds exactly like Velcro scritching apart.

The battles that go on right underneath our noses! Who would think that a conflict between the forces of light and darkness is going on in Wendy's right now?

Pull an equal amount of air into the syringe, inject it into the bottle. Draw in the insulin. Flick, flick the side of the syringe. Squirt, while it's still in the bottle. Draw it in again.

"What's that for?" Andy asks.

"Gets rid of the air bubbles."

I take a quick glance around the restaurant. No one else seems to be watching. I lift the edge of my shorts, pinch a little fat, give the shot.

"Doesn't that hurt?"

"Not as much as the poker."

Cap the needle, put it away, put the meter in the bag. Zip. Sling the bag over the back of the chair. Take one last check of the other patrons.

No one threw up.

Alright, maybe it's not hacking up a bunch of green gerbils, and maybe it's not as conspicuous as an oxygen mask. Maybe it's not as scary as wigging out or turning blue, and maybe it's not as annoying as walking too slow in a crowded grocery aisle. Maybe diabetes is a little easier to do in public than C.F. But it's a start, isn't it? Hold on, jesus, I'm trying.

Create in me a fresh heart O God
And renew a sturdy spirit within me
Keep me in your care and
Restore me to the joy of your salvation
Uphold me with a new will
And teach me the way I should walk
Show me how to be proud in your love
Secure among strangers
And gracious with my kin.

Lambda

Dateline: Jerusalem.
9:30 a.m., Palm Sunday

And you always wondered what drew the crowds.

Mark gawks down the street with a look bordering on panic. "What's he doing?"
"Riding into town," I shrug.
"I can see that," he snaps. He turns to Philip and appeals to him instead, pulling on his shirt. "What's he doing?"
Philip just looks confused, shakes his head.
Andy rubs the back of his neck and frowns uncertainly. "He usually rides bareback," he says. "I wonder what the cloak's for?"
"To cover up the rope."
"Rope? What rope?"
"The rope holding their waists together."
A man runs down the street, calling for his wife to come look. People hear the commotion, and do surprised double takes. The local foot traffic comes to a stop. Children are pointing and giggling. Some adults get it right away, others are confused.
"Who is this?" a tailor frowns. "What's the fuss?"
"jesus, the prophet from Nazareth," someone else answers.
"They have strange customs in Nazareth," the man remarks, looking closer. "I'd like to see their saddles."
The sound of a donkey braying splits the air, and Judas flinches at the sound. A little kid laughs with great high shrieks. jesus smiles and throws him a piece of bubble gum. Candy!
All hopes of a quiet entry are permanently hosed. The children swarm around the clown coming down the street. James groans. "It's going to be a regular parade," he laments. "Has he no shame?"
"No, I don't think so," I reply, a little wistfully.
jesus cries out to us, waving from his unsteady perch. His legs are just long enough to straddle the two beasts, which are of very different height. Kind of like

sitting on a chair and a barstool at the same time—you can't do it with dignity. "John! Luke! Come join us!"

John and Luke are rooted in place.

"James? Peter?"

They look at each other uncertainly, each waiting for the other to commit himself. Neither moves.

Matthew walks proudly at jesus' side, stroking first the head of the colt, then the head of the mother. He's the only one unsurprised by it all. Kids flow around him like a chaotic torrent, and he recites snippets of the prophets to them, in his glory.

"It could be worse," I tell Mark, remembering Zechariah's text. " 'A donkey, a colt, the foal of a donkey.' At least Matt didn't make him ride all three."

"I don't think his legs are long enough to ride three," Philip observes.

"I won't play along with it," Mark pouts.

Luke agrees. "It's absurd," he says, pinching his lips together distastefully. "We should make him change it."

"It's worse than absurd. It's denigrating, unbecoming of God," moans John.

Peter is so embarrassed it's painful to watch his flushed face—but he finally walks over to stand by Matthew anyway. What can he do? This is where he finds jesus.

The rest eventually tag along, like grudging boys asked to play with dolls. As the last of them fall in line, a strange shift in the air occurs. The colors become more vibrant, the shadows deeper, the wind fresher. Everything seems more... real. In a distant part of the city, far over the ancient temple walls, a cannon suddenly booms out, marking the decision, and the echoes seem to reverberate forever.

"Couldn't happen to a nicer guy," Andrew says.

"Yes," I sigh.

The new inductee beams like a borderline student at graduation, lets loose a holler that sounds something like "Whoosh-aya!" Someone else shouts back "Hosanna!" corrupting his text. The chant is quickly taken up enthusiastically by the crowd.

"Hosanna!"

"Hosanna!"

Congratulations, Matt. You'll never know how much grace you've been given.

Mary and Martha bring sacks of ammunition from the local Qwik-Piq. They found Milky Ways, M&Ms, Tootsie Rolls—some of the Tootsie Rolls are already gone—and, of course, Gummi Worms. Gummi Worms are an important symbol of the church.

The Ashpot Gate is closed for repairs, so we process through the Water Gate. People laugh and spread their cloaks on the road. Cover it up: mud, ropes, stupid mistakes... Cover it all up. Scripture, Politics and Sausage Making all have something in common: you don't want to see how the product is put together, or you might very well lose your appetite entirely.

"Hosanna!"

"Hosanna to the Son of David!"

I wonder what that means. I ask Luke, but he just shakes his head morosely and bites into a Milky Way. He's lost all sense of harmony today—call it a diminished chord.

The crowd doesn't care, though. They're cutting branches from the trees and spreading them on the road. They wave them, tickle other's ears with them, whop each other over the head—and that's just the grown-ups. The kids goggle at their elders, wondering what's gotten into them. A fresh wind is blowing through old Jerusalem; people blow down the streets like litter, flutter up against the procession.

"Hosanna!"

"David's back!"

"Hey, Mr. Savior! You got any treats left?"

"Hosanna in the highest!"

"Hosanna!"

We'll have to figure out something, I think. You can't let everything slide…

Let's see, there's the Hebrew imperative *hosa*, to save, augmented by the enclitic precative particle *-(n)na*, which adds a note of urgency. Hmm… a little strange, in context. I wonder what the scribes are doing with it. Sneaking up to the back of the colt, I pull a large red volume out of jesus' robe. It begins to speak as soon as I open the cover.

> There is, however, no evidence whatsoever that Hosanna in biblical or postbiblical Jewish usage was ever an acclamation of praise. It was Christian misapprehension of a well-known Hebrew term that has confused even scholars to this day. The difference between acclamation and a stark cry, "Help, please!" is too great to be glossed over…[32]

Martha groans, seeing me burying my nose again, and sneaks up behind my ear. "Give it a rest," she says. "Put the book down. It's Sunday."

"Just a minute," I say. "One more minute… coming."

She's heard that before. She wanders off to walk with jesus.

"Pipe down!" a woman screams, leaning out of a second-story window; she's far louder than anyone on the street, but not in the mood to notice. "I have children sleeping in here!"

"I thought there was supposed to be a white horse," mutters a shopkeeper.

"Donkeys are royal around here," a scribe explains. "Good footing in rocky country."

"Oh." The man falls silent, but looks vaguely unsatisfied.

"Hosanna!"

"What's all this foolishness?"

"Hosanna to the Son of David!"

"You're disturbing the city!" a nearly apoplectic Pharisee complains. "Quiet!"

"If they were quiet," jesus replies, "the stones would roar." He offers the Pharisee a Milky Way, but the Pharisee stomps away, unimpressed. This is not good order, it's disruptive, it's nonsense. The mountains could snicker, for all he'd care.

> ... How could such misapprehension occur? Why did not the gospel writers look to the G[ree]k of Ps[alm] 118:25 and some thirty other passages where the Hebrew imperative is duly rendered by the Gk imperative *soson*, "save"? The crux of the problem lies in the nonsensical cries "hosanna to the son of David" and "hosanna in the highest" which indicates that the cry was not understood because of the Semitic particle l- before the addresses "Son of David" and "highest."
>
> C. C. Torrey (1933) surmises that in the original cry the Aramaic use of the proclitic particle l- as the object marker was mistaken for dative sense...[33]

Martha's face appears above the edge of the page. "Weighty words?"

"Like an anchor," I admit.

"Have an orange slice."

There's an idea...

Poof. The hand-wringing volume disappears in a puff of smoke, and the kids take up a chant, drowning out the last echoes of the scribe's voice.

> jesus loves me,
> this I know,
> for the Bible tells me so...

The disciples begin to sing along with the kids, hoping they can still remember the words.

> Little ones to him belong
> They are weak,
> But he is strong.

jesus lifts his face and arms up to the sky; he breathes deep, laughing and crying at the same time.

The wedding dance, the party. What Jew can resist a laugh under the eyes of God when a marriage is taking place?

> Yes, jesus loves me,
> Yes, jesus loves me,

Not funny. Decorum.

Incense.

> Yes, jesus loves me:
> The Bible tells me so.

Gummi Worms.

Mu

Martha has been going through a high-growth, high-stress season. She is changing careers, trying to build confidence, saying slow-motion goodbyes to her husband—who stands on a boat that's always leaving the dock at unpredictable speeds—and exploring her past. She is trying to discover new voices that will tell her she can make it through all the changes whirling around her. She is making it, yes, a little bit each day. When you pursue healing with *pistis*,[34] the only variable to God's response is the delivery time. Her yes is coming more quickly than mine, but we're all rowing to New Jerusalem one way or another.

"Did you ever see one of our family devotionals?" she suddenly asks. We've been talking about the past, and she's referring to the strangest phenomenon in religious life I'd ever encountered.

"Yes," I smile. "I don't think I saw the worst of it. But I do remember one night, hearing your dad downstairs, rousting out the boys…"

"Did you hear the screaming, and pounding on the walls…?"

"Oh, yeah," I chuckle. "Couldn't miss it."

She mimics the scene in a bestial voice:

DAD

Get up! We're going to have a devotion.

KIDS

Dad!

DAD

Shut up now! Get up!

KIDS

It's eleven o'clock! We're in bed!

DAD

Get up! I said get up!

SOUND EFFECTS ON WALL

wham-wham-wham… thunk

"Uh-huh. I remember listening to it and thinking, 'Oh, this ought to be peaceful.'"
She laughs.

"Then you all trudged in and flopped down on the couch with a fuming, 'O.K.-here's-my-body' expression..."

As I speak she recalls the pose, crossing her arms resentfully over her chest, sticking her lips out far enough to support a vase. By this time both of us are starting to laugh uncontrollably.

> MOM
>
> Oh, I don't know why you have to do this...
>
> DAD
>
> We're going to have a devotion!
>
> KIDS
>
> Dad, let Mom read. Please?
>
> DAD
>
> What's the matter with the way I read?
>
> KIDS
>
> You're boring!
>
> DAD
>
> Stop that stupid talk! Shut up, now. We're going to have a good time.

"Yeah," I say. "It was kind of like orc spirituality."

Martha howls. "That's it, that's it!" she cries, slapping the table. Tears start to stream down her face. "Orc spirituality. Oh, my stomach hurts..." We roar, giggle and carry on for a while—"Grishnak, hand me Bible axe" kind of stuff—then gradually settle down enough to speak again. She's tempted to call her brothers and tell them, but most of them never read *Lord of the Rings,* so they wouldn't get it. Too bad.

"Did you guys ever have any devotionals?" she asks, wiping her cheek.

"I don't think so."

"Guess that makes sense; that fits your Presbyterian, corporate style. Separation of church and state... separation of church and family..." That sets off another round of giggles. Lord, our beginnings are absurd, aren't they?

Separation of church and family. Well, it wasn't quite that bad. Separation of God and Creation, maybe. That's more accurate, if you're keeping score.

I grew up a Deist. I didn't discover the term for another ten years, but that's what I was. I believed that God just wound up the Universe, and then let it run like a broken clock without further intervention.

It's a classic scheme. God builds the perfect clock with one fatal flaw—*us*—and after we gum up the works He (always a He, the ultimate engineer) goes off to sulk. After a few million years of doodling on sketch pads, he comes up with an attempted repair. A new gear called Christ! God drops him into place, and the machinery pretty much runs the same way it did before—clank, whirrr, boing—but with one essential difference: our souls have been saved. The clock still keeps lousy time, but hey, we've been pardoned from hell.

Well, I think you can see the dynamics that went into that. Churchwide, it created an answer to the tension between the claim that jesus has already saved us, and the easily available contrary evidence. Move the "saved" portion into the invisible realm, and the contradiction moves with it. Forget the Feeding of the Five Thousand, forget all the healing stories: those brief flashes of material power were only meant to establish his credentials. The real work was in the invisible realm of the spirit—you know, the part that didn't hurt as bad as my brother's and sister's broken bodies.

For me personally, all this shielded God from my anger. If God was an absent engineer who cared not a whit for the broken gears, but only for the outcome of our souls, then he wasn't especially singling us out. God's job description only included the stuff we didn't immediately care about, right here, right now. That's one way to raise your annual performance review.

When I went to seminary, I studied the basic marks of Gnosticism, an old religion which is being repackaged these days for our brave, bold new age. One of the basic characteristics of Gnosticism is a belief that matter is evil and spirit is good. Gnostics say our spirits are imprisoned in the material plane, and the goal of life is to free our trapped souls, become elevated to spiritual perfection. Many Christians are Gnostics and don't even know it. We are angry with matter. It decays, rusts, gets sick. Our pets die, our roads develop potholes and even the pyramids are looking shabby these days. Surely, we think, God must be just as disappointed as we are! When we imagine heaven, we have visions of disembodied spirits, drifting through a nebulous fog of shifting lights: ephemeral, half-real, dreamy.

When you think about it, Earth is actually twice as real as heaven, for it has both matter and spirit. But most of us have so given up on matter we figure God might as well write it off, take the deduction. When the author of Revelation talks about streets of gold and gates of pearl, we blush and say, "Well, that's probably a sign of spiritual purity…"

I think the author of Revelation was trying to communicate something to his readers about what matters to God. I think he was trying to say that heaven was *more real.* Imagine a heaven that is more solid, vibrant, everything so clear and sharp that this earth seems wan and faded. The colors startle; the dullest rock gleams. Blacktop seems to shine with light… and metal gates, Lord, look at the sparkle, I can't describe it. The closest I can come is to tell you it's like gems, like gold, like precious and exotic metals. Everything has extra depth to it, as if it's poking out of space, as if time pools around it, like a quiet pond. And it's not so much that everything is made out of precious stones, it's that the *stones are precious.*

Look. Stand here a moment, at the bottom of time: harmony is starting to happen in the New Jerusalem, the city at the end of the Universe. The world is starting to dance to God's tune, and even the rocks are beginning to get the hang of it. Not spiritual perfection, but ultimate rockishness. Rockishness without the random Void crawling through it; rockishness with a definite beat, the pulse of God's heart.

The discordant notes are not erased but resolved; not undone but brought into the whole of the composition. It's not the evil nature of the world that jangles, it's the *incompleteness,* the unfinished state of the work.

Grab somebody that can read music… you have to hear this.

—Oh, I know; you'll say you did, and just continue to lie there on the couch—

No, *Really.* Go get someone. You'll like this, it's cool, it's part of the real world and it's a message from God. Play this on a piano:

chart 1

Ugly, right? Makes you want to shove those notes around, doesn't it? It's *bad.* But this is how God resolves the tension: with more notes, not less. Those very same notes are still present and unchanged in the following chords.

chart 2

You don't resolve the tension of great, diverse reality by cutting it down; you add *more* reality. Together these diverse, jangly notes make rich, complex chords: G7, Cmaj7, Cm11, Eb6, a beautiful Amaj9… Cool huh?

God made music (a personal invention for my benefit; I let the rest of you folks borrow it from time to time). What if music revealed God's methodology?

What if God didn't bend your basic nature at all—even the parts that currently make you wince—but simply added in the missing notes you haven't yet heard? What if it wasn't the *nature of the notes* at all, but the Void still hanging between them that created the awful noise?

It's impossible to imagine, isn't it? Until you hear it played, you can't fathom it. When you hear chart 1, it's hard to believe that it could ever be beautiful without fundamental Augustinian surgery—just as, when you hear chart 2, it's hard to believe the offending notes are still there. But they are. They are singing with a full throat. Just like you, and you, and you.

Lord, let me roll through that gate of yours with the rock of ages. Resolve my discordant notes by adding in the missing ones. Teach me to be something better than a purified ghost.

Teach me to be Nathaniel.

Filling in the missing notes; call it a synonym for love.

When Martha came into my life, she was such a Pollyanna. She thought God still liked matter, still cared for body and soul, still actively loved the world. I thought the evidence of my family's life would quash that right quick. She'd wise up as soon as she met the *real* world.

But I was the unsophisticated one, the Gnostic, the Deist. After being married to her for several years, her faith began to rub off on me. I began to toy with the idea that maybe God *wasn't* an absent clock maker. Maybe God was still poking around in this mess.

The more I toyed with the idea, the more I saw; and the more I saw, the more I came to believe. I met a God who was standing in the middle of the river with us, getting as cold and wet as we were... and still hustling, still trying to make things happen.

That was a mixed blessing. God was not only released back into Creation, God was also shorn of the protective shield I had erected around the material world. If God was still *here* and willing to lift a finger to help us out, why did that finger refuse to touch my disease?

I began a long, slow journey of discovery, a journey I'm still taking. First I saw, through Martha's eyes, the physical care that was there. It may come as a surprise to hear that a man who's lived more than twice his life expectancy should not notice that... but there you go. That's what estrangement will do to you.

And then I saw the amazing ways in which our finances always veered off the edge of a cliff. My career was constantly blessed with the happy accident and chance connection—and, of course, even the skill that used those chances was a free gift, a currency called "talent." Programming was hidden like an Easter Egg in my head. I was entirely "self-taught," to use a vastly inappropriate term.

The truth was, more literally and correctly, serendipity: a happy, effortless discovery. I was a budding musician, trying to make the local circuit. I "just happened" to build a synthesizer kit that "just happened" to have an optional computer controller; "just happened" to discover a weird affinity for 6502 machine code, which "just happened" to be the heart of the first home video game system; "just happened" to do a game for my own enjoyment and "just happened" to see an ad from a new Atari division, looking for products... and "just happened" to discover a career that could be done at home, at my own body's pace and schedule. The royalties, savings and disability insurance I "just happened" to make from that career just happen to feed us to this day.

Ah, the self-made man; how did you knit those neurons together, anyway? Did you keep the blueprints?

I never thought I'd have a job or a spouse, or a house, or anything that most little boys think is their birthright. This was the *rational expectation*. One day, after being married to Martha for several years, my eyes were opened, and I saw what I had, rather than what I feared I would not have. In fact, I had to admit that none of my fears had panned out. I kept waiting for doom to fall, and bounty kept falling instead.

It's all just a trick of the eyesight, you know. It all depends on what you're looking for. As a new acquaintance of mine, Ed Rose, has remarked, you can just as well ask why *good* happens in the world. In the worst of situations—he served in Vietnam—good keeps breaking out with insane persistence.

Maybe we need a doctrine of Original Charity to balance the weight of Original Sin. Correct the assumptions. In a universe where all the facts seem to point to evolutionary aggression, self-interest and evil, maybe we need to start wondering why this place isn't *worse,* rather than better.

After the scales fell off my eyes, I decided my only real burden was fear. That was unstable, of course—it was built upon the bearability of my condition, and the realization that, up until then, my main burden had mostly been in the realm of the nonphysical. I took that truth into a reverse spin on Gnosticism. Suddenly my *matter* was cared for, and it was only my *psyche* that was in trouble.

The pendulum swings that go on in the human soul! It was inevitable that the pendulum would come back down, wasn't it? Time and gravity, the decay of my body, was on its side.

I entered seminary with a hope both true and false at the same time. True, because I *truly had* been materially cared for by an alive God, far beyond what skeptical reality would allow. False, because my heart had abandoned its doom for the first time in its life, and in that giddy freedom forgotten that I was truly going to die—and die painfully, in a theodicy-shaking way.

My mouth and brain still knew the words, but that season was a time that death forgot, and my heart forgot death.

Yes, all theodicies are unstable. We move from one to another like stones in a fast river. We step on each to get us a little further across, leaping before the unsteady perch topples. It's nothing to be embarrassed about; it's human. We're just built that way.

But this needs to be said for that old, worn stone: it restored me to conversation with God. When my doom returned with its teeth bared, I was now caught in a relationship that had known both love and hate, anger and joy. God and I were old road warriors, sometimes in league and sometimes in enmity, but always in direct contact, looking each other in the eye.

I could no longer pretend abandonment or peace, hell or heaven. I had to be real now, both body and soul. I was in a land where neither God nor Devil held full sway; in a place where "saved" language was a laughable churchman's fantasy, and Deism a hopeless rationalization. Redemption would either involve all of my pain, or none of it. I had come, in other words, to inhabit Earth.

That's a serious piece of healing, there. It's not every day you experience incarnation.

Martha, you are the gift of God to me. I am convinced that at the very time my genes were knitting together, God was knitting you together to begin my healing. You were the note that filled in my most discordant hole, the beginning of the end to all the noise and emptiness. When you came into my life, the noisemaker howled and wept to see his work come undone. You were the leading tone to God's patient refrain. Thank you, from the bottom of this strengthening heart.

And yes, my good friend Joan: I will admit the possibility you raised when I confided this to you. Maybe God was thinking of Martha's needs when I was being formed too. We fill each other's staves.

In the middle of all her internalized voices…

> "You can't do that."
> "What's that foolishness?"
> "People will pay money for that?"

…there are new voices growing in her chest, saying "Yes, you can"; and one of them, I am glad to say, is mine. It is the gift I'm trying to leave, as this balky boat drifts away from the dock.

This boat is drifting, make no mistake about it. I'm going to die like everyone else; no special exemptions. Whether I like it or not, God is going to bring me over the river.

Damn.

Indeed, what was once splendor is now no splendor at all; it is outshone by a still greater splendor. For if the fading and transitory had its moment of splendor, how much greater is the splendor of that which endures! *(2 Corinthians 3:10–11)*

Listen: Martha and I are being born, and born again, from head to toe, in a very real physical and spiritual way. As jesus told Nicodemus, it's the only way we cross into the realm of God. It's what happens to us all.

When we're done, I think we will move on to something deeper and more colorful than what we know—the angels, they say, always assault the eye like burnished bronze—and this current flimsy thing will have done its job.

It's not evil, and it's not immaterial. It's not unimportant, but not ultimate, either. It will be, as Martha told me just a few days ago, like a discarded umbilical cord.

When you look in my casket, world, I want you to remember this word, please:

Afterbirth.

It will probably be the truest word you say all day.

Creation is not a six-day—or ten-billion-year—flash in the pan. It's not fixed in the past at all. Creation is in our *present and future*.

There is a time coming when all 450 of the mutations linked to cystic fibrosis will be resolved, and the gene will be heard as God hears it; when War and Holocaust will be a memory of the noisy darkness; when alcoholism, cancer and crippling shame will all be part of the senseless foam that was conquered.

There is a time coming when people will still be people, but they will be at peace with that awful truth. There is a time coming when we will no longer flinch and cower before the thought of a God we're told to fear, but stand in the real warmth of the Holy Spirit and sway, sway, sway, like wheat on a Kansas summer night.

I have dearly loved you since the most ancient of days, and still keep my unfailing care for you. I will build you up again, O virgin Israel—yes, you shall be rebuilt! Again you shall adorn yourself with jingles, take up your tambourines, and go forward with a throng of joyful dancers.

Again you shall plant vineyards on the hills of Samaria; your farmers will plant them and enjoy their fruit. There is a day coming when the watchmen on Ephraim's hills will cry out, "Come, let us go up to Zion, to the Lord our God!"

...See, I will bring them from the northernmost reaches; I will gather them from the ends of the earth. The blind and the lame will be with them, and expectant mothers and women in labor... oh, what a company! They will come home, weeping as they come, but I will comfort them and be their guide and escort, leading them past the flowing streams and the smooth paths, so they shall not stumble.

(*Jeremiah 31:3–6, 8–9a*)

Nu

Then Mary brought a pound of very costly perfume, pure oil of nard, and anointed the feet of Jesus and wiped them with her hair, till the house was filled with the fragrance. Judas Iscariot (the disciple who was to betray him) objected, saying, "Why was this perfume not sold and given to the poor? She spent nearly a year's wages!" (John 12:3–5)

"The way I figure it," Judas says, "this is the time to capture the Big Mo."

"The big what?" Mary asks.

"Mo. You know, Momentum. You saw the crowds at the gates, after that little stunt. I thought he was committing political suicide, but I can see now what he was doing. It really humanized him, made him a Man of The People."

Judas is the kind of guy who Really Can Pronounce Capital Letters.

"The kids had fun," Philip says, mildly.

"The parents are the ones that count. And they were ready to crown him right there! We have to capitalize on this, ride the wave. By Tuesday, I figure we'll have enough momentum to crash right over the Romans." He makes a sweeping motion with his hands, in the general direction of Herod's Palace. "The Kingdom of God is about to touch down, and we're standing right at Ground Zero."

"Have you got your position picked out?" Mary asks, archly.

Judas opens his mouth to speak, but then catches her tone, and closes it again. He narrows his eyes at her and reaches for a fig.

No wonder we do not lose heart! Though our outward humanity decays, day by day we are inwardly renewed. (2 Corinthians 4:16)

Mary's been getting more outspoken lately, and Judas has been catching the brunt of it. I don't think he's too crazy about her beloved Rabbi's efforts to improve her confidence.

James is a little nonplussed, too. Two days ago, we were getting ready to move, and James asked her to go grab a pack from the living room. Mary was already descending the steps with her hands full, and she gave him a look that would shrink a stone.

"Your arms painted on?" she asked.

We managed to hold our laughter in until James got through the door, then Philip and I roared. Mary kept on going as if nothing had happened.

But the whole truth is that none of us escaped unscathed. I certainly didn't get away scot-free. When I said I didn't know how to do laundry, she asked me if that trait was linked to the Y chromosome, or if it was just a *localized* brain defect. I didn't think that one was quite so funny. I did learn how to separate the whites from the reds, though.

We're sitting in the shadow of a doorway, waiting for jesus and eating from a gift basket from the Ladies' Auxiliary. Lots of fruit and nuts, a spray of flowers. Nice.

"He did seem to make quite a splash," Philip says, hopefully. "Maybe the lawyers will go easier on him, now."

"I hope so," I sigh. "Then he'll go easier on us."

"Take it from me," Judas says, "the hard part's over. Getting here was a hassle, but it will pay off. He's built his base."

Andrew frets into the basket, digging around for another glazed date. "I don't know. He keeps talking about being murdered."

"He's alright. Did you see their faces? He's just a little edgy, that's all." Judas waves his hand casually. "He'll be O.K., as long as he doesn't overextend himself."

"I don't think he's doing anything that isn't God's will."

"Well, you have to choose your battles. This thing with the Pharisees, for instance: I wish he'd cool it a little. There's no point in wasting your energy on them. Once you have the empire, you just convert everyone by fiat. Order the Pharisees to preach what you want, or you'll shut them down. That's the way to do it. When you're dealing with these kind of people you don't debate them, you just let them know who's holding the cards."

"That's how you win people's hearts and minds?" Mary asks. "By force?"

Judas flicks his eyes over her. "Well, you wouldn't know," he says. Mary's jaw turns hard, and Andrew winces. I can tell she's about ready to cut him down to size—but that's just when the door opens, and jesus plows off down the street, with a cloud of grim Apostles trailing behind him.

Judas grins broadly. "See? Time to storm the gates." He leaps to his feet and runs off before Mary can respond.

We stare dumbly after him, then pull ourselves into gear and join the chase.

Breaking Silence

In the great dark cavern of
suffocating stillness
and
stale spirits
the children drifted into Silence
but never Quiet

The rustle of brown feet
frippered over the endless tile
of a mosaic they could only feel
with bruised hands

The Silence was a
Void
in every word

Just
the vowels
missing out of respect to an
old
stone lion
who hated the
Oh
in their lives

So they learned to say I
in dogged, humble tones
where there should have been
something more like a
cry
with round lips

and who knows maybe it was a cry of joy
but without the
Oh
You'll never
Know

They only
Knew

They knew
what was sacred
by the feel of the
floor beneath their feet
and the pounding
yearning in their
blood

And the ones who
Lit Up
were disturbing because
some began to
Glow
with the heat of
swallowed vowels
and
displaced passion
which grew to a
Fire
in their throat

And they sang their names
with all the vowels

The Ay in Allelulia
the Eee in Egypt
the Oh of their Howling Cries
and a strong, sure I
which offended
U

You didn't recognize the name
YHWH
anymore
But it was
GOD
clear and surely
with the pain and passion stuck back
between two
consonant visions
of the
Good Deity
laid out there before you
On the stone floor
which sparkled with
reflected flame
and lit up the
cavern
Which was as
beautiful
as a young woman
and all of the children
which
you'd
forgotten

The roof was like
glinting
salt
and the walls were
sparkling
diamonds

The mosaic was
colored
brown and orange
yellow and green
red and all the colors
in between

Showing scenes of love
and pain
and life
that had never been painted
but always existed
right
under your feet
in the
silent cavern
Which now fairly
screamed
the name of
God!
God!
God!
Like the blare of Chinese trumpets
or a thundering
Niagara
of
black water
or the cry of high-pitched agony
under the void
which only slowly
eased
into laughter
as the froth of
a pent-up river
comes into its pond

You never saw the waters
Sparkle
and you never heard the
Quiet
that comes from what's been
Said
And you never saw
the cavern
so
full of light
before

You gazed in open wonder
at all the
hidden secrets
and all the
sorrows bared

so it took a while
to notice

—but look
wait
spin around—

the frightening old
stone lion

was never

really
there.

Omicron

We struggle to catch up. jesus *is* storming through the city, crackling hot as a June thunderhead—and is it my imagination, or are the shadows moving against the wall as he passes, as if a competing sun is burning through the ancient streets?

But the way doesn't lead to the Romans.

"What's he doing?" Judas cries. "jesus, wait!"

He tries to snare jesus by the robe, but the way is narrow and choked with onlookers. They close about him like brambles. jesus thunders on ahead, unheeding his cry, though the echoes of it resound in the face of the other Apostles.

Down the avenue, cross the plaza. He's heading to the temple. Oh dear Christ, don't do this. It's the beginning of the end. Can't we put this off for another week or so? I made my peace with Andrew for you.

I can see Peter's face; he's as upset as ever. I can tell he wants to stop jesus, but he's also afraid of getting in trouble again, so he follows at close quarters, hoping to find some opening to speak.

John looks as nervous as a horse in a crowd, but he's behind his Master. *Whatever he chooses is best, whatever he chooses…*

James is ready to punch someone. Just one word and he'll go off like a bomb.

> Give thanks to the Lord, for he is good;
> His love endures forever.
> Announce it, house of Israel;
> Declare it, house of Aaron:
> His love endures forever.
> Let those who fear the Lord say it:
> "God's love endures forever!"
> When distressed I called to the Lord,
> and his answer was to set me free!
> The Lord is with me; God is my helper.
> I should not be afraid
> —what can mere mortals do to me?
> The Lord is with me, my aide and companion;

and I shall have the last laugh over my enemies…
It is better to find refuge in the Lord
than to trust in princes and rulers.
(Psalm 118:1–7, 9)

We reach the parking lot. I am panting, heart pounding. There's a heaviness in my chest. Sludge today, going green. Philip comes back to get me.

"You O.K.?" he asks.

I nod, too breathless to say anything. He clasps my arm to steady me, and we pause for a moment. jesus has already reached the temple. "Come on," I say, chuffing out the words. "I don't want to lose him." We cross the parking lot, avoid the greeters, refuse name tags.

I have become a stranger to my brothers, an alien to my own mother's sons. For zeal for your house has swallowed me whole. The insults of those who would insult you land upon me now. *(Psalm 69:8–9)*

There are money-changers in the narthex, just past the point of the stairs. They are doing brisk business today: turtledoves and crackers; naked blood, veiled bread. jesus glowers at them.

"Go learn what this means," he says. "I desire mercy, not sacrifice."

They don't even stir to reply. Their faces say it all: *Who are you to tell us what to do? This is sanctioned, fella, move along.*

jesus' hand automatically reaches for his belt, but his gaze passes over them with a scowl, and he moves on without saying another word. Another time, another place, and they would all be scrambling out onto the parking lot—but this is a different time, a different place. He crosses to the wide hall just outside the sanctuary, the narthex.

Let Israel say this:
"His love endures forever."

There is an ornamental fig here, looking haggard and root-bound. It has outgrown its pot, but no one has been willing to replant it. jesus shakes his head and searches for fruit, but finds none. He curses and puts his hand on the doors.

Let the house of Aaron say this:
"His love endures forever."

He enters an enormously empty cavern. Stone. The sanctuary soars to the sky with a tremendous gasp of stone. The people inside are lost peas in an upturned bowl. The pulpit floats halfway between earth and heaven, trying to get some control over the space. Row after row of seats march away from the altar; the first rows are empty, as if they had been scoured by its presence, as if someone had thrown a grenade. Two robed figures stand in the middle of the blast pattern.

Let those who fear the Lord say this:
"His love endures forever."

The windows are stained like wine and leaves. The light coming through them is colored and fractured. It glints off the delicate silver implements on the table, then reflects on the face of the assisting minister who, with hands raised, is midway through her prayer. She looks up, sees jesus and stops, confused. This isn't in the liturgy.

O Ephraim, what should I do with you? How shall I deal with you, Judah?
Your love, it is like a morning mist, like dew that vanishes early. Therefore I lashed you with prophets, and tore you to shreds with words.
Steadfast love is my desire, not sacrifice. Know me and bring that to the altar, rather than burnt offerings. (Hosea 6:4–6)

jesus just stands there and watches.

The priest frowns at the intrusion, and motions for his assistant to continue. She hovers uncertainly above the text. The congregation twists around uneasily to see what's happening.

jesus walks halfway up the aisle. Stops. The storm has retracted into his center now; it no longer flashes at the edges.

But listen to the Son before he sets: he is standing in the middle of the aisle, somewhere between the collection plates and the altar. He has three parables to tell.

"There was a woman who had a large attic under the roof of her house. In it she kept all the things her husband had left her. She was not a widow, but she lived like one.

"People felt sorry for her, so they brought her presents. They were all very pretty and well designed, and they all would have looked right in somebody else's house, but they did not fit her age. Nevertheless, she could not bear to part with them— even the ones that were clearly not right for her—so she stored them in her attic.

"In time, her attic became so full that it could not hold any more trinkets. So she opened the doors to her attic and let the collection spill into her upper rooms. But that did not solve her problem, because she still could not throw anything out. So soon the upper rooms became full, and she started to store things in her living and dining rooms.

"When visitors came into her home, they were shocked by the garish assembly of furniture and trinkets. They all thought she was crazy. She made them sit on chairs that were too rickety to support them; she wouldn't let them shift the knickknacks to get space to stand. If the chair broke, or if they stumbled over a piece of rubbish, she said it was their fault and grew angry. Very few visitors kept coming to her home. But her family loved her and made excuses for her, so she never got any help or changed.

"One day, however, a rude stranger did come by, and openly laughed at the unsightly jumble. It infuriated her. To stop up his mouth she sent her grandchild up into the attic to retrieve the most beautiful thing her husband had left her; but the attic was so full that her grandchild could not find the pearl. He did, however, find a pair of cheap tin buttons that looked like chocolate candies. The child tried to eat them, choked on them, and died."

The first parable ends, and the congregation waits unhappily for a better ending. But when jesus starts speaking again, he starts a second parable.

"A man once told a story about how we sin.

"In it, a man named Dusty is allowed anything at all—complete freedom—except the one thing that will hurt him. He is forbidden to try to make himself like God. But Dusty, in consultation with his wife Dawn, a serpent named Loophole and their son Will, decides that is the one thing they must do above all others.

"Estrangement breaks out between the conspirators. When God comes to view the damage, he hears four different stories:

"'It's Dawn's fault,' says Dusty.

"'It's Loophole's fault,' says Dawn.

"'It's Will's fault,' says Loophole.

"'It's your fault,' says Will.

"And so the man finished his story, showing how sin always passes the blame, always leading back to God. His listeners loved the story and told it to their children. It was a perfectly truthful story about how we sin. But just to make the point, as the story was handed down from generation to generation, the children, and their children's children, changed it to a reason *why* we sin.

"'Why do you sin?' the stranger asked.

"'It's Dusty's fault,' the children said.

"And so the story was proved true, even by its false retelling."

The congregation is becoming restless. An usher moves up the aisle to restore order, but jesus stops him with a glance, and tells his final parable.

"A man planted a vineyard, rented it to some farmers and went away for a long time. At harvest time he sent a servant to the tenants, to fetch some fruit of the vineyard. But the tenants beat him and sent him away empty-handed. He sent another servant, but that one also they beat and shamed and sent away empty-handed. He sent still a third, and they wounded him and threw him out.

"Then the owner of the vineyard said, 'What shall I do? I will send my son, whom I love; perhaps they will respect him.'

"But when the tenants saw him, they talked the matter over. 'This is the heir,' they said. 'Let's kill him, and the inheritance will be ours.'

"So they threw him out of the vineyard and killed him. But the inheritance was not theirs, and their consciences convicted them again and again. So they put together an alibi. This is what they said: the owner of the vineyard *wanted* them to kill his son. It was part of the owner's mysterious, psychopathic ways, which none of them could fathom. It was an instrument of the owner's intention to give them the vineyard, they said, and they drew up a Last Will and Testament to prove it. They drew this new testament in the very blood of his son, and bound it up with other important documents. They forbade the unbinding of any of them, and passed it on to their children as if it were the truth. But it never was a true will, and when it went through probate the judge recognized it as a forgery.

"'This is an offense,' said the judge, 'and a libel against the victim and his father.'

"'It's a paradox,' they appealed.

"'It's a sham,' the court replied, and threw the case out at once.

"Now, what do you think the judge will do to those wicked tenants?"

There is a stunned silence in the sanctuary. For an unbearable length of time, the only sound is the faint whisper of dropping leaves coming from the narthex. It is a weeping fig tree, merely ornamental. jesus turns and walks out of the sanctuary, across the falling leaves and into the hills. He doesn't stay for the wine today.

I have a true story to tell you. It's actually Martha's story, brought home from church. Martha was teaching Sunday school. She had a very small class, but she worked very hard. Her kids loved her. They had, in fact, a very special kind of freedom with her, the kind of freedom that feels safe to share any kind of thing they think. They knew they were secure in her love. If you ever met Martha, you would know why.

One Sunday, Martha asked her kids what they thought about God. They did what kids usually do when you ask an open-ended question. They rolled their eyes and looked dumb. It always takes some work to get the water flowing.

"Well," she said, going for the most basic thing she could think of, "is he good, bad, or what?"

One of them—we'll call him Timothy—looked at her and said something a lot of Sunday school teachers will never hear, because they are not Martha.

"Well," Timothy said, "God killed his son."

Shut your ears, Timothy! You're listening too well. That fig tree won't bear you any fruit, Tim. You just hold on to the notion that God is good, not evil, and that loving you doesn't mean he wants to kill you. If you let that filth in, you'll spend the rest of your life trying to scrape it off. When they start to bleat their poison in the big room, you just plug your ears and chant with me: *God is good. God is good. God is good.* That will be our measuring stick, you and me. If anything doesn't measure up to that, you'll know it's broken. This is your basic wiring, child. You won't be able to bulk-erase it later, take it from me I've tried and tried Tim you just stay away from that piece of hate and don't ever let it touch your heart or you'll end up as crippled as I am can't you see the way I've struggled and I'm still being dragged down down to hell...

Don't believe that God is the Devil, no matter what your church says.

God is good
God is good
God is good
God is good
God is good
God is good
God is good
God is good
God is good
God is good
God is good
God is good
God is good
God is good
God is good
God is good
God is good
God is good
God is good
God is good
God is good
God is good
God is good
God is good
God is good
God is good
God is good
God is good
God is good
God is good
God is good
God is good
God is good
God is good
God is good

God is good
God is good
God is good
God is good
God is good
God is good
God is good
God is good
God is good
God is good
God is good
God is good
God is good
God is good
God is good
God is good
God is good
God is good
God is good
God is good
God is good
God is good
God is good
God is good
God is good
God is good
God is good
God is good
God is good
God is good
God is good
God is good
God is good
God is good
God is good
God is good
God is good
God is good
God is good
God is good
God is good
God is good
God is good
God is good

Priest and prophet reel from beer and wine. They clamour in their cups and stagger; they misread their visions and err in judgement. Every table is covered with vomit, no place unspoiled.

"Who is it that the prophet hopes to teach, to whom will they make sense? Babes newly weaned, just taken from the breast? For it is command upon command, line after line, rule after rule, a little here, a little there."

So people will think they hear God speaking barbarously, in a strange new tongue, this people to whom he once said, "This is true rest; let the weary have rest"—but they did not hear, so this will be the only word of the Lord to them, in harsh cries and raucous shouts: "A little more here, a little there!" Rule after rule, command upon command, do and do and do… and so, as they walk, they will stumble backwards. They will be injured, caught and trapped.

Listen, then, to the word of the Lord, you arrogant men who rule this people in Jerusalem:

You say, "We have made a treaty with Death and signed a pact with the grave, Sheol. When overwhelming disaster sweeps by, it shall leave us untouched, for we have refuge in the lie, a hiding place in falsehood."

Listen, then, to the Lord God's reply:

"Look, I am laying a stone in Zion, a block of granite, a precious corner-stone for a firm foundation; he who has faith shall not waver. I will use justice as a plumb-line and righteousness the plummet; hail will clear away your refuge of lies, and flood-waters will carry off your shelter. Then your treaty with Death will be annulled and your pact with the grave will fail. When the raging disaster passes through you will be beaten down by it. As often as it sweeps by, it will take you; morning after morning it will come, day and night."

This message is sheer terror to those who grasp its meaning. Your bed is too short for you to stretch out on; your blanket too narrow to fully cover you. *(Isaiah 28:7b–20)*

Pi

"The lamp of your body is the eye. When your eyes see well, you have light for your whole body; but when the eyes are bad, you are in darkness. See to it, then, that the light within you is not darkness." (Luke 11:34–35)

It's 2:45 a.m., and the house is quiet. Martha, Mary, Lazarus and Philip are sleeping. I'm running 3.5 liters of oxygen—high for me—and it feels like dirty Chicago air rather than a fresh arctic breeze. Bad sign, that. It's not the air that's changed, but the gerbils. They're getting aggressive.

My blood sugar is 149. I just took 7 units of insulin, and I'm waiting 45 minutes before I eat my breakfast. The temperature is 82, and the humidity is 90 percent...

Numbers! Complicated, real-world numbers, and every one of them a factor, no matter how strange-seeming.

It's now 3:10. Just finished hacking up a few gerbils. They didn't stick Chicago air in that tank, after all. (Have to cancel the lawsuit.) Now it feels like Flint. Maybe if I work really hard, I can get it up to Corpus Christi before I go back to bed. But my ribs feel bruised, and I'm sick of vibrating. I just want to sleep, sleep.

That's a bad sign, too. When you most want to just lie down and rest, that's the worst time to do it.

"I could never do that," people sometimes say to me.

Oh, yes you could.

I used to run cross-country when I was younger. I learned a few mental tricks to finish the race. When you're about to fall over, you don't think about the next three miles. You play dumb little games to shorten the distance: *See that tree, about a hundred feet down? Just make it to there, that's all. That's all you have to do, is just make it to that tree...* Then, when you get to that tree, you look at the bush on top of the hill. *See that bush? Just make it to that bush, that's all...* The last three miles are run one hundred steps at a time. It's just what you have to do.

Lately, I've shrunken to praying for good breath and low pain for the day. If I'm feeling especially greedy, I'll ask for some time to get some work done.

I'm not the only one that knows the trick of long-distance running. The A.A. motto is "take it one day at a time." Cancer patients come to it, too. Everyone comes to it when they have to. Call it a gift of God, advice from the Spirit.

I remember, back in my rubber chaplain days, sitting with folks who had to do physical therapy to stretch and strengthen their limbs. It's such a struggle for those good people. They can know, intellectually, that a little pain right now will prevent a lot of pain later on, but after a while the spirit just loses steam. That's when they have to dig down deep and find the steel that lies in every human heart. Some folks don't know it's there. But it is.

Maybe if Christians saw that side of folks, they wouldn't think humans were so bad; maybe we ought to send them on field trips to P.T. and A.A. rooms across the country.

Trees growing out of the rock. There are *millions* of them.

Communion is tonight. I don't know if I can make it. I have a doctor's appointment this afternoon, and though I can technically make it back in time, I'm so washed out after that, I'm rarely good for anything. All that vertical time, you know. I have to make up for it with horizontal time: postural drainage with my head down. These days I can only go two to four hours without the bat couch. Drives me crazy.

I'd really like to go. I've been missing so many events lately I'm beginning to feel like a stranger. Guilt always circles about my head like a vulture when I've missed too many services.

The most deadly phrase in church social-speak, by the way, is *we missed you*. Even if by some miracle you use it sincerely, the listener's ear will still hear *I noticed your absence*—because that's what it usually means in Christian circles, where guilt-trippers and guilt junkies feed upon each other like fish and bugs in a small pond. If you ever say that phrase, I will come back and haunt you. I will stand at the foot of your bed, moan and rattle chains. I'm not kidding.

jesus can't sleep, either. He sits beside me on the couch, watches me write.
Scritch, scritch.

I always use a pencil for the first draft. There's not enough resistance to a word processor—it's like trying to blow up a balloon with no balloon. After I've smudged up real paper, I'll type it in and digitally process the revisions. I've got a computer setup on the bat couch that lets me type upside down.

Sometimes I look at my strange computer accommodations and think of those awful Sunday supplement articles on the handicapped. Can this really be my life? It must be someone else; there must be some mistake. I'm *me*, not one of *them*.

"Got an appointment today?" jesus asks.

I nod.

"Good. Hope they find something."

"Yeah. You know I'd really like to go—"

"—I don't want you to come."

That stops me short; I don't think I've ever heard anyone say that before. "No?"

"It'd be stupid. Stay, take care of yourself."

What a wonderful combination of words. I'm dumbfounded at such unexpected grace. Permission to be healthy!

I've tried letting people know that C.F. patients respond very poorly to stress. I asked them to not increase the pressure on me, because that brings on my pneumonia quicker. It shaves off the life-time I have left with Martha, and that makes me angry, because she deserves better.

Even something like "We don't know what we'd do without you" can be very controlling—especially when you're begging to get some help, as I was. I'd made a direct request. But it never works. They just don't seem to get it—or maybe they do, and just don't want to set down a familiar tool.

"Nathaniel, did you ever hear the story about the king who hurt his foot on a stone?"

"No."

"He demanded that the whole world be covered with leather, and his feet got very bruised and sore while he waited for the kingdom to be completed; some say he might have been better off to buy a pair of shoes."

I sigh.

"Why is it that your graceful word is always followed by a reproving one?"

He looks surprised by the accusation at first; then recognition hits his sleepy face. He ruefully kneads his forehead. "Because I'm getting testy too, maybe. You folks wear me out..." His eyes are bleary and red; he pinches the bridge of his eyebrow. "Forgive me if I push hard. I love you too much to leave you in the womb."

"I know," I say. "But it's not easy... I could as well ask you why the cobbler's shop is strewn with broken glass, if that's where we're supposed to find shoes."

He grunts and concedes the point. You don't have to tell *him* about what's on the floor; he's been wielding the broom for three years.

But it's really no contest. Both points are true at the same time. That's what makes real life so cussed.

He looks eroded, beaten down. He hangs his head, closes his eyes and falls still. His elbows are propped on his knees, his hands clasped together in a half-hearted gesture that might be prayer, might be simple support. He waves slowly in a barely perceptible orbit, like an unsteady reed. For a while I think he has fallen asleep, but eventually I catch the strains of an ancient melody, a chant from the evening service.

Hear my prayer, O Lord;
Listen to my cry.

> Keep me as the apple of your eye;
> Hide me in the shadow of your wings.
> In righteousness I shall see you;
> When I awake,
> Your presence will give me joy.

Be present, merciful God, and protect us through the hours of this night,
so that we who are wearied
by the changes and chances of life
may find our rest in you...[35]

Compline. It is perhaps the most lovely service in the world. I can't tell you how many times it got me through when nothing else would. So many long nights in chapel, I would come in aching and wondering... and then the warm, beautiful music of Compline would pray for me. The requests I could no longer make; the hopes that were dying on the vine; the sense of protection and the ability to approach God for surcease...

Dear God, if you hadn't made that service for me I would have put a gun to my head years ago. I was so desperate at times.

I sing the canticle back to him:

> Guide us waking, O Lord,
> And guard us sleeping;
> That awake we may watch with Christ
> And asleep we may rest in peace.

He smiles and sings the reply:

> Lord, now let your servant go in peace;
> Your word has been fulfilled.
> My own eyes have seen the salvation
> Which you have prepared in the sight
> Of every people;
> A light to reveal you to the nations
> And the glory of your people Israel.
> Glory to the Father, and to the Son,
> And to the Holy Spirit;
> As it was in the beginning,
> Is now and will be forever, Amen.[36]

We sit in the new quiet and listen. I set my pencil down. He breathes in deeply, savors the air and slowly opens his eyes.

"Do you know why I picked Peter?" he asks, curiously.

"Sometimes I have to wonder. He seems so rock-headed."

He smiles. "Yes, he is—and you haven't seen the worst of it."

"But he is human, Nathaniel. And every one who follows in his footsteps will be human, too. That's the material we've got to work with. Sometimes it looks like that's not good enough. But it will be.

"Look at me: I am becoming the son of every one of you, the picture of what God is making. When you look, you will see what it means to be fully human.

"What do you see right now? I still weep, I still get tired. Weakness and fear. You can't put the flesh on without it. But the other side is true, too. It's possible to have a foundation that is unshakable, rooted in the confidence of God's love: leather for your soul, even here on this rough earth."

"I do not look to other people for honor. With you it is different, as I know well, for you have no love for God in you." *(John 5:41–42)*

The Pharisee said to Jesus, "You are witness in your own cause; your testimony is not valid."

Jesus replied, "My testimony is valid, even though I do bear witness about myself; because I know where I come from, and where I am going. You do not know either where I come from or where I am going.

"You judge by worldly standards. I pass judgement on no one. But if I do judge, my judgement is valid because it is not I alone who judge, but I and the One who sent me. In your own law it is written that the testimony of two witnesses is valid. Here am I, a witness in my own cause, and my other witness is the Father who sent me." *(John 8:13–18)*

"Don't give up yet, Nat. We'll make it."

I look down at the floor. "Hard to believe."

"We will. It's just growing pains."

He stretches, gathers his strength. "Yarrgh! I can't believe you do this all the time—you're one, I guess, that won't fall asleep in the garden..."

He gets up and walks to the window. His robe makes a little breeze as he passes. I long, oh how I long, to reach out and touch it. But I keep my hand still.

Three times, Paul wrote. Three times he asked to have the thorn in his flesh removed, and three times the answer came back: "Is not my grace sufficient for you?"

Why not four times, you ask? Because each time you approach the robe, it's a little like dying. We all get tired of dying. After a while we just stop.

"I get tired, too," he sighs, looking out the window.

I know, I know. Dear Christ, I don't want to crucify you. Forgive me for my anger. I don't know what to do with it.

"I'm struggling with myself to carry out my Father's will," he says, "and the message is getting heavy. I am praying hard, Nat, and I'm also getting answers that I don't like. 'Speak what I have spoken,' says the Father, 'and I will raise all humanity up with you.' That's something that will sound a lot better once I've passed through it! But right now, it makes me tremble."

He puts his hand to the window frame and grasps it. I can see every vein pulsing in his hand. His voice is like the scrape of a cinder block.

"But," he vows, "I will do it."

He looks into the night and sees—what? Darkness? The void? The next tree? Whatever it is, he stares at it long and hard without flinching.

"By tomorrow," he says, his eyes brimming, "you will know that God is not the author of pain, but the victim of it. Pay attention, Nat. I'm only going to do this once."

He is not immune to the taunting of his adversary; he is not removed from the world. Far from it. The difference is a subtle one, I think. He is like an adult who makes a hard choice for the benefit of his family, knowing what is best. Others may describe the mystery of his being differently, but I can only find one word to describe what I see: mature.

"I have a baptism of fire waiting for me. I have to enter your burning hearts. I wish it were already done. I wish we could just leap over this moment… You don't really know me; I look forward to the day when we might have more time, when this—fever—is gone. I would like to relax, to just eat a meal with you without this tension between us…"

He turns from the window and faces me with a wan smile. It sounds like a gentle fantasy in the middle of a storm; not very real to either of us tonight.

I can't think of anything to say. There is a part of me, so frustrated with my discolored heart, that can't open up to him. How easy for him to talk about the love of flawed beings! He doesn't know how warped I am inside… my body isn't the half of it. It is the picture of perfection when compared to my soul. I am infected through and through, crippled beyond hope.

He moves away from the window and opens the door, with no reply to his wish. I have disappointed him again. The most deserving man I have ever met, the greatest, the person most worthy of respect, and I have let him down once more. I can picture the hurt on his face…

…but he pauses at the threshold, turns, and *smiles*.

"Not infected, Nathaniel. Incomplete. Like the spine of a week-old fetus. That's all."

Then the door closes.

I rush to the window and watch him pass quickly out of the window's light. The darkness swallows him up. He will not speak to me again until he comes into his inheritance.

How dare he do this to me? He won't even give me the benefit of his anger.

It accuses me even more.

I don't understand
said Pastor Trim
why their faces
are so long
and the eyes
so sad
at the rail
where their sins
are forgiven why
aren't they
dancing there should
be joy because
jesus died for
them
they are free why
do they
look so
condemned
I don't
understand

Another time, another world. Tuesday night under the fig tree. A night class. Styrofoam cups and slouching students. Snow coming down in white fluffs out the window. I remember the smell of coffee.

"Guilt," said Rabbi Halverstadt, "can be forgiven. Shame cannot."

I was new to this, still eating figs furiously and leaving them undigested. "What do you mean?" I asked. "I thought they were the same."

"Guilt is the consequence of sin. It comes when you do something wrong. We all sin. When we see it, guilt tells us that we violated our own basic identity. It's like a child who knows he shouldn't get into the candy drawer, but does it anyway. He knows he's acting against the way he's been raised; so he feels guilt. Forgiveness heals guilt. If you confess to your Mom, she forgives you—and you go out to play."

"Shame is a different feeling. When you do something wrong, it tells you that you *fulfilled who you are*. You are a bad kid: you just proved it. You are simply working out your destiny. Forgiveness has no effect on shame. If you confess to your Mom, she forgives you for this infraction, and sends you off. But the wound is unhealed; you still believe you are bad at root, and you know it will only be a matter of time before you reveal your true nature again.

"The church is full of people looking for healing of their shame, but getting forgiveness instead. They keep coming back even worse, because it's not working for them and they think it should."

The lights finally come on; I nod.

"I remember a Thanksgiving service I saw in a distant church," I said. "The message was such a double-whammy: God loves you, but you don't deserve it. God loves you, but you are evil. God forgives you, but if he had any sense he'd just wipe you off the face of the earth right now. So you just better be grateful, you low-life scum, that God loves you."

"Exactly," the Rabbi smiled.

I've been digesting all I ate in Chicago for nearly two years, and the more I've digested—and the more I've worked inside the church—the more I've come to believe that the Church's basic mechanisms are broken. Christian theology induces shame and hands out forgiveness, much the same way Internet companies hand out free software and sell access time. The gift of shame is the Trojan Horse that keeps you coming back for more.

This needs to be said: I have belonged to churches which, led by the Spirit, created a healing place founded on good love. Pastor Bob Walters and Calvary Lutheran Church; Pastor Bob Klonowski and Lebanon Lutheran Church; Rector Ed Rose, Father Reese Friedman and St. Peter's Episcopal Church; you have all been the gifts of God to me. You were part of my healing.

But I have also seen plenty of sickness break out, in a recognizable pattern. A syndrome, if you will. It's something more regular than the random wounds of a random population, something that might yield to a little epidemiology. And I think the most telling diagnostic clue is this: the sickest churches have been the ones that followed our inherited tradition most closely. The healthy ones were always silently leavening the tradition, weeding, de-emphasizing, spin-doctoring.

We've come to depend upon such exceptions to the rule of shame. We are like a car company releasing vehicles with no bolts on the wheels, hoping people will find and install their own.

Listen to the basic language of redemption:

• God clothes us in Christ's righteousness.
• We are forgiven for jesus' sake.
• God credits Christ's goodness to our account.
• When God looks at us, God sees jesus.

I want you to imagine the following dialogue from a parent to two children:

"You are bad, Billy, and there is nothing I can do about it. But Sally, your sister, is good. She does everything right, and I love her. So I tell you what I'm going to do, Billy, so that I can stand to let you live in my home. Whenever I look at you, I'm going to pretend that I'm looking at Sally. Whenever I see you and get nauseated, I'm going to close my eyes and think of Sally instead. I'll think about how lovely and pure she is, and that will calm me down. Then, as long as I can hold the image of Sally in my head, I might be able to be nice to you. But never forget, I'm not really looking at you, Billy. I'll never look at *you*, or love you for your own sake; only Sally's sake."

Now I want you to imagine how Billy will grow up. When he acts out who he is, how will he act? Will he ever feel truly loved for himself? Will he act as a rational adult worthy of love, able to let his "yes be yes and his no be no?" And what kind of complicated feelings will he have toward Sally? Will he ever be able to truly be at ease with her—or will her presence always stand as a subtle accusation, no matter how graceful her words?

Rho

Joanna is a little-known disciple of jesus, recorded only in Luke's account.[37] That's a shame; she's a nice lady with few airs, a shrewd manager by trade, a minister by natural vocation.

After jesus cured her of her health problems, she became a major patron of the movement, supporting the Apostles with her own money. Yet you'd never know that if you met her; she prefers to stay in the background. She works harder than three other people and waves off any recognition for it. You may not have met her, but you would recognize her. She holds up a mission near you.

Since I was unable to attend, I've included Joanna's account of the Last Supper, and her reflections on jesus' last days.

"Oh, Lord! That's going back a ways, Hon. You're going to tax this old girl's head. You really want me to…?

"…Alright.

"Well, first off: I don't recall it being much of a to-do. It was just another Passover, and not a special one at that. We were a bunch of kids, eager to get it over, get back to the revolution, you know. It was looking back, that's when it picked up more meaning.

"It was the same way with my Grandma, too. The last time I went out to see her, it was just a plum day. Then she died, and everything we said took on this hazy glow. You know how it goes.

"I'm not saying we deliberately changed things; it was—um—more natural than that. You've got to keep in mind we all went into shock; took years to work it out, years. We'd been building something wonderful! The Son of David was back! Can you imagine? We were on top of the world for a while… and we were young, too, of course. Then it was all dashed against the rocks. It hurt. Still does, I guess.

"Anyway, none of us enjoys reliving it. Some pretty it up. But we were ashamed of jesus for letting us down. Executed with two thieves! No angels, no kingdom; after all the power he'd poured out on others, he just hung there.

"He just hung there. Can you imagine how humiliating that was?

"Oh, I got hacked off. I called up for him to *do something*. I hate to say it, but I swear most of the yelling came from me…the *goyim*, they didn't care enough to taunt. He was just another felon to them. To us, he was the betrayer. I could kick myself, now.

"Mary says, well, at least you were there. Right: I was there to scream. Some comfort! Been better if I'd run out with the men, but I was just so angry, I could have killed someone.

"Mary, she could barely stand up. I can remember hearing her moan 'not again,' over and over. Not that she'd ever watched a crucifixion before—she hadn't. Neither had I. But there's been plenty of times when she started to hope and then it was ripped away from her. Same goes for me, too, I suppose. jesus wasn't the first promise to jump into the sky.

"Let me tell you: we were entirely centered upon ourselves during all of this. It was mostly what was happening to me, how dare he do this to me, that sort of stuff. jesus died *alone*.

"Guess it shouldn't be too surprising if later on we found meanings that were all about us. What did we get out of it? How did we turn a profit? Nobody really wanted to admit we'd *lost* anything.

"I don't know when I first heard the phrase 'Good Friday,' but I hope I won't hear it again. It pretty much sums up the pose they settled on. They took the worst day of the world and called it good. Pretty sick. Those folks would be great around an airplane crash, hey?

"Thomas never went along with any of that. He grieved hard, and wouldn't let anyone stop him. That's when the nickname 'Doubting Thomas' stuck—everyone else hated him for not playing happy. He didn't spend much time with the others after that; he rarely came around. I haven't seen him in years.

"Oh, we're a sorry lot, aren't we? If I came out of a tomb to find the kind of friends he had waiting for him, I think I'd just leave town with no forwarding address; let them muddle through on their own. But I'm not jesus, of course.

"—bless your heart. You're quite a smoothie when you want to be.

"By the by—this story they're telling about Tom? Let's set the record straight. They're telling the facts all right, but the spin they put on it is just plain mean. jesus wasn't wagging his finger at Thomas. Thomas said he needed to put his fingers in his wounds before he trusted him again—and jesus gave him exactly what he needed. That's all it was. They're making him an object lesson about doubt. Well, listen to the punishment, for once!

"jesus knew what was going on in Tom's mind, and he took care of it. Then, when Thomas believed and felt terrible, this is what jesus said, honest to God: 'Thomas,' he said, 'don't worry about it. Those that can believe what they haven't seen are truly blessed.' Some trip to the woodshed! But people always get their digs in, don't they?

"Well, at any rate. I'll rant all night. I bet you're regretting asking me."

"The supper."

She taps her finger on her upper lip.

"There were two things I can remember. First off, jesus was sad. We all felt it, but we tried to ignore it. He'd try to bring it up, but we'd find something else to talk about. We did the same thing to my Grandma; makes me wonder what on earth's wrong in our heads. Same thing to a tee. She knew she was going to die and kept on trying to say goodbye—and we wouldn't let her; it just made us too uncomfortable, so we'd pat her on the hand and say something like 'Oh, don't be silly!' or 'You'll be fine,' or 'You're not going anywhere.'"

I murmur in recognition, and she smiles. "You been there, too? Why do we do that? Do you know?

"Well, you can guess what the atmosphere was like. False cheer, lots of tension; people getting angry with jesus for being so down. Not a great holiday. At one point he said something that yanked our chains for a minute. 'I've changed this supper forever for you,' he said. 'From now on, when you drink this wine or taste this bread, you won't be able to stop thinking of me.' You can imagine how well that went over with the party.

"I think Bart made a joke about mounting a plaque on the table. Then we all went back to eating, more on edge than ever. You could have cut the air with a sword.

"The other thing that happened, though—that made more of a happier impression on me. Peter, James and John were woofing and barking over some stupid issue or other, and jesus had enough. He got up, stripped himself near naked and got himself a bowl of water. Then he started to wash everyone's feet."

She takes on a spark I haven't seen in her before; her eyes widen, she holds up her hand without thinking.

"'Men are always trying to climb to the top,' he said. 'But God is at the bottom. God is under the lowliest beetle, serving it life and love. Children, if God stopped thinking of you for one minute, you would all disappear.'

"—All this time he's moving and dipping, moving and dipping, whispering quietly—

"'The farther you climb to the top,' he said, 'the harder it is to be close to God. God is at the bottom. If you must compete for seats near God, you must sink lower and lower—and no matter how low you sink, you'll never be closer than the least of your littlest children. This is why I am free to sink beneath the earth,' he goes. 'Because I know who is waiting for me. God is underneath you all, like bedrock, like earth. God is at the bottom...'

"I remember when he said that, I got a chill down my spine. I suddenly saw everything turned around, and realized that all the things jesus had been talking about weren't sacrifices, but *privileges*. You know, you keep thinking you're supposed to be dirt... and then one day you realize you're supposed to be fertile soil. It's the same, maybe, but then again maybe it's not.

"When I came back to attention, he'd gotten to Peter. Peter started to compete over that, then, trying to be lowlier than jesus—well, you've heard the rest. Poor Pete. He's always out of the oven before the crust is hard.

"Anyway, that's how I remember it. Somehow, when they tell that one, they put more of a spin on the need for jesus to wash us. Us washing each other, that part fades. But that's not what I heard that night. And they're real big these days on putting something together to commemorate the dinner. I guess Bart's joke wasn't too far off. Funny which event they want to highlight, huh? Well, you can't have people yanking their socks off, I guess… might slip a little dignity. God forbid we might come down a few rungs…

"I don't know. I just don't know about all these ceremonies. Thomas, last time we talked, he said ritual was supposed to work like a rehearsal. We're supposed to act out the community's wishes, he said, then go out and actually *do it*. I'm trying to think of an analogy from real life, but I can't think of one right now. He had a real good one. Tom's a thinker. The only thing I can think of is my cat, who scratches outside the litter box rather than in it—but I guess that doesn't make the same point, does it?"

She laughs then—an innocent sound behind sparkling, shrewd eyes—and rises. She's getting dinner ready for a Wednesday hymn-sing at the shelter, and she's already wasted too much time.

"Thanks for asking me, Nat. Good luck with your book, now—and don't show it to anyone around here, or I'll skin you alive."

Sigma

Every moment
A thick beat
In a heavy chest
I waver on the table
Try to remember
What
This was for
Stalactites
In my breath
Droop
To the floor
Ah don't
Move
Wham
Wham

It's frightening how fast an infection can pick up speed and tip over into something resembling a death spiral. Frightening, too, how fast a doctor can move in those conditions. Martha and I sometimes dread my innocent little clinic visits. I can walk into that room and not walk back out.

So it is this time. My system is sagging like an overloaded power line, and Dr. Pettigrove can see it. He hooks up the pulse-ox, and even that little traitor agrees, in sad, slow boops, that I'm not feeling well.

That's scary. Because I'm a "compensated" lung patient, the pulse-ox doesn't indicate much. We usually have to go to arterial blood gasses to see what's going on.[38] If the pulse-ox is unhappy, I don't even want to think about my A.B.G.'s.

Suddenly the nurse is on the phone arranging a hospital room...
...a blue-suited man is here with a wheelchair...
...and Martha is clutching her purse the way she does when she's scared.

Martha, I'm so sorry to let you down. It's this body of mine. You just didn't know, did you, what you were marrying? Sometimes I feel like a car dealer who passed off a lemon on a young lady.

The gentle man wheels me toward the tunnel. Martha follows.
"I'm sorry."
"Don't apologize. It's not your fault."
"O.K.… sorry."
She gives me a squeeze on the arm.

I've always tried to stay healthy for other people's sake. It's the way I'm wired. Until I married, the pressure was greatest with my parents. It makes me angry that they've had to endure so much. I want to shield them from more heartbreak. Even before I became a teenager, it had become my life's goal: I was going to die *after* them. They've had too many goodbyes already—surely I should be able to shoulder a few. If the Universe *were* fair, it would let me do that, don't you think?

Bad news, Nathaniel. The Universe ain't fair.

White Water Days
Your raft dips
And the quiet stream
Is gone
Hang on
For dear life
And look
For Jesus
In the waves
Dry Days
Dry Days
Oh come again
Seamaster, Windbreaker
Stormslayer, Peacemaker
Your feet are
Drier than mine.

Let me show you the core of my belief. Everyone who survives seminary has one; after the Bible is run through the meat-grinder of analysis, we all come out with some little chunk of bone to cling to. Mine is derived from the fifteenth chapter of First Corinthians. Biblical scholars believe it is the earliest written record of the oral witness that built the church.[39] If the Christ story accumulated barnacles upon its immersion into the sea of thought, this little piece of scripture represents the lowest level of barnacles we can hope for. It is what I came out of seminary deciding to proclaim. It has few reasons behind it, which is one of the reasons I like it. It has all the rational analysis of a UFO report.

> I would remind you, sisters and brothers, of the Good News that was brought to us, and which we received. It is the story upon which you stand—if you hold fast to the message that was proclaimed to you—or fall, if you come to trust in vanities.
> It is of the first importance that you remember this: Jesus the Christ died as a result of our sin, as scripture and prophecy predicted. He was buried, and on the third day he was raised, as was also predicted, and he appeared to many people, more than five hundred. *(1 Corinthians 15:1–6)*

There you go. The Gospel According to Nathaniel. I've rendered it as I believe it, scraped down to the level that is right for me. This is the piece of bone I carry with me, after seminary, church work and thirty-six years of cystic fibrosis. There are other things that are useful and instructive, certainly, but this is the chunk upon which I shall either stand or fall.

Ninety-nine words.

I suspect it's pretty obvious why I hold onto this scrap. If not, I'll let my friend Paul explain it. He says it so much better than I ever could:

> Now, if Christ is proclaimed as raised from the dead, how can some of you say there is no resurrection of the dead? If there is no resurrection of the dead, then Christ has not been raised; and if Christ has not been raised, you have believed in lies. If Christ is not alive, we are of all people most to be pitied.
> But in fact Christ has been raised from the dead, the first part of a great harvest. This is your faith; this is what you hold on to. *(1 Corinthians 15:12–20)*

Boy, he sure captured the essence of it, didn't he? That's our hope and predicament all rolled into one. Like it or not, the only thing the Church has in its hand is a set of embarrassing UFO reports. We dress it up and try to make it look impressive, but that's what it gets down to. The first creed was *He is risen.* That is what built Christianity. The rest is just a footnote, and usually bad theodicy, besides.

As one of my professors at seminary (Pete Pero, another gift of God) had a habit of saying: "I'm going to stand over here with you people—and I sure hope you're telling the truth!" That's the crux of it. Kind of scary, isn't it?

I have a UFO report of my own. It helps build my confidence in the first report, even as it changes my perception of its meaning. It's kind of weird, but I'll share it with you anyway. (I've already betrayed the fact that I'm a wild-eyed loose cannon, as loony as Matthew. Too late to stop now...)

> I am obliged to boast. Although there is nothing to be gained, I will go on to tell of visions and revelations granted by the Lord. I know a Christian man who fourteen years ago was caught up to the third heaven. Whether it was in the body or

out of the body I do not know—God knows. And I know that this same man—
whether in the body or out of the body I do not know—God knows—was caught
up into paradise and heard inexpressible things, things that man may not repeat.

(2 Corinthians 12:1–4)

Scholars think the context of the above passage indicates that Paul was talking
about himself. We all get a little embarrassed about talking about this stuff. Even in
seminary, the students have to undergo many secret handshakes before they pull out
the *real* reasons why they're there. No one likes to look like a crackpot.

O.K. Here goes…

About eleven years ago I developed a cycle of apnea that came and went unpre-
dictably. I would stop breathing while I slept. The pause would not usually last
long—just long enough to jerk me awake with a bang. Memory and awareness
would get switched on at the same time, a jolt of aliveness and simultaneous sensation of deadness freshly fled. It would thud into me from deep sleep, arcing my
body, sometimes waking Martha with the convulsion, and then it would be over. I
would lay there and listen to my heart pound, and wonder what *that* was all about.
Then I'd eventually go back to sleep, because there was nothing better to do.

One morning the second half of the cycle forgot to happen. I just stopped
breathing. No switch of adrenaline, no defibrillator, just a long, long, empty space. I
remember waking up about two inches off the bed, floating up like a soap bubble
on a slow wind. It was a pleasant way to come to consciousness; there was no pain.
No pain at all.

Imagine you've heard a buzz all your life. From the moment of your birth there
has been an incessant, high-pitched whine so ever-present that you didn't even
know it was there, until it disappeared.

A flood of emotions washes over you: joy at the wonderful quiet, grief that
you'd never heard it before. It's a release from bondage never known, and its relief
is coupled—almost exactly matched—with the shock of recognition: *I was living
with that? I've been suffering with that all my life and never known?*

But the pain I'm speaking of was not physical.

This happened eleven years ago, long before my life became overrun with the
hurts I now know. I was amazingly healthy for a C.F. patient, not yet hospitalized.

The pain was the feeling of separation. It was the cost of this body, the burden of
putting on the flesh. I felt like a waterdrop falling into a vast bucket of rainwater, losing my sense of loneliness.

It's terribly lonely to be alive. No matter how many friends you have, there is an
aching spot somewhere that wonders if you are the only person who feels the way
you do. Are there other dreams, fears, hopes and failures in the world like yours—or
are you truly an orphan? As soon as we move from infancy to early childhood we discover a suffocating sense of estrangement, of having been thrown out of the garden.

Music is a salve for that spot. In fact, all good art is a hand across the waters, a message that says, "No, you're not alone. I feel this way, too." Poetry does that for some; and painting; dance and theatre; we keep inventing ways to reach across the void that separates us.

That's why people sing hymns in church. For a few minutes, we beat and move as one—still individually created, but now confident that we are also part of something larger, something that is feeling the same thing.

> This leaky boat
> Oh it won't float
> No, it won't float without You
> When I'm captain I keep asking
> For the Lord to be the crew
> I keep wishing for some fishing but the
> Bailing's all I do
> Now I'm praying cause I'm ailing
> And only You know what to do
> I'm sick of sinking and I'm thinking
> That I need a hand or two.[40]

We long to know this for sure and forever, to drop the fear and reproach of being a single, lonely child in a vastly indifferent world.

Are you there?

Is anybody out there?

Does anyone feel as stupid as I do?

The only cure for existence is everlasting, infinite love, applied minute by minute like an ointment. We call it God and wait for it to happen to us.

This was the bucket I felt myself drop into. My lonely skin just seemed to dissolve away, like silence in the face of a song. It struck me that I should be frightened to be so naked, so shorn of defenses. Intimacy is scary; we're not sure we'll survive it. Will we completely disappear? Yet in spite of thinking I should be afraid, I wasn't. The "skin," in fact, *was* the fear. It's the thing that keeps us from bonding completely, this devil's voice that whispers "you will be hurt by love." This is our separateness, our estrangement from God and each other. We feel it so naturally that we never even know it's there.

We place secret limits on our most intimate relationships, we commune and then clear our throats, we imagine qualifications, demands and contractual fine print for love—whatever we can to get a little safe distance. Always circling what we yearn for, we are stuck in a constant orbit of distrust, never able to come to ground but never willing to abandon sight of it. Ambivalence, literally: stuck between two attractive poles, love and fear of being swallowed.

Death changes all that. At the moment you die, you are born into a world of constant, streaming love that strips away the barriers—and it's *all right*. It's completely all right. The fear and shame are a lie, and suddenly you know it. You are like a butterfly coming out of a grey, lonely cocoon. You float in this startling notion, amazed at how warm Creation is. How had it ever seemed so cold before?

That's what it feels like.

For I am convinced that there is nothing in death or life, in the realm of spirits or superhuman powers, in the world as it is or the world as it shall be, in the forces of the universe, in heights or depths—nothing in all creation that can separate us from the love of God in Christ Jesus our Lord. *(Romans 8:38–39)*

Eternity is only changeless in one significant way: you can't be unsecured from love and fellowship. Once you know that completely, all the other changes become unthreatening. It is the missing note that resolves all possible chords.

That's another word for the rain bucket I fell into, maybe: Harmony—but none of these words capture it. I keep groping, and missing.

Three inches… four inches… five inches above the bed—though *above* isn't quite the right word—I sensed Martha lying beside me, and knew she would wake up to find me gone. This worn-out husk would be lying there like an old pair of jeans I'd changed out of to go to church. I couldn't do that to her. We'd just been married a couple years.

Sorry, but I can't do this right now. That was all it took; no argument, no stern warnings or cloaked figures, nothing to sign. I pounded back alive with a kick-start that made our whole waterbed slosh.

The whine switched back on. I was separated again, and it seemed twice as acute, now that I knew what heaven sounded like. Imagine crawling back into the womb after having experienced light and music and candied orange slices. It's suddenly too small, too dark, too isolated, too bitter. I lay there and ached and wept and felt all the terrible immensity of the choice we make, to live here and be part of this place. It wasn't until that moment that my life felt like exile.

I grabbed Martha's sleeping hand and told her it was alright. She settled back into dreaming. I stared at the ceiling for the rest of the morning.

Pretty hard to go to sleep, after dying.

Kind of wakes you up.

The next year I kept trying to make sense out of what I'd felt. The most disturbing thing to me was that it didn't feel very Christian. Not that it felt anti-Christian, it just felt different. More uncontrolled, organic, crazy, untamed. It certainly didn't feel very Presbyterian, which was the bulk of my heritage, nor did it feel very Lutheran, as I'd recently become. Where was the Book of Life, the Judgment, the Trial, the Acquittal? Where was the awful filmstrip reviewing all my failures? Where was the sense of condemnation only narrowly avoided? Where was the trumpet blare, the angel's shout?

Nowhere. I was just a waterdrop sliding into a vast bucket of rainwater—and everything was going to be alright.

Waterdrop
Waterdrop
You love your waterskin
Keeps the salt out
Keeps the air out
Your waterskin
    But the waterdrop knows
    The waterdrop knows
        When to lose its waterskin

                Where'd the skin go
              In the puddle, in the pond?
                Where'd the skin go
              In the river, in the sea?

        The waterdrop knows
        The waterdrop knows
        When to lose its waterskin.

I think the feeling was similar to what the Gnostics were trying to get at: a sense of liberation from chains. It makes me suspect that the genesis of Gnosticism lies in that near-death experience, although their sense of "pure spirit" doesn't seem quite right. That's only half of the truth.

I think Paul has a closer grasp of what can only remain a mystery in human words:

But, you may ask, how are the dead raised? In what kind of body? A senseless question! The seed you sow does not come to life unless it dies first; what you sow is not the body that will be, but just a seed, perhaps of wheat or something else. God clothes it in a body of his choice, each seed with its own particular body.

All flesh is not the same: there is human flesh, the flesh of animal, birds and fish—all different.

There are heavenly bodies and earthly bodies. The splendor of the heavenly bodies is one thing, and the splendor of the earthly bodies is another. The sun has a splendor of its own, the moon another and the stars another, for stars differ in brightness...

The first human was made "of the dust of the earth": the second is from heaven. The one made of dust is like all those made of dust, and the one from heaven is like all those from heaven.

Just as we have worn the earthly likeness, so we will wear the heavenly likeness.

(1 Corinthians 15:35–41, 47–49)

As to the Gnostic notion of how you're supposed to get there, that's all rubbish. Purifying yourself through higher levels of consciousness, working yourself up the cosmic ladder—balderdash. God saves, God creates. No one else. Legalism just doesn't work, no matter who's pushing it. All you have to do is die. Simple.

...Wait a minute: surely we must have to do something to claim credit for our existence. That would be terribly unfair, to let *God* be responsible for our creation... How can we justify taking up space, unless there's something for us to do?

Well, I kept trying to reinterpret it, but the experience kept reinterpreting *me*, instead. It formed a magnetic pole that kept drawing all my other compasses. Theology and scripture had to align with the UFO report, or else they seemed silly, childish, half-real.

Hear the bad news, folks: the Universe just ain't fair. There's nothing you can do to claim credit for your birth... either one of them. God's God, and you're not.

Sorry. You'll just have to get used to it. I'm still trying to.

Martha and I talk about all of my weird experiences, of course. She's told me that the next time I get a train ticket out of here, I'm free to take it. We'll see. It will probably take one heap of pain and weariness to make me stop playing Mr. Shield. I keep playing out my own god-wish, trying to protect folks from pain and sadness.

I'm not proud or ashamed of this, it's just a fact. I live because of other people, even though I know it's an awful burden to hang on them. I should be responsible for my own life: I know this. But there is nothing else strong enough to keep me going. My love for people here is the tether that keeps this balloon tied to Earth, even when I'd rather just float away.

I keep thinking about Martha wanting to know something about our computer system—"How do I get it to give me the quarterly tax report?"—and not having me to ask. I'm teaching her, yes, and she's learning. I'm proud of how far she's come. But there is no way to duplicate this Easter Egg in my head, this weird affinity for the electronic, and I know that no matter what I do the day will come when she will want to call out "Bill" and I won't be able to answer. This breaks my heart—and I would destroy the earth if I could, just to prevent it from happening—but the Apocalypse is late and I'm running out of time.

(For the director of music. To the tune of "Lilies." Of David.)

Save me, O God, for the waters have risen up to my neck. I sink in muddy depths and have no foothold; I am swept into deep water, and the flood carries me away. I am wearied with crying out, and my throat is raw. My eyes grow dim as I wait for God to help me. *(Psalm 69:1–3)*

The gentle man wheels me to the elevator and swings me around with easy grace, like a shoreman handling a barrel. His stamina amazes me.

As we wait for the doors to open I ask him about his job. I get the orderly answers I expect—*oh, it's not so bad—well, I'm not crazy about these carpets—yessir, just running like this all day—nosir, don't really mind*—and then the door opens. He nods to a friend, lets the box empty out, and rolls me in. I hang my head again and fall silent.

I'm talking too much, using too much breath. Nathaniel's Chipper-O-Meter, calibrated in cramps, is clicking. My muscles are all yearning for oxygen, from my neck to my calves. When I've been starving for air for a long time, my whole body winds up like a steel band spring. Martha massaged my shoulders for a while in the doctor's office, and it felt so good I nearly cried.

I try not to whine, I really do. I know you must be tired of hearing about it by now. But it's just so *relentless*.

The wheelchair moves me into an isolation ward. My file shows I have had methicillin-resistant staph—leper, unclean!—and so I will stay by myself. No roommates to chat with. For the next few days I will see no one's smile. I will see blue masks under clinical or fearful eyes. Too bad.

Most of the staff handle isolation patients unanxiously, but not all. The eyes of the anxious ones are wide and black, alert, checking distances and gloves repetitively. They rush through their duties in controlled alarm, trying to do the best they can under the circumstances, and escape to the airlock with evident relief. They're not necessarily selfish or uncaring. I suspect they're thinking of their children, wondering if they're going to bring my uncleanliness home to destroy their family. They see me as an object, a unexploded bomb.

I do understand the fear—shoot, you don't think I thought about infections during my rubber chaplain days?—but it's still very dispiriting to be the object of such fear. I suspect I have seen only one-tenth of what an HIV-positive patient sees, and that makes me shudder.

The room is large for a single patient, but small for a self-contained universe.

Without exercise, it doesn't matter how many miracle drugs you pump into me; it takes hard work to get these lungs clean. I normally do a lot of walking up and down the halls. But to get my exercise here, I will have to pace like a lion at the zoo.

Oh, well. I slowly pace off the steps, to calculate how many passes equal a mile. "Three hundred and seventy-seven," I announce, after scribbling on the back of my admission form.

Martha laughs. "Better get started," she says.

The window, at least, looks onto a green world of plants and trees. That's nice. It'll be O.K. We've done this before.

Martha stays for a while, then decides to head home to pack my things. She leaves reluctantly, even though she'll be coming back this evening. It's too long a drive to make twice in one day, but she will do it…for better or worse, in sickness and in health, 'til death do us part.

Yes, I believe in the Resurrection.

Tau

"To the angel of the church in Ephesus write: 'These are the words of the one who holds the seven stars in his right hand and walks among the seven golden lamps: 'I know all of your ways, your hard work and your perseverance... Yet I hold this against you: you have lost your early love.'" *(Revelation 2:1–2a,4)*

Hospitals have their own rhythms. You get used to them. The best time to sleep, for example, is in the afternoon, a little after lunchtime. Sleeping at night is quite impossible: too many people march in and out, needing to get their work—that's you—done.

Half past five to nine in the morning is, perversely, the busiest part of the day, all abustle with linen and blood samples and orange juice. Nine to lunch is the time for the great slow whales, the doctors, to drift by, trailing schools of lesser fish. Respiratory therapists come at all hours of the morning, evening and night, looking harried and apologetic. But that stretch of time between one to four, there's your chance for some rest. Charting, giving report and cigarette breaks are the precious plot of dirt in which you may plant yourself and sleep, sleep, sleep.

Back when hospitals were noncompetitive, that was where they placed visiting hours, to keep the civilians from getting in the way of the troops. Patients who had friends had to choose between company or sleep. That's why so many people came home looking like towels that had gotten unaccountably wrapped up in the gears of a ten-speed. Things are much better, now that the visitors can come and go with more freedom.

Still, you can pretty much kiss your admission day goodbye. It takes a while for your body to remember hospital rhythms. It's too keyed up to sleep in the afternoon, and it has this unreasonable notion that nighttime will be a perfectly fitting time to lie down—and you can argue with it all you want, but if it were really interested in your opinions, you wouldn't be in the hospital in the first place, would you?

So you generally spend the first day looking around the room, trying out variations on the same thought, which is "Well, here I am." It's not a great time for profundity, either.

The nurse introduces himself to me. He's a Canadian, which makes me wonder just what is happening to that country. I've met ten times more Canadians than when I lived fifty miles from the border. We discuss that for a bit—yes, their economy is going south, both literally and figuratively—then we review the salient details of my care. I tell him the pharmacy won't have my enzymes, but I've brought my own. He doesn't believe me—that's highly irregular—but he's too professional to argue. He makes a note on his clipboard, and moves on to asking about my insulin regimen. We talk about that, he takes more notes.

I like his relaxed manner. He's a nice guy, neatly trimmed, probably a little wild-living off-duty, but you'll never know it here. He finishes his assessment casually, then wanders into the airlock and throws his robe into the bin marked "unclean."

Back to prowling again.

The strange thing about first days in a hospital is that you don't actually have to *be* there. I could stay at home the first night and phone it in. Maybe it's different when you come in with a heart attack. Hope so.

I wonder what Martha's doing, wonder how the cats are. We'll have to get someone else to do the bulletins for the weekend. I'd phone somebody about it, but communion's probably done by now. I wonder how the dinner went. Shame I couldn't be there...

Blah, blah, fret, blah.

The telephone watches me with twelve little eyes, wondering when I'm going to call my parents and tell them that I've let the family down again.

Later. I'll let the church down first.

I really don't know how to tell people. I would like my friends to know what's going on. Not that they could do much. Just because it's lonely, I guess. Sometimes it feels like Martha and I are on one side of the scale, and the rest of the universe is on the other. I feel so outgunned.

But how do you bring it up? "Hi, John, just thought I'd let you know that in the last year my condition has really slipped. I'm running out of lung area, and right now I hurt so much I wish I were dead. What's up with you?"

Uh-huh. Sure.

Even worse, when friends ask me how I'm doing, I use the devil's own word: *fine.* Talk about being in isolation. What the hell's wrong with me, anyway?

Seeing that I've spurned the telephone's amorous advances, the little blob of white plastic on the bed beckons me instead. There's always an electronic suitor calling, when you're hospitalized.

It's the Remote Control of Hell.

We gave up TV about six years ago. It was the largest single quality-of-life improvement we ever made. It's just too ironic to bemoan disease but continue to watch life rather than live your own.[41] We couldn't maintain the hypocrisy any longer, so we ditched it.

TV, to my mind, is nothing but an electronic fear and desire amplifier. The newsman's cynical joke—"if it bleeds it leads"—is all too accurate; that's what people swallow every night, interspersed with entertaining commercials that let them know *they don't have enough, they need something more*. Then the whole country processes the input, cultures it like an infection and serves up the results to eat again. Yuck.

I'd rather go to the beach and have peace and contentment amplified instead. That's the thing I need more of. Let me feel the froth of the whitecaps fizz on my legs; let me hear the sea whisper like a freshly opened soda.

More watts! Turn up the goodness!

Dinner comes, with a little cup of pills that are exactly the wrong kind of enzyme. I buzz the nurse and tell him, then eat and take my own pills. Ten minutes later, the nurse buzzes back. The pharmacy has told him that his patient is quite mistaken: those are the pills the doctor ordered. I tell him to send the pharmacist over so we can do our little dance. There's no point in making it a threesome.

An hour later the pharmacist shows up with a condescending air. Yes, she knows these pills *look* different, but they are still pancrelipase and they should work just fine. I nod and tell here that I'm intimately familiar with the enzyme market, thank you, because my previous drug was orphaned and I had to run all of the other products through my stomach. Each brand has different proportions of lipase, protease and amylase, none of them has the bile salts of my old pills, and many of them—including the ones laying in our cup of contention—include a narcotic, for reasons that escape me. These pills, in fact, give me cramps that make me scream for hours on end and make me want to kill either myself, or—when I'm thinking more logically—pharmacists who won't listen to their patients. It is, after all, my body.

Her head is buzzing by this point. Hospital patients aren't usually so well rehearsed. They haven't had too many C.F. patients down here, so this is all very new and uncomfortable for them. In bigger cities, C.F. patients develop a good/bad reputation. Staff who like informed partners love us; the rest loathe us.

She writes "cotazym" down on a scrap of paper.

I repeat that it is "cotazym-S."

She nods and doesn't write anything more. I tell her the original cotazym won't do me any good, it's not enteric-coated and the formula is weaker. If she doesn't write that little "S" down, we're going to end up doing the same dance again tomorrow. She compresses her lips together and writes "S" down, then leaves the room, hurling her mask and robe into a bin labeled "unclean."

Tomorrow, after talking to my doctor, she will be embarrassed and apologetic. She could have given me something that would have completely locked up my digestive system. If that goes on for long, it's a major crisis. My crisis. My body.

This is all very routine, and I try to stay firm, dry and polite during this phase. It's no longer outrageous, just wearing. I've never stayed in the hospital without at least one med error. I've even had a wrong I.V. bag hung, which is big-time stuff. I hate to think what happens to patients who don't know their own meds. Is my sample accurate, statistically speaking? Is there that much error going on? Horrifying thought.

But I've seen the other side of it, too. I remember the time Martha made a med error. She had to file an incident report, and her confidence was shaky for a week. It's a terrible responsibility, caring for people's lives. When I worked with computers, the worst possible bug meant turning the machine off to reboot. When you work with humans, though, you really, really hate to hit the off switch.

One more battle to fight, and we'll have the territories marked out.
Cue the music from Psycho, please…

The Dietitian!

The Dietitian!

The Dietitian!

I don't even want to think about it.

It's not that they're especially noxious people. Forgive me if I sometimes give that impression. I get frustrated, I start to demonize them. I am unredeemed. It's really the system that trained them. That's what drives me crazy. They're taught to think in terms that just don't work for C.F. patients. We have absorption problems, which means calorie counting is hopeless, we have mega-colon, which means that bulk is critical, and we need ridiculous amounts of salt in our diet, unlike every other two-legged creature in the universe.

Out of all the other aspects of checking in to a hospital, I hate wrestling with dietitians the most—and that doesn't even take my new, exotic insulin schedule into account.

Argh!

Well, take it one battle at a time, Nathaniel, and in a couple of days you can start recuperating.

I think this is the thing I find most annoying about hospitalization. The time when you're at your weakest is when you have to fight all these turf battles to keep them from making you worse, rather than better.

Dr. Pettigrove helped me considerably, on my last stay. He told them, rather pointedly, to pay attention: I knew my body more than they did. If you don't know your body and you have C.F., you don't get to be thirty-six years old. It's that simple. We are like flying machines built out of toothpicks. You can't just depend on occasional maintenance from the mechanics on the ground, or you'll come apart in the air. You fly with one hand on the stick, and one hand on the glue.

The beast I saw resembled a leopard, but its feet were like a bear's and its mouth like that of a lion. The dragon gave the beast its power and rule, and great authority.

(Revelation 13:2)

Draw close to me, children, and I will tell you a mystery, a cosmic conundrum of the first order: *Hospitals are made up out of the same good folks that do medicine elsewhere.* Really. The nurses on this floor are no less caring that the ones in my doctor's clinic. The pharmacists here are no less decent than the ones near home, whom I appreciate so well. So why is a hospital so often infuriating, when my local care isn't? And why is it that churches are made up of people I love, whereas the Church as an aggregate makes me foam and spit?

Even insurance companies—Lord, I'm going out on a speculative limb here, increase my faith—must be made out of many decent people, just doing their jobs.

Why is it that the Aggregate Human turns out so much less than the sum of its parts?

Revelation can be read with an interesting spin: as a judgment upon the institutions that enslave us and fail us.

The beast also forced everyone, great and small, rich and poor, slave and free, to be branded on the right hand or forehead, and no one could buy or sell without the beast's mark, either the name of the beast or its number. *(Revelation 13:16–17)*

With a mighty voice the angel proclaimed, "Babylon the Great has fallen! She has become a dwelling for demons, a haunt for every unclean spirit and loathsome bird. All the nations have drunk deeply of the fierce wine of her fornication; the kings of the earth have fornicated with her, and merchants the world over have grown rich on her bloated wealth."

Then I heard another voice from heaven say: "Come out of her, my people, so that you will not take part in her sins and share in her plagues. Her sins are piled high as heaven, and God has not forgotten her crimes. Pay her back in her own coin; pay her back double for her deeds! Give her grief and torment to match the glory and luxury she gave herself. She says in her heart, 'I am a queen on my throne! I am not a widow, I will not mourn.' Because of this her plagues will hit her in a single day—pestilence, mourning, famine and burning—for the mighty Lord God has pronounced her doom!

"The kings of the earth who fornicated with her and wallowed in her luxury will weep and mourn over her when they see the smoke of her burning. They will stand at a distance, in horror at her torment, and cry, 'What a shame for the great city of Babylon: the city of power! In a single hour your doom has come!'

"The merchants of the earth will also weep and mourn over her because no one will buy their cargoes any more..." *(Revelation 18:1–11)*

The whore is not a person at all, but a city, a principality. The same is true of the seven-headed beast. (Well, probably. You never know. Maybe God's special-effects department is better than George Lucas and Stephen Spielberg combined. But this is what we *think*, anyway...)

Revelation finds the locus of human evil in the institution, rather than in the individual. The images struggle to say something every one of us senses: that there is a shadow world of titans stomping about the earth, distorting us all. It has terrific resonance with us because we have formalized it. It is no longer metaphor or vision; we have literalized the dream. In our world, we form aggregates that have the legal status of people. A corporation can own property, take on debt, pay taxes, assume legal responsibility for wrong-doing and contribute to political candidates. There are very few rights these artificial people don't have.

When a suit is filed against General Motors, or when a mega-corporation slips money to a senator, we all step into John's increasingly solidifying world. The titans rumble out of the mist.

Who conducted the Inquisition?
Who caused the nuclear arms race?
Who killed this coast?
Who made these children poor?

The answers increasingly lie in the Aggregate Person, and the consequences of individual choices seem to shrink in comparison.

I've said I've never encountered a classic description of the "root sin" of pride that wasn't supported by a rotten foundation of shame. I was speaking about biological people at the time. What about synthetic people?

In the realm of corporate creatures, classic pride is all too easy to spot. Disney, IBM, governments, hospitals, denominations... here pride abounds; and the root shame no longer seems apparent. I think it's still there, though. It's simply distributed among its shareholders: the citizens, workers, baptized.

Organizational pride is like a counterweight on an elevator. The heavier the shame-weight of its members, the more massive the pride-stone must be. We build it in to lift us up.

Nazi Germany is the archetype. It was born in the humiliation, depression and defeat following World War I. Such an enormous weight required the myth of the "Master Race" to lift it up: a massive, unspeakably evil stone.

At the Nuremberg trials—the war-crimes tribunal conducted at the end of World War II—the world discovered the depths to which such a stone could sink. During the course of the trial, an American film was shown documenting the horrors liberating troops found at the concentration camps of Dachau, Buchenwald, and Bergen-Belsen. The courtroom suffered through stomach-churning images of the

Holocaust's trailing edge; movies so shocking that even one of the accused, Hans Frank, was struck with grief that he'd supported "that beast"; yet to others such as Hermann Goring, it was all merely an annoying end to what had been a pretty day.[42] Even the discomfort he'd felt was something to be shoved on to an Other.

That these marvelously brilliant, brittle people have been the focus of two world wars seems like an obvious warning to me; the other end of the Axis, Japan, was counterbalanced with similar weights. But you don't have to look far from home to find these elevators being built. They're all around us. I remember the first time I heard the incessant, scary chant of "U.S.A., U.S.A." resound through Olympic competitions. It was in the first event held after our humiliation in Iran. The chant has continued since then. I keep hoping it will go away, but it's not.

In fact, now that we think we're the only Superpower left, it's getting worse.

The whole world followed the beast in wondering admiration. Men worshiped the dragon because he had given authority to the beast, and they worshiped the beast also, and chanted, "Who is like the beast? Who can fight against it?" *(Revelation 13:36–4)*

In an age where our titans hold global death in their hands, can we afford to ignore the warning we've been given? We have to *do something*, or there will be a lot more hurt in the world. Even the fish and birds will suffer, which is surely not fair.

Does God recognize corporate law, too?

Lord, we hope so.

This little beast certainly hopes so: all of my medical savings are in mutual funds! They're the only investments that can even hope to keep pace with medical inflation. When the stock market rallies because unemployment went up ("calming fears of inflationary pressures," the analysts always say) or a company celebrates record profits by *laying off* 10,000 workers, I find myself staring at the back of my hand just a tad uneasily.

Revelation is actually my favorite book in the Bible. Its expression of hope against despair is so much more ringing than anywhere else. People who find it depressing, I think, haven't yet absorbed the fact that their world is going to end, regardless. (No shame there; we're built that way. Normal development requires that kind of womb, don't you think?)

But once necessity brings this bit of unhappy information home to the heart, John's Bad News becomes Old News, and his Good News stands out like bright yellow against midnight blue. He spits into the world's wind with remarkable courage, the blessed old crackpot. Thank God for him.

Yet I have to admit that John also scares the hell out of me. Even while he honors the gut feeling I have about the titans that rule us, he lays an even heavier challenge at my feet. John says that God does not know corporate law. When I push the blame upon these synthetic people, John pushes it right back.

You made those titans, John says. *Own them.*

A third angel followed them, crying out in a loud voice: "Whoever worships the beast and its image and receives its mark on the forehead or hand, will drink of the wine of God's wrath, poured undiluted into the cup of vengeance: tormented in sulfurous flames before the holy angels and the Lamb. And the smoke of their torment will rise for ever and ever. There is no rest day or night for those who worship the beast and its image, or receive the mark of its name."

Here, endurance is called for on the part of God's people—in keeping God's commands and remaining faithful to Jesus. *(Revelation 14:9–12)*

What am I supposed to do, Brother John? How shall I buy my air? This little hospital stay could easily run me twenty grand. I have no health insurance. What shall I do next time? Shall I call up Dr. Kevorkian and take that way out? Your "pro-life" friends tell me that's a sin, too. Am I supposed to asphyxiate for the Glory of God? Is that it?

Then I heard a voice from heaven say, "Write this: Happy are the dead who from now on die in the faith of Christ."

"Yes," says the Spirit, "they will rest from their labors, for their deeds follow them." *(Revelation 14:13)*

Gee, thanks.

Dear God,

I have to be part of the system if I want to breathe. If it's a sin to want to breathe, then I have no hope.

Please don't blame me for the twentieth century. I inherited it. They do a lot of things here that I don't like, but no one ever asks for my permission. I try to clean up my little space, but it seems that just living makes me dirty up other spaces. Everything is out of whack.

I'm fresh out of ideas, here. Speak clearly, and I shall do my best.

The same goes for most of my friends. They can breathe without a stamp from the beast, but eating isn't optional for most of them and no one knows how to get out. A lot of us dream about it, but nobody can pull it off. It's awfully hard down here.

Sorry.

Your failed disciple,

Nathaniel

They did not deem their lives too valuable to give up. *(Revelation 12:11b)*

I look out the window, watch the leaves blow in the mercury vapor lights. I feel very tired, very old. I was planning on living until thirteen, which was all the warranty they gave any of us. Imagine being 193, and you'll understand the strange sense of astonishment and fatigue that often overtakes me. It's not being dead that bothers me so much, it's getting there. It's the long drag of the bag over your head—and abandoning Martha, of course. Those are the hardest parts. Otherwise, heaven sounds like a pretty decent option. It's not like I'm terribly fond of the current equipment.

They're starting to use the "T-word" again. Transplant: heart and both lungs all at once, install a new engine. They've discovered that the heart is so intimately connected with the lungs, you have less rejection problems if you just gut the whole cavity.

My doctor has admitted that his main goal is to keep me going until my Medicare waiting period ends. You don't buy new organs with your own pennies, no matter how many you saved for a rainy day.

What shall I do?

It will be a battle.

When I was in Chicago, a pair of hotshot surgeons swooped down upon me while I was hospitalized. I had not asked for the consultation, but my stats had merely tripped off their alarm systems. I was admitted for pneumonia, and they descended upon me like wolves. They were looking for proper C.F. candidates for another heart–double lung transplant. They were simultaneously flattering and insulting as they discussed the criteria for their candidates. They wanted people who would "make something of themselves" and not "just lie down and give in." They thought that since I was in a master's degree program, I had the Right Stuff to further their research.

When I explained, in patient detail, that I only wanted truly life-giving procedures—not merely death-avoiding ones—they became hostile and argumentative. Toward the end I began to guess that the operation had more to do with their careers than my life. I was the raw material necessary for their work.

The interview left me feeling slimed and denigrated.

Every one of my hallowed institutions has occasionally turned Beastly. As John warns me, there is no escape.

I don't want a transplant.
It makes me want to scream.

This is not meant to criticize all of those who opt for transplants. It's purely personal. But my gut reaction is this: I'll go through all the pain of having my ribs cracked open (diabetics heal very slowly); the long convalescence and the antirejection drugs (hiding from the sun and dealing with constant infections); the therapy and expensive drugs (which I shall surely pay heavily for)…

…and for what? So my diabetes can make me go blind, or I can lose my hands or feet. I am extraordinarily brittle; I've seen what happens. I've looked at the charts.

The only man I've talked to who truly understands my position is a man who had part of his lung removed, also a diabetic. He's always healed from other surgeries well enough, but just the recovery period made him vow *never again*. He would rather say goodbye.

The goodbye is the hard part, of course.

Martha doesn't want me to do it, either. She knows I would only do it because of her, and she doesn't want that kind of burden. She also saw some truly disgusting travesties related to donor "harvest" that soured her on the dream. It was one of the first major shocks that started her on her journey out of the nursing profession. It's not always as humane as it's painted in the Media.

But will this feeling hold when I really start to suffer? Will I get desperate, and grasp at any chimera, no matter how futile?

Maybe.

> The shape of the wall before you
> Is different from the
> Stone in your hands
> The color of the mountain
> Is not the texture of the land
> You can't know, you can't know
> Before the sun falls
> How the stars will shine.
> It's not the vision of the granite
> That scrapes your bloody heel
> Or the sparkle in the water
> That makes your body feel
> So cool when it was sweaty
> So wet when it was thirsty
> It's not the blue that cleans your hair
> You can't know, you can't know
> About the river
> Til you're there.

10:00. Martha isn't back yet, and it's getting late. I have no books to read, no notebook to scribble in, and the brochure on living wills has gotten pretty old. I'd pop out to the bookstore for a newspaper, if it weren't for the isolation-leper-unclean-M.R.S. status. My doctor has told me not to worry about it: I can still walk up and down the halls if I want to get exercise. But I've seen the looks of panic in the eyes of the staff. I can't torment them like that.

Desperation sets in. I reread the living will brochure, and wonder for the thousandth time who draws those civic cartoons. Did they grow up saying, "Momma, I want to draw people with little round heads for the government?"

I write a poem on a Kleenex box, using the circle of the cutout as a rhythm-determining element. I pace across the room twenty times—count 'em, what the heck. I stare out the window. The twelve-eyed monster watches me. *You could always call someone.*

"Hi, Aunt Meg. I'm just in the hospital for a quick stay. Don't think of my brother and sister, O.K.? I'm not dying yet, this is just a little clean-out..."

Yeah. Maybe in a while. I wonder where Martha is. I wonder how the cats are doing.

Oh, all right. I reach for the remote control, feeling like an ex-junkie grabbing a needle.

Upsilon

Then I saw another beast, which came up out of the earth. It had two horns like a lamb, but spoke like a dragon. It wielded all the authority of the first beast in its presence, and made the earth and its inhabitants worship the first beast, whose fatal wound had been healed. And it performed great miracles, even making fire come down from heaven to earth before the people.

It deluded the inhabitants of the earth with the signs it was allowed to perform in the presence of the first beast. It made them set up an image in honor of the first beast that had been wounded by the sword and yet lived. It was allowed to give breath to the image of the first beast, so that it could speak and could cause all who would not worship the image to be put to death. *(Revelation 13:11–15)*

A news bulletin is on: local reporter, standing in the dark. A lighted porch shines in the distance, palms waving back and forth in the breeze. She's chattering about a breakthrough in an "ongoing investigation," using the voice women reporters must use, a voice that sounds perpetually annoyed.

See what's on another channel. I poke the remote control.

Click. Same scene, different reporter.

Click. Ditto.

Click. WJHN has a slightly different feed, but it's the same story. As I watch they cut to a pencil sketch of a man standing in a circle of people, his head sagging low. He looks like he's been beaten, like he's about to fall over.

The reporter is complaining that they won't let cameras into the courtroom.

Click. On WMRK, the reporter is hounding a man. He's holding his hand up in front of his face, trying to plow through a press of bodies. Floodlights and flashbulbs are going off all around him. Glare on skin, harsh light: the exposed man looks ugly and sweaty, as we all do under floods without makeup.

He is shaking his head furiously now, cursing everyone around him. He pushes one of the reporters, and there is a scuffle. Flash, pop! A feeding frenzy now. Violence, of a sort. The video jiggles a little, there's some more shouting. A local sheriff wades in to break it up. The trapped man is yelling that he's just a bystander, he doesn't know anything, will you just please leave him *alone*. The camera gets one good look at his enraged, snarling face, and my jaw drops open.

It's Peter.

Landslide is the devil's child.
I remember plans
like deep breaths in full laugh
of life lived in giant steps of promise

We were big then
weren't we Peter
On the slope of glaciated soil

It was far too thick to hold

And it makes me ache
to think of all the talk we scattered
on the Holy Mount of Service
back when it was fun
to make petty sacrifice
of home and tawdry job
The unending whine of all we
missed but did not treasure
I gave away old synthesizers
and you gave up your dad's boat
which you hated anyway
but you never told
that part as loud
at the evening
get-togethers

Oh, landslide
You're the devil's child
who hears the mumbled reasons
and waits for the step that comes

to rest on what we truly value
the log that's not so easy
and the not-so-facile soil
the moss that slips on gravel
and the rock that starts to roll

Another minister
is falling from the heavens
Bright Star they called you

He was such a faithful stone,
My Lucifer.

Martha arrives, breathless, telling me to turn the TV on, she's been listening to the radio reports. Tears are in her eyes; she's in shock. She caught the news just as she turned onto I-35.

The TV's already on. She blinks up at it: oh. She's too flustered to comment. Turn it up. The tape is mesmerizing. Show it again.

He's cursing himself, to prove the lie. Peter, how could you? Did you have to go so far? Is your own life so important to you?

> But I am a worm, less than human. I am abused by everyone, scorned by people. All who see me jeer at me, make faces and mock me. They wag their heads: "He threw himself on the Lord for rescue; let the Lord deliver him, since he holds him so dear!" (Psalm 22:6–8)

Can you believe it? They've got it all wrong, they're calling it a plot against the government, a radical sect, a bunch of nuts. One of the anchormen nods knowingly and recalls the crazies in Waco. They had to burn down that ranch, even though there were children inside. Dangerous, to let that kind of thing fester. National Security. People can get hurt.

What about the healings, Tom?

Well, they've got someone looking into that. It may be an elaborate fraud, hard to say.

A medical expert comes on the screen.

Click.

Another courtroom sketch. The accused is being struck by a bailiff. He tried to escape at one point, they say. Just like those wetbacks last month, the ones the police had to fire on. Some folks just won't abide by the rule of law—

—listen, if they weren't guilty, why did they resist?

Click.

> Be not far from me, for trouble is near, and I have no companion. A herd of bulls surrounds me, great bulls of Bashan beset me. Ravening and roaring lions open their mouths wide at me. (Psalm 22:11–13)

Yes, it does look like jesus, although the sketches are hurried. There's one of him blindfolded. Must be to keep him from running away again. They have to do that, sometimes.

One of the guards has his hand raised into the air, as if poised to strike.

"The man says he is a prophet," the voiceover intones, "but the claim is not holding up under examination."

There may be a bomb involved, according to an unidentified source close to the investigation. He fits a standard FBI profile: single Palestinian male, a loose collection of working-class friends, travels a lot, few connections to stabilizing organizations…

Click.

WMTT is excited. They have some live, exclusive footage purchased from an unnamed source. It shows a fight in a garden, badly lit. A sword flashes in the air—the camera loses sight for a moment—then blood. A policeman lost his ear.

There you go, they're violent and dangerous.

They loop that clip over and over, like the explosion of the shuttle *Challenger*. You never see what happens at the end of the sequence. Just that little five seconds: jerk, slash, jerk, slash. My stomach turns, and I hit the channel selector.

Click.

WMRK has some garden footage, too. This strip isn't quite as exciting. It shows disciples running away in every direction. Dimly lit shapes in the dark…

I lean forward, horrified to recognize John's retreating back.

Look, there's James jumping over a rock. James, how could you? His foot catches and he falls. He comes up with a bleeding cheek and terrified eyes, then vanishes into the night.

There's Philip's shirt. I'd know it anywhere.

There's Andrew, stumbling backwards.

And there's a young man who has lost his cloak. He looks dazed, disoriented. The camera catches him for just a brief moment, but they repeat it because he's naked. The clip loops over and over for a nation of voyeurs—hey, it's news, isn't it?—and I have time to lean up against the screen and examine the mad flock of teeming dots. It is very grainy in the low light, but some of the facial features are recognizable.

Dear God, it's me.

Phi

"I can't believe it," Martha says, eyes glued to the screen.

"No," I say. "No."

I rise and look out the window. The trees bob innocently up and down in the same wind that was blowing an hour before. Now it all looks different. But did anything change, really? I don't know.

A woman steps into the courtyard for a smoke. I see the quick arc of the match, the start of the red glow. Destroy yourselves, the demon commands.

I remember an old blues song by Paul Simon, "Everything Put Together Falls Apart"; it was musical entropy, the chords always breaking down, hypnotic. I used to play it constantly, before my body took up the tune.

Look at that woman, there, throwing away her free lungs. Life is like gold, you silly, frivolous human, it is rare and precious beyond all belief; and air is silver in your blood when it shimmers and makes you want to stretch like a warm Saturday in bed—

—but death looks cool when you're an adolescent. So sad.

The reflection of the TV hangs in the upper left corner of the window, a fury of color. The news report gives way to a car commercial, a beer commercial and something that moves so fast that I can't even tell what it was for. Destroy yourselves...

"Can you turn it down a little?"

Martha thumbs the blue knob.

"Thanks."

The reports are confused, and they get worse as the night grinds on. jesus has been handed over to the Romans. No, he's being seen by Herod. No, he was sent directly to Rome...

jesus has been released! The anchorman speaks hurriedly. It's just come in. He has been sprung on a technicality—

—then two minutes later, he comes back on the air with a retraction. It was Jesus *Barabbas*, a renowned revolutionary. *jesus of Nazareth* is still being held by the authorities. The anchor is embarrassed by the slip-up; he actually snaps at his director about it, on camera.

The anchor's lapse makes me laugh, imagining myself in the hot seat. An old T.J. Waters song starts up in my head, accompanied by battered dulcimer and slide guitar… blues, of the mountain variety. The bass notes warble d*oomp, doomp, down/doomp, doomp down.*

> I seen you yell
> At the chillun
> I seen you smoke and fire
> and belch the name of whiskey
> I seen your woman
> running to save your boy
> I seen you naked
> I seen you naked
> And I ain't lied
> with you[43]

…that's what this is all about, isn't it? We're all naked there, all looking for some cover… *I seen you yell…*

This happens to me all the time, when I get disoriented, I have these prophets, they start to sing in my head and tell me what's wrong, give me a grip on life again. It's another gift from God… prophets… I read science fiction sometimes, too, and think this is where they went, they understand. A long time ago, long, long time ago, art was sacred, and sacred was art… *I seen your woman running…* What album was that, anyway? Don't remember. It had another one on it, one we used to play…

"I don't think I can take anymore," I say. "Turn it off."

"We might miss something. Something might happen."

"O.K.," I sigh.

How dulled is the gold, how tarnished the fine gold! The gems of the sanctuary lie strewn at every street corner.

Look at the precious sons of Zion, once worth their weight in the finest gold, now they are worth no more than a clay pitcher made by any potter's hand.

Even jackals offer their teats to nurse their young, but the daughters of my people are cruel… (*Lamentations 4:1–3*)

The fear and blood roil in the water. I see the flash of a fin, the froth in the mouth. The world feeds.

At about 3:30 A.M. I decide to take a shower. What am I trying to wash off? Not sure. I just need to get under the water. Baptism, cleanliness. But the soap in the little packet is perfumed, so it leaves as much gunk as it removes. It makes me want to cough. Real flowers don't bother me, but these artificial scents, they just seem like more particles in the air. They promise to sweeten, but it's just sweet pollution. I would rather stay dirty. I dig out the shampoo and use it all over my body. Wipe the fake stuff off.

I stand in the shower for a long time and let the water hit my face. It runs in and out of my mouth, down my chin.

I seen you naked… The tune is stuck in my head.

Pilate replied, "Do you wish me to release the king of the Jews for you?" He knew that it was out of malice that they had brought Jesus before him. But the chief priests incited the crowd to ask Pilate to release Barabbas instead of Jesus.

Pilate spoke to them again and asked, "Then what shall I do with the man you call king of the Jews?"

They shouted back, "Crucify him!"

"Why? What harm has he done?" asked Pilate.

But they shouted all the louder, "Crucify him!"

Wanting to satisfy the crowd… (*Mark 15:9–15*)

"Nathaniel! Come quick!"

I'm toweling off in the bathroom, standing on the runoff tile near the sink. I've been looking at a stranger in the mirror, wondering how he feels. He's been looking back without much expression.

"Just a minute," he says.

"Hurry, or you'll miss him."

"Alright, alright…"

I walk back out and flop down on the bed, still drying my hair. The TV is babbling quietly, too quietly to actually hear the words, but the excitement and annoyance are still audible. The video shows a stern-looking woman in front of the county courthouse, holding a microphone in front of her mouth.

Another person is standing next to her with the body language of importance just screaming from every tight move, begging us to notice that he's on television: *Look, Ma, you said I shouldn't study rabbinic law, but now the world is hanging on my every word.* He is staring at the reporter with a careful expression he hopes will appear polite, but he actually looks impatient and frustrated. The woman is speaking too much.

He is a prop, not a real point of interest. You have to have these authority signatures when you're doing a complex story, but you don't want them to go on very much, because they don't know how to speak concisely. The ideal authority prop is as voluble as a griffin on a flag.

The reporter finishes her summary and waves her wand under the griffin's chin to collect a "yes." He tries to give her a "yes, but." She reluctantly gives him a few more seconds of glory, then suddenly puts her hand to her ear in the universal sign: *Wait a minute, this just in.* She twists her body and rips the wand from him in mid-sentence, indicating the scene behind her even as her eyes stay locked on the lens.

The camera zooms between their bodies and leaps up the steps of the courthouse. A phalanx of dark suits emerges from the portico. jesus is in the middle of them all, head bowed and bruised. His hair is long and bedraggled, his shoulders sagging. His cheek is bleeding slightly. Flash bulbs go off around him like anti-aircraft guns in an air raid.

They pause at the top of the steps for a moment while a black sedan slides into position. jesus raises his weary head and looks around in confusion, blinded by the fusillade. He seems to be searching for someone, but finds no one: just dark suits, strobes and babblers.

The camera angle alertly shifts as he is hustled down the steps, catching the oozing red welts on his back.

My God, for what? What did you do?

What did you say to enrage us so?

A caption appears under the live feed. Someone in the studio has typed in these words:

Jesus of Nazareth—"King of the Jews"

It blinks on in white offensive letters, then blinks off.

What a terrible thing, for your only crime to be who you are.

The phalanx pushes its way down to the waiting sedan. One of the guards puts his hand to jesus' head and roughly shoves it down. Another forces him into the back seat. It has all the brutal efficiency of a mafia kidnapping. The doors slam shut, and jesus disappears behind dark, bulletproof glass. The sedan creeps forward into the pulsing mob.

It was I whom he led away and left to walk in darkness, where there is no light.

He has turned against me alone and it is like this all day long.

He has wasted away my flesh and my skin and broken all my bones; he has built up walls around me, and has cast me into a place of darkness like a man long dead.

He has walled me in so I cannot escape; he has weighed me down with chains. Even when I call out or cry for help, he rejects my prayer. He has barred my way with blocks of stone; he has made my paths crooked.

He lies in wait for me like a bear or a lion lurking in a covert. He dragged me from the path and lamed me and left me without help.

He has strung his bow and made me the target for his arrows. He has pierced my vitals with arrows from his quiver.

I have become a laughing stock to all nations, the target of their mocking songs all day long. (*Lamentations 3:2–14*)

4:00 A.M. Racking horribly by the bed. Martha is pounding on my back. The sludge disconnects slowly, like that slime toy Nickelodeon sells. Awful.

Where is God, Mark?

Faith. Have faith…

At last some air returns: I huddle against the side of the bed and pant, until a knock comes on the isolation room door—we were so busy, we didn't notice the movement in the air lock—and here I am, only wearing a bath towel. I leap up and stumble into the bathroom, dropping my towel in the process. Martha brings in a shirt and shorts.

I gasp at the sink for a moment, trying to find enough energy to put them on. The nurse calls in to see if I'm alright. I groan and pull on the shorts.

"Coming."

It's Sarah, one of the LPNs, come to collect a sample for culturing. She's a nice lady, always smiling. She hands me the cup and puts the bed into position for me. I can't see her smile today because of the mask.

"You should be in bed," she reproves, "getting your rest."

I wave at the TV in explanation, too busy with gerbils to talk.

Her eyes follow my gesture to the screen.

"A shame, isn't it?" she says, and Martha murmurs agreement. "He looked like such a nice man, too. You never can tell, I guess." Her eyes linger wistfully over the image, then return to her work. "You need me to pound on your back?"

I grunt something like "Mmm-hmm," and she whops me a few times until the gerbil is born: very bright green, almost glowing. Bad, but at least it's not slate grey.

I hand the cup back to her. She replaces the top, labels the contents with my name and bids us goodbye. In the isolation air lock she strips off her mask, robe and gloves into the bin marked "unclean," then makes off down the hall with her pet.

The PBS law correspondent is on WMRK, explaining the arguments before the authorities. She has her ironic face on, the one she uses when describing a process gone sour. Apparently the original charges did not hold up; they could not get the witnesses to coordinate their stories.

"I heard he was going to destroy the temple," says the lady drawing my blood work.

Well, that's not true on several counts: he said if people destroyed the temple he would raise it again. But he was speaking metaphorically anyway, always a mistake when dully ferocious adversaries are listening. The only true charge that could be drawn is that he's not a politician or a lawyer, two pluses in my book. He's a *healer*.

Of course, I shouldn't expect the politicians and lawyers to get that; they think all of Creation is law and politics. It would take... what? A miracle; a disease? A death in the family? Probably not even that.

I should explain all of this to her, but Martha is napping and it all seems so point-less to get into. My eyes are getting blurry from lack of sleep, my mouth is dry, and I'm sick at heart. It's obvious it's too late; the fever is raging and the patient is dying. Who cares what one more onlooker thinks? I just shake my head, and thumb the volume down to silence.

She finishes filling the last vial, pops the needle out of my arm and picks up her tray. The door closes, the garments go into the bin marked "unclean," and I stare at the flickering images without comprehension. It's just video wallpaper now, a succession of talking heads. The effect is oddly hallucinatory. I drop off without knowing it, and the remote control crashes to the floor. That startles me awake long enough to pop the lights off and slip into bed; but I let the electronic visions dance in the box, like a weird, colorful campfire. The shadows of the bed railing lurch back and forth on the wall as the scene cuts from one camera to another. The room dances with demons.

The next woman to enter disturbs me only lightly. She takes my blood pressure, counts my respirations and heartbeats, and lets me slide back into the void.

> My strength pours out like water, and all my joints are loose. My heart, turned to wax, melts within me. My mouth is dry, sticking my tongue to my jaw. I am laid low in the dust of death, with hunters all around me; I am ringed by a band of ruffians, some of whom who have already pierced my hands and feet. I can count all my bones.
>
> People stare and gloat over me. Some divide my garments into shares and cast lots for my clothes.
>
> Do not remain so far off, O Lord; O my help, hasten to my aid. Deliver me from the sword, my precious life from the axe. Save me from the lion's mouth, my poor body from the horns of the wild ox. (Psalm 22:14–21)

Every power, system, creative force or dominion can be used for good or evil. Look at evolution: the same thing drawing me out of the dust is also raging in my breast, trying to draw me back down into it.

Or medicine: sometimes it promises to give life but it prolongs death instead.

Or the courts, which promise justice and deliver lawful games; or democracy, which promised the end of tyranny but gave it to mob will; or Christianity, which promised the realm of God and gave us bomb-throwing nuts.

There is no hope in the old games.

Picture the world as a heaving storm, a tangle of hope and pain. Every new thing can be picked up by all players. It does not change the conflict in the heart but merely amplifies it. The battalion that delivers food by helicopter is charity writ large; yet there are normally bombs in her belly. We cling to technology to save us, but it just escalates the war inside us, makes every turn more hopeful and more deathful. The contrast on the picture tube goes up: the world is a better place; the world is an evil place.

Today the shadows deepen and seem to overwhelm us.

But there is this single dot of light flaring in the middle, brilliant as magnesium, painful to look at.

He emerges slowly, like a wounded ox pulling a heavy load. He is bleeding from the head, where he's been struck repeatedly with a policeman's club. Someone has made a little joke and pushed it into his hair, a pathetic circlet of intertwined briars: Hail, King. The insult and abrasions it leaves are meaningless—might as well pinch a dead man. He is too far gone to care where the pain comes from. His back is aflame with flogging, his joints are stiff with a full night of abuse.

Every time he has been transferred, his protectors have seen fit to dole out their own brand of justice, out of range of the cameras. Now their eyes watch their handiwork behind dark glasses, their faces carefully neutral. They have sheathed themselves and settled, the way a man will just before he leaves the restroom, all cool and perfect again, nothing exposed to the light.

Zip up your anger, man, before people suspect you are an animal. Aspire to be a mineral: rock-hard, strong as steel, eyes like flint... you hate yourself, don't you, and you strike others.

jesus stumbles and falls. A second time, a third.

One of the older guards, not quite iron, stops the procession and surveys the situation. Are his kids watching television today? He feels dirty inside, like he has swallowed something unspeakable. *Oh God, keep me from throwing up... we need to get this over.*

He waves impatiently at one of the younger studs, a piece of smirking quartz, to grab the cross and pick it up. *See how much fun it is,* he thinks, angrily. He'd do it himself, but his colleagues would suspect it was from weakness. He might be exposed. He'd lose discipline, he tells himself, that's the thing.

The kid won't bear any crosses—he's into giving them. He fulfills the command by grabbing a man out of the crowd: Simon, of Cyrene, the father of two boys named Alexander and Rufus. The gentle father with hulking shoulders is pushed away from his children, shoved into the ground.

Pick it up, nigger.

He does, though in a fair fight alone he could have crumpled the young snot. He does not, however, have a billy club, a band of cohorts and the full force of Rome behind him, so he quietly picks up the shameful cross in front of his children and balances the weight on his back, fiddling to get the feel of it.

He is astonished how heavy it is; the criminal doesn't look that strong. He shakes his head in wonder and grief. Then the impatient kid plants a foot into his rear to get him moving, and he lumbers along.

The young guard swells inside; he's just bullied a man twice his size. The power of a uniform! *Take that, Dad, what do you think of your runt now? I am the size of Rome, do you see that?*

He hopes the camera is watching. The older guard hopes it isn't.

The camera is watching.

"Look at that," says my physical therapist.

She's been working on me since half past eight, thumping on my back and watching the television. I'm inhaling a mixture of oxygen and traffic accident, spitting up with increasing vigor. We're making progress.

Cindy is pretty good; if I ask her she'll do it the *real* way—with her hands—rather than use the vibrator. They don't have to do this. Most don't, anymore. It takes enormous stamina. I'm always grateful to find one willing to use her hands.

"What?" I say, unable to see the screen.

"They've got a black carrying it for him."

I twist to look at the picture. She's right; a big man, yet his back is bent with the weight.

"I can't believe he can carry it," I say, shocked and outraged. "Why don't they use a wagon?"

"One mule's as good as another," she sniffs, and returns to whopping my ribs.

What a terrible thing, for your only crime to be who you are. My heart sinks. I'm always disappointed to discover that kind of ignorance in people I like. If only humanity itself was enough… I struggle to formulate a reply, but I'm afraid of simply offending her—it doesn't help, does it, to get people angry?—and before I can find anything suitable her pager goes off for a second time. She grunts and pulls it out of her pocket, looks at the number and sighs. The old biddy in room 138 wants her again.

"Got to go," she says. "Keep breathing until it's done, and I'll come back and finish you." She slips the beeper back into her pocket and gathers her things. In her haste she steps on the towel I'd dropped after my shower.

"Sorry," she mumbles, "I'll tell housecleaning."

Then she whisks away and drops her garb in a bin labeled "unclean."

I stare at the towel for a long time. It is laying exactly how the linen lay in Mark's film clip last night.

The alarm clock rings.

Time to wake up.

I don't know how Mark's cameras caught it. What magic crept across time and space to nail me so? Nathaniel the Truth Teller, the one in whom there is no guile, a child of God… look, there he is: fleeing from the light, hoping not to be exposed. A skulker in the dark, escaping the garden.

I, too, denied who I was three times. For what?

For nothing, really. Weariness and embarrassment. Not wanting to get into it. Peace-keeping, some would say. Approval. Wanting to be liked, fear of embarrassment…

…*I seen you naked, I seen you in the daylight, and I ain't messin' with you…*

I don't know which is worse; to be frozen forever in Mark's camera, or to be frozen forever anonymously, without a caption.

Judas, you were remembered by the ages as a traitor, and so you rest in truth. The rest of us live in a lie, passing the blame on to you: *The apostle you gave me, Lord, he betrayed you. The one* you *chose.* You let out your life in a potter's field, before jesus could get to you, so we will never know, will we, what the Master said?

What do you think, Peter?

Chi

A great vision appeared in heaven: a woman robed with the sun, beneath her feet the moon, and on her head a crown of twelve stars. She was pregnant and cried out in the pain of her labor as she was about to give birth.

Then a second vision appeared in heaven: an enormous red dragon with seven heads and ten horns. On his heads were seven crowns. With his tail he swept a third of the stars out of the sky and flung them to the earth.

The dragon stood in front of the woman who was about to give birth, so that he could devour her child the moment it was born. *(Revelation 12:1–4)*

A number of women were also present, watching from a distance. Among them were Mary of Magdala, Mary the mother of James the younger and of Joseph, and Salome, who had all followed him and waited on him when he was in Galilee. There were also several others who had come up to Jerusalem with him.

(Mark 15:40–41)

Eve returns.

She knows, doesn't she?
Yes, she knows.

She did not appear in the courtroom, though her healer saved her. She took the miracle but did not repay the favor. Her testimony died in the darkness, the words blown out of her mouth by the storm.

But she will not pass it on, no; not this time. She will claim it.

The temptress, the whore, the junkie: she knows the litany. *It is the one you gave me, Lord, that is my sin. Your fault. Your own most grievous fault.*

She knows where it leads. No more: stop the cycle. She returns, in ones and twos, to own her half.

The hill is called Golgotha, the Place of the Skull. It is ringed, slowly, with beaten flowers, abused children, battered wives, punished dreams. They assemble spontaneously around the three crosses, keeping a timid distance, afraid to claim too much or too little, unsure where to stand.

He healed us, he told us God loved us, he saved us from the stones, he gave us crumbs from the table. And we did not come to his trial.

But they are there, now. Where are the others? Where are the apostles?

A wail hits the sky. It flutters into the air suddenly, like a flock of flushed quail, and the heavens boom in reply. A flash of lightning cracks across darkening clouds. The wail grows stronger, more insistent, demanding to be heard over the storm. It stirs the back of my spine to hear it.

This is who we pierced, you and I, it cries. *You and I, we held the words in, we stopped up our throats.*

And now all the throat can do is wail without words, a long, keening sound, agony untamed. Women stand all around the scene, weeping toward heaven, caught in the sudden flash. It is an awesome sight. Mark's camera records it, but the commentators say, incredibly, not a word.

Not a word.

We all say not a word.

At three in the afternoon on the stupidest, cruelest Friday the world has ever seen, jesus descends into Hell.

"My God, My God," he cries. "Why have you forsaken me?"

And then his spirit departs, leaving the womb empty and dark, dark, dark.

One of the correspondents, caught off-camera by an open microphone, says these words he would not say in front of the lens. "Truly," he whispers, "he was the Son of God."

Yes, and so are you. That's what he was trying to tell you. Try listening to the prayer he gave you sometime, as it rolls senselessly out of your mouth.

I turn the TV off, weary and nauseated. It blinks into darkness. The clouds outside the window rumble. Martha turns to me and we give each other a sad, inexpressible hug.

Then the owner of the vineyard said, "What shall I do? I will send my son, whom I love; perhaps they will respect him."

Then the owner of the vineyard said, "What shall I do? I will send my son."

Then the owner of the vineyard said, "What shall I do?"

The Accuser will tell you a different story than what is recorded here. The Accuser will tell you that God was very angry with us, because we weren't God. He will tell you that God was so angry, there was only one thing that would make things right: that we point a gun at the head of jesus and pull the trigger. That is what would make God feel kindly to us, the murder of his innocent son.

And when your very soul cries that this is evil, horrible!—Satan will tell you that God's ways are not our ways. Mystery, paradox, ineffability, sacrifice, atonement: the words will buzz around your head like angry bees.

Translation: You cannot tell God from Satan, lowly mortal. What is evil to you is good to God. Fall down and fear us both.

You must be my child, Satan says. *You obviously have nothing in common with God.*

Enough. I've had enough.

There is no greater love than this: that a man lays down his life for his friends. If you do what I command you, you are my friends.

You are not servants anymore because a servant doesn't know his master's business. I call you my friends because I have told you everything that I've heard from my Father. *(John 15:13–15)*

This is the truth: jesus came to fetch us. We are the lost sheep, the prodigal sons, the scattered chicks, the lost coins. It is not a slaughtered lamb you see, but a fireman who was willing to walk into a burning building. That is the only sacrifice you find in this accursed place: the sacrifice of a fireman for a child. He put his own life on the line for love, not for law—and not to die, but to rescue life.

Why must you look to Romans for mysteries, when you have the words of the Savior himself? If the roof collapses upon his head, don't profane his intent. He made *no secret* about what was going on! He came to call us home, and we reduced him to raw meat. Stop doing it: stop reducing him to raw meat.

If we take the evidence of God's love and call it proof of anger, what can God possibly do? I ask again: *What can God possibly do? What will get through? What will make us* stop?

"You are my children," God said, "and I love you. You are acceptable to me. Your sins are forgiven easily; I did it for you countless times. Why do you say I am murderously angry? *You* are the ones who are angry, *you* are the ones who are the judge. Come home!"

But we didn't want to hear that. So we put the muzzle to the temple of the Holy Spirit and fired. We finally found a target for our rage, and we took full advantage of it. *Bang. Bang. Bang.* And every time we share Satan's version of the story, we fire again and again. We won't even admit that the gun is in our hands.

Tell them, "As I live, says the Lord God, I have no desire for the death of the wicked. I would rather the wicked mend their ways and live. Give up your evil ways, Give them up! Oh Israelites, why should you die?" *(Ezekiel 33:11)*

God finds no pleasure in the death of the wicked, but finds pleasure in the murder of *innocents?* What nonsense, what utter filth! We can hardly claim surprise that we spawned the Children's Crusade, with that kind of sick, sick view of the world.

Am I angry?
Yes, I am angry.

I am angry the way a reformed alcoholic gets when you push liquor down his throat. I'm trying to stay on the wagon, and this poison is not helping me. I will chant it to my last dying breath: God is good, God is good, God is good. If you want a different God, you're welcome to him. As for me, I will choose the God of goodness, the God who calls us out of the demonic. That is a God worth following, not fleeing.

This is the proof of God's love: not that jesus died, but that *we live*. After all we have done, God has not removed the breath from our nostrils. The rain still falls on the just and the unjust; the sun still shines.

Look here, this ground that soaked up Jewish blood: it blossoms in wildflowers. See the corn growing from an entire continent stolen from Sioux, Iroquois, Illinois, Arapaho… it is the breadbasket of the world. We deny who we are a thousand times, God reinstates us a thousand times. There is *no other scheme necessary*. If you cannot feel the truth of that debt, no mechanism will truly matter to you, either.

Praise God for blood? Yes: the blood that runs in your veins. By human laws it is forfeit, a million times over. Yet it runs and runs, even while you search the altar for mercy.

Peter was sitting outside in the courtyard, and a serving maid accosted him and said, "You were also there with Jesus the Galilean."

Peter denied it before all of them saying, "I don't know what you mean." Then he went out to the gateway, where another girl saw him and said to the people there, "This fellow was with Jesus of Nazareth."

He denied it again, saying with an oath: "I don't know the man!"

Shortly afterwards the bystanders came up to Peter and said, "Surely you are one of them, your accent gives you away!"

At this, he broke into curses and swore to them, "I do not know the man!"

At that moment a rooster crowed. *(Matthew 26:69–74)*

After breakfast, Jesus said to Simon Peter, "Simon son of John, do you love me more than anything else?"

"Yes, Lord," he answered, "you know that I love you."

"Then feed my lambs," he said.

A second time he asked, "Simon son of John, do you love me?"

He answered, "Yes, Lord, you know I love you."

"Then tend my sheep."

A third time he said, "Simon son of John, do you love me?"

Peter was hurt that he asked him a third time, "Do you love me?" He said, "Lord, you know everything; you know I love you."

Jesus said, "Feed my sheep." *(John 21:15–17)*

Oh God, you conceived us.

We are your children.

May we follow your name out of the dark. May we treasure it and keep it untainted from the void that clings to our souls. May we never, ever besmirch your reputation among others.

Let us say this: you are Holy, and the void does not claim you. There is no shadow in your heart. You are the Maker of Light.

When you come, the Darkness and the Silence recede, as it does in your own house. It flees from you, it fears you.

We depend on you for all that is good. Never stop your servanthood, or we shall simply die.

Heal us as we heal others. Work your life into our life with our own hands. Build us up with building.

Lead us out of the void, out of destructiveness, out of the swirling storm. If we stumble, pick us up. Carry us when we can't walk, and teach us your ways. Let us be born as you intended. For all goodness is yours, and your love endures forever.

Amen.

Psi

Look.

The sky grows pink, but the ground isn't playing along yet. The world is wool grey.

There's a new tomb, freshly covered—but "new" isn't a nice word around here, not the kind of thing you splash on your detergent box. "New" means "cut off from your ancestors." It's a mark of eternal shame. You're supposed to be gathered in to your people, buried with your folks. An old tomb, a rooted place, is your right.

I have suffered scorn for your sake. I am a stranger to my brothers, an alien to my own mother's sons. (Psalm 69:7–8)

What kind of person deserves this disgraceful treatment, this final rejection?

A convicted criminal, executed by the State at the Church's urging. A rabble-rouser, blasphemer. A fraud, a megalomaniac. A wild-eyed crazy person who knows the truth.

Truth! scoffed Pilate. *What's truth?* Truth is what men do, not say. And these men pounded the claims of a madman to dust. There he lies. You'll smell him soon.

He showed his dirtiness in the end. Just before they squeezed the life out of him, he betrayed his humanity: screamed accusations at God, he did. All the fire and mud of the human heart came pouring out of him. God, he said, is an absent father who forsakes his children, abandons them to suffocation on a hard piece of wood. That's what he said: we have the tapes to prove it. He confessed.

We know what it means to reveal such hate; we know what the punishment is for such enmity, blasphemy. Hint at it, bend all your thoughts to it, but never admit it, because it's the confession that will damn you.

Look: here's the example! A son who spouts such filth at his father—no wonder he lies in a new tomb.

Shameful. What on earth will God do with such an Ungodly child as this?

Look. The sky is brightening to orange and red. The ground hauls itself out of damp wool blankets. The first direct light falls over the rocks and grass. It touches on a boulder. The boulder is very heavy. Not the kind of thing a man would easily move. It should take a crew of three, sweating and straining.

But look...

The finger of dawn presses lightly, and the shameful rock shifts forward, splitting the darkness inside. The secret things, the things which are hidden, the things we reject, despise and crucify; these are the things that the light uncovers. It brings them back into the world, rejects our rejection.

And when brought into the full light of day, it pronounces an astonishing word. Look.

The word is moving out of the tomb again.

Omega

Sometime after they had lost hope
Of seeing the sun again
Sometime after the world had turned
To a permanently sodden, miserable bog...

                    The Storm Broke.

They crawled out of wet holes
And soggy shelters
And blinked at the strange sight
They didn't know what to say
Or even name it anymore, it had been

                                        So long, so long.

They moved slowly and
Picked their way among the wet leaves
As if lost, as if blinded
As if they'd forgotten something—

                                        —Which they had:

Sometimes
        Sometimes
                Sometimes
                            The storm
                        is not the death
                        Of the sun.[44]

It is late afternoon. I am drowsing in my bed, a book at my side. Today's lunch
was salisbury steak, not bad. This hospital feeds better than most.

Martha is at home, trying to get some work done. She is still anxious, and will be
until she gets me back safe at home. But there are hopeful signs. The gerbils are scat-
tering, turning yellow. The culture results have come back, three days after we started
the antibiotics, and it turns out that we're using the right one. Dr. Pettigrove, he's good.

The TV is off. I've got books and papers now, and no excuse not to read them.
Heaven, of a modest nature. When I take time to read, I tend to heal.

Why don't I do that for myself, without checking in to this expensive hotel? I don't know… always have to have a project, I guess.

There is a light knock at the door. I jerk myself awake, look expectantly. No one enters.

"Come in," I say.

A figure comes into the room, looking a little unsure. The mask and the gloves are mandated, yet…

"Nat?" the figure asks. "Do you really want me to wear all this?"

I wave my hands. "It's up to you. Martha doesn't. My doctor says the hospital is too skittish. I'm not carrying anything I wasn't carrying a month ago… but whatever makes you comfortable."

The mask comes down in relief.

"Good," he says.

It's only at that moment that I recognize who it is.

Who is it that touched the leper?

Who is it that walked onto troubled waters?

"Have a seat," trying to hold my bursting heart together.

> You came!
> You did not abandon me.
> When I was sick, you visited me.
> When I was in prison, you freed me.
> When I was naked, you clothed me.
> When I was thirsty, you watered me.
> When I was hungry, you fed me.
> When I was a stranger,
> you invited me in to your house.
> You came![45]

"Christ, I'm glad to see you," I say.

He laughs. His body eases into the chair with evident relief. His face is worn and creased with the week's sorrows, and his shoulders sag a little, with the burdens of the world on them; but the smile is still there, the eyes still warm. They're the eyes of someone who has just been through hell and back again, but still cares enough to see his brother in isolation.

It's family. You gotta visit family when they're in trouble, right?

"Rough week?" he asks.

I nod. "Getting better, though."

His smile is quick. "The antibiotics are working already?"

"Yes, but that's not what I meant. Thanks for coming."

"Sorry it took so long."

"You've been pretty busy yourself."

His smile fades a notch. "Yes."

I fidget a little in the sudden silence.

"I have something to tell you."

It's different this time. I'm not sure I can explain it, but it's different. Maybe it's the way he finally came down from heaven, and the hope it gives me. This one who calls himself the Son of Man… it always rang a little hollow, you know. He was so faultless; I was pretty sure he was no relation of mine. The angels heralding his birth; the kings kneeling before the babe; the crowds and the glory; it all sucked him up into an unreachable heaven. The claim that he'd become one of us seemed unfathomable to me.

The closest I could come to understanding it was an old rich kid's game called "slumming." Sure, he set his crown down for a while—but when you can pick it up again, it's really not the same, is it?

But he finally convinced me. He showed his union card. It was at the very last, but he finally came down to stand with me in a way that told me he truly was irrevocably, nakedly human—and you can't take this away; I won't let you. I hold it in my hands like a gem I never thought I'd see.

jesus unleashed the Accuser in his heart. He, too, had it hiding within him. It took all the power of Hell and Earth to pry it loose, but it finally came out.

The lowest bedrock shared by all of us; the very function of being turned into flesh; the question that bends our spines in either spoken or unspoken ways; it was really there. jesus wasn't slumming. He truly became one of us.

The most graceful words in the New Testament are these:

> *My God, my God,*
> *Why have you forsaken me?*

I have his confession on tape. You can hear it if you like.

And now I know two things.

This kin I have, he screamed his throat bloody raw at God…

> *And he survived.*

Not only did he survive, he was rescued, lifted up, brought out of the tomb!

There is no silence that can overtake me, no truth that can slay me; no wrath that can separate me from the love of God. I can come to God with anything—*anything*—and speak as freely as he. There is no prosecutor taking notes in heaven. There is only a loving God who wants to love truly and honestly, no holds barred. God wants no lie between us; no fakery. Somehow, that makes me want to scream a little less.

Dear Christ, you are the greatest gift of God to me, out of many, many gifts.
You rescued this burning child and bathed him.

You brought me back to the table, found me on the ledge. You found me in a pack of wolves and lifted me to a high rock instead. You restored me in truthful relationship to the one I could not live without.

I will praise and defend your name for as long as I am able. I will shout it to the hills. I will tell the rocks, trees and oceans. I will sing with whatever breath you give me, and I will try, Lord, to sing about love.

Come! Let us raise a joyful song to the Lord, a shout of triumph to the Rock of our salvation. Let us come into his presence with thanksgiving, and sing him psalms of triumph.

For the Lord is a great God, a great king over all gods; the farthest places of the earth are in his hands, and the folds of the hills are his; the sea is his, he made it; the dry land fashioned by his hands is his.

Come! Let us throw ourselves at his feet in homage, let us kneel before the Lord who made us; for he is our God, we are his people, we the flock he shepherds. You shall know his power today if you will listen to his voice. *(Psalm 95:1–7)*

The second thing I learned is as important as the first. It's a lesson in genetics. jesus taught me something new about recessive genes. I thought I knew how they worked, but I never really understood them theologically. Recessive genes, you see, can be tricky; they can lie unexpressed in each of us, unseen, unsuspected. When you look at a carrier of a recessive gene, you can have no clue that they've got it inside them. All the evidence lies in the other direction until the right time, until the gene meets its match—but then the truth is finally unveiled in the progeny, and you know what was there all along in the parents.

This is what I learned from the Messiah, this Son of David, Son of Mary, Son of Adam, Son of Eve: If the Son of God claims to be our Son, then we must be Children of God. If jesus is your son, then you must be a child of God. If jesus is my son, then I must be a child of God.

For the created universe waits with eager expectation for God's children to be revealed... we know the whole created universe has been groaning in labor pains until now; and not only creation, but even we, to whom the Spirit has given the first fruits of the harvest, are groaning inwardly while we wait to be made children of God and to have our whole bodies set free. *(Romans 8:19, 22–23)*

He listens to everything I have stored up, without rushing, without making me feel like something that should be thrown out with the trash. It's astonishing the things you can say to him, and he doesn't look surprised at all. He's been to hell, too; there's not much left after that.

I am a pot, I am a pot, I am a broken pot...

When I run out of things to say, he takes a deep breath and walks over to the window. It is Easter Day: he looks out onto it, silently. Time to take it in. The world looks very alive and real when you've just left a graveyard.

There are two birds fluttering in the air, arguing over a piece of bread. A cleaning lady sits under the tree, throwing her lunch to the wind. The sunlight through the pane is mottled by waving branches, painting his face with faint grey stripes. The trees have a few buds on them. More will come.

"I never answered the question about the wicked tenants," he says. He turns around and leans against the heater. "What do *you* think will happen to the wicked tenants?"

"If they got what they earned—"

He interrupts me, quickly, holding up a finger. "—let those who fear the Lord say this: his mercy endures forever."

I stop and rephrase my answer. "Give them the vineyard anyway?"

He's not convinced. "Why? The sham document's been thrown out. Why does the landlord give the inheritance to his children?"

"Because that was his intention all along."

"Really?" he asks, severely. "That's it? Surely something must force his hand."

"Love," I reply.

"That's it? It's hard to believe that love could be reason enough. There must be something else."

"No," I say, "That's it. I'm sure of it. Love forces God's hand. Nothing else is needed."

He smiles. "Thank you," he sighs. "I was beginning to think I'd never get through."

Then he returns to his seat.

First fruit of the harvest
First man in the house
First citizen of Jerusalem
First born of Israel
First out of the tomb
First hope for the nation
Struggling out of the womb
A vision of the
Future
Sent back to the weary
First message in a bottle
First unobstructed view
Hold on, hold on
This is the reason we're
Walking the shattered plain
We will all get there
Cross the mountain, Messiah
Show me what lies
On the other side

Of pain

jesus

is

What

Happens.

We talk, for three times as long as we should, twice as long as he'd planned and only half as long as I might have wished. I talk a little failure, he spots a little success; I complain about others, he asks me what I'm doing about it. Back and forth, never ceasing, the midwife never rests.

"It's time to leave that church," he finally observes. "You can't even make it to the service anymore, and you've done enough chores. You need a fresh start."

"Where will we go?"

"I'll find you a place. Trust me."

"I could go to them again…"

"You've gone many times."

"I need to give it another try—"

"—Nathaniel, relax. This isn't about good and bad. This is about two kinds of wounds that fit into each other, like a crowbar into a window. Your doctor wants you to separate, so you can get some rest."

"Rest? But you're supposed to live for others, not yourself," I object. "How can I put my hand on the plow and look back? You're the one who's always talking about sacrificial living."

His eyes blink slowly. "Trust me. In a month, this will be a sacrifice. Once you get your breath back, it will practically kill you to just worship without endless busyness. But you're entering a new stage of life, my friend. The last inch takes up all your energy. You need to stop."

"But service, servanthood—"

"—Nathaniel, stop playing God. That will be one amazing service for me. I might stop worrying about you for two seconds—might even be able to focus on someone who doesn't drive his own thorns deeper."

"O.K." I mumble. "Sorry."

"No you're not," he says, evenly.

He considers me with a look I've seen on Martha's face before: it's the look of someone who is not quite satisfied with the line on a canvas. Some bemusement, some vexation, but certainly no surprise.

"Look, you're not done yet," he sighs. "I'll find some things for you to do. Let me think about it."

"I'd appreciate it," I say.

"Wait until you find out what it is before you thank me."

Then he looks at his watch and grimaces. He has to be at Emmaus in an hour, and the freeway is going to be stacked. Looks like McDonald's over the steering wheel again.

He touches my hands and holds them for a moment.

"God loves you," he says.

"I know," I say.

And I do.

Sister in the pickup truck, are you listening? This oxygen mask that offends you, it is not a problem but a solution. I pray for air; it comes in a bottle. I can't help it if you think it is a shame. I will not apologize for it any longer.

jesus *is* healing me, in ways you refuse to understand. The most important healing is going on far below. Down in the tangled wiring of my being, neurons are starting to zag, kinks are coming out. You can't see any of this, and I can't explain it as well as I would wish. But somehow, the Son touches me where it really hurts. My spine is starting to unbend.

When he prays in the garden and his prayer is answered "no"; when he feels forsaken; when he cries against God; this is when I know I am not alone. He walks into hell with me; he breaks the bonds of my lonely pain. I know that I am feeling nothing that he has not felt. I know I am not more disgraceful, disgusting or blasphemous than he. And I know his resurrection is not just one more perk that the rich kids get—that his punishment will be my punishment too.

This is the punishment for being human:

We will be saved from our wrath, our pain, our silence, our disgrace, our void, our death. We will be brought into the New Jerusalem, where our healing will be made complete.

The body that is sown in the earth as a perishable thing is raised imperishable; sown in humiliation, it is raised in glory; sown in weakness, it is raised in power; sown as an animal body, it is raised a spiritual body. *(1 Corinthians 15:42–44a)*

God loves the despised things of this world. The very things we reject are the things God brings out of darkness. We are all convicted criminals, deviants and lepers in the eyes of the world—and the world tries to pronounce that judgment with the voice of God—but on Easter we hear the true voice. God does not share our condemnations. They mean nothing, and *even our executions will be undone.*

God is not ashamed to be making me; God is not ashamed of the tools working this clay; and God is not making me for dishonor like some Augustinian pot, either.

I am not God… but that is no dishonor.

I am not yet complete… but that is no dishonor.

I am going to be born someday, and that birth will look as messy as any of God's children… but that is no dishonor.

It is no disgrace to be wounded or imperfect. It is no shame to be human.

jesus moves among the very lowest of us, the most despised, just to make the point: the traitor, the tax collector, the leper, the whore, all the weakest ones who bear the focus of our condemnations. These are the first to bear the touch of healing, the first to receive the easy wave of the hand: *You are acceptable, infinitely forgivable, completely loveable. I am unsurprised by what I've conceived.*

If God does not want to hide me, what right do I have to skulk in the shadows? I must confess to something astonishing about myself: I am unwhole and unwell, but nevertheless worthy of love. I am free to come home without fear. The table is set, the family waiting.

When God reaches down to the earth to raise up this precious thing we smashed, it is not to pronounce our condemnation, but our acceptance. It is the moment of God's vindication, when the Accuser's charge is exposed as a weak and petulant lie. The gates of hell are burst by a single, unexpected word. After all we did to it, the word remains the same. Even crucifixion will not harm it or alter it. You can't change the message, even when you kill the bearer.

Do you hear it now?

It isn't his death that heals you, or his suffering, or even the empty tomb. It is the word spoken *before* the tomb that heals you, and the word spoken *after* the tomb that heals you… as Peter, as Thomas, as me. It is the Alpha and Omega Word, the word that cannot be stopped.

As it was in the beginning, is now and ever shall be: the love of God is more powerful than death.

As the nations streamed like water
Through the vale of many thunders
And the burnished bronze of angels
Held back the cracks of doom; "It is I"
Set Lords to weeping; "It is I"
Made warriors cry; "It is I"
Sprang from east to west
Like a flash of ancient memory
Stark the angel's trumpet
His sudden shout a
Waterfall
Twelve billion names in a instant
Twelve billion
Names in all
Oh, can't you feel the pulsing

And the earth is quaking, too
His eyes are flaming jasper
His feet like diadems
This Feast
Is the Victory Supper:
My Lord,
He's back again.

"Take care," the midwife says. "I'll see you soon."
"You'll be back?" I ask.
"Yes," he smiles. "I'll be back. I'll pick you and Martha up, O.K.?"
"O.K."
He walks into the air lock, strips off the blue garments and deposits them into a bin marked "laundry."
And then he is gone.

This is the word recorded in the book of Genesis, describing the moment when God first conceived of all Creation. Through it all things are coming into being; not one thing comes into being without it. It shines in the darkness. The darkness does not understand it, but nothing can overcome it. It will conquer everything in the end.

This is the word of God, and the power of life over death:

God saw all that he had made, and it was very good. *(Genesis 1:31)*

Rebirth

An old dry juniper
Brown with drought
Dripping needles
Roots on a ragged hill
Where the old dry walls
Wait for dust
And the city sits silent
The empty husks of angry days
Hang on clotheslines
Like discarded suits of forgotten
Disgrace
That suit was never you.

Sky blue
And monarchs in the air
Like snowdrifts so many
They flutter

White clouds
Angels on the ground
Breaking up the
Soil for new planting

Here comes
Rain

And the butterflies
Flurry

Disgrace?
That suit was never you.

Mountains green
And the walls they tumble
Lord, they fall
Through no hand but their own
Sand billows
Into the air
Over dancing streets

A drum beats
And the pulse fills the valley
That suit was never you
The monarchs blizzard
Over indigo colors
Straw turns
Into gold and the bricks quiver
A new city
From an old cocoon
That suit was never...

I hear voices

Look
In the window
Of the upper room
A maid sits
With her new baby
Who looks like all babies do
But this one is special to Mom

She plays with
Newborn fingers
As soft as anemones
And the fist
So chubby
Waves
ah ah ah
Back and
ah ah ah
Forth

Do you want to know
A secret
Your Mom was never
Frightened
That you'd
Be any different
And your Dad was never
Anything but proud
And your brothers and sisters
Couldn't wait to get a playmate.

Disgrace?
That suit was never you.

Look I see
Monarchs
In the heavens:

Butterflies.

Appendix A: Update

It is now ten months since I began the journey recorded here, six since I finished the first draft. Readers may wonder how things are going.

Well, my body hurts more than it used to. No surprise there.

I'm still a Christian. Looking back, I realize, with some surprise, that it was a near thing. The old balance had become so intolerable that it couldn't survive. The process of writing this book was like undergoing theological meltdown.

How surprising, then, to look at what came out of my molten faith. It is more resilient to cystic fibrosis than the old one. It seems to survive this universe better. I started out with nothing more than desperation and pragmatism. It wasn't until I got up to revision four that I began to realize that I had better reasons than that. Conviction grew, and I began to achieve a coherence of soul I'd never had before.

For many years I would sit in church and respond erratically to scriptures about the Carnivorous God. The adult in me would disagree, but the child would fear that it was really true. But then we took this walk together, this journal; and after the fourth revision, the child finally got it. It finally collected all the poison together and understood what the adult was telling him: if this junk was true, *no one* has any hope. He began, too, to have more confidence in the contrary vision which also exists in scripture, the affirmation that God is truly loving.

In short, he began to trust God.

A weird thing happens to me in church now: when scripture starts to prattle on about God the Crazy Boy, *both of us*—both adult and child—wave our hands and say, "No, thanks. Been there, done that."

We've walked this ground together, and we know where it leads. Coherence of soul. Conviction that it's O.K. to come home. Faith.

Healing!

I am being overtaken by a startling sense of reality these days. I want to shout it to the world: this is *real*! God is *real*!

I have had many prayers answered, excepting the central thorn which remains locked.

I have little patience for foolish pondering that bears no relationship to life as I have met it. People think too much.

De-emphasis of baptism—restoring it to its proper dimensions—has been a significant source of healing to both Martha and me. When you're actually dying, all this "death" talk surrounding baptism is obscene. It is similar to calling high tax rates "rape"—works for you, maybe, but don't you *dare* say that around somebody that's truly been raped, or you'll get an earful. You will realize how dreadful your overspeak was, how little you really knew about the subject, and feel very, very small.

Baptism is a washing. Limit your talk to the realm of cleansing, and you won't obscenely devalue the concept of Death, which is very real, very painful and very different than having a spot of water dunked on your head.

The Birth of the Spirit—the concept of being born again, shorn of its church barnacles—has become a powerful way to make sense of this experience, for both of us. Birth is painful and bloody, there's no denying it. There comes a point where the womb makes it clear it's time to go. In fact—and I have this on the good assurance of many cancer patients who have gone on before me—there is a point where it makes that so abundantly clear that you're *damn glad* to go.

And this is true even for the survivors. The one thing that seems to make sense of their grief is this: the sense that the person they love has stopped suffering.

Don't build that into a theodicy, please; don't make pain the point of the universe. God help us from that bit of wisdom! But don't ignore it, either. It is another bit of grace salvaged from the rocks. We can't minimize the screams. But we can, at least, hold on to the hope that lies at the other end of it; and even more than that, we can feel free to scream without fear.

I know that in the end, I will likely say and think some pretty ugly things. It's my way—don't go looking for some holy saint departing in peace, alright? It's not my history.

But God will, I suspect, be no more surprised at this than a father standing next to his birthing wife, hearing moans and curses fly with abandon. If he has any sense at all, even a *human* father knows enough to say, when his wife calls him an S.O.B., these words of ancient wisdom, handed down from father to son:

"Hmm… I think this is contextual."

The day I became free to wail without punishment was the day the word grace came to mean something real to me; and it was only after digesting that word that I came to the point where I could say, quite simply and truly, "Do you know I love you?" and have it be the beginning, middle and end of a prayer. It was no longer something dragged out of me by the play-acting of liturgy, but an honest emotion.

Murderous fury is a terrible dragon to encounter in your own heart. But the unleashing ends an un-dead, un-live stasis, pushes you back out to the world of living relationship. Growth returns; conversation returns; prayer becomes searingly real.

The vision of the spirit waiting to be born from this fleshy husk means so much right now. It captures the inevitability of a process that is undeniably built into our very design, like the shedding of a nut.

It gives me greater patience with the birth pangs. It gives me a hopeful thing to look forward to; the flight of the New Being, release, soaring. To stretch out from the ground like a young shoot...

Almost sounds worth it.

Anyway, that's where I am right now.

Sitting on the runway.
Waiting for clearance.

Appendix B: Feasts of Joy and Sorrow

The original Hebrew feast was an eating of unleavened bread. What did the bread mean? It meant that sometimes the world moves too fast for your bread to rise. When freedom comes you must leap for it, not tarry or be cautious—or you may never leave. It was a symbol of freedom, of release from bondage. When you ate it, you contemplated the fact that God had rushed you out of slavery as fast as divinely possible.

The original Christian eucharist was a feast shared by the faithful, a true meal. People brought food and shared it; those who had less ate with those who had more. The modern Church Potluck, oddly enough, is the repository of much of the original experience!

There was, however, a ritualized thanksgiving included as part of the meal (possibly at the end), following the command to "do this."

> It is, one fears, worth pointing out that the referent of the explicit "Do this" cannot be the eating and drinking, since only the Pauline and Lukan texts have "Do this" and in them there is no mention of eating and drinking...[46]

According to Jenson, the command refers to the thanksgiving itself, but he goes on to point out that the technical distinction is rather moot, since the act of thanksgiving implies that people are going to be eating the Passover meal.

When the thanksgiving was performed by the early church, what did it look like? The best, earliest example comes from the *Didache* (possibly as early as thirty years after Easter). It explodes with gratitude for life; it may also surprise modern Christians with its symbology.

First with the bread:

> We give thanks to thee, our Father, for the life and knowledge which thou hast revealed through Jesus, thy son. To thee be glory forever! As this bread was strewn over the hills and is now gathered into one, gather thy church from the ends of the earth into thy Kingdom. *(339)*

The broken bread was the bread of "life and knowledge." The scattered teachings of the Traveling Preacher; the life the Wandering Healer dropped all over the countryside... this was the heavenly bread, new manna, gathering now together into congregations. Can you hear the excitement of the young church?

Then (possibly with the wine):

We give thanks to thee holy Father, for thy holy Name that thou hast made dwell in our hearts, and for knowledge and faith and immortality which thou has given as food and drink to human creatures, that they might thank thee, and to us thou hast given spiritual food and drink unto eternal life through Jesus your son. To thee be glory forever! Remember, Lord, thy church, to defend it from all evil and perfect it in thy love. Gather it, sanctified, from the four winds into the kingdom prepared for it. For thine is the power and the glory forever. Amen. *(339)*

Knowledge, faith and life; strong wine poured out from the hand of the Christ.

Oh Death, where is thy sting—and where is thy heavy presence? You are only here as a defeated foe, negated and scorned. We have been liberated from you, Death. We will never fear you again. Run off and hang your head, while we gather the power of Christ's life into our presence.

Once again, a celebration of liberation.

Modern communion poses as liberation. It says it forgives your sins; but does quite another thing. It is actually a ritual that intentionally reapplies guilt.

Don't be surprised. If you set church rhetoric down for a moment and think about what you know about humans, it will come to you. It is certainly something any married person can tell you. Imagine you've done something that has come between you and your spouse. Your spouse tells you that you've been forgiven for it. Yet every time you meet at the dinner table, year in and year out—she reminds you of it. Have you been forgiven?

Talk to an average person in the pews and listen to what they remember. Listen to the top half of what they say, but listen to the bottom half, too: the underlying messages they've received.

This is the decoded meaning of the memorable portion of the liturgy:

Christ suffered because you are bad. Eat his body, broken because of you.
Christ died because you are bad. Drink his blood, shed because of you.

When outside of the moment, your survey subjects may describe this with a cheery face and top-level confidence that it is as it has been advertised: a feast of liberation. But watch their eyes at the chalice, please. What are they saying in their private moment? How much joy do you see? How much release?

Do you see relief?

Look!

This is how another branch of God's church—medical science—works. The Healers pay attention to both data and theory, and as a result, they've been able to carry their half of the Teacher and Healer's mandate with more effectiveness.

Can't the Teachers do the same?

Or am I dreaming again?

"Is there a father among you who will offer your son a snake when he asks for a fish, or a scorpion when he asks for an egg?" *(Luke 11:11–12)*

Jesus retorted, "Yes, you lawyers, it won't be any better for you! You load people down with intolerable burdens and will not lift a finger to help them." *(Luke 11:46)*

No one can say what truly happened at that Last Supper. The Gospel accounts differ—a point often lost in our harmonized portrayals—and the inserted liturgical formulas stretch credulity. I believe the Guiltfest is a later development in one off-shoot of the Church, influenced by a particular theodicy that gained ascendancy as time went on. That offshoot generated the book of Mark. It is obvious that Mark was written with that particular theodicy firmly in mind.

It is commonly believed that Mark was used as a source for Matthew and Luke. Thus the apparent numerical superiority of the three Synoptic Gospels does not necessarily indicate an accurate sample of what was happening out there on the ground, in the hurly-burly of early Church growth—as the *Didache* illustrates.

The Church, as it expanded the ritual, freely accentuated that strand to its own advantage, giving in to its own power and control issues. This should not be a sur-prise, either, if you've spent much time around wounded humans—or studied Church History. The Reformation had something to say about the pristine motives of the Church. Let's not pretend the Church's descent into brokenness all happened at once, please. The New Testament itself makes that point with depressing preci-sion (Luke 9:54–55, 2 Corinthians 11:13–15, 2 Peter 2:1–2, etc.).

It's notable that the Gospel of John was left in the dust; he gives little fuel to those who want a club to beat the faithful. Poor John shows Jesus washing the feet of others, with a command to do likewise, and then shows Jesus dipping the bread with his betrayer! This is hardly the stuff to excite humans who want to manipu-late others.

We have to face up to this. Our communion liturgies do exactly the opposite of what Christ was trying to do: bring forgiveness to the world. Christ died defending people's right to be *genuinely cleared* of such burdens.

If we had the courage to give up the bondage and guilt money that (we fear) sup-ports our budgets, we might return to his intentions. Wouldn't that be a real shocker? Wouldn't that be radical?

Jesus repeated, "Peace be with you!" Then he said, "As the Father sent me, so I send you." Then he breathed on them saying, "Receive the Holy Spirit! If you forgive any-one's sins, they are forgiven; if you pronounce them unforgiven, then they remain unforgiven." *(John 20:21–23)*

Just imagine a church that ended its fascination and addiction with the second clause of that charge. What would it look like? What would it be like to be married to someone who forgave you, and meant it? Would it be like love?

The following pages include an experiment for your community to run, if you're interested in real-world data. It is a communion service that celebrates the impact of Christ's *life* upon the world's life.

It shouldn't upset people frightened by change, because it's meant for church potlucks. It reconnects the prayer to the meal, leaving the sanctuary liturgy unthreatened.

I would be overjoyed if you tried this celebration at your next church dinner, and pondered the results. Pay attention to what you see, and let the Spirit guide you. Is it possible to do communion in such a way that people are not visibly burdened by it? Is it possible to actually lift people's burdens instead?

Be bold.

God is still present in this world!

God is still coming to this world!

God be with you!

—*Bill Williams*

The Potluck Prayers

Following the practice of First Century Christians, the following service is intended to be used before a common meal. The presiding minister should have a bowl of water, a hand towel, and some of the bread, wine, and grape juice that will actually be used during the meal. The minister should use them as she or he sees fit during the Thanksgiving Prayer. It is not necessary that the congregation partake of the elements while the Thanksgiving proceeds; they will have plenty in just a moment.

This service may be distributed and used without permission from the publisher, with proper credit given. May it nourish your good spirits and build you up in God's love. The Gospel was adapted for liturgical use from John 6:22–40. The imagery was inspired by an early eucharistic prayer recorded in the *Didache,* and John's Gospel.

Gathering Our Spirits
(A hymn may be sung, or special art shared.)

Apostolic Greeting
Presiding Minister: The grace of our Lord Jesus Christ, the love of God, and the communion of the Holy Spirit be with you all.
Congregation: And also with you.

The Gospel Reading
(The reading may be done by either one or three lay-readers.)

1. The day after the feeding of the five thousand, the crowd came searching for Jesus. Boats from Tiberias came to where they had eaten bread after the Lord's thanksgiving. When they did not find Jesus there, the crowd got into the boats and went to Capernaum, looking for him.

2. When they discovered that he had reached the other side of the lake without a boat, they asked him, "Rabbi, when did you get here?"

3. Jesus answered, "I tell you the truth, you are looking for me because you ate your fill of the loaves, rather than because you saw heavenly signs. Do not work for the food that perishes, but for the food that endures forever, which I will give you. I have the seal of God."

1. They asked him what they must do to perform the works of God.

3. Jesus answered, "Have faith in the one whom God has sent."

2. Then they asked him for another sign so that they might believe, saying, "What work will you do? Our ancestors ate the manna in the wilderness; as it is written, 'He gave them bread from heaven to eat.'"

3. Jesus replied, "This is the truth: it was not Moses who gave the bread from heaven, but God who gives the true bread. For the bread of God is that which comes down from heaven and gives life to the world."

1. They asked him to always give them this kind of bread.

3. Jesus declared, "I am the bread of life. Whoever comes to me will never go hungry, and whoever trusts me will never be thirsty. But as I said, although you have seen me, still you do not rely on me. Everything God has given me will come to me, and anyone who comes to me I will never drive away; for I have come down from heaven, not to do my own will, but the will of the one who sent me. And this is God's will, that I should lose nothing of all I have been given, but raise it up on the last day."

Congregation: May God's will be done!

The Thanksgiving

P: Ever-lasting and ever-loving God of all Creation,

We praise you for the bread of life you bring to us. You scattered manna to the Israelites and healing to the Palestinians; you preached to the Jew, Gentile, and Samaritan; you covered every hill with bread. You held out your hand, and we gathered like birds. You still hold out your hand, and we still gather. We flock to your hills, we feed from your palms, we stand in your presence with trust and dependence because you made us, know us, and understand the wounds that cause us to go wrong. You are the source of light, life, truth, and healing, wherever we may find it. You are the one who will never, ever leave us.

C: We praise your name!

P: Israel ate your unleavened bread with a full heart, saying, "This is a sign of what the Lord did for us, when he led us out of slavery." You have always been the path out of bondage, our true freedom.

C: We praise your name!

P: Before your Son celebrated the Passover with us, he washed our feet, and led us to do the same for each other; to serve and cleanse; to wash away the hurts of the world. Even as the hand grows clean that bathes the foot, we touch the water for others, and wash away our own sorrows as well. Once again you led us out of the wilderness. You are the way, the truth, and the life of all Creation.

C: We praise your name!

P: He also gave bread to us as a sign of your undying and infinite love; he became our New Manna, our new Passover, and changed all our feasts forever. We can no longer eat without his presence, we will no longer settle for the fare that fades. You are the life that endures forever.

C: We praise your name!

P: In the same way he gave us wine from water, grape, and Passover cup. He said he was the true vine, and we his branches. He bid us abide in him and bear good fruit; to never cut ourselves off from him; to share the life that will defeat even death itself. You are the vine that will never wither.

C: We praise your name!

P: For these great gifts, O God, we praise you; for you are the author of all life, knowledge, and faith, the source of all bread, wine, and water. You change us as you touch us, you draw us forth into the birth of the spirit. We truly thank you for these free gifts, as well as for others we name before you now, with both eager tongue and silent heart:

(A time for personal thank offerings.)

P: We remember, too, O God, the cares of our lives, knowing that you will walk with us, catch us as we stumble, and lift our burdens as quickly as you can, moving both heaven and earth to bring about your healing. We wait for you even as the night traveller waits for the morning sun to rise. Come quickly, Lord, to these good people:

(The Community prayer list is read.)

P: And we offer our personal griefs and worries to you now, both silently and aloud, even as our spirits ache and groan for your help:

(A time for other petitions.)

P: We thank you, Lord, for the freedom to come to you and eat without fear. We pray that, having nourished ourselves with all of your gifts, we will spread them with your grace and wisdom. You are a lovely God, a marvelous Maker. Give us the power to represent your love well, and correct our occasional mistakes. Enable us to serve without anxiety, to answer your prayers, and complete the joy of heaven. We ask all these things through Jesus Christ our Lord, who taught us to pray…

(The Community may then finish with their preferred version of the
Lord's Prayer.)

A Brief Order of Confession

This service may be distributed and used without permission from the author. Special thanks to the good people at the Lutheran School of Theology for prompting its creation.

Apostolic Greeting
Presiding Minister: The grace of our Lord Jesus Christ, the love of God, and the communion of the Holy Spirit be with you all.
Congregation: And also with you.

The Answer to Our Sins
P: If we say we are perfect, we stand in the dark and hide. But God is merciful and just. If we stand in the light and confess our sins we will not be punished, but forgiven for our broken ways. In the light of Christ we will find right relationship with God, ourselves, and the whole of Creation.

(Silence for reflection and self-examination)

P: Most merciful God,

C: We confess that we are enslaved to sin, broken and incomplete. We cannot free ourselves. We sin by what we do and choose not to do; we do not love you or your works as well as we ought; we do not treasure the love you have shown us. Free us, renew us, and lead us to walk in your holy ways; help us know your forgiveness through Jesus Christ our Lord, Amen.

P: God loves you more than you have imagined; and God forgives you all your sins. To those who believe in Jesus Christ, God gives the power to grow beyond their sins and become children of God, trusting in mercy. God declares you and your neighbor both acceptable and lovable through the power of the Holy Spirit; do not be convinced otherwise.

C: Amen.

Notes

1. All poem and song excerpts are from material by the author unless otherwise noted.
2. I've made a decision that will annoy you to no end. I'm not going to capitalize jesus. Arghh! This is my bone-headed reason: I'm convinced it will signify that this is typography, not the real thing. You may accuse me of putting words into jesus' mouth, but you can't complain that I'm doing it surreptitiously.

Those of you who suspect others of playing the same trick without adequate disclaimers may now heave a sigh of relief. The rest of you may heave a brick.
3. Raymond F. Collins, "Nathaniel" (definition 3), in *Anchor Bible Dictionary* (hereafter *ABD*), ed. David Noel Freedman, vol. 4 (New York: Doubleday, 1992), p. 1030.
4. Dr. Richard Rubin, quoted in *The Monitor* Newsletter, a Johnson and Johnson Publication (Palo Alto, Calif.: Johnson and Johnson Company), 6, no. 3.
5. Diogenes Allen, *Christian Belief in a Post-modern World: The Full Wealth of Conviction* (Louisville: Westminster/John Knox Press, 1989), pp. 23–26.
6. "Augsburg Confession," in *The Book of Concord*, ed. Theodore G. Tappert (Philadelphia: Fortress Press, 1959), Article II: 1–2n.
7. "Apology of the Augsburg Confession," in Tappert, *Book of Concord*, Article IV: 33, 35b.
8. "Apology of the Augsburg Confession," Article II: 14, 42.
9. "What Wondrous Love Is This," American folk hymn.
10. Robert W. Jenson, "The Triune God," in *Christian Dogmatics*, 2 vols. (Philadelphia: Fortress Press, 1984), p. 141.
11. Jenson, "The Triune God," pp. 148–49, emphasis and insert mine.
12. *Lutheran Book of Worship*, 1979 pew version.
13. Justo L. González, *The Story of Christianity*, vol. 1 (New York: HarperSan Francisco, 1984), p. 400.
14. "When a woman bears a son she shall be unclean for seven days, just as she is during her monthly period... The woman must wait thirty-three days to be purified, and she must not touch anything that is holy or enter the sanctuary until her days of purification are completed.

"If she has a daughter, she shall be unclean for fourteen days, and shall wait sixty-six days to be purified from her bleeding.

"When the days of purification for a son or daughter are over, she shall bring a yearling ram for a burnt offering and a young pigeon or dove for a sin-offering... This way the priest will make atonement for her and she will be clean" (Leviticus 12:2–8).

15. "In the same way, the Spirit helps us in our weakness. We do not know what we ought to pray for, but the Spirit himself intercedes for us with groans that words cannot express. And he who searches our hearts knows the mind of the Spirit, because the Spirit intercedes for the saints in accordance with God's will" (Romans 8:26–27).

16. Chaos is not complete randomness. (The modern word is shifting from its earlier roots.) If you graph chaotic data, it might look random under certain views, but in other views it will look wonderfully beautiful, systematic in a way our minds can barely comprehend.

The key to plotting chaos is to include delta (change) as part of the plot. Suppose you have a chaotic system that bounces a steel ball on a hopping plate. If you plot the positions of the ball, it may look very noisy and unpredictable. But it you plot the changes in the position (it went from 4 inches to 9 inches, so plot a 5), a near-miraculous transformation in your view of the data may occur. It might still look marvelously complicated, but in a weirdly beautiful way.

I have seen rotating 3-D plots of the human brain's electrical activity that have made me gasp. A normal plot of the activity looks senseless; but a chaotic plot is as awesome as a cathedral. When you put the lens of chaos to your eye, you can't help but feel you are glimpsing a holy secret.

That's a worthwhile observation to hold onto: nature doesn't make sense if you reduce it to static form. Change is part of God's process, not some pollution of a Greek god's timeless ideal. It is the difference between what God *made*, and what God is *making*.

17. Paul Tillich, *Systematic Theology*, vol. 3, (Chicago: University of Chicago Press, © 1963), p. 409.

18. Taken from O. Michel, "Faith," in the *New International Dictionary of New Testament Theology*, by Colin Brown (Grand Rapids, Mich.: Zondervan, 1975), pp. 599–600. Used by permission of Zondervan Publishing House. Available at your local bookstore or by calling 800-727-3480.

19. Saint Augustine, "The City of God," bk. 15, chap. 1 excerpted in William C. Placher, ed., *Readings in the History of Christian Theology*, vol. 1 (Philadelphia: Westminster Press, 1988), p. 120.

20. Obviously, jesus' roots lie in the culture that produced such distorted understandings of God's will. But if jesus had been perfectly aligned with that culture, none of us would remember him today. The same burden lies on those who claim his name: to repudiate an anti-Christian view of God wherever it is found—especially when it occurs in the Bible.

I am not arguing for a "neo-Marcion" Bible cleansed of certain elements. I hope by now my attitude toward silence and censorship is clear. It is, in fact, the very silence that permits biblical evil to fester in our church's soul.

It is only when the church actively removes the log in its own eye that its vision becomes clear. A church that does not present the anti-Christ in the Bible and actively *preach* on it with regularity is not Christian, not prophetic, not even alive. It's not enough to disagree with a passage and then remove it from sight; that's been an outmoded tactic ever since the first Gutenberg Bible was printed.

We don't have to vilify or demonize the authors, and we should certainly let them speak for themselves; the Psalms and laments are perfect examples. But when they project their personal and cultural wounds onto God's face we have to talk about it, put it in context and explore it—from the pulpit, for that is the authoritative center of the community. If we do that, we can *minister to the diverse situations of people.* We can model how to understand and survive scripture.

We can free Christians by giving them the power of a very simple but very scary sentence: "The Bible says this—and I disagree." As long as we rely on more timid tactics from the pulpit—especially the interpretative equivalent of "Well, he really didn't *mean* that"—we will be coauthors of hidden pain.

The trick of presenting three scriptural lessons and only preaching on the one you prefer is another way to commit Christian malpractice. (Yes, when I was preaching, I did that for a while, too, until my conscience started to act up.)

It's scary to say "Peter says this, and Peter is wrong." We won't do it without leadership. That's what it means to be the leader of a flock: to walk in front, show the way.

21. "Baptism," in *Baptism, Eucharist, and Ministry* (Geneva: World Council of Churches, 1982), Section II.A.3, E.7.

22. David Rhoads, *The Challenge of Diversity* (Minneapolis: Fortress Press, 1996), pp. 3, 19, 22.

23. Diagnostic Related Group; used for determining the length of a hospital stay.

24. From *A Brief History of Time* by Stephen W. Hawking, copyright © 1988 by Stephen W. Hawking. Used by permission of Bantam Books, a division of Bantam Doubleday Dell Publishing Group, Inc., p. 135.

25. Hawking, *A Brief History of Time*, pp. 137–38.

26. There are other issues, such as the setting of certain "magic" physical constants that are necessary for life, that might need some help from God; please read Mr. Hawking's book to explore them.

There is also the issue of the force that is working against entropy. Evolution itself seems to be heading in the wrong direction... Increasingly complex systems that generate life and intelligence, growing in their ability to manage and direct energy, do not immediately spring to mind as a natural partner of entropy. A believer can easily read into this the stuff of faith; but science is attacking the problem with a new field called "complexity theory." Check out articles on that field to see what's happening there. It should be a fast-moving field.

Quantum physics has other features that challenge scientific reductionism; I think every believer should keep tabs on it. It is well known, for example, that quantum entities, having once interacted, can continue to influence each other, no matter how far apart they may be. Light, in one famous experiment, can either reveal itself as a waveform or particle, depending upon the test performed—and once an individual photon has "chosen" its identity, it must then retain that state. But the interesting thing is this: if you make a twin of the photon, then perform an experiment forcing the photon to identify itself, it will also "choose" for the other, no matter how far they've parted! How is the data conveyed? Through what media? No one knows. Yet we now have a scientific experiment verifying that the most fundamental entities of matter can instantaneously affect each other across time and space. (For more information, you might be interested in the book *From Physics to Metaphysics* by Michael Redhead [New York: Cambridge University Press, 1995].)

Finally, it should be observed that beauty, symbiosis, community, synchronicity, spirituality and miracle are the personal arguments to the heart of a believer; hard things to measure or debate scientifically. For a well-written approach to the general interface of science and belief in the modern world, you might enjoy Diogenes Allen, *Christian Belief in a Post-modern World: The Full Wealth of Conviction* (Louisville: Westminster/John Knox Press, 1989). I did.

27. The first draft on progressive theology was a little rough. It received a body blow called World War II. How could one say things were getting better?

Yet one can challenge Jesus the same way—where is the realm of God in the Holocaust? Does the mustard seed grow in Hiroshima?

The thing that made the vision brittle, I think, was losing sight of apocalyptic tradition. Daniel, John of Patmos and Christ himself are far less naive than early progressivists. They have a hope which is resilient, even after Dachau, Nagasaki and Bhopal. Their testimony is not of machine-like processes turning down the noise, but waves of chaos, struggle, victory.

The marriage of process theology to the concept of birth pangs produces much stronger children.

Even chaos theory suggests birth pangs: when you put new energy into a chaotic system, the model does not immediately slide to a new balance on the graph, but spirals into equilibrium. Hence the greenhouse effect produces both colder and hotter seasons for a while, obscuring the general trend. (Chaos scientists predicted this several years before Reaganauts started using hard winters as an excuse for obstructionist environmental policies.)

I would have thought that process theology was a natural choice to those who seek a view of God harmonious with our view of Creation; yet I've been terribly surprised. Ever since I declared my allegiance to the notion that God does not create evil, it's amazed me how often I have encountered strong resistance to even simple challenges to *ex nihilo*. Can it truly be nothing more than our allegiance to the lessons of our youth? (I am reminded how long plate tectonics endured hazing from the scientific community.)

Why this bit of trivia stirs such strong emotions is beyond me, especially when its concurrent data—that God is the source of evil—inspires not half as much passion. Can familiarity truly generate such willfully peripheral vision? Or is the passion of my life blinding me, instead? (Let's be fair.) Some further thoughts I would like to leave behind for pondering, if you find these issues personally engaging or troublesome:

1. There is, among my Christian friends, the impression that the Big Bang has settled the issue. Quite the contrary. We are still uncertain as to whether or not the universe is in a cyclic state of bang/contraction or infinite expansion. A cyclic bang/contraction takes away our clean sheet at the "beginning of time"; that is, we can no longer take for granted a period of universal nothingness that God fills. Instead, we just have moments where the universe shrinks to a singular point. (If you're interested in that line, do some reading on the astronomical topic of "dark matter.")

2. I would be uncomfortable drawing such confident conclusions from Big Bang theory until we could also easily handle questions like this:
   a. What are angels made up of? If immaterial, how do they interact with material objects? If material, was that material's appearance part of the Big Bang sequence? If so, why are there no missing particles in the Standard Model of Physics? (We'll leave the matter of angels' sandals and pinhead metallurgy aside for the moment...)
   b. What was the Big Bang God's principal means for bringing material into the universe? Was it completely controllable, or was there a paradoxical limitation inherent in the process? As Stephen Hawking reminds us, the entire universe was at that moment a singularity subject to quantum probability behavior. Does that make the "cleaning-up" process of creation a necessity demanded by probability?

3. It is easy enough to blame moral evil on humanity, but evil's boundary is far larger than that. Disease puts the problem in stronger light. You can, of course, take the tack of Genesis: these natural evils were added onto our punishment or our moral evil. If so, you shall have to explain, to people like me, how the punishment fits the crime.

Well, I have willingly flaunted my foolishness here to make a point; there are many *simple things* that we still don't know. That ought to produce a response, don't you think?

I would suggest a response of humility, playfulness... and an absolute refusal to build high walls defending obscure doctrines—especially doctrines that suggest God is the inventor of cystic fibrosis and its million other evil twins.

Another thing I need to clarify, while I'm clearing my throat: I really don't want to imply a Shirley MacLaine-style individual progressivism. Please don't hear me saying that we enter this life to learn a lesson or any such nonsense. The process I am speaking of is of all Creation; the building of New Jerusalem. Perhaps, if we are blessed we might help lay a stone or two while we're here on this planet, by the grace of God. If so, that's well and good—building itself is a healing act. I don't think Christ meant any other thing in his own preaching. We are meant to sow as well as we can.

But by far the most important point is that each of us is the *beneficiary* of God's ongoing creation. We will all die, and most of us will die in a pretty unfinished state. Some folks are just going to see a blur of helpless pain on this planet. Living and dying is not a personal "evolution," by all the evidence. The order in which we're taken does not back up the notion.

But I do believe that the finished New Jerusalem will be a healing place. I also believe that the Old Jerusalem must find its culmination in the new, that they are related somehow. If the Omega is a complete discontinuity from the Alpha, the theodicy issues become hopelessly numbing.

The "brought here to learn a lesson" stuff, by the way, is another function of misunderstanding the Birth of the Spirit. Have you ever read those little fantasies about babies in heaven, eagerly waiting to be born? Have you ever wondered, if their soul was already in heaven, why God would insist that they go down and suffer Earth?

If the spirit is born in heaven, then the whole process turns into a ridiculous version of summer vacation—intolerable, insulting.

28. E. Gordon Rupp and Philip S. Watson, *Luther and Erasmus: Free Will and Salvation*, translated and edited by E. Gordon Rupp (Philadelphia: Westminster Press, 1969), pp. 1–2.

29. Or, to put my canon more explicitly: If I can think of someone on Earth who is more loving, wise or merciful than the God you're telling me about, you're not talking about God. It's scary how often that clause has to get invoked.

Some folks quickly move on to *My ways are not your ways* talk, when I suggest my canon. They are the same ones that will—on a different day—tell you that we have the knowledge of good and evil in our hearts, that the Spirit has written the law into our souls, and that's why we deserve damnation for the evil we do...

In other words, you know and recognize good and evil—unless, of course, you can't. It all depends on what issue we're debating and what will throw people into hell the quickest. If you're feeling ornery, I bequeath to you my response to *My ways are not your ways*. You may use it without royalties: You're right. We're judgmental, mean-spirited jerks, and God isn't anything at all like us.

30. Rhoads, *Challenge of Diversity*, p. 157.

31. David G. Myers and Ed Diener, "The Pursuit of Happiness: New Research Uncovers Some Anti-intuitive Insights into How Many People Are Happy and Why," *Scientific American*, May 1996.

32. Marvin Pope, "Hosanna," *ABD*, vol. 3, pp. 290–91.

33. Pope, "Hosanna," same passage continued.

34. "Faith, trust"; see Chapter Tsadhe.

35. *Lutheran Book of Worship*, p. 157.

36. *Lutheran Book of Worship*, p. 159.

37. Luke 8:3, 24:10.

38. If you move to a mountain range from a low-lying land, you'll be breathless for a while, but eventually your body will adjust. There are plenty of little tricks your system can do to squeeze more oxygen out of the air. That's "compensation."

I've already used all those tricks up, however.

One of the systems that flops over is the mechanism for determining breathing rate. Most folks breathe fast when they have too much carbon dioxide in their blood: the emphasis is on eliminating waste products. (That's important, because too much carbon dioxide turns your blood acidic, and that can kill you.)

A compensated lung patient, however, has switched to focus on the oxygen in his blood. He breathes fast enough to get his oxygen level up. That's why the pulse-ox gives inadequate pictures of what's going on for us. We're tuned to make it into a little liar.

Compensation is also why my oxygen mask can't fend off C.F. forever. I can pump in all the oxygen I want, but if my lungs can't get rid of the carbon waste products, I can't sustain life. Both sides of the system have to be flowing—you just can't keep jamming more into the input without a corresponding output.

39. The New Testament is not arranged in the order in which it was written. Of the Gospels, Mark was probably first; and it was written after Paul's mission began. Even Paul's letters are out of order: Romans represents a much more developed theology, and the "collection for the poor" project (Rom. 15:16; 1 Cor. 16:1; 2 Cor. 8:4, 9:1) implies the chronological sequence of Corinthians 1, Corinthians 2 before Romans.

40. Anonymous.

41. Calculate (honestly) the waking hours you spend watching TV, spread across a week. Include the shows you didn't intend to watch, but did. Here's an example:

2.5 hours a night + 1 extra hour on Saturday + 1 extra hour on Tuesday = 19.5 hours

This example lands smack in the middle of the pack. The average American watches 1,019 hours of TV a year ("1996 National Science Board report to the President," quoted in "Phenomena, Comments, and Notes," *Smithsonian*, November 1996, p. 34).

O.K., now guess how long you've got to live. Be positive. The average male can expect to live to 80, the average female 83. We'll do a 35-year-old guy:

80 - 35 = 45 years

You're going to spend how many more hours with the Great Blue Eye?

19.5 hours a week x 52 weeks x 45 years = 45,630 hours

That's a big number. Let's give it a scale that can be grasped. If you sleep 8 hours a day, you have 5,840 hours of consciousness in each year.

$$45,630 / 5,840 = 7.8 \text{ years}$$

That's nearly eight years straight through, *full-time communion*, and we're not counting how much time you've already sunk into it. If you're younger it's even worse. Quit today and you'll get them back.

You don't want them?

Can I have them?

42. Robert Shnayerson, "Judgment at Nuremberg," *Smithsonian*, October 1996, p. 134

43. "T. J. Waters" is a fictional musician created by the author. Lyrics copyright © 1997, William P. Williams.

44. Excerpts from "Sometimes" © 1995 Bill Williams.

45. It is said that at the end of days, this will be the way Christ's followers will be recognized (Matthew 25:31–40). Lord, may it be so!

46. Robert W. Jenson, "Tenth Locus, the Means of Grace, Part Two: The Sacraments," in *Christian Dogmatics*, p. 338. The subsequent page citations are also to this article.

Works Cited

Allen, Diogenes. *Christian Belief in a Post-modern World: The Full Wealth of Conviction.* Louisville: Westminster/John Knox Press, 1989.

Anchor Bible Dictionary. Edited by David Noel Freedman. 6 vols. New York: Doubleday, 1992.

"Apology of the Augsburg Confession." In *The Book of Concord,* edited by Theodore G. Tappert. Philadelphia: Fortress Press, 1959.

"The Augsburg Confession." In *The Book of Concord.*

Baptism, Eucharist, and Ministry. Geneva: World Council of Chursches, 1982.

González, Justo L. *The Story of Christianity.* 2 vols. New York: HarperSan Francisco, 1985.

Hawking, Stephen. *A Brief History of Time.* New York: Bantam Books, 1988.

Jenson, Robert. "The Triune God." In *Christian Dogmatics,* 2 vols. Philadelphia: Fortress Press, 1984.

Lutheran Book of Worship. Pew Version, 1979. Copyright © 1978 by Lutheran Church in America. Minneapolis: Augsburg Publishing House.

The Monitor. Palo Alto, Calif.: Johnson and Johnson Company. Lifestyle journal and promotional tool.

New International Dictionary of New Testament Theology. Edited by Colin Brown. Grand Rapids, Mich.: Zondervan, 1975.

Rhoads, David. *The Challenge of Diversity.* Minneapolis: Fortress Press, 1996.

Reuther, Rosemary Radford. "Mother Earth and the Megamachine." *Christianity and Crisis,* 13 December 1971. Reprinted in *Readings in the History of Christian Theology,* edited by William C. Placher, pp. 200–203. Vol. 2. Philadelphia: Westminster Press, 1988.

Rupp, E. Gordon, and Philip S. Watson, ed. and trans. *Luther and Eramus: Free Will and Salvation.* Philadelphia: Westminster Press, 1969.

Saint Augustine. *The City of God.* Excerpted in *Readings in the History of Christian Theology,* pp. 228–21. Vol. 1.

Tillich, Paul. *Systematic Theology.* 3 vols. Chicago: University of Chicago Press, 1963.